The beautiful but haughty Duchess of Herridge is known to all the *ton* as the "Ice Queen." But to Ian McNair, the exquisite Emma is nothing like the rumors. Sensual and passionate, she moves him as no other woman has before. If only she were his wife and not his captive . . .

Little does Emma know that the dark and mysterious stranger who bursts into her bedroom to kidnap her is the powerful Earl of Buchane, and the only man who has been able to see past her proper façade. As the Ice Queen's defenses melt under the powerful passion she finds with her handsome captor, she begins to believe that love may be possible. Yet fate has decreed that the dream can never be—for pursuing it means sacrificing everything they hold dear: their honor, their futures . . . and perhaps their lives.

By Karen Ranney

KAREN RANNEY

A Highland Duchess

AVON
An Imprint of HarperCollins*Publishers*

This is a work of fiction. Names, characters, places, and incidents are products of the author's imagination or are used fictitiously and are not to be construed as real. Any resemblance to actual events, locales, organizations, or persons, living or dead, is entirely coincidental.

AVON BOOKS
An Imprint of HarperCollins*Publishers*
10 East 53rd Street
New York, New York 10022-5299

Copyright © 2010 by Karen Ranney
ISBN 978-0-06-177184-2
www.avonromance.com

First Avon Books paperback printing: August 2010

Avon Trademark Reg. U.S. Pat. Off. and in Other Countries, Marca Registrada, Hecho en U.S.A.
HarperCollins® is a registered trademark of HarperCollins Publishers.

Printed in the U.S.A.

10 9 8 7 6 5

Prologue

Chavensworth, outside of London
January, 1864

Emma, Duchess of Herridge, approached the great house of Chavensworth feeling sick. Her palms were damp inside her gloves; her skin was clammy, and nausea had been her constant companion since leaving London.

Her maid, Juliana, said nothing as they entered the long drive sweeping up to the house, but then, Juliana wasn't married to the Duke of Herridge.

If Emma could have invented any excuse to avoid this meeting, she would have. She should have told Anthony that she was sick in the mornings, that her stomach did not agree with her, leading him to think—erroneously—that there were hopes of an heir.

She hadn't thought that quickly. When she'd received the summons, she immediately left London for Chavensworth.

The tersely worded note from the housekeeper had been a surprise but regardless of how Anthony had summoned her, he'd done so, and she was not fool enough to anger him by being tardy. Anthony was even more vindictive when she did not obey him instantly. Whenever she thought she'd experienced the depths of his depravity, he managed to shock her again.

If only Chavensworth were a greater distance from London. If only snows had blocked the roads. If only ice had made the journey dangerous. If only . . . if only . . . if only . . . the wheels of the carriage seemed to sing that refrain as if mocking her.

The coachman halted in front of the north façade, the most dramatic face of Chavensworth. Here, the three story, yellow stone structure was topped with a pediment adorned with Greek statues in various poses. The fact that all of the figures were barely dressed should have given her some hint about Chavensworth.

Emma nodded to Juliana, attempted to rearrange her features in an aspect that would be pleasing to Anthony, and waited for the footman to open the carriage door. He did so a moment later, and all too soon she was walking up the steps to the massive front door, her maid a few steps behind her.

Williams, the majordomo, greeted her now, his bald head ringed by a tuft of white hair, his stocky figure immaculately attired in the Herridge livery.

"Your Grace," he said, his usual sepulchral tones even more muted.

"What is wrong, Williams?" she asked.

Please God, don't let Anthony have planned another entertainment so soon.

"Your Grace?"

She turned her head to see Mrs. Turner, the housekeeper Anthony had employed just weeks before their marriage. In a sense, she and Mrs. Turner had learned the secrets of Chavensworth together.

"Mrs. Turner," she said, greeting the other woman.

"I'm very sorry, Your Grace."

"Sorry?" She began to remove her gloves, ignoring the sudden plummeting of her stomach. "Whatever for?"

Had some housekeeping emergency called her to Chavensworth? The housekeeper's look, however, did not lend itself to relief.

"His Grace has expired."

For a moment Emma didn't understand. It took Juliana's gasp behind her for her mind to race to the unthinkable.

"Anthony?" she asked. "He's dead?" How very calm she sounded.

The housekeeper nodded. Williams moved to stand beside her. An armed front?

"He was found in his library this morning, Your Grace," Williams said. "Slumped in a chair."

"Anthony is dead?"

Williams's face was smoothed of any expression as he nodded, an indication that the impossible had become possible.

Slowly, Emma removed her bonnet and gave it to Juliana. Soon she would go to the Duke's Suite or to a dozen or so rooms that were comfortable in their way. At the moment, however, she couldn't move at all.

"If I may speak to you in private, Your Grace," the housekeeper said. She looked pointedly at Juliana. So, too, did Williams.

Emma nodded, and followed Mrs. Turner down the hall to the main corridor of Chavensworth, saying nothing as they passed the Yellow Parlor with its welcoming fire and entered the Chinese Parlor. There, on the other side of the room, was a bier, already erected by the carpenters.

Emma began to tremble.

"He's really dead?" she asked softly.

"Yes, Your Grace."

"We shall have to cover the mirrors," Emma said, all too familiar with funeral customs since her father's death two years earlier. "And close the curtains and set the clocks."

She would need to have some dried lavender, grown in Chavensworth's own fields, moved into the Chinese Parlor, arrange to have some beeswax candles burning. Should she have laurel wreaths adorning all the doors, or only those on the north façade? Did she have enough black-bordered stationery or would she need to order some? She would have to give instructions to Cook to prepare the funeral favors, biscuits wrapped in white paper and sealed with black sealing wax. Did she have enough black sealing wax on hand? If Anthony died this morning, the funeral should take place in four days. So much to do in so short a time.

"We've already begun preparing the body, Your Grace," Mrs. Turner said, pulling Emma from her thoughts. "Which is why I needed to speak with you privately."

Again Emma thought she might become ill. What had Anthony done to shock the middle-aged housekeeper, and put such a look in her eyes? What horror had he committed at the last moment of his life?

"What is it, Mrs. Turner?" she asked, dispirited at the very moment she should begin feeling some joy.

Anthony, Duke of Herridge, was dead. Anthony, satyr and despot, breathed no more. Anthony, who'd done everything in his power to squander the fortune she'd brought to her marriage, was to be interred behind stone blocks in the family chapel. Anthony, about whom people spoke in scandalized whispers, would never summon her to Chavensworth again, never insist that she perform in his revels to her disgrace and shame.

"We were beginning to remove the headband from His Grace," the housekeeper said.

Emma was all too familiar with that task because of her father. As close after death as possible, a three-inch-wide band of cloth was placed under the chin and then tied at the top of the head to keep the mouth closed as the body stiffened. Once the body was bathed— beneath a sheet in order to shield the naked limbs of the deceased from view—the headband was removed and the body dressed.

"Something appeared on the body, Your Grace, that was not visible when we began to prepare him."

Mrs. Turner reached out and gripped her arm, something she would never have done at any other time. But the woman no doubt sensed that Emma would not advance on the bier without coaxing.

The coffin looked quite sturdy, and was covered in black cloth. Did Chavensworth's carpenters have a store of coffins waiting for all of them?

Anthony looked restful but not asleep. In sleep he'd still worn that half smile of his, as if he knew that she watched him sometimes, wondering at his capacity for evil.

"You're sure he's dead?" she asked.

Mrs. Turner looked at her. "Yes, Your Grace, he's dead," Mrs. Turner said, her voice warm with sympathy. Because of her loss? Or because she had been married to Anthony for four years?

Did they know, these loyal servants, of the activities that occurred in the ballroom on the third floor? Of course they did. Were they horrified? If they were, they had been careful not to reveal their emotions around the Duke of Herridge.

"This is what I want you to see, Your Grace."

Mrs. Turner leaned into the coffin and unbuttoned three buttons of Anthony's shirt.

Emma stared, uncomprehending. Understanding came in a rush. She looked at Mrs. Turner, then back at what the housekeeper had revealed.

"Dear God in Heaven," Emma said, an oath no proper lady should utter.

Of course Anthony could not simply die like anyone else.

She couldn't breathe; the air would not travel past her constricted throat. She swayed on her feet and was caught by Mrs. Turner. Emma began to laugh hysterically, the sound echoing around the Chinese Parlor until at last it faded, choked off by panic.

Chapter 1

London, England
Late June, 1865

"**I** have found another husband for you, Emma."

Emma, Duchess of Herridge, did not look up but concentrated on her needlework. A spot of blood bloomed beside a pink peony. If she stood now and went to the washbasin to blot it with cold water, the stain would surely come out.

She remained seated.

A ball of ice was forming in her stomach, growing until it chilled her chest, spread through her arms and down to her legs.

"Did you hear me, Emma?"

She clasped her hands together, the needlework abandoned, and bowed her head.

"Emma?"

"I heard you, Uncle," she said, forcing herself to look up at him.

Her uncle resembled her father so much that it was always a shock to look at him. His face was narrow and thin, his chin sharp, his mouth full. Unlike her father, however, her uncle seemed unaccustomed to smiling.

The tips of his ears pointed through his thinning blond hair. Her father's hair had been slightly darker, and fuller. Nor had he ever smelled of camphor like her uncle did, even now. The dish of potpourri at her side was no match for his overwhelming odor.

"There's no need for me to wed. I have my own income, Uncle."

He knew exactly how much money was at her disposal. Although Peter Harding had become the Earl of Falmouth at her father's death, the earldom had not been accompanied by her father's wealth. That had come to her, at least what had not already been spent by Anthony. After Anthony's death, she'd been informed by her solicitors that her uncle had become her financial guardian.

She hadn't cared at the time nor did she now.

All she'd wanted was to ignore the reality of the past four years as well as the circumstances of Anthony's death. She'd planned to occupy herself with her needlework, her flowers, becoming an example to all how rumors could be false.

Not that they were, in her case. Another reason to adopt a decorous mode of living. Now, however, her uncle was putting all those carefully made plans in jeopardy.

"Regardless of what you want or don't want, you have no choice in the matter."

She stared down at the stained peony. The blood had spread, her fingertip only now beginning to sting. Odd, she hadn't thought it that great a wound.

Was he correct? Did she have no say in this matter? She'd not been able to convince her father that Anthony was not the right husband for her. Her father had been so pleased to find a duke, no less, who would protect her, who would see to her long after he departed this world, that he'd paid no attention to her pleas.

Had he known? Sometimes, Emma thought her father had died two years after her wedding because of his shame.

"At least this time," her uncle was saying, "you will have a young man for a bridegroom. Not one thirty years your senior."

She did not want to talk about Anthony. She didn't even want to *think* about Anthony.

For all these months, she'd been spared a husband. Now, it was going to happen all over again. She could barely breathe. Was she going to fall into a faint? After the last few years of being resolutely conscious, how very odd to want to collapse now.

Her fingertips felt numb, and her feet were oddly cold. A soft buzz hummed in her ears. Perhaps she was simply going mad. At least insanity would spare her a marriage, would it not?

"I will send for the dressmakers in the morning," he said. "You will feel better about it once you have a new trousseau."

"I am in mourning, Uncle," she said, looking up at him. "Have you forgotten?"

"You are to be a bride again, Emma. What bride wears black?"

One who does not wish to wed?

"It is not proper, Uncle. I can't marry now. At least not until I have begun half-mourning."

His narrow face was mottled, his color high.

"When, exactly, will that be?"

"It has only been eighteen months since Anthony

passed, Uncle. Another year at least. It wouldn't be proper to marry earlier than that."

"Why do you care about propriety, Emma?"

She forced herself to face his gaze. Her face warmed but she didn't speak. Did he know? Had he known, all these years?

The ice ball in her stomach seemed to crack, causing her to tremble. She held both hands together so tightly she could feel each separate bone.

"You will marry, Emma, and when I decree it, not when you feel it best."

He turned and, without another word, left the room.

Why did she care what society said?

Because a semblance of reputation was all she had. Because Anthony had stripped everything from her, decency, dignity, pride, and all she had remaining was her reputation for being cool and aloof, above the fray. She was the Duchess of Herridge, Ice Queen.

Anything but Emma, a bride again.

The moment she was alone, Emma lay her head back against the chair and sighed. She closed her eyes and willed the last ten minutes away, but they would not vanish. Nor would her uncle's announcement.

She'd not even asked her bridegroom's name. In all honesty, it hadn't mattered. Marriage had been a hideous experience for her and she would not repeat it.

Emma opened her eyes, put aside her needlework, stood, and walked to the window.

Her suite of sitting room, bathing chamber, and bedroom had been designed for a duchess. The house had been a gift from her father, on the occasion of her wedding. She'd wondered, at the time, if it was a gift of apology, a way of conceding that perhaps his decision to accept the Duke of Herridge's suit had been a poor one.

What had he known before her marriage that she'd discovered weeks later?

The furniture in this room had come from France, delicate pieces crafted of mahogany with cabriole legs footed with delicate lion paws. A vanity, four-poster bed, armoire, and *prie dieu* furnished the bedchamber, while several tables and a *bonheur du jour* writing desk complete with two secret drawers sat in the sitting room. The upholstered pieces—love seat and two chairs—had been covered in a delicate blue floral pattern she'd selected herself, thinking her father wished advice for his own home. The walls were covered in silk the same color as the background of the floral pattern.

Unlike the homes of her contemporaries, in which fabric draped everything from cachepots to furniture, this room was nearly sparse. Clutter had been set aside for space, and the few items that remained were those reminding her of better times. A pair of Minton Parian figures sat atop the mantel; a large Chinese red lacquer vase sat beside the fireplace.

The day after Anthony's funeral, she'd left the house he built not long after their wedding, a quite impressive town house not far from here, and moved to this house on Alchester Square. If people speculated on her actions, they'd probably thought that grief had driven her from the home she'd known during her marriage. They would be right in one respect—she couldn't bear to be around anything that reminded her of Anthony.

Soon after she'd come to live here, her uncle had moved into her home, taken over its management, including hiring a new staff, altering the library to fit his needs, and generally running the establishment. At the time, his presence seemed to fit her plans.

She should have rebelled. Against what? Propriety? Residing with a relative was more acceptable than living on her own. Society? Getting her good name back was the one goal she'd had since Anthony's death.

If she were proper enough, decorous enough, she'd be accepted once more into society. People wouldn't stare at her carriage or turn away when she attended a gathering. When her mourning ended, she'd actually be invited to a gathering or a dinner party. Unless society expected her to be more like the Queen, inconsolable since Prince Albert's death a few years earlier.

Her hand gripped the curtain as she stared out at the square. The night was a stormy one, the flash of lighting against an ebony sky curiously absorbing. The cobbles were wet, and the wheels of the carriages made a *ssshhh* sound as they traveled through puddles. The streetlamps were blurred, shielded behind a curtain of rain.

Emma would have liked to go to the country, to leave London behind, but she wasn't allowed to leave the city, tethered to this place and her role in life as if a rope were wound around her waist and tied to the foundation.

She didn't close the drapes. She loved the night, loved the softness of it, the gentleness of the darkness. One of the lamps close to the house was suddenly extinguished, then another. Was the wind truly that fierce tonight? No matter, the watchman would come by in an hour or so and light them again.

Emma leaned her forehead against the glass and wished herself one of the people passing through the square in a carriage. Let her be on her way somewhere, anywhere but here. Let her be anyone but who she was.

If she were brave enough, she might walk among the shadows, become anyone she wished. Someone who wasn't the widowed Duchess of Herridge. Someone who was simply Emma.

A woman who felt as if she were a spot of blood in a pool of water, flowering slowly before disappearing forever.

What would the world say to know that she'd loathed being the Duchess of Herridge? Her predecessor was reputed to have been a lovely, charitable woman whose death Anthony did not mourn at all. They'd married less than six months after Morna's death. Perhaps Fate had a sense of humor, after all, or an ironic sense of justice. Society would be scandalized, again.

She sat in the chair beside the window. Dear God, she could not do it. She could not marry again. Did the youth of the husband truly matter?

Anthony was forever dining on oysters and other foods he claimed were powerful tonics for his manhood. He smelled of the sea, a beast of the ocean, equipped with a living trident that wasn't particularly pleasant.

Please, God, save me. The prayer was one she'd uttered before, in just such a tone of resignation. Panic, however, laced the words with more emotion now. *Please, God, save me. Please, I beg you.*

For most of her life, she'd done what propriety

decreed was right. For the whole of her marriage, she'd maintained a rigid control in order to survive what was happening around her. In the last eighteen months she'd become a hermit, a proper and silent ghost dressed in black, not simply to redress the horror of her marriage, but to be overlooked by society.

She knew too much.

For her efforts, she'd been rewarded, not with freedom, laurels, or commendation for her sense of decorum, but with the prospect of another husband, another marriage.

She turned and noticed her reflection in the window. Several tendrils of hair had come loose and were framing her face. Her maid did not have to use an iron on her hair, it curled on its own, and rain only made it worse. She removed the hairpins and her snood.

A gloved hand slammed against the window-pane.

She stared at the window, her heart pounding rapidly from the fright. The hand had abruptly disappeared, and for a moment Emma wondered if she just imagined what she'd seen. No, it had been real.

She stood, quickly walked to the bellpull and was reaching for it when a voice spoke behind her.

"Please do not do that, Duchess."

She whirled to find a man standing in front of an open window on the other side of the room. He was dressed all in black, not unlike her own garments. But she doubted it was mourning that dictated his attire as much as a wish to escape detection from the watchman.

The intruder was a tall man, too large for her delicate sitting room. Black hair tumbled over his brow and might have softened his features if they hadn't been so strong. A proud nose, squared chin, and full lips marked his face as one she would not easily forget.

"Who are you? What are you doing here?"

She pressed her fingers against the mourning cameo at her neck. A solitary adornment in her widowhood, it reminded her of her mother, of her family, and at this moment, her own mortality.

Her heart was beating so quickly that she could hardly breathe. Nor did she think it possible to blink; her eyes were wide open and staring at the intruder.

The rogue had the temerity to smile at her. As if she were impressed by an attractive smile. As if she could ever forgive him this unpardonable intrusion.

"I've come for the Tulloch Sgàthán," he said.

She frowned at him. "The what?'

"The Tulloch mirror."

She took a step backward, closer to the bellpull. "I don't care what you've come for, leave my house."

He frowned. "You are the Duchess of Herridge, are you not?"

She nodded.

"Emma Herridge?"

She nodded again.

"Where is it?" he asked, looking around the room.

Dear God, he was a thief.

She had little experience with histrionics. At this moment, however, she was giving some thought to screaming, loud and long, a sound to summon her uncle, if not a footman or two.

The intruder looked as if he knew exactly what

she was thinking, because he strode across the room, grabbed her wrist and pulled her closer to him.

"Duchess," he said softly, "if someone enters this room right now, I might be compelled to do bodily injury to them. Or to you."

Was this how God answered her prayer?

Chapter 2

She wasn't quite ready to die.

"I don't know anything about a mirror," Emma said, forcing a calm into her voice that she didn't feel.

"It doesn't belong to you, Duchess."

Was he not *listening* to her?

"My jewelry is in my vanity," she said. "You're welcome to it. Take anything you want. Take all of it."

She pulled her wrist free, twisted off her wedding ring, and held it out to him. "Take it, I'm certain it's the equal of any mirror here. Now go away."

He grabbed her wrist again, walked her over to the window, pushed her into a chair, and sat opposite her.

"I don't want any of your jewelry. Just the mirror."

"I don't care what you want. Leave me," she said. "Immediately." She accentuated the command by pointing at the window.

He raised one eyebrow and regarded her almost in amusement, if she read his expression correctly.

"No one told me how beautiful you are," he said.

She stared at him. Was it entirely proper to accept a compliment from a thief?

"What is this Tulloch mirror?" she asked.

He sat back in the chair, folded his arms and regarded her. It was rather disconcerting to be the object of that direct stare. Now she knew how a pigeon felt when faced with a hawk.

His mouth was full, and easily curved into a smile. His eyebrows were black slashes above eyes so brown they appeared almost black as well. His skin was tan, as if he labored outside when he wasn't engaged in thievery.

"It rightfully belongs to the Tullochs of Perth."

"Scotland."

He nodded.

"My husband's daughter emigrated to Scotland."

He smiled at her but she ignored the expression. She was not that easily charmed.

"I hardly think the word emigrated applies to Lady Sarah," he said.

"You know her, then?" She'd never met Lady Sarah, either at her wedding or Anthony's funeral.

"I do," he said.

"Did she send you here?" she asked.

"Duchess, where is the mirror?" he asked softly.

She turned her head and looked out the window. Now she wondered if he had caused the lamps to be extinguished, the better to climb up onto the roof and not be seen.

"I don't know anything about the Tulloch mirror," she said, glancing over at him. "I must insist you leave. If you do so now, I'll not call the authorities."

"You're very brave, Duchess. Aren't you worried

that I could harm you?" He sat impassive, arms still folded, watching her.

She folded her arms in an identical posture and frowned at him.

"If you're going to harm me, then do so now, because I'll not help you steal from me."

"I don't consider retrieving the Tulloch mirror to be an act of thievery, Duchess. I am merely attempting to return that which was illegally taken."

She wasn't the least bit reassured about her safety. She looked around for a weapon but there was nothing nearby. The lamp would have to do. She could break it over his head.

"I've never been guilty of violence against a female, Duchess," he said, as if guessing her intention.

"But you have, against a man? Is that supposed to reassure me?"

"No," he said. "Nothing I've said tonight was meant to reassure you."

She blinked at him, surprised at his honesty. "You mean to intimidate me."

"Of course," he said, smiling at her again.

She had had enough.

She stood, and before he could grab her, marched to the door, and would have opened it had he not seized her from behind. One arm wrapped around her waist, lifting her. His free hand pressed against her mouth as if he guessed, rightly, that she was about to scream.

"You're the most surprising woman, Duchess," he said.

She kicked him.

He laughed and she kicked him again.

"Your Grace?"

Her maid was on the other side of the door.

The intruder reached out and locked the door before Juliana could turn the latch.

"Your Grace? Are you all right?"

"Tell her you're fine," he whispered into her ear.

Emma shook her head.

He made an exasperated sound.

"Your Grace?" Juliana said. "Do you not need my help readying for bed?"

"Tell her no," he whispered, "or I shall have to hurt you." He turned her chin so that she could see him. There was no humor in his gaze, and not one speck of amusement on his face. "Perhaps I haven't been guilty of harming a female up until now, Duchess, but I'm certainly capable of it."

Emma reluctantly nodded.

Slowly, he released his hand from her mouth, resting his knuckles against her cheek, almost a reminder that he would not hesitate to use force.

She took a deep breath.

"I don't require any assistance tonight, Juliana. Go ahead and retire for the night if you wish."

"Are you certain, Your Grace?"

"I am very certain," she said, making her voice firm and strong. "Sleep well."

"Thank you, Your Grace, and you as well."

Should her maid sound so surprised? She'd bid her good-night on many occasions.

The thief moved back from the door, releasing her.

"Very good, Duchess," he said.

Emma sent him a look that should have scorched him in place before sitting on the chair beside the window once again.

"Take every mirror in the house. I, personally, will see to it that a wagon is loaded up with every single mirror I possess, if it will banish you from my home."

"It's not any mirror, Duchess. It's a hand mirror made of gold. It's quite old, with Latin writing on the back. I understand that the most recent addition to it is a ring of diamonds around the glass."

He stood leaning against the wall, his arms folded in place, his ankles crossed. He looked as if he were perfectly comfortable standing there for as long as he wished, and she had the sudden and disconcerting thought that he probably could and would.

She lay her head back against the chair, closed her eyes, and simply ignored him.

He studied the Duchess of Herridge and knew that this errand had been foolish. What he should do was leave the same way he'd come and vanish from her sight.

However, he wasn't about to leave without the Tulloch mirror, sensibility be damned.

The chance of her recognizing him was relatively low. He and the Duchess of Herridge did not move in the same circles. He was given more to science, and she was a recluse due to her mourning.

"How old were you when you married the duke?"

She opened her eyes and looked at him. "Is that any of your concern?"

"Put it down to curiosity," he said. "Add to that the fact that you don't look more than seventeen now."

She only frowned at him.

"How old?" he asked, wondering why he insisted.

One hand peeked out from the material of her skirts. She clenched it into a fist as if the question were a painful one.

"I have no intention of discussing personal matters with you. Leave my house."

"He was in his fifties."

"You needn't tell me my husband's age," she said.

"When did you meet? At the altar?"

"Again, I see no reason to discuss personal details with you."

"Emma!"

They both turned toward the door.

"Juliana says that you are acting oddly. Are you ill?"

"Who's that?" he whispered.

"My uncle," she said, her gaze fixed on the door.

The sound of the key in the door had him looking for a place to hide. Well, now, he had truly gone and done it. He could just imagine the headlines in the newspapers. *Earl of Buchane Found in Lady's Boudoir.*

Evidently, the Duchess of Herridge was as loath to be found with a man in her chamber as he was to be discovered there, because she pointed to a wardrobe in the bedchamber. He made it into the wardrobe just as he heard the door open.

He pushed aside a few of the dresses in order to make room. What was the perfume she wore? Something that reminded him of spring nights. And what was this silky garment in his face? He brushed it aside, his fingers straying across the lace.

Had he gone insane? He was Ian Hamilton McNair, Earl of Buchane, Laird of Trelawny, and he was hiding in the Duchess of Herridge's wardrobe.

"What is this about you not requiring your maid, Emma?" a masculine voice asked. "Are you feeling ill? Or are you simply being rebellious?"

"I'm not ready to retire, Uncle," she said. "I merely wished to spare Juliana the hours of waiting for me."

"Nonsense," he said. "The servants are here for your convenience, not the reverse."

"Nonetheless," Emma said, "I am not fatigued as yet, Uncle. Or are you now dictating when I rise and when I go to bed?"

"That attitude does not become you, niece. Everything I've done since I've arrived in London has been for your greater benefit."

"Does that include gambling away my fortune, Uncle?"

Ian heard the slap and for a moment debated leaving the wardrobe. To do so, however, would be to make the situation even worse than it was.

The second slap, however, rendered the point moot. He was hurtling out of the wardrobe and toward the tall figure standing in front of the duchess, even now raising his hand to strike her again.

The look of shock on the older man's face was almost worth the disaster of this night. Ian gave himself a second to contemplate it before letting loose with a right hook. The man stumbled, gripping his jaw, but came back at him faster than Ian would have believed possible. Evidently, Emma's uncle had some boxing experience.

Ian had more.

Two quick left jabs, another right hook, and the man was sprawled on the floor, arms flung out, his hands still curled into fists.

Emma remained silent, simply looking at him over her uncle's supine body. The man moaned and blinked a few times. In a moment he'd be back on his feet.

"Well, hell, Duchess," Ian said, the enormity of what he'd done just now striking him.

He grabbed her wrist, pulled her out of the room and down the stairs to the front door before she could say a word.

Chapter 3

All in all, Ian's escape from the Duchess of Herridge's house was easier than his entrance, and a damn sight safer than scaling the roof.

He led her to his carriage parked across the square. When she looked at it, then at him, he knew she was probably wondering if he'd stolen the ebony vehicle with its brass lamps.

Ian stepped aside and allowed her to precede him inside, but before he followed, he needed to give instructions to his driver. The rain-soaked wind was chilling. Ignoring his own discomfort, he stood at the head of the carriage, trying to decide where to take the Duchess of Herridge.

His own town house? He needed time to figure out how to get out of this situation without doing any further damage to the duchess's reputation. Taking her to his home wouldn't be the wisest decision. However, a hotel was out of the question, and he didn't know of any lodging houses. His only other alternative was to call upon one of his friends. What kind of man would engage an innocent bystander in an act that was, at its heart, illegal? The same kind of man who would abduct a woman. No, he couldn't involve anyone else in this ill-conceived, idiotic situation.

He called up to his driver. "Home, Thomas." He would just have to find a way to ensure that no one knew who she was.

Ian entered the carriage, closing the door behind him. He sat back against the cushions and studied her, wondering what it was about her that was so appealing.

She was willowy and of average height, but so were a hundred women he'd met. Her dark brown hair was thick and springy, curling in tendrils around her temples as if to call attention to the perfect oval of her face. Her eyes were almond shaped and such a piercing blue that they reminded him of summer skies over Lochlaven.

"I find your perusal of me rather insulting," she said.

"Do you? Even more so than your abduction?"

He reached over and pulled the shade down, covering the window close to her before doing the same on his side of the carriage.

"They are both equally as distressing," she admitted.

"I have the feeling, Duchess, that I am going to do a great many things that will end up distressing you. Let me proffer an apology now for all of those acts."

"I'm not your confessor," she said. "Instead of apologizing, why don't you simply stop your carriage and allow me to exit?"

"How will you explain my presence in your wardrobe to your uncle?"

Instead of answering him, she placed her hands together and rested them demurely on her skirts.

He had never been given to studying a woman's hands before but hers were lovely, with long, slender fingers.

She seemed suddenly intent on the small compartment fitted with a clock and a traveling quill and ink. A moment later her attention was directed to the window shade. Why he was irritated about the fact that she thought anything was more interesting than conversation with him, he had no idea.

He'd abducted the woman; he wasn't here to converse with her.

The sooner he could figure out a way to get her back to her house without any damage to her reputation, the better.

The rain on the roof punctuated the silence between them.

She folded her arms in front of her chest and it was then he noticed she was shivering. Her dress was dotted with rain, and until this moment he'd not considered that she would be cold.

He took off his coat, bent forward and arranged his jacket around her shoulders. She didn't move or make it easier for him but became a solid block of flesh, her arms close to her sides. He simply ignored her fierce frown, pulled her forward and arranged the jacket so that at least her shoulders were covered.

"I haven't much practice in the art of abduction," he said. "If I had, Duchess, I would have ensured that you brought your shawl or coat."

She didn't answer but her frown lessened a degree or two.

"We have a dilemma, you and I, one in which I need your assistance."

There, the full fury of her frown was back.

"You have intruded upon my privacy, assaulted my uncle, and taken me from my home. Now you wish my assistance?"

"I will concur with your litany of charges, Duchess, all except for the one about assaulting your uncle. Your uncle needed assaulting. Your cheek is still red from his blow."

Her hand went up to her face, her palm cradling her cheek.

"What do you want?"

"A piece of your petticoat."

If her expression was any gauge, he'd evidently startled the Duchess of Herridge.

"We are returning to my lair, Duchess. It would be best if you didn't know where it was located."

"Else you will torture me?"

"Or kill you," he said, smiling.

Her eyes widened and her hand dropped, curving into a fist.

"Only to keep you quiet, you see."

She didn't appear horrified but did look at him with some caution, which still had the effect of annoying him. Couldn't the woman see that he was no more a killer than he was a torturer? The only sin to lay at his feet was that he didn't accept obstacles. If given a task to perform, he would complete it, regardless of the time or effort it cost. Perhaps he was tenacious to a fault.

She grabbed his coat and hugged it to her before turning away and leveling her stare on the shade again.

Was she trying to be irritating? If so, she was succeeding.

He tilted his head back, expelled a breath, and

rubbed the nape of his neck with one hand. "If you please, Duchess. Else, I will have to rip your petticoat myself."

She frowned at him. But she pulled up her skirt an inch or two, revealing a black taffeta petticoat. Quite a lovely thing it was, too, with ruches and lace. The proper mourning garment for the wealthy lady of leisure.

"The bottom tier should do," he said. "Would you care to rip it, or would you prefer that I do it?"

"I would prefer that you not touch my garments, sir," she said, bending and working at one of the seams. He reached into the compartment beside him, pulled out a small traveling quill, and handed her the nib.

"You might want to use this to rip the stitches," he said.

She took the nib from him without another word. A few minutes later she handed it back to him and began to rip her petticoat. In no time at all she had a long strip of black taffeta, which she balled up and threw on the seat beside him.

Sitting back against the seat, she closed her eyes, no doubt pretending that he was nowhere in sight.

If he were being fair, or in the mood to be impartial, he would admit to himself that she had every reason in the world to be disdainful of him. After all, he'd invaded her privacy and then abducted her. But he'd also treated her with what kindness he could, including protecting her from her uncle.

He would simply have to ignore her opinion of him. He didn't know her and it was quite evident that she didn't know him, either. Perhaps it was better if it stayed that way.

A few moments later he flipped the shade back with one finger. They were nearing the square where he lived.

"Your Grace, give me a few hours to figure out a way to get you home with no damage to your reputation."

She turned her head, finally, to look at him. "If you send a note to my uncle, and state that I have been abducted, he would give you almost anything for my safe return."

"Your uncle didn't seem overly concerned about you earlier."

"My uncle resents me," she said. "Every cent he spends, even gambling, comes from my inheritance. A man grows to resent such things."

The statement was so calmly uttered that he wondered if she'd heard it before, perhaps from her dearly departed husband?

"There's no excuse for a man to take advantage of those not his equal," he said. "Whether it is status or wealth or physical stature."

She only looked away again.

"Tell him to give you the Tulloch mirror."

He folded his arms and stared at her.

"The one you don't know anything about?"

She had the grace to look a little shamefaced. "I did not, when you first asked. It was only after you described it that I remembered the mirror. It was a wedding gift from my husband."

He didn't particularly want the image of the Duke of Herridge and his fresh, innocent wife in his mind. He'd met the man only once, but the memory, and rumors, furnished him with all he needed to know about the Duke of Herridge—pompous, arrogant, given to self-indulgence and easy cruelty.

"Where is the mirror now?"

"At Chavensworth, I believe." She glanced at him and then away. "My husband's family home."

"How far is Chavensworth from London?"

"An hour or two."

He looked up at the grill separating him from the coachman and considered changing destinations.

"You cannot think to travel there at night," she said.

He glanced over at her.

"You would've made this entire situation a great deal easier if you had remembered it earlier, Duchess," he said.

"I cannot command my memory," she said. "I put the mirror away the moment it was given to me."

"It belongs in Scotland."

"So you've said." Her remark was accompanied by a frown, quite an imperious expression.

Ian reached for the length of taffeta and then changed seats to sit beside her. He could smell her scent again, the same one he'd experienced in the wardrobe. He wanted to ask her what she wore, if the perfume was something developed especially for her, or if the origin of the scent was something else. Powder? A sachet? The questions, however, were intrusive, and too personal.

Without a word, he placed the taffeta over her eyes and then wound the cloth around her head twice, tying it in a knot at the back. Not only would she be unable to see but she would be difficult to recognize.

Abruptly she held her hands out, wrists together.

"What are you doing that for?"

"Do you not wish to bind me? I am your prisoner, am I not?"

"I don't think that's necessary, do you?"

She dropped her hands, bowed her head.

"If you're disappointed, perhaps I could engage in some very small acts of torture," he said.

"I do not believe you have any experience at torture at all," she said.

"Why would you say that?"

"People who are very good at torture rarely talk about it beforehand. They seem to derive great pleasure in surprising you with it."

Now *that* was a revelation. He didn't know what to say to that comment. Besides, she was right in one aspect. He'd no experience in torture at all.

At that moment he felt a surge of pity for her. No, something more than that. Compassion, certainly, but something else, an emotion he couldn't readily identify.

"I am doing this for your protection as well, Emma."

"I have not given you leave to use my Christian name," she said stiffly, straightening her shoulders.

How very proper she appeared, and annoyed.

He moved to sit opposite her again. When the carriage slowed and came to a stop, he opened the door before a footman could do so, assisting Emma down the three steps.

"There are stairs here," he cautioned her, guiding her hand to the iron banister.

The door opened above him, and his majordomo

stood there, a look of surprise replacing Patterson's usual impassive expression.

Ian waved his hand in the air as if to caution the other man not to speak. Patterson nodded in response, thrusting an arm out to hold back the footman when he would have crossed over the threshold.

Ian took Emma's free hand, entering his house with her.

In the next moment he would have to explain to his majordomo and at least one footman why he was standing in the foyer with a woman wearing his jacket. A woman who was also blindfolded with a length of taffeta petticoat.

He would somehow have to do this without revealing his own identity or hers, and in such a way that would not send one of his servants running to the authorities.

"We are playing a game," he said, winking at Patterson. "Beyond that, it would be ungentlemanly of me to explain."

Emma thought him a torturer and murderer, and now Patterson and a footman thought him a satyr.

Would this night never end?

Not before he figured out how to obtain the Tulloch Sgàthán and how to return the duchess to her home with no damage to her reputation. His impulsive gesture for his friends was demanding a very high price indeed.

"Brigand," Emma said, startling him. "What happens now?"

Patterson smoothed his face of any expression, but the footman smirked.

Ian had never thought himself capable of embarrassment but he felt it now, a curious burning sensation flushing his skin.

"Now, lady," he said, "I take you to my lair and ravish you."

He headed for the stairs, hoping to God and all His angels that she kept silent until they reached his chamber.

Chapter 4

The wind had begun to escalate, coming in through the front door and up the steps as her abductor hurried her up the stairs. Emma could feel the chill piercing her clothes like tiny knives.

At the top of the stairs he hesitated, then unknotted the silk from around her eyes. She could now see that the corridor was dimly lit by brass wall sconces, shadows pooling over the striped wallpaper and the crimson runner covering the dark oak floorboards. A small sideboard stood beside the landing, a jar of potpourri infusing the air with a sandalwood scent.

The thief lived well.

When he put his hand on the flat of her back, Emma felt her blood chill. She did not like to be touched.

His jacket fell, but when he retrieved it and would have placed it around her shoulders again, she shook her head. His sound of exasperation was the only communication between them.

He halted in front of one of the doors in the corridor, reached out and turned the handle of the door. After opening it, he stepped back, allowing her to precede him.

Emma squared her shoulders and prayed for courage.

"I have no intention of entering a bedchamber with you, sir," she said, pleased to note that her voice didn't tremble at all.

"Your virtue is safe enough with me, Emma," he said. "But my majordomo and probably most of the staff, at this point, believe that you're my plaything for the night."

Her cheeks flushed, a sensation of warmth traveling to her temples and the spot in front of her ears.

She shook her head, still refusing to enter the room.

Annoyance shimmered in his eyes. She didn't care. Although he was several inches taller, much larger, and the outcome of any struggle in little doubt, she was more than willing to fight him.

He startled her by simply picking her up and depositing her in the middle of the room, releasing her just as quickly.

She jerked down her bodice, frowned at him, and took several cautious steps away.

"You need to change into something warmer."

She only frowned at him. She had no intention of taking off her clothes.

He raised one eyebrow but didn't respond.

For several long moments they simply stared at one another.

"Do you have a name?" she asked finally. "Or shall I just refer to you as my abductor?"

"Ian," he said.

"Ian. It's Scottish. That's where you're from, isn't it?"

"Have you any objections to the Scots?"

"Only if they take me prisoner," she said.

The room was shadowed, the windows buffeted by the increasingly fierce wind. Despite her resolve, she began to tremble.

He approached her, but before he could touch her, she placed both hands on his chest. When she realized she could feel his body's warmth through the finely woven fabric of his damp shirt, she pulled her hands back. For safety's sake, she took a few more steps backward.

"Is this your bedroom?"

"It is."

"I have no intention of sharing this room with you," she said.

"Nor am I asking you to do so," he said. "I merely ask that you pretend to do so. Your identity, of course, will be a closely guarded secret."

The furniture looked French, the wallpaper a watered ivory silk. The bed was taller than most, making her think that it was a double mattress. Was this brigand a hedonist as well?

Two armoires and a bureau shared the space, in addition to a small writing desk covered with papers. What occupied a thief?

Emma moved to the side of the room, taking the chair in front of the desk, giving him such a fierce look that he knew not to approach her.

He only smiled in response. "Are you hungry?"

"I've already had my supper."

"Would you like some wine?"

"I don't drink wine," she said.

"Something warm, then? Some tea, perhaps."

She focused on the oval rug in front of the bed, its pattern of flowers and entwined vines quite lovely. Was it Scottish?

"You win high marks as a jailer," she said. "If anyone wants to know if you were kind, then I'll say you were. If anyone questions me as to your hospitality, I'll say you were a grand host."

"You think me kind?"

She glanced up at him.

"I haven't been appreciably kind, Duchess, since we met. What disturbs me is that you think I have been. It makes me wonder what other treatment you've had in comparison."

"Must we continue to talk?" she asked. "I find that I am excessively fatigued."

"All of a sudden?"

"It has been building," she said, biting off the words. "Ever since I was forced from my own home."

"I would convey my apologies for that, Duchess," he said, his tone just as terse, "except for one fact. The house you claim as a home didn't seem excessively comforting to me. No one will strike you here, Duchess. No one will threaten you."

How very strange that it was easy to smile. "You have threatened me from the moment you took me from my home, sir. It does no good to say you have not done so. Actions count louder than words. Anyone can be a brute and say he hasn't been."

"Like your husband, Duchess?"

She didn't answer.

"I shouldn't have taken you from your home," he said, surprising her. "Frankly, I didn't know what to do at the time. But it's been done, and we must work with the situation as it stands now. Not as we wish it might be."

He smiled, and she wished he wouldn't. The expression rendered him even more handsome, a darkly beautiful creature who confused her.

He turned and walked toward the door. On the threshold he glanced back at her. "Forgive me, Emma," he said. And then he was gone.

Emma stood, walked across the room and pressed her hand against the closed door. A kind manner could hide a perfidious heart; she knew that only too well. She turned and looked around the room, searching for something she might use as a weapon. The poker in the fireplace tools would do nicely.

She would never again be caught unawares.

Rain sheeted the glass, creating an intimate and watery prison. The only good thing about this entire situation was that she couldn't be married as long as she was a prisoner.

How quickly would her uncle ransom her?

When a knock sounded a quarter hour later, she stood at the door with the poker in hand, more than willing to defend herself.

It wasn't the thief, however, but a young maid holding a tray.

"Begging your pardon, miss," she said, bobbing a curtsy, "but I've been told to bring you something to eat. I've bread and cheese, and some of Cook's biscuits."

Emma wasn't hungry but didn't think it necessary to explain to the young girl that the circumstances of her abduction had stripped her of any appetite she might have had.

"Thank you," she said, pulling the door open and propping the poker behind it.

Anthony had admonished her at least once a day not

to thank the servants. *They are there to do your bidding, Emma. Thanking them undermines your authority.*

She'd never argued with him. Yet to say *thank you* was a small thing, an inconsequential rebellion, and therefore one she continued.

The maid disappeared, bobbing yet another curtsy. London servants were more jaded than that young girl, making Emma wonder if she'd come recently from the country. Or from Scotland?

The maid knocked again. This time when Emma opened the door it was to find herself face-to-face with Ian.

Since leaving her, he'd changed. He was no longer dressed in solid black. Instead, his shirt was white, his gray trousers dry and pressed. He no longer wore boots but well-polished shoes with elegant silver buckles. His hair had been dried as well, no longer falling forward across his brow. If she'd met him anywhere but in her sitting room, she would've thought him a peer of the realm, or at the very least a gentleman of the merchant class.

Instead, he was a thief with immaculate manners, and a taste for gentrified life.

"I've brought you a nightgown," he said, and only then did she realize that he held a folded garment in his hands. He halted a few steps into the room.

She took the precaution of stepping to the back of the door, the poker once more in her hand.

"You have the most horrified expression on your face, Emma," he said. "Why?"

"Is your mistress in residence?" she asked.

He frowned at her. "Mistress?" He placed the nightgown on the end of the bed before returning to the door.

"A ménage à trois? Is that what you think I have planned? If you hadn't been married to the Duke of Herridge, I might have asked you where you got such an idea."

She gripped the poker tighter.

"I'm not the Duke of Herridge," he said, his voice strangely kind.

She was trembling in earnest and it had nothing to do with the chill she felt or the residual dampness of her clothing.

"The garment belongs to my mother," he said. "She has never worn it. It was delivered after she returned to Scotland. I'm certain she would not have any objection if you took advantage of that fact."

"I'm in mourning," she said.

Amusement danced in his eyes. "Must a widow wear everything in black?"

"I really have no intention of discussing my garments with you."

"Even your . . . " He was obviously struggling to find an acceptable word.

Emma remained silent, enjoying his discomfiture. "Everything," she finally said.

"Would the world know if, for one night, you didn't wear black??"

Instead of answering him, she asked a question of her own. "What would your mother say about my being here?"

"She'd be horrified," he said, smiling. "You see, I haven't had a very long history of abduction. No doubt she'd have some recommendations. She comes from a long line of border reivers."

He turned and without another word left the room, closing the door firmly behind him. She knew, and yet couldn't say exactly why she knew, that if she wished to leave this room, or this house, there would be no barriers to her doing so. He would simply stand aside, his dark eyes revealing nothing.

Kindness, however, often masked a cruel nature. Another lesson she'd learned from Anthony.

She took the precaution of locking the door.

Emma moved to the bed and stared down at the nightgown. It wasn't black, and at this moment she didn't care. She could remain dressed in her damp clothing but that didn't seem reasonable. She could easily catch cold, and the very last thing she wanted was to be ill while a captive.

Turning, she glanced at the door and then back at the bed, then moved the desk chair to the door and wedged the back beneath the handle.

Slowly, she began to undress, placing her dress on the chair by the window, hoping that it would dry overnight. Once attired in the pale blue nightgown—silk, by the touch of it—Emma sat on the edge of the bed.

What was she to do?

Today she'd been informed she was to marry again, but she couldn't face that horror right at the moment. Instead, she thought about her abduction, how Ian had struck her uncle in her defense, how she'd been so startled by that act that she allowed him to grab her and escape from her own home.

A home that wasn't truly a home, just as he'd said. But if the town house wasn't home, then what was? Not her childhood home of Graviston Park. Her uncle now owned that as well. Certainly not Chavensworth; it had gone to Anthony's cousin. Even if the great house had not been entailed, she would never have returned, willingly, to Chavensworth.

Where did she belong?

Ian made it to his library before he began to swear. He closed the door, leaned both hands against it, then clenched his fists into palms, bruising his knuckles against the hard wood. If he could have disinterred the Duke of Herridge at that moment, he would have gleefully pummeled his corpse.

At the moment, however, he was more annoyed at himself than he was the dead duke.

He rounded his desk and sat behind it, extracting a piece of his stationery and loading the nib with ink. He closed the letter with:

Your niece will be surrendered upon receipt of the mirror. A man will call upon you in one day, sufficient time to obtain the mirror from Chavensworth.

Rest assured that the Duchess of Herridge is being cared for and will suffer no harm.

He sat back. He'd never written a ransom note before but it seemed to cover the matter suitably. Of course, he'd never abducted a duchess before, either, both actions entirely out of keeping with his nature and his inclinations.

He'd send the note by messenger tomorrow morning, instructing one of his staff from Lochlaven to ensure it was done with some anonymity.

At least no one would expect Emma to appear anywhere. She was in seclusion, in mourning. All that he had to do was ensure that no one in his home knew who she was, or if they did discover her identity, that they not speak of it.

Most of his employees had come from Lochlaven, returning home when their taste of London was surfeited. He'd counted on their loyalty many times before tonight. Patterson, however, was a different story. The majordomo was so stiffly English that it was a wonder the man had deigned to be employed by the Earl of Buchane and the Laird of Trelawny. He knew he had to keep Patterson suitably occupied and ignorant of Emma's identity.

Until Emma's uncle retrieved the mirror and returned to London, she would be his guest. In the meantime he would ensure that her stay was as comfortable as possible, that no further talk swirled around her.

He banished the thought that perhaps it wasn't altogether wise to feel protective of the Duchess of Herridge.

"Is there no sign of her?" Peter, Earl of Falmouth, asked.

"No sign, Your Lordship," the majordomo said, standing in front of Peter's chair with head bowed. "Nor of the carriage."

"No one knows in which direction it traveled?"

"We were unable to discover that, Your Lordship," the majordomo said. "Would you like us to keep looking?"

"No," Peter said, holding his hand to his jaw. "The rain has gotten stronger. I doubt there is a soul abroad who would've seen the carriage at this point. You say you didn't get a good look at him?"

"Your Lordship, I was not in the front hall when they left."

"And you have no idea how he got into the house?"

Neither the majordomo nor any of the footmen ringed behind him had any idea. But then, he knew that anyone who would allow a stranger to come into his house wouldn't admit to it.

"Shall I send for a physician, Your Lordship?" the majordomo asked.

"No," he said. His jaw felt as if it were broken, but it wasn't, merely sore. He would have a mark on his face for days, courtesy of the stranger who'd stolen his niece away from the house.

If she didn't marry, then he'd be unable to pay his blackmailer. The young fool would talk. Someone might begin to think that the man was more than a sot and there was some truth to his assertions.

The very last thing he could afford was a bit of inquiry. He had to find Emma, and marry her off with all possible haste.

Chapter 5

The knock on the door roused Emma from a surprisingly deep and restful sleep. She rolled over onto her back, blinking several times before realizing where she was.

She'd been abducted. Should she have slept quite so well? For that matter, should she be as ravenously hungry as she was?

The knock came again, and she sat up, tossing the covers aside. After moving the chair, she unlocked the door cautiously and opened it, peering around the edge. It wasn't Ian but the same young maid who'd brought her a tray the night before.

"I'm to tell you, miss," the girl said, "that the master would like you to join him for breakfast. I'm to make it in the form of an invitation and not an order."

She repeated the words with such diligence that Emma knew she'd been coached.

Perhaps it would be better to request a tray in her room. Or were prisoners given such flexibility?

At home, she wasn't. Even if she did not feel like facing the day, she was expected to be at breakfast when the bell rang every morning, to share the time with her uncle, to pass the minutes in conversation of some sort.

One day, perhaps, she would have a single establishment of her own. She would be the one to dictate if she came down to breakfast in the morning or chose to take her lunch in the evening. There would be no one but her to decide how she might spend her days.

"You need to give me a few minutes to get dressed," she said.

"Then I'm to take you to the garden, miss."

"The garden?"

"The master eats in the garden on fair days."

"A moment, then," Emma said.

The maid bobbed a curtsy and left.

Emma did not call her back to help her dress. She'd disrobed the night before; she could certainly dress herself this morning. For the first time in her life, however, she had no choice of garments to wear. In her armoire at home there were at least a dozen dresses suitable for half-mourning, some with touches of white about the collar and sleeves. One or two were ornamented with jet beads or delicate little ruches across the bodice. Small touches of femininity to remind her that even though she mourned, she was alive.

Emma slipped into the bathing chamber attached to the bedroom, performing her morning chores before beginning the uncomfortable task of outfitting herself for the day ahead. Her chemise was still a little damp from the night before but she ignored the discomfort. She left the top three eyelets in her corset unlaced, a small concession to comfort. Her petticoat was damp as well, and looked sadly bedraggled, as did the small at-home hoop she'd been wearing last night. The skirt

48   Karen Ranney

came next, the black looking almost rusty in the morning light, then the bodice, fitting too snugly, perhaps, because she didn't tighten her corset as well as her maid might have.

When she was finally dressed, she was left with the problem of her hair. On top of the bureau was a silver handled military brush resting on an ornate silver tray. She'd never used such a personal object belonging to a stranger but had no choice at the moment. There was a mirror above the bureau but she brushed her hair without looking at her image. She simply had to trust in the fact that she was clean and presentable. Any additional concern about her appearance would be vanity, and she'd never been overly vain.

What did her appearance matter? She had no control over it. She could not dictate why her cheekbones were higher than those of her peers and more pronounced, or why her eyes were that shade of blue, odd enough to be noticed in a crowd. She had no ability to change the shape of her nose or the angle of her chin or the curve of her ears. She was, simply put, just who she was.

True, there were times when women of her acquaintance augmented their good qualities, and attempted to confuse the eye so lesser traits were not noticed. A smudge of kohl just below the cheekbones made them look more pronounced. A tiny vertical line of white near the nose made it appear more patrician. There were unguents a woman could use on her lips to make them more prominent, and drops for the eyes so they appeared radiant and sparkly.

She'd never used any of those artifices. This morning

she didn't even have her reticule and the little pot of rose salve she sometimes used to offset the paleness of her lips.

Perhaps it was better that she didn't look in the mirror.

Whatever her appearance, she was ready, and the ferocious growling of her stomach—rude and unpardonable in the best of circumstances—drove her from the room.

As she closed the door behind her, the maid stepped out from an alcove, smiled brightly, and bobbed yet another curtsy.

"There you are, miss," she said, and with that, smartly turned on her heel, leaving Emma to follow.

Last night she'd thought this a hallway, but it was a column-lined corridor overlooking a courtyard. She walked to the waist-high wall and looked down.

A walkway of crushed gravel stretched from one corner of the courtyard to the other, creating an X. Where the two paths intersected sat a small round table, its bright white cloth undulating in the soft breeze.

"The master is waiting, miss," the young maid said, turning back impatiently. Evidently, the master could not be made to wait.

Emma was tempted to inform the young maid about the kind of person she served. A bounder, a cad, and although she didn't know his behavior well enough to fit the label of rake to him, she didn't doubt that it applied as well. Any man who invaded a woman's bedroom should certainly be called to task for his actions.

However, she kept silent, having had years of experience at biting back words that more wisely should be left unsaid, and followed the girl.

The house was not as grand as hers, yet it was certainly not ill-appointed or lacking in beauty. The banister was truly a lovely thing, with its sweeping wood curves and heavily carved balusters. She followed the maid down the stairs, noting the niches along the way that held bits of statuary that looked quite old.

The maid led her down a covered walkway lined with a series of columns, reminding her of the Roman ruins in Bath. She stopped beside one arch and stepped aside, motioning to Emma to precede her.

Secluded from traffic sounds, lined with tall trees swaying in the gentle breeze, the courtyard was a small and perfect green oasis. A profusion of Sweet William, Hypericum, and another bed of strange plants greeted her.

Emma hesitated at one, bending down to examine one of them more closely. A long, strong, straight stem ended in a bulge, and above it bloomed a purple spiked flower.

"It's a thistle," he said.

She looked up to find Ian standing on the gravel walk.

"A thistle?" she asked, straightening.

"A symbol of Scotland," he said. "A little bit of my home, brought to London. Besides, the butterflies seem to like it."

In the morning light he was even more handsome than he'd been last night, and despite the fact that she was the Duchess of Herridge, she felt unaccountably shy, incapable of sitting and eating breakfast across from this incredibly handsome man. Nestled in her unaccustomed awkwardness was wonder that she could feel so terribly young once again.

"Will you join me?" he asked, leading the way down the path.

On the table two small covered silver domes glinted in the morning light. Beside them sat a book, open but turned upside down, as if her abductor had been engrossed in it prior to her arrival.

Who was he?

He pulled out a well-padded chair that looked as if it belonged in the dining room.

"It's a bright and sunny day," he said. "I always think the air so much clearer after a storm, don't you?"

She only nodded as he assisted her with the chair. Despite the fact that last night had been chilly, this day was temperate, hinting at warm.

"I am torn between wanting to ask if you rested well and being aware that the question is not one normally uses to begin a breakfast between strangers."

"I slept well," she said. "Thank you." In fact, it was odd how well she did sleep. As restful as a baby. There were no sounds from the streets, no cautions in her mind.

"Then as your host, however unwittingly," he said, smiling, "may I tell you that you certainly look well rested. Quite lovely, in fact."

She ignored his words, directing her attention to the bright white plate with its gold trim, a pattern she recognized as Royal Dorchester. She had a similar pattern at home.

"It's unusual to have a garden in London," she said, when the feeling of warmth had faded from her cheeks. "We have a little plot of land behind the stables, but we use it to exercise the horses when necessary."

The rather vacuous nature of her comment made her wince inwardly.

He only continued to smile. For some odd reason her gaze kept returning to him and not the table, or the plate, or the scenery around them. She was not even captivated by the pattern of shadows on the tablecloth caused by the swaying branches above them.

Today he was attired in a white shirt and black trousers, the plainness of his attire a perfect backdrop to his appearance. His eyes were brown, so darkly brown they appeared almost black. His features were finely chiseled, and he was tall and lean with broad shoulders. A very impressive appearing man.

"I have always liked this house," he said.

At her quick look, his smile broadened. "No, I didn't steal it. This house has been in my family for generations."

"Who are you?" she asked.

Instead of answering, he only shook his head, as if to negate her curiosity.

He raised his right hand, and a footman suddenly appeared, as if he'd sprung full-grown from a nearby bush. He carried a small round tray heaped with a selection of toast and rolls. She selected two pieces of toast, and some kippers from the covered container on the table.

After the footman departed, she glanced up at him. "I've never had the opportunity to dine alfresco," she said.

"Did you never have a picnic?" he asked.

"Is that your price for this meal? Details about my private life?"

"Can we not converse?"

"Why should we?" she said.

He shook his head.

"You cannot simply shake your head at me," she said. "Not when I'm certain there is something you wish to say."

"Let's just say that my comment would not have been complimentary." His smile took none of the sting from his words.

He laid his spoon on the edge of his saucer before slowly and deliberately picking his cup up and drinking from it, all the while regarding her.

She could feel the flush emanate from her toes and travel all the way up to bloom on her cheeks. She picked up her cup, mimicking his movements, studying him with the same intensity.

"You're quite annoying," she said, placing the cup down on the saucer.

"Am I?"

He raised one eyebrow in such an imperious gesture that she almost smiled.

She preferred to study a hedge a few feet away rather than look at him again. Whoever cared for this garden had the ability to coax even the boxwood into lush profusion.

"I've taken your advice," he said.

"What advice did I give you?"

"This morning I sent a note to your uncle informing him that you'll be returned once I have the Tulloch Sgàthán."

"That's very bold of you," she said. "What if he tracks you down first?"

"From what I've seen of your uncle," he said, "I doubt he'll make the effort."

"What if he refuses to surrender the mirror?"

"Never underestimate your value, Duchess."

She'd four years to know the true extent of her worth. It lay in her womb, not in her person.

"I'm nothing without a husband, and with a husband, I was less than nothing. Society does not value women. They value women who accommodate."

"Did you accommodate, Emma?"

She stared at her plate without speaking for several moments. "Yes," she said finally.

"I often take my meals out of doors," he said, returning to the previous topic.

"Therefore," she said, grateful for his easing her through a difficult moment, "you've had vast experience at picnics."

He smiled, the expression charming.

"My home is near a lake, and on the lake is an island. Ever since I was a little boy, the island has been my refuge, my lodestone, as it were. I can remember eating many a meal at the top of the hill on that island. Inconsequential moments but ones I still recall."

She cut her toast in half, busying herself with the knife. "So you've created an island in London."

He looked around, as if suddenly viewing the courtyard differently.

"Perhaps I have," he said.

Breakfast occupied them both for a few moments, the time passing in a surprisingly pleasant interlude.

She glanced at him from time to time, unsurprised that he had excellent table manners. He possessed a quality, something arresting that drew her eyes over and over. Perhaps it was a sense that he knew his place in life and his purpose, had a goal, and was determined to achieve it.

Against that, what were mere good looks?

"Where is your home? Your island?" she asked.

"Where is home to a Scot if not Scotland? But the world comes to London, doesn't it?"

"The world doesn't necessarily live here."

He smiled again, a little effortless charm to mask the fact that he had not answered her question.

"Where in Scotland are you from?" she asked more directly.

"Shall I say the Highlands?" he asked. "And in doing so immediately be characterized as one of those warriors that are so popular of late. I'll be a laird, shall I?"

"Are you?"

"Scotland has existed all these hundreds and thousands of years," he said, deflecting her question. "But it's only in the last twenty that there's been so much written about my country."

"The Queen has a great fondness for Scotland," she said.

He only nodded.

"Am I not to know?" she asked. "Or are you simply trying to be mysterious?"

"Perhaps I'm trying to be more like you," he said, "revealing little of myself. They gossip about you, you know."

"I'm the Duchess of Herridge. People will say what they will."

His hand brushed close to where one of hers rested on the table. When Anthony was near, she only felt aversion, and a sickening kind of fear. Now, her skin tingled and her stomach fluttered. She dared herself to leave her hand where it was. When he made no further move, she didn't know if she was disappointed or relieved.

The sun warmed the top of her head, and the air was clean and sparkling. The equanimity with which

her abductor treated her was unusual, and yet as re-
freshing as the breeze. She could have been anyone,
anyone at all. Not necessarily the Duchess of Herridge,
or a woman in mourning. She was simply herself,
simply Emma, the person she'd yearned to be for so
very long.

She would revel in this freedom for as long as she
had it, knowing that it was short-lived. A day, perhaps two at the most, and she would return home,
and take up the role that Fate had decreed for her,
becoming the widowed Duchess of Herridge until
she was married again.

The thought of marriage almost made her ill.

She stared down at her plate, realizing that her
appetite had abruptly vanished.

"Is something wrong, Emma?"

She looked up at him. "I'm to be married," she
said. She'd not intended to say that. Ordinarily she
would never have revealed something so personal
about herself. But then, these were not ordinary
circumstances.

He was looking at her, his gaze so direct she almost
glanced away.

"So am I," he said. "In a matter of months."

"Are mutual congratulations in order, then?" she
asked.

"By the look on your face, no," he said, his voice
too soft, too kind.

He shouldn't be considerate. If he were, she would
start to think of him as more than an abductor. A
friend, perhaps, in a life devoid of friends. Or something even more dangerous—a handsome man who
interested her a little too much.

Chapter 6

"**D**o you know her?" she asked. "Your betrothed?"

"Her father is one of my oldest friends. My mentor, as a matter of fact."

"Do you like her?"

He looked startled by the question.

"I shouldn't have asked that, should I? Perhaps I envy you. I'd only met Anthony once, and didn't even remember it. He did, however, and appealed to my father that very night. He said meeting me was one of his fondest memories. Wouldn't you think I would be able to recall it as well?"

"Perhaps not. Evidently, you made an impression, while he did not."

"It was a party, I think. Perhaps that's why I don't remember. I dislike parties," she said. "Mourning isn't onerous for me, for that very reason. It gives me an excuse to be by myself, in my own company."

She was prattling—she could hear herself. What had gotten into her?

"Rebecca, my betrothed, is just the opposite," he said. "She knows everyone's names and the names of their brothers and sisters and mothers and fathers.

And as far as liking her, we've been acquaintances for a great many years."

"Then I wish you the very greatest happiness," she said.

"And I, you," he replied, smiling at her. "Who is to be your next husband?"

"I haven't any idea," she admitted. "I never even inquired as to his name. My uncle made the announcement last night, before you arrived."

"Quite an adventurous night."

She sent him a look.

"Perhaps he will be the best of husbands," he said, watching her over his cup.

"Perhaps he shall. And we will grow old together in loving matrimony."

He put the cup down. "Your tone seems to make a mockery of marriage, Emma."

She was silent for a moment. When she did speak, her voice was faint, as if she were ashamed to say the words. But she felt, strangely enough, that they needed to be said.

"You've listened to the rumors about me. Have you heard anything said about Anthony, then?"

"I have, yes."

"Can you imagine, then, if half the rumors you heard were true, what my marriage was like?"

It was his turn to remain silent. "Yes," he said finally. "I can."

His look was too sympathetic.

He reached out and touched the top of her hand with the tip of his forefinger. A delicate touch, one that somehow managed to feel almost intimate. She should draw her hand back but she didn't. Instead, she stared at his finger, feeling oddly mesmerized.

She'd never sat so close to any man other than her husband. No man, including Anthony, had ever been so charming. A few of Anthony's friends had whispered lurid suggestions to her but no one had ever been so pleasant.

She didn't know what to do. Should she leave now? Prudence demanded that she do so, yet the impulse warred with her very real wish to remain exactly where she was.

"After you get the mirror," she asked, pushing aside her thoughts, "will you return to Scotland?"

"Yes," he said.

"Tell me what your home is like," she said, then softened her request. "Please."

Even as she sat there, she knew she wasn't being wise or proper at all. She should retreat to her chamber and act the part Fate had given her. If not prisoner, she should play the role of widow. On this bright and shining morning, however, she couldn't find it in herself to pretend to grieve for Anthony.

For a moment they sat in silence, before Ian began to speak.

"Lochlaven is a few hundred years old and my family has lived there since it was built in 1606. It's perched upon a promontory," he said, his voice soft, almost melodic. "Overlooking a lake on which there's an island, the site of the first castle. Behind us is Ben Cuidan, and a range of mountains. Lochlaven itself faces west. Each day as the sun sets we're treated to a show of pink and gray skies. When I was a boy, I used to think that we were the last spot on earth, the last ones to see the sun set, but then, everything in my life revolved around Lochlaven in those days. It wasn't until I went away to school that I understood it wasn't the center of everyone's world."

The more she knew about him, the more mysterious he became—a thief with a castle in Scotland and a large home in London.

"Yet you left your home for the sake of a mirror," she said.

"Not exactly," he admitted. "I was due to be in London on business, and decided to take advantage of the opportunity." When she didn't respond, he leaned forward. "You aren't here because of a mirror, Emma," he said softly. "I didn't want to leave you alone to explain the presence of a man in your chamber to your uncle."

She nodded. "That would have been difficult," she said. "But not impossible. I doubt my uncle cares much for my reputation."

"Can you trust him to choose a husband for you?" he asked.

She turned her head and looked at the profusion of plants surrounding her. Crimson lilies and deep red roses contrasted with the brighter oranges of the vivid gerberas. What a lovely place this was. Indeed, an island in the midst of London.

She would have loved to talk to the gardener about the plantings. Anything but answer Ian's question. In the end it didn't matter what she thought or believed. Only that she was subject to her uncle's will.

He leaned back, folded his arms and regarded her steadily.

"I haven't heard many good comments about you, Emma. You surprise me."

"From Lady Sarah? I can understand only too well.

Any woman who would attempt to take her mother's place would be looked upon with disfavor."

"She never said a word. Other than to comment that she didn't know you, had never met you."

"Ah, rumors, then."

Women had been among some of the most dissolute guests at Chavensworth. Women who were doyennes of society, showing a serene and flawless face to the world. No one saw the rot beneath the surface. Would any of those hypocritical women have meekly acceded to another marriage?

The appearance of virtue was truly its own reward.

She didn't even have that—no woman married to Anthony would have.

"You've been an exemplary prisoner."

What would he say if she told him that she'd had four years of imprisonment?

"Perhaps I should abduct a duchess more often," he said. He was trying to be charming again, and succeeding only too well.

"You mustn't relegate yourself to only duchesses," she said. "There are few enough of us. You might consider a countess or two, or even a baroness."

"In all honesty, I doubt I shall do this again. The journey across your roof was a little more adventure than I choose to have. I'm a better scientist than I am a thief."

"A scientist?"

He nodded.

"What do you study?"

"Water," he said. A moment later his smile deepened. "You have the most amazing look on your face.

As if you're deciding whether or not to ask—why water?—or to remain silent."

"Why water?" she asked.

He began to laugh, and she had no choice but to smile with him.

"Omne vivum ex ovo," he said.

"Every living thing comes from an egg?"

"You know Latin?"

She nodded. "Not extensively," she admitted. "But my governess considered that a woman should know a great deal about many subjects."

He evidently didn't consider that important enough to comment upon, or perhaps women in Scotland were educated in a similar fashion.

"Do you know anything about spontaneous generation?"

She shook her head, finished her tea, and set the cup down.

"I presume, however, that you've heard of Aristotle."

' "You are what you do,' " she quoted.

His surprised glance amused her. "The governess?"

She nodded.

"Aristotle also believed that living things could be born from nonliving things."

She sat back, interested. "Or spontaneous generation," she said.

He nodded.

"Aristotle's theory is being proven wrong. Instead of spontaneous generation, there is something called a bacterium, an organism we think capable of producing disease."

He leaned toward her, turned his hand over and stretched out his index finger. "Imagine, if you will, that on the tip of my finger there are hundreds of thousands of tiny little animals that you cannot see. These are bacteria, so small that they aren't visible to the human eye. But they're there all the same, and it's their presence that can make us ill."

He straightened and pulled back his hand.

"How do you see them?"

"With a microscope," he said.

"And you study this? Isn't it dangerous?"

"A great many things can be dangerous if care is not taken."

"But why?"

"Because it's there? Because I can? Because whenever people become ill I want to know why?" He shrugged but the intent look in his eyes belied his affected nonchalance.

"Are you a physician, then?"

"No, but I work with a physician. My betrothed's father, as a matter of fact."

She envied him his enthusiasm because she'd never viewed the world with such delight.

"I must be about my work now," he said, placing his napkin on the side of his plate. "But I have no needlework to occupy you," he said. "I noticed the needlework in your room."

"I do not require occupation," she said. A moment later she corrected herself. "I do not require needlework as an occupation."

"My sister deplores it," he said. "Ever since she was eight, and required to rework her sampler numerous times, she's refused to take up the needle."

"Your sister sounds like someone after my own heart," she said. "However, I've always thought it a failing of mine not to have the patience or the skill."

"Perhaps your talents lie in other directions," he

said. "Unfortunately, my library is filled with scientific treatises, but perhaps my sister has left behind a novel or two. I'll see if I can find something for you."

"You are very solicitous for an abductor," she said. "For all that you say you've had no experience in it."

"Much less than you've had at being a duchess."

"There isn't much to being a duchess," she said, looking away. "One must simply have the capacity to endure."

She hadn't meant to say *that*, either.

He reached out and touched her hand again. She didn't withdraw it but left it there, fingers straightened and pointing toward him.

She tilted her head slightly and regarded him with some intensity.

He smiled once more, an expression that was evidently commonplace for him. Was it also a routine occurrence for him to attract women? She couldn't help but wonder.

A very mysterious man, this brigand, and one she'd do well to avoid.

She stood, pushing back her chair rather than waiting for him to assist her. She placed her napkin to the left of her plate, checked to see that she'd left the silverware in the correct position. The training of a lifetime served her now, as it had so often in the past.

Yet she'd never taken nearly an hour to eat her breakfast. Or eaten it in the bright light of the morning sun or with such an enticing stranger.

A great many things can be dangerous if care is not taken. Including wanting something one mustn't have. Although she may wish it, she could not turn time on itself. She couldn't become someone other than who she was. It was not four years ago; it was today.

"Thank you for breakfast," she said. "But until my uncle sends you the mirror, I think it would be better if I ate in my room."

He'd stood when she did, and now she had to tilt her head back in order to see him. Not an easy thing to do since the sun was behind him. She shielded her eyes, wishing she could see his expression.

"But it's not my room," she said. "It's yours. Where did you sleep last night?"

"There are ten bedrooms in this house," he said. "I simply took another."

"Wouldn't it be better for you to have your own chamber back? I'd be happier in another," she said.

"I have no objection to sharing what I have with you, Emma," he said softly. "Whether it's breakfast or a room."

"Yes," she said, an answer to a question he hadn't asked. She felt foolish and silly and too young. Without another word she left him, nearly running down the path and up the stairs to the room that was less a prison at this moment than sanctuary.

As she did so, in that space of only seconds, Emma allowed herself to feel the pain of regret and something, strangely, like longing.

Chapter 7

A few minutes after Emma left him, Ian made his way back to his library. There was work he needed to do on the paper he'd present to the Royal Society of London tonight. The gathering was to be a small one, hosting a few visiting members of the Académie des Sciences from France. The document was more theoretical than empirical and was the basis for his current study of the bacterial content of the natural springs around his home in Scotland.

The first of three missions he'd had on this trip to London. He hoped the first—his paper—would be well received. He still had not succeeded in the second—obtaining the Tulloch Sgàthán. The third—that of contacting his cousin Bryce—was not going to be pleasant.

His cousin had remarked, on more than one occasion, that he didn't wish to be saved. If he chose to travel down the road to perdition, it was his damn choice. A decision that Ian would have been more than happy to leave to him, had it not been for his mother. His mother was fond of Bryce, and more than a little concerned for his welfare.

He needed to find Bryce, and find out just how much money he owed this time. He'd also attempt to urge Bryce not to contact his mother for money. Every time he did so, the Countess of Buchane was upset, and determined to do something to aid her adopted son.

He'd planned to be in London less than a week, having come to learn, to be educated, to share his own knowledge. He had not come to London to be flummoxed, to be confused, or even worse—to be concerned about a woman he barely knew.

"Your Lordship," his majordomo said, "this just came for you."

Peter reached out his hand and took the missive. His name was written in distinctive script but he didn't recognize the handwriting. The stationery was a good quality, easily equal to that he'd recently ordered for himself.

"Who did you say brought this?" he asked of his majordomo.

"A young boy, Your Lordship."

"Is he here now?" Peter asked, having opened the envelope and scanned the contents of the letter.

"No, Your Lordship," the majordomo said. "He gave the envelope to me and then ran away."

"Pity," Peter said, rereading the message.

His niece had been abducted. He knew that. If he did not produce a certain object—a mirror, purportedly at Chavensworth—she might very well be in danger.

Peter sat back against his chair, stretched his feet out on the footstool in front of him, and folded his hands across his stomach, trapping the letter beneath his hands.

He was damned tired of feeling powerless. Something would have to be done. First that idiotic young fool and now this. He needed Emma back now.

The message stated that he would be given one day. One day to produce an object he'd never before seen, and whose location was a mystery to him.

Dearest Emma, his niece, the darling daughter of his older brother. His brother should have ensured that his fortune had accompanied the title. After all, what's the worth of a title when there are no funds to accompany it?

He was too old to marry again. His wife had borne him three children, none of whom had survived childhood, before she finally died a few years ago. An heiress might have solved the Duke of Herridge's money problems but Peter wasn't the Duke of Herridge. Nor was he interested in courting some young girl.

If something happened to Emma, he would have more than control of her money. He'd have all that lovely fortune to himself.

He'd had to abandon his plans the minute that young fool showed up. Now he was being forced to pretend to care.

Damn it. He had to get Emma home, and quickly.

When Emma was a child, she had no dreams of being a princess. Perhaps because her father had treated her as if she were one in truth. Anything she wanted, he bestowed on her with generosity and love. He'd purchased a very expensive horse from a next-door neighbor because she'd admired him in the paddock. He'd given her a carriage of her own when she was sixteen, a pretty little thing of midnight blue, with an interior of pale blue velvet upholstery.

"You and your maid can go calling in that," he said. "A carriage befitting its occupants."

Perhaps she might have been spoiled had not her mother's death brought sorrow into her life. Perhaps her father thought to make up, in a small way, for the loss of her mother, a sweet and calm-faced woman with an eternal smile.

Emma remembered being grateful that her father had not remarried. Yet now, as she sat in a strange room in a strange house in the middle of a city she knew well, she couldn't help but wonder if her father had regretted not marrying again. He'd devoted himself so completely to his interests and to his daughter that there had been no room for anyone else in his life.

Had he been lonely?

Why had it taken until now for her to wonder? Perhaps she had been spoiled, after all.

She sat on the chair beside the window, wishing it would storm again. The weather was calm, however, the view from the window serene. Her life had been like that, until Ian entered her sitting room window. From that moment onward, everything had turned upside down.

Even a scientist from Scotland had heard the rumors. Of course people talked about her—she was the Duchess of Herridge. She was Anthony's wife. More than that, she was the Ice Queen.

Could she have escaped? Could she have simply walked away from Chavensworth?

If she'd told her father only a fraction of what had

gone on in Anthony's house, he would have gladly offered her sanctuary. But then, she didn't doubt that Anthony would have attempted to punish her father for doing so. Anthony answered to no authority but his own.

And now, to the Devil's.

Could she have refused to attend his entertainments? Doing so would have delighted her husband—hadn't he said, more than once, how he relished a little spirit and fire? In the end she'd survived, the cost for doing so no doubt taken from her immortal soul. She'd hated in a way few people could, and feared in a way that no woman should.

How could she possibly explain that to anyone?

Perhaps she had been spoiled as a child, and paid for it as a woman.

A knock interrupted her thoughts, and when Emma answered the door, it was to find the same young maid who'd summoned her to breakfast. Now she held a small square basket in her hands and a selection of books under her arm. A selection of novels, Emma was delighted to discover, that she'd not read; all books she could not wait to read.

No one in her entire life had ever given her a book, not even her father. No one had encouraged her to sit and read. Instead, she'd always been told that she must busy herself with those occupations befitting the daughter of an earl. If no one would be disturbed, she should practice the pianoforte. If silence was required, she should work on her needlepoint. She was to be a lady of leisure but her time should be spent in a manner that would bring credit to her family and to her husband.

Wasting the hours in fascination, in being transported to another time and another place, was hedonistic, at best, and at worst encouraged a woman to think beyond her role in life.

The girl disappeared into the bathing chamber, emerging to finish dispensing the contents of the basket. She placed a long handled silver brush and mirror on top of the bureau before bobbing a curtsy and leaving the room in silence.

Emma settled on the bed, arranging the books before her like plates at a feast. *Bleak House*, *Pride and Prejudice*, *Silas Marner: the Weaver of Raveloe*, and *Wuthering Heights*, all books so exciting that the words must surely singe their pages.

She felt curiously lighthearted. For the first time in years she wasn't expected to be anywhere, to be doing anything in particular, and most importantly, no one demanded that she act in a certain way. For a day she didn't have to worry about her upcoming marriage. In the safety of this room, she didn't have to pretend to mourn her husband.

For the first time in years—in her lifetime, perhaps?—she was entirely and completely free, and she was a prisoner.

Lying back on the bed, she grabbed *Silas Marner* and began to read. Immediately, she lost herself in another time, another place, and another person's experience.

Once, she found herself agreeing with poor Silas.

It seemed to him that the Power he had vainly trusted in among the streets and at the prayer-meetings, was very far away from this land . . .

How many times had she felt that God was very far away, especially on those nights when Anthony entertained in Chavensworth's ballroom? Emma pushed that thought from her mind and concentrated on Silas's world and not her own.

She put her book down when summoned to the door by a knock.

"Your dinner, miss," the girl said, entering the room nearly bent over from the weight of the tray.

"Is it that time already?"

Although she hadn't done anything but read all day, Emma found herself remarkably hungry. The tray was laden with a slice of beef, vegetables, pudding, a small serving of fish, potatoes, and an individual pear tart. The meal looked delicious, and the serenity of not having to face her uncle across the table was even more wondrous.

This day of imprisonment had been pure bliss.

She'd been interrupted only once, when a young man had knocked.

"Begging your pardon, miss, but I need to get some clothes from the wardrobe."

She opened the door wide, and he'd gone to the armoire, selecting several garments. He'd left with an armful of clothing and a smile.

"It's a little early, miss," the young girl said now, placing the tray on the table near the bed. "But Cook is having hysterics on account of the dinner tonight, and the master just now returning to the house. My mother always said that what cannot be helped must be put up with." She shook her head, smiling.

"A dinner?" Emma asked.

"Oh yes, miss, the master is having a grand to do. Twenty people in all, and all the staff to wear their best bib and tucker. It's a very particular occasion."

Emma moved to sit on the edge of the bed.

"Is there anything else I can get for you, miss? With all the to do downstairs, it might be a bit of a wait if you ring for me."

"Who are the guests?" Emma asked, tamping down her sudden, insane panic.

"I'm not sure, miss. Mostly gentlemen, I think. Friends of the master."

She bobbed another curtsy and left. Emma stared at the closed door, then forced her attention to the meal.

Although she was certain the meal was wonderful, and more than a prisoner had a right to expect, she found that her appetite had abruptly vanished.

She might as well have been eating sawdust for what she tasted. When she'd eaten enough to satisfy her hunger, she slid from the bed and walked to the window. While she'd been reading, day had surrendered to night. This view was of a brightly lit square, not unlike her own neighborhood. But unlike her more sedate square, a line of carriages sat waiting for their passengers.

Her brigand evidently had guests.

Ian was not Anthony. This was not one of Anthony's entertainments. Her stomach, however, still clenched, and her hands trembled at her sides.

Ian would not take advantage of a lone woman. Had he not been concerned for her comfort from the first?

Still, she might be wrong. She would know in a matter of time, wouldn't she? Someone would come for her. Someone would tell her lies to reassure her. Someone would hold her down while another person—

or two—would strip her clothes away, before leading her to a place where she would be displayed, naked, for everyone to see.

That's how it had happened the first time.

Every other occasion, she'd simply been told that an entertainment was planned, and she'd performed in silence and utter calm, determined not to cry or plead or allow anyone to see her revulsion.

At first she'd been terrified of Anthony. Then, when she simply could not summon enough energy to care about what he would do to her, he told her that he'd disclose everything to her father, a man who was already ailing. When her father died, slipping beyond Anthony's grasp, her husband had threatened to tell the world what she'd done.

In the end it was simply easier to become someone she wasn't, the Ice Queen, no so much unaffected by what she saw as uncaring. In the last few years, she'd suspected Anthony had drugged her wine, but even that would have been unnecessary. She was an instrument of his will, his plaything, and his toy.

And she didn't think she could ever forgive herself for it.

This time she was not going to wait for them. Nor was she going to cower in this room. Instead, she would investigate, and if Ian's entertainment was anything like Anthony's, then she would flee this house, alone and in the darkness, if necessary.

Turning, she grabbed the latch and opened the door.

Shadows filled the corridor, and from far away came the sound of masculine laughter. This laughter was neither boisterous nor did it have a tinge of drunkenness to it. Instead, it sounded almost polite, as might a gathering before the Queen.

Slowly, she left the room, the flagstones abrasive on her bare feet. How shocking she was being. Her dress was badly wrinkled from lying on the bed most of the afternoon. She'd unbound her hair and it now fell in a mass past her shoulders. She'd removed her hoops and her corset was loose.

A lady never appeared in public without being perfectly dressed, even down to her gloves.

How idiotic that society decreed a great many rules for a woman's behavior and comportment, and almost none to a man's.

Yet she'd tried to obey those dictates when she could. She was to wear an endless assortment of petticoats if she did not wear her hoops. If she wore her hoops, she was not to complain about the itchiness of the tape fastenings. Her corset was to be laced at exactly the tightness required to both give her a womanly shape yet conceal that womanly shape from prying eyes. Even in the midst of summer she was to wear stockings, a most regrettable rule since even the delicate ones made at a convent in the south of France were unbearably warm—and itchy.

She was not to walk but to glide. Her breath was to come in soft, feminine pants, so as not to give the appearance of being too hearty or strong. Without a corset, a woman could breathe as well as a man, but every morning she laced her corset as prescribed. Only in the past months had she instructed Juliana to begin lacing at the third set of the eyelets and cease before the top two. In this manner, she allowed herself some freedom of movement, of breath, and relief from pain.

As a woman, she was to be meek and mild mannered. She was to defer to a man at all times, taking a man's judgment over her own, a man's reasoning over her own, a man's opinion over her own. At no time was she to consider herself a man's equal. After all, was not man created first, and woman second, from man's rib?

If, for some reason, she was to lose all her wits and forget those lifelong lessons, then a woman's husband was to show her where she'd erred.

Her mother had instilled those lessons in her from the time she was a child. An elderly aunt of her father's had added her chastisement as well, rapping Emma's knuckles with the crook of her cane when she wasn't quick enough to obey.

For all that, she still had fond memories of Aunt Ethel, a widow for so many years she claimed not to be able to recall her husband at all.

Would she be the same? In a matter of years would someone ask her about the Duke of Herridge only for her to be confused? Would she search her memory and be unable to remember the husband she'd so hated and feared for four years?

No, memories of Anthony were forever lodged in her mind, burned into her brain by shock and horror.

The laughter was closer, and she halted behind one of the columns. From here she could see down into the courtyard, that lovely space where she'd breakfasted with Ian only this morning. Light shone behind several windows lining the courtyard, and shadows flitted against the draperies.

Her heart beat rapidly, her hands grew damp, and her feet felt encased in blocks of ice. For endless moments she stood watching and waiting, a prayer trapped in her mind. How foolish she was—God had not helped her at Chavensworth.

Perhaps she thought that if she watched the door to the courtyard, it would remain shut. The men would stay inside with their party guests. She wrapped her arms around her waist, unable to push back the fear.

The stairs were barely illuminated by a lamp in the corridor below her. She clung to the banister with a hand while she gripped her skirts with the other and took one step at a time.

At the bottom of the steps she moved across the gravel, the stones biting into her bare feet, stopping at a spot close to where she'd breakfasted that morning.

The door opened.

She stepped back, behind a tall bush. A stream of men left the room. All of them were dressed in evening wear, and most of them appeared to be smoking a cigar. The smell of tobacco, a not unpleasant scent, wafted through the air.

Ian emerged finally, dressed in a similar fashion as the others. He was handsome enough in his everyday clothes, and even more so in black and white. But some people had considered Anthony a handsome man as well. They hadn't looked into his eyes and seen his withered soul.

Ian was intent upon shaking the hands of the men clustered around him.

"No, Sir Eustace, I will be unable to attend," he was saying.

"A pity. You have a first-rate scientific mind."

"Coming from you, Sir Eustace, I consider that a great compliment. Thank you."

"Keep up the good work, my dear boy. I think you're on to something."

One by one the men walked to a door on the other side of the courtyard, once more entering the house. Ian and another man followed them, Ian's hand on the man's shoulder.

There were no women in sight. No cancan dancers or scantily clad women of society.

Several maids and two footmen entered the room the men had vacated, evidently gathering up the dishes and straightening the chamber. She heard them laughing, the kind of camaraderie that went on in well-run households.

"If I'd known you were so curious," Ian said from behind her, "I would have invited you to dinner."

Chapter 8

She turned to see Ian standing in the shadows.
He took a few steps toward her, slowly, as if not wishing to startle her.

Her heartbeat was so rapid she was faint with it.

"If you had attended, I'm afraid someone would have recognized you," he continued. "Not to mention the fact that you would probably have been exceptionally bored."

"Was it an exceptionally boring dinner?" she asked, feeling absurdly close to tears. Relief because he wasn't like Anthony?

He moved out of the shadows and to her side. "Parts of it were," he said. "But I've learned to take the bad with the good. Some speeches were quite illuminating. My guests are members of the Royal Society, very learned men, all in all. True, some are boors, but you find that in any group."

"I've no affinity for science."

"Do you know that for certain?" he asked. "Or are you only saying that because you've not been exposed to much of it?"

"I'm not even entirely certain I know what science

is," she said. Why was she always so lamentably honest with him?

"I shall have to show you one day," he said. "Perhaps after all of this, we'll have the opportunity."

"A friendship between an abductor and his prisoner."

"Perhaps," he said, smiling.

"Brigand and scientist. What else do you do?"

"A great many things," he said.

"Do I have your word that I will be safe here, Ian?" she suddenly asked. She hadn't meant to ask the question but she was still conscious of the fear she'd felt earlier.

Was she always going to be just a little afraid?

He frowned at her, then just as suddenly his frown eased and a look came over his face that she couldn't decipher.

"I give you my solemn word, Emma, that you are safe here."

He didn't speak or ask the reason for her question. She was more than a little embarrassed for having spied on him, as well as insisting upon his reassurance now. A man's word was worthless if he had no honor. People in Anthony's circle were cleaved in two: a private persona and a public one. No one was truly honorable in either guise.

She shouldn't have considered this man who'd invaded her home, who'd abducted her, an honorable man. Yet she believed him, and strangely, trusted in his word.

"Thank you for the books," she said.

"You're welcome. I'm glad my sister is such a prodigious reader."

The silence was oddly intimate, as if each held back thoughts they shouldn't say.

"I haven't heard from your uncle, yet," he said. "But I'll send a man to your house tomorrow."

She nodded. Uncomfortable with the silence, she spoke again. "Did you give a speech tonight?"

"I did," he said, smiling. "Perhaps that's why parts of the dinner were so boring."

"I should like to hear it," she said.

"You wouldn't."

"I very much would," she said. The startled look on his face, coupled with his obvious reluctance, encouraged her to insist. "Truly, I would."

"The sun's light reveals its track when passing through a dark room by the dust floating in the air. The same particles are invisible by candlelight," he said.

She glanced at him in confusion, then understood. He was reciting his speech to her.

"In my research on decomposition by bacteria, I was troubled by the appearance of floating matter, and compelled to remove these atoms and dust. I wanted my experiment to have no taint of these diffuse particles."

Two maids walked along the corridor, and he leaned closer, his voice dropping to a whisper. His mouth was only an inch or so from her ear. She could feel his breath on her skin.

She shivered.

"I therefore constructed a box to track these atoms before the air which contained them reached my experiment." His voice was low, the words less important than his delivery of them. He could have recited the

Book of Common Prayer and made it sound like a decadent and forbidden volume.

"The box was lined with a vitreous solution."

She heard the sound of laughter, then he moved still closer and she couldn't pay attention to anything but him.

"As I had postulated, within a day the air coming into my experiment was devoid of these particles."

"It sounds like an enormously interesting speech," she said when he'd finished. In truth, she'd barely heard a word of it and understood even less.

The air around them was still, the courtyard silent. Not a leaf stirred. Not a bird sang. The servants were gone, all but two of the lamps extinguished. The two of them stood alone in the garden.

"I should leave," she said. Why was it suddenly so difficult to breathe?

She took a cautionary step to the side, then another, but he only turned to face her, the faint light illuminating the side of his face, the curve of his smile.

"Have I given you any reason to fear me?" he asked.

"Besides entering my sitting room? Other than crawling across my roof?"

He chuckled, holding up his hands as if in surrender. "Other than that," he said.

"Other than that. You've been a gentleman. A kind and generous host."

His smile faded. Had she insulted him?

"Emma," he said, then stopped.

She waited but he didn't speak further. Instead, his attention was captured by something across the courtyard. A flicker of light? The movement of the branches in the gentle night wind? Or perhaps he just simply wished himself away from her. She took another step to the side, gripping her skirts with both hands.

If nothing else, she should be mindful of the sheer romance of the night, of the moonlight casting shadows onto the walkway, the scent of roses, the whisper of wind through the branches, and the far off call of a night bird.

"Your guests will be missing you," she said a few minutes later, her eyes on the shadowed forms of the bushes and the flowers.

"I've plied them with spirits and tobacco," he said. "I doubt they will miss me unless either runs out. Scientists are largely a parsimonious lot. They spend most of their money on their experiments. To be treated to a fine dinner, cigars, and brandy is a luxury."

"Are you truly a thief?" she asked. "Is that how you've managed to acquire money for a fine dinner, cigars, and brandy?"

He didn't speak for a moment.

"Shall we be relentlessly honest with one another, Emma?" he said finally. "Shall I confess to you my identity? If I do so, then I want the truth from you as well."

The truth was an ugly thing, and this garden was too lovely to be soiled by it.

She shook her head.

"Then can we pretend, for however long we're destined to be in one another's company, that we are who we choose to be?"

"Who would you choose to be, Ian?"

"A scientist, a man who might be independently wealthy, with myriad responsibilities but a love of learning new things. And you? Who would you be?"

When she was a child, Cook had prepared pattern biscuits for her on special occasions or when she was ill. She would roll out a certain measure of dough, and using a wooden die, press a design into the soft dough. The biscuits were spicy, sweet, and uniform, each like the other.

During her marriage to Anthony, Emma had wanted to be like a pattern biscuit. She hadn't wanted to be singled out, made special or unique. She simply wanted to exist, anonymous and unseen.

Here and now, she was being given a chance to be anyone she wanted to be.

She could be the woman she'd been for the last four years, silent, reserved, pretending to be untouched by Anthony's depravities. Or she could be the Emma she'd never been, the woman grown from her girlhood, someone capable of kindness, generosity, compassion. A woman with excitement about life, enthusiasm about each coming day.

The Duchess of Herridge whispered to her to remember who she was. But Emma spoke. "Emma," she said. "I'll simply be Emma."

A footman passed not ten feet from them, and Ian turned his back to the man, effectively shielding her. The tinkle of glasses on a tray echoed loudly for a moment before fading away.

The air was warm, sultry. The soft breeze of the morning had acquired heat and a delicate and powdery scent from the roses.

He reached out his hand and touched her wrist.

"Who is Emma?"

Dear God what did she tell him? That she wasn't quite certain herself? One thing she did know—Emma was a girl much more approachable than the woman she'd become.

He took another step toward her, and she wanted to warn him that he stood much too close for propriety. But she kept her hands in front of her, still linked by his fingers on her wrist, as if he measured the effect of his touch on her.

Her heart was beating almost as fast as when she'd left the room and crept down the stairs. But this was not fear. Instead, it was something else, another sensation she'd never felt—longing.

She moved her hand, turning it just slightly so his fingers rested against her palm. Another movement and she would have entwined her fingers with his, until they stood linked by hands and silence.

Did Ian feel the way she did right at this moment? As if something strange were happening? As if by simply declaring herself to be someone other than the hated Duchess of Herridge, she'd somehow truly freed herself to become that person?

He took one more step, bending his head down until she could feel the warmth of his breath on her forehead.

"Who is Emma?" he asked again.

"Does it matter?"

"Do you never talk about yourself, Emma?"

What was there to say? That she'd once been a foolish girl, an improvident one, who'd run through the house with her voice raised in laughter. Years of training had modified her behavior until she was decorous to a fault. She could restrain herself so much that people who'd witnessed her demeanor under intolerable conditions labeled her Ice Queen.

Except now, here, in this place, in this darkened garden, with this man standing too close, she suspected that the Ice Queen might be melting inside. The woman who was beginning to emerge was not as restrained or as capable of resolve. At least, not around him.

He was not Anthony—that thought rose above everything.

Anthony was cruel and vindictive. Ian was solicitous and kind.

Anthony was old; Ian was strong, vigorous, and young.

Anthony delighted in the debasement of others. Ian thanked his servants.

Anthony had made her shudder in revulsion. Ian stole her breath.

Anthony lived his duchy. No one within his sphere was allowed to forget that he was the Duke of Herridge. Ian cloaked himself in mystery.

Anthony was incapable of humor unless it was at someone's expense. Ian laughed at himself.

Ian was much taller than she. Her chin came barely to his shoulder. She might reach out and kiss his throat if she wished.

The Ice Queen would never do something like that. The Duchess of Herridge would never kiss a stranger.

The Emma of her girlhood, the optimistic child with shining eyes and bubbling laughter, had not breathed life, had not emerged for so very long that her sudden reappearance now was startling.

She should put her hand on his chest and push gently, so he understood he was much too close.

Then he did something surprising. Ian stepped

back and stretched out his hand, simply that. A gesture of conciliation? Friendship? Or something more?

He beckoned her, welcomed her, urged her without a word spoken.

She should have excused herself and returned to her chamber, burying herself in the books she'd been given. Instead, she placed her bare hand on his palm, stretching her fingers over his hand, feeling the calluses on his fingertips. When he gripped her hand tightly, she didn't pull free.

He urged her out of the shadows into the faint illumination from the lamps in the corridor.

"I should not have brought you here," he said. "Not to my home. Not to this garden."

What did she say to that? Was he warning her? Should she flee now? How strange that she didn't want to, that her blood felt heated and her cheeks flamed with warmth.

He glanced downward, stopped, and turned to her.

"Where are your shoes, Emma?"

To be confused was one thing. She tucked that emotion away to examine later. To feel embarrassment was another thing entirely.

She looked down at her bare feet as if surprised to find them suddenly shoeless.

"My room," she said. "Your room."

He was smiling. "I didn't notice you were barefoot," he said.

The Duchess of Herridge would never have appeared in public in such a shocking lapse of decorum. Emma, however, might well have tossed her shoes away in a show of freedom.

Perhaps she'd become Emma, just Emma, from the moment she'd been abducted.

"I'll see you to your room," he said.

Your room. For the first time, she fully realized that she slept in his bed, slept where he had slept, put her head on his pillow.

He led her to the stairs, as if she were a child and couldn't find her way, or perhaps they were both children, giving each other comfort in the night.

No, nothing so innocent. This brigand was temptation himself.

Chapter 9

Slowly and together, they mounted the stairs, then wordlessly continued down the corridor, still linked by their joined hands. He saw her to the door, opened it for her, and stood aside.

This moment felt as if it were a beginning, not unlike a dance when musicians tuned their instruments in the corner of a ballroom. First came the discordant notes, then the sudden rich weeping of a violin, sweeping the dancers onto the floor, shoes sliding across the waxed boards.

Her heart beat in time as if to make up for the lack of music. Her feet ached to dance across the space between them, demand he hold her in his arms and make proper her wish to be embraced.

How very handsome he was, his Celtic heritage showing in his high cheekbones, sharply angled jaw, and chiseled features.

Who was Ian, the brigand? Scientist, abductor, or simply a sorcerer, conjuring up a spell, throwing up a handful of dust and having it return as diamonds?

If she didn't move, he was going to kiss her. If she didn't say something now—something strict and proper—he was going to embrace her.

When he reached for her, she didn't step back, and when he lowered his head, she only closed her eyes and waited.

He kissed her as if he'd never kissed anyone before, as if a kiss were something to be savored, a rarity. Tenderly, delicately, slowly, he explored the shape of her mouth with his.

She was almost dizzy from it, enough to reach up with both hands and rub her palms against the soft fabric of his jacket, to feel the firmness of his muscles beneath the cloth, sensing the strength and the tension in his shoulders and neck.

The door frame pressed against her bottom, but she wouldn't have moved had someone shone a lantern on them. This shadowed and silent moment, near desperate with desire, was something she'd never forget.

She swayed, a helpless sound escaping her.

Kiss me more.

He kissed her as if he'd heard her entreaty, as if he were starved for kisses and she was the only one he would ever kiss for as long as he lived. She hooked her hands around his neck as he gripped her waist.

She could feel the heat of his palms as if her clothing were not a barrier.

Abruptly, he pulled back, his mouth no longer on hers. His breathing was harsh, his eyes dark.

He reached up slowly, giving her time to understand, and unlaced her hands from around his neck, allowing her to step down from her toes.

"Do not presume upon my honor, Emma," he said, his voice rough. "It's not made of stone. I'd say it's more like sand around you."

She lowered her head, closed her eyes, and willed her heart to cease its riotous race. What had she done?

Kissed a man. Kissed a man in utter delight and desire. Instead of shame, she only felt wonder.

She clasped her trembling hands together, taking a step back. Should she feel ashamed? She didn't, and she wouldn't.

She glanced up. His look was so intent it seemed to vibrate between them.

"From the moment I climbed into your window I've wanted to kiss you senseless," he said. "I didn't know that just being around you would render me the same."

"Senseless?"

His lips quirked in a half smile. "Without a doubt," he said.

He bent, pressed his lips against her forehead, an avuncular gesture that managed to be tender, also.

Turning at the door, he gave her one last look. Instead of speaking, however, he simply left her, closing the door behind him.

She thought about the kiss all night. She thought about it when she should have been sleeping. Instead, Emma paced from one side of Ian's bedroom to the other, conscious of two things. She'd never before shared a kiss that left her so confused, and she wasn't acting like a prisoner.

The fact was, ever since she had been abducted from her home, she'd been treated with greater care than at any time in the last five years.

Why wasn't she afraid? Why wasn't she terrorized?

Not every man in the world was evil. She'd had the

misfortune to be married to one of them. Nor was her uncle a sterling example of character. But her father had been a good man, a man who cared for those around him, and acted with decency toward all. Ian seemed to be of a similar nature.

He was to be married. So was she, if she acceded to her uncle's wishes, which she had no intention of doing. She'd made that decision earlier this evening.

No longer would she be subjected to a man's will.

She lay her forehead against the door, feeling the wood cool against her skin. She huffed out a breath, impatient with herself. Longing kept her awake. Longing and something more, a need, a wish, a yearning.

She was no stranger to passion. She'd witnessed its effects on people from the very beginning of her marriage. She'd seen the dark side of passion, as well, and watched what people would do in order to express it, to feel it. She had felt it herself, sometimes brought about by Anthony's herbs and potions. Sometimes, despite herself, her body had experienced pleasure.

But she'd always felt dirty afterward, as if she'd surrendered something more important. As if, in experiencing ecstasy, she'd relinquished part of her soul.

The kiss she shared with Ian had promised something more.

She checked the lock again, a habit from her marriage. Such an action was silly, since Anthony could easily have commanded a footman to break through the door. He'd never done so, but she knew better than to ever expect her husband to act the same from one day to the next.

What about Ian?

Would he be the same tomorrow?

And would she?

In two months he'd become a husband. No doubt soon after that he would find himself a father. Both roles decreed that he behave with some correctness. He'd acted rashly, with an impetuousness he'd never demonstrated, even in his earlier years.

First, he'd abducted a duchess. Secondly, he'd kissed her. Now, he was prowling the corridors of his home, his mind fixed on doing more than that.

Although it was too damn late—both in matters of time and inclination—to be regretful of his actions, he could use these sleepless hours for something worthwhile. Namely, finding his second cousin.

If anyone else other than his mother had asked him to check up on Bryce, he would have politely declined. But when his mother set her mind to something, both he and his sister obeyed. Bryce was the only one capable of ignoring the Countess of Buchane.

But then, Bryce was capable of a great many things, not many of them admirable.

When Bryce wasn't attending one of his favorite clubs, he unashamedly frequented music halls. Ian visited two before he found his cousin at the third, a place no more substantial than a roof over an inn yard, its interior consisting of one long gallery, and twice as many people as it probably should hold.

The audience, predominantly working men and women with a smattering of aristocrats and women who plied their trade on the street, was robustly singing "Champagne Charlie" at the top of their lungs. The air was smoky, the noise cacophonous.

A great many people were looking up, and following their gazes, Ian understood why. A woman dressed in little more than feathers and netting was balanced on a horizontal bar supported by two cords hanging from the center of the ceiling. She swung back and forth, occasionally raising a leg to expose the degree of her undress, inciting a roar of approval from the crowd that drowned out the singing.

People weren't standing as much as leaning against each other, or draping themselves over chairs and tables. Most of the patrons were drinking beer. Evidently, if a man came to a place like this it was for one of two reasons—to drink his weight in beer, or find himself a companion for the evening. When he finally found Bryce, it was to discover that he was well on his way to doing both.

Bryce, however, was doing his best to ignore him.

His cousin was seated at a small round table, its three male occupants being entertained by a young woman who was nearly naked—the acrobat above them had on more clothing. She was sitting on Bryce's lap, her feet on the table, her legs half spread, her giggling accompanying Bryce's attempts to wedge his hand down her bodice.

Ian stood on the other side of the table, watching the tableau and finding himself curiously unmoved.

Even though they were second cousins, there was some familial resemblance. He and Bryce were roughly the same height and weight. Bryce, too, had the dark brown eyes prevalent in the family. His hair, however, was nearly blond. Despite the fact that Bryce was five years his junior, his cousin looked older. Years of dissipation had given him pouches beneath his eyes and faint red lines around his nose.

His cousin's greeting—about five minutes after Bryce had seen him—consisted of raising a beer in his direction.

"Why, if it isn't my cousin. Here to join the merriment, Ian?"

The other two men saluted him with their mugs. Ian ignored them, pulled out a sum of money and placed it on the table in front of Bryce. Was he too intoxicated to take advantage of his offer?

"What the hell is that?" Bryce asked, staring at the money as if it were a hissing snake.

"Passage to Inverness," Ian said. "Or Edinburgh, if you prefer. You can stay with Mother in the house there."

"Why would I want to do that? The gambling's not as good there as here, cousin," Bryce said. "Everything is better here, don't you agree?" He gestured with one hand, the other still firmly fixed in the bodice of the woman on his lap.

"I imagine everything looks better from the bottom of a bottle, Bryce."

His cousin laughed. "The night is advanced, the moon beckons, and I've won a fortune at cards."

"Mother is concerned for you," Ian said, annoyed at the smirk on Bryce's face.

"Which is the only reason you're here, of course. The dutiful son, the Laird of Trelawny."

"Stop soliciting her for money, Bryce. If you need any, come to me. Leave her alone."

Bryce sat up, pushing the woman off his lap. She

fell with a snarl, rising up on her knees, her hands on his thigh.

"Do you ever stop being responsible for everyone, Ian? Take your money, cousin, I don't need it. I'll never need it again."

"I don't believe in luck, Bryce. It's a pity you do."

"You're the one to be pitied, cousin. You're too young to be so old. I, on the other hand, lead a charmed life."

His two companions nodded.

"A carriage nearly ran him down last week," one of them said. "Nearly killed the bugger."

"He's a damn sight luckier than me, that's for sure," the second man offered.

"Go to Inverness, Bryce."

"So you're close enough to take care of me, cousin?" Bryce said. "I must decline such a gracious invitation."

Ian was fast losing his temper. "Then find an occupation for yourself, Bryce, other than soliciting my mother for money. Something, preferably, with a future. Gambling won't suffice."

"I have," Bryce said, leaning back in the chair and reaching for the woman.

She crawled into his lap again, stretching over him like a kitten, before draping her arms around his neck and turning her head to smirk at Ian.

"I've been giving my future a great deal of thought, cousin. And I've made plans accordingly. You might say that I've guaranteed my future."

His smile didn't reassure Ian one whit.

Ian folded his arms and restrained himself with some difficulty.

Bryce was at an age to make something of himself.

But there was no passion as fierce to him as the game of chance. If Bryce could have parlayed that into a career, he would have been his cousin's greatest supporter. Instead, Bryce was going out of his way to destroy his future. Or drink it away.

"How?"

"Congratulate me, cousin, I'm about to become a bridegroom. And not to just any bride."

"And who is the fortunate woman?" Ian asked.

"An heiress."

Bryce smiled at the woman on his lap while molding his hand around one of her globelike breasts. "God save the moneyed classes," he said, and the others raised their mugs in agreement. "God save my heiress."

"God help us all," Ian muttered.

Chapter 10

Emma slept well into the morning. When she awoke, her first thought was that she'd missed breakfast, which was probably for the best. The less time spent in Ian's company, the less temptation.

She debated whether she should leave the room, or remain inside like a proper prisoner. The storm ended her confusion. She opened the door and peered out into the corridor and beyond to the walled garden. Any thought she might have had about spending some time in the garden was moot because of the downpour.

A few minutes later the young maid arrived with a breakfast tray.

"It's a soggy day, isn't it, miss?" she asked, placing the tray on the desk. "The master said that he's busy with his work today, but if you need anything at all, you've only to ring and one of us will come."

She gestured to the fireplace, and to the bellpull hanging beside it.

"I'm also to ask if you'd like a fire, miss. Because of the day."

"I'm fine," Emma said, feeling absurdly disappointed that she wouldn't see Ian. How paradoxical of her that, at the moment she was denied his presence, she yearned for it.

"Could you tell me who's in charge of the garden?" Emma asked.

The young girl straightened in the act of removing the dishes and cup from the tray and blinked at her.

"I don't think we have anyone in charge of the garden, miss. It's always been just the way it is. Oh, the master's mother comes occasionally and fiddles with things. She plants a few bulbs and trims a few branches but it's allowed to grow just the way it wishes. It's a Scottish garden after all."

"Are you allowed to do whatever you wish, being Scottish?"

"Aye," the girl said with a smile. "That I am."

When she was done arranging the dishes, Emma thanked her. Once again the young maid smiled at her, and it seemed to Emma that there was something in her eyes. A touch of compassion, perhaps. For being a prisoner, or for not being miserable in her prison?

This chamber would do as well as her own.

She ate her meal, more lunch than breakfast, and as tasty as the dinner had been last night. She must congratulate Ian on his cook. Perhaps that would be enough of a ruse to go in search of him. How foolish she was to want to see her jailer. How silly could she be? But none of the books in which she'd been so absorbed yesterday captured her attention now. She tried to read, one after the other, and ended up closing the covers, dissatisfied and slightly disconcerted by her inability to concentrate.

What was he doing? What was occupying him to such

a degree that he hadn't even come to check on her?

Had he regretted their kiss? Is that why he stayed away? Had he been secretly appalled by her cooperation? Or would it be more correct to call it eagerness?

Emma lay back on the bed, staring up at the ceiling. Two days ago she'd been perfectly content with her life. Two days ago she might have even called herself happy. Granted, there were days when sadness seeped in or when memory overwhelmed her.

She'd been fortunate to escape Anthony's domination. If her uncle attempted it from time to time, it was a small price to pay. There were enough small victories in her life to compensate for the difficulties. For the most part, people left her alone. Until now, she'd resigned herself to a very quiet and sedate existence.

Suddenly, however, the life she'd planned didn't seem to be enough. Now, she wanted more. What else she wanted was not so easily defined. The brush of a man's hand on hers. A masculine glance of appreciation. The whisk of a night beard against her cheek. She wanted a kiss and more.

Passion, ecstasy, bliss—without the price she'd always paid for them.

Ian worked on his notes until nearly midday. Perhaps it was the hours searching the music halls for Bryce the night before that had taken a toll on both his concentration and his linguistic abilities. Or perhaps it was simply the fact that the Duchess of Herridge was still his guest and occupied too much of his mind.

He'd given the Earl of Falmouth a day to obtain the mirror. He should send a footman to recover the mirror, then arrange to send Emma home. Each minute on the clock reminded him of his duty, even as it increased his dread.

He didn't want to send her home. His reluctance was not solely based on the fact that he'd been overwhelmed by her, by one simple kiss.

The Earl of Falmouth had struck her, hardly the act of a caring relative.

The notes finally done, he walked around the courtyard to the small laboratory he'd created here in London. The equipment was not as expansive as what he had at home, but it would do to occupy him. He needed something to divert his attention from Emma.

Ian lit the sconces against the gray day, then uncovered his microscope. After polishing the lens and arranging the slides in order, he checked the settings and opened his notebook. His work would eat up the hours.

He should talk to her, see if there was anywhere else she could go. Perhaps she had friends with whom she could stay. Or acquire her own establishment. She was a widow, after all, and not entirely subject to the same rules that governed a single woman's life. Besides that, she was an heiress. Her father had left her a fortune. Surely she had the money to do what she wished.

Anything but live with someone who had struck her.

Why, then, didn't he simply ask her? Why was he avoiding her?

He should not involve himself in the Duchess of Herridge's life. Nor did he have any business feeling protective of her.

Strange, that the woman he'd abducted had almost

nothing in common with the rumors that circulated about her. Her beauty was undeniable but he'd known other beautiful women. Her intelligence interested him, as did her rarely seen sense of humor. But it was the look in her eyes he found fascinating. Almost as if emotion were buried beneath emotion, layers of secrets hidden in their blue depths. He'd glimpsed fear there, and worry, and more than once a little sadness. He'd been tempted to ask her if he was correct, then counseled himself that it wouldn't be wise to learn more about her.

What had she been like before her marriage? Had she awakened in the morning eager to explore the day, knowing, somehow, that only good things would come to her? Had she seen each new adventure as something to be treasured, to learn from, to experience? In the intervening years, had all of that joy, all of that excitement and wonder, been leeched from her?

His curiosity about her was unwise and perhaps dangerous. He was due to be married—he should remember that fact.

Before he could change his mind, he summoned the young footman. After giving him an explanation carefully crafted in innuendo and vagaries, he sat back.

"Do you know what I expect of you, Jim?"

The young man was from Lochlaven, a Scot, and therefore loyal. "I am to say that I'm there for the mirror, sir. And then bring it back to you, straightaway. I'm not to let the man know your name or the lady's whereabouts but only to tell him she's fine and in good health. Once I have the mirror, she'll be returned home."

"Exactly," Ian said.

He inspected Jim's attire. The footman was dressed as any young man might be in bustling London: black trousers, white shirt, and a loose-fitting jacket.

"I'm depending on you, Jim," he said. "Both for this errand, and your discretion."

The young man nodded. "You have it, sir."

"Off you go, then."

After Jim left the room, Ian indulged in a moment of self-congratulation and tried to ignore the fact that it was tempered with regret.

The rain had lasted all day, the intensity of the storm varying depending upon the hour. Darkness came early, with the clouds obscuring the last of the sun and thunder heralding the approach of night.

Emma left the dinner tray untouched, feeling very much like a prisoner indeed. She stood, leaving the bed where she'd finally become interested in *Jane Eyre*. Perhaps there was too much of a resemblance between the two of them. She was as lonely as poor Jane and just as certain that the condition would never be rectified.

She opened the door, glorying in the fresh breeze from the rain-drenched air. The sconces on the other side of the building had already been lit and appeared blurry through the curtain of rain.

Several windows were lit on the first floor, and a door open as well, almost as if it were an invitation.

If she had any sense, she would simply close the door and retreat to Jane Eyre's world, one that seemed—even deprived and sad—safer than her own.

She'd been sensible all day. Besides, she had an acceptable reason to seek out Ian. She needed to discover if he'd heard from her uncle.

The staircase was slippery, wet from the rain, and she held tightly to the banister on her descent. She loved storms, loved the majesty of them, the sheer power of God and nature. When the ground trembled from the thunder, she halted on the steps, looking toward the garden. A bolt of lightning flashed across the sky like the claw marks of some atmospheric monster.

Storms made her conscious of her own humanity, of her infinitesimal ranking in the world. She had no power, was as subject as any person to disease or death. Religion taught her that she was prone to sin, frail by the nature of humanity. Yet the same realization of her weaknesses made her conscious of her strengths. She had survived a great many things, from illness as a child, to the death of her parents, to the horror of her husband and his entertainments. She'd persevered even when she'd doubted her own capacity to do so.

The light flickered, caught by the increasing wind, as if the storm overhead was as suddenly anxious as she felt. Her anxiety was fueled not by fear but anticipation, a shiny soap bubble ready to burst.

The voice of her conscience, her keeper, whispered warnings. She ignored them.

A few minutes later Emma stood in the doorway of the strangest room she'd ever seen. Two long oak tables stood parallel to each other in the middle of the room. On the table at the farthest end was a series of glass boxes, each large enough to hold one of her bonnets. The table closest to the door bore several beakers and jars made of glass, a mortar and pestle, a large leather book, and a peculiar structure made of brass standing nearly two feet high that she guessed was a microscope.

Seated in front of it on a tall stool was her brigand. This afternoon he was neither abductor nor thief but a scientist. Two of the four wall sconces were lit, creating pools of flickering light and shadow. Beside him sat another lamp, tall enough that it rained light down on him.

For several moments she watched him. His face was tight in concentration. He would periodically press his eye to a long cylindrical tube, then frown, sit back, and make a notation in a small notebook at his side. Twice, he did this, each time adjusting a knob on the side of the eyepiece.

Finally, he reached up to pull the lamp closer and saw her.

For long seconds neither one of them said a word. She should have asked if he minded the interruption. Or perhaps she should have inquired as to his study. Instead, Emma was frozen to the spot, overwhelmed by the sheer masculine beauty of him. He sat ringed by light, his dark hair a little unkempt, the intensity on his face fading to something like caution. His eyes were unreadable but they weren't cold. Instead, they seemed to blaze with emotion.

She'd never before considered that a man might be viewed as more than he was because of his actions. Did she see him as more handsome because he had been kind? Because he had been decent and honorable, was he more attractive? No, Ian would be considered handsome by any female, even viewing him the first time.

"I've sent a footman to your house," he said. "But he hasn't returned yet."

There, the answer to the question, the reason she'd searched him out. Now she could return to her borrowed chamber. She didn't move.

"Is there no one else with whom you could live?" he asked. "A friend? A relative? Anyone who wouldn't strike you?"

Surprised, she could only stare at him for a moment.

"Must you return to that house?"

"I have no friends," she said, "and my uncle is my only relative."

"Must you live with him? Couldn't you set up your own establishment?"

"My uncle controls my funds. I have a quarterly allowance but little else."

"How did that come about?"

She shrugged. "I'm not certain if it was Anthony's wish or if my uncle simply assumed that role."

"He hasn't evinced a great deal of interest in your well-being, Emma. Nor can I forget that he struck you. Does he do it often?"

"Not often," she said. She'd learned to avoid her uncle when he was in one of his tempers.

The anger in Ian's eyes didn't frighten her because she knew it wasn't directed toward her.

"I have no right to be concerned for you," he said. "But I am."

His voice was low, warm, and too alluring. But, then, so was the man himself.

"Thank you," she said. No one had been concerned about her for a very long time, and for that alone she was grateful to him.

"But you have no intention of doing anything else but returning to Alchester Square."

There was nothing else she could do. Her uncle, for all his flaws, was not as hideous a companion as Anthony, and she'd endured him for four years.

She only shook her head.

He blew out a breath, obviously exasperated. Her brigand was evidently free to do what he wanted when he wanted. Were all Scots the same?

"I've been wondering what you've been doing all day," he said finally.

"Reading," she said, grateful that he'd changed the subject. "But, then, the rain made me melancholy."

"I told myself not to seek you out. It wouldn't be wise. And here you are, come to my lair."

"Ah, the infamous lair. I was blindfolded once, to prevent my knowing its location." How very easy it was to smile at him.

She took a few steps into the room, placed her fingers on the edge of the table at the corner. A good six feet separated them. Neither moved to close the gap.

"I think it's a laboratory, instead," she said, looking around her. "Tell me, do you bring all your prisoners here?"

He laughed, charming her. "I've only had one," he said. "And she's more a guest than prisoner. Still, I wouldn't want to bore her."

Emma shook her head. "I doubt the work you do would bore anyone. The men last night seemed fascinated, at least from what I heard."

"Yes, but they are easily fascinated. Give them a speck of a germ, and they can pontificate on it for hours." He stood. "I, on the other hand, have been fixated on something else all day."

"Have you?"

A dozen sensations, each one of them startling,

seemed to drift over her like fog. Awareness, not only of herself, but of him. Heat, from his look and her own body. Confusion, that she should be able to feel such things. Fear, that she might have changed in the last four years, become a creature instead of a being. Loneliness, that seemed to make a mockery of anything else.

"You should go," he said, coming toward her.

Yes, she should. Oh, yes, she should.

She stretched out her hand, and it trembled in the air. He regarded it for a moment, then met her eyes.

"Emma," he said, his voice low, his tone warning her. Suddenly, his gaze shifted. He stared beyond her, then uttered an oath.

"What the hell happened to you?"

Chapter 11

❧〰〰❧

Ian moved to the doorway and pulled his footman inside.

Jim looked as if he'd been in a brawl. One cheek was bruised and his left eye was badly bruised. Tomorrow it would boast a shiner. A sleeve had nearly been torn from his coat, and the front of his shirt was badly ripped.

"The earl, sir, he wasn't for letting me go."

Ian pushed him onto a stool, conscious that Emma had come to stand beside him.

"He said he didn't have any damn mirror, sir, but that he was holding me hostage for his niece." Jim sent a cautious look in Emma's direction, making Ian think that the earl had a great deal more to say than that.

"I take it you didn't approve of the plan."

Jim grinned, showing where one tooth had been lost to the cause of freedom.

"I've four brothers, sir. If I couldn't fight off an Englishman, I'm not worthy of being a McNair."

"Take yourself off and have Glenna look at you," Ian said. As the footman made his limping way to the door, Ian called after him. "Have you had your fill of London yet, Jim?"

The young man turned and grinned again. "Not yet, sir."

As he watched the footman leave, Ian made a mental note to have his factor increase Jim's pay and give him a bonus besides. God only knows what complications would have arisen if Jim had been the Earl of Falmouth's guest.

Now what the hell did he do?

With Jim returning empty-handed, Ian's choice was threefold. Either he could threaten Emma's uncle further, which wouldn't be reasonable. He could go to Chavensworth himself and retrieve the mirror, if he was still set on obtaining the Tulloch Sgàthán. Or he could simply forget about the damned mirror, take Emma back to her home as quickly as possible, and hie himself back to Scotland.

Of the three choices, returning to Scotland was the wisest.

Why, then, was he so reluctant to do exactly that?

Emma turned and walked away from him, moving to stand at the door looking out at the rain and the darkened garden. He knew the view well; there was nothing in the scenery to occupy her thoughts to such a degree.

"I'm sure there's some reasonable explanation," she said.

How very calm she sounded. How very composed, as if she'd retreated to her Ice Queen role. Yet he wanted to see her eyes, to see what kind of emotion she struggled to hide.

"It's time for you to go home," he said.

"And the mirror?"

"It no longer matters, Emma."

At that remark, she turned to look at him. In her

blue eyes was such misery that he wished he was more sorcerer than Scot. He would've pressed his hand across her eyes to close them, then banished that look with a kiss upon each eyelid.

"No," she said, surprising him. She held up one hand in an almost queenly gesture. "We'll go to Chavensworth," she added.

She looked straight at him, her stare direct and intent. "It's what began the whole thing, isn't it? If, as you say, the mirror belongs in Scotland, then that's where it should go. I don't want it."

He should have refused the offer, sent her home and planned his departure for Lochlaven in the morning. But he knew only too well why he was willing to go to Chavensworth, and it had nothing to do with the errand he'd wanted to perform for Lady Sarah.

She walked toward him, hesitating only a few feet away. Her face was flushed.

She was a widowed duchess; he was a betrothed earl. She was wealthy but so was he. She was hiding from life; he embraced it in all its wonder, wanted to study it, learn it, understand it, and perhaps even document it.

Yet despite their differences, and in concurrence with their similarities, he felt a bond to her. Perhaps they might become friends. True and valued, loyal friends to whom each might say anything, from whom each might ask anything. Or perhaps they would become lovers, stepping too close to a precipice and a danger against which neither of them was prepared.

The scent she wore, one of lilies and roses, hinting at springtime, would forever remind him of her, and possibly this moment of sadness and regret, layered over a strange and exultant kind of joy.

She looked down at the floor, rather than at his face. He wanted to reach over and tilt her chin up so he might see her eyes. Instead, he remained where he was, not impinging on the invisible wall she'd erected around her.

Ian realized, suddenly, how difficult returning to Chavensworth would be for her.

"We don't have to go," he said. "I've already written Lady Sarah and told her that it was a fool's errand, and one I regret attempting. I don't like to see that look of sadness in your eyes," he added. "Nor did I have any intention of saying that to you." He shook his head. "I seem to say and do idiotic things around you, Duchess."

"Am I to blame, then, for your insensibility, brigand?" Her small smile robbed the words of their tartness.

"What if I should say yes to that? Yes, Emma, it is all your fault. I lay all of my flaws at your feet."

"Then I would say it's a weighty burden for anyone to take on, let alone a mere duchess."

He laughed, delighted with her sense of humor.

She stepped closer, reached out one hand and touched his arm. He covered her hand with his, knowing that he should have moved away.

The Duchess of Herridge was going to prove to be difficult to ignore, not to mention forget.

"I don't mind going back to Chavensworth," she said, and he could see the lie in her eyes. But he didn't question her on it.

"Tomorrow, Ian."

He nodded, allowing her hand to drop, wishing that she would leave before he dishonored himself.

Being proper reminded Emma of being the Duchess of Herridge, the Ice Queen. Dear God, she wanted to erase every single one of those memories. She wanted to feel desire without debauchery. She wanted to feel passion, unencumbered by shame or humiliation. She wanted his honesty and her own.

Slowly, so he would not think this a thoughtless act or one she'd not fully considered, she took another step toward him, placed her hand on his chest and smiled.

Ian shook his head.

She nodded.

Ian took her hand, brushing a kiss across her knuckles. The look in his eyes created a fire inside, heat so molten that she felt as if she were melting from it. Still, he didn't move, other than to brush his thumb across her knuckles slowly.

Must she seduce him? She'd never done so before. How very strange that she was quite willing to do so now.

"Are you very certain, Emma?" he finally said.

More so than at any time in her life, but how did she tell him that, without telling him the rest?

Without speaking, he dropped her hand, turned, and extinguished the sconces and the lamp on the bench. When he reached her side, he took her hand again. Within moments they were racing up the steps, caution forgotten, prudence buried beneath excitement.

She was first inside the room. He closed the door

firmly behind her, the click of the latch imprisoning them in the room together.

He bent his head and kissed her again, softly at first, then deeper. His tongue traced her bottom lip, exploring, enticing. She'd no choice but to open her mouth to his, a soft gasp escaping her.

His hips moved against her, pushing subtly, the hard bulge between his thighs leaving no doubt of his desire. The rhythm of his advance increased, slowly at first, then matching the movement of his tongue in her mouth.

He pulled back and left her then, and she heard a lamp being lit. In the soft glow, he began removing his jacket, then the shirt, his torso revealed as he stripped himself bare. Small bronze nipples peeked through the black hair covering his chest. Her gaze followed the trail of hair down the center of his stomach and then veered away as his hands went to his trousers.

A moment later she heard the sound of his shoes hitting the floor. Her gaze returned to the sight of him removing the rest of his garments. When he was done, and gloriously naked, he made no move to cover himself.

Muscles shaped his upper arms, rippled down his sides and stomach, and thickened his thighs. The most arrogant part of him, even now throbbing and swelling, rose from a nest of hair as black as that on his chest.

She'd never considered masculine beauty but now was in awe of it.

Her brigand was a proud Celtic warrior who might have been frightening under other circumstances. At the moment, however, he was simply magnificent.

Emma held her hand to her throat, thumb and

forefinger splayed, as if to test the beat of her blood there. The Ice Queen was not feeling appreciably frosty. Instead, her heart was beating too quickly, her lips felt too full, her breath was rapid and shallow.

Above all, she was not afraid.

He walked slowly toward her, giving her time to flee. In the seconds it took for him to reach her, she could have easily reconsidered. She might have claimed idiocy, or resorted to tears, begging for his understanding.

The Ice Queen did nothing but watch him, her body heating at his approach.

He stopped only inches from her, bent his head and kissed her again.

Her hands explored his chest, his shoulders, and ran down his arms to measure their strength.

He reached out and touched her skirt, gripping the material with both hands, as if he wished to tear it from her. Before she could urge caution on him, the skirt was falling to the floor, accompanied by her lone petticoat.

As he kissed her again, she could feel the buttons of her bodice loosening. His fingers were so infinitely talented they divested her of her clothing without her assistance.

Brigand, Scientist, and Ravisher of Women.

Well, she certainly hadn't needed to seduce him.

He began to unlace her corset. The air on her bare skin should have summoned her to reason, but she only welcomed the coolness against her heated flesh. She looked down to see her corset floating to the floor to join the rest of her clothing. A moment later he bent, grabbed the hem of her chemise, and pulled it over her head.

Naked, she stood still as his gaze raked her.

"Emma, you're beautiful," he said. "More beautiful than my poor imagination made you."

Dare she ask how long he'd been envisioning her naked?

The thought vanished the moment he effortlessly lifted her, taking her to his bed, sweeping the books off the counterpane. At another time, perhaps, she might have chided him for his treatment of the volumes, but now she only wanted to kiss him again. To feel him against her, and to have him touch her with his talented hands.

A second later she got her wish. His palms were soft, his fingertips surprisingly rough, tracing a slow and sensuous path up her thighs and hips to her rib cage.

She trailed kisses along his jaw, his throat, reveling in the taste of his skin and the prickliness of the stubble on his face. He was so completely masculine that he made her feel small and dainty and feminine beside him.

His chest was hard, muscled, and slightly damp. When he moved from side to side, the rough hair brushed her sensitive nipples, urging them to tighten and harden.

Her pulse jumped as he bent his head to kiss the curve of her breast. Her muscles quivered as he trailed a line of slow kisses around the nipple, then finally licked her, his tongue hot. She arched involuntarily, needing the touch of that clever, talented mouth.

She thought she knew everything there was to know about the coming together of men and women. She thought that the education she'd received at Anthony's entertainments would have prepared her for any encounter. This night, however, scented with roses and touched with mystery and passion, was beyond her experience.

The light was dim, shadows pooling around the bed, sheltering them. His touch was like a miracle, chasing away any memory or thought.

Ian kissed his way back up her throat, and down. His hand cradled her right breast as if to ready it for his mouth.

"You're very experienced at this," she managed to say between gasps.

His eyes glittered at her in the faint light.

"I've thought of nothing but this since the moment I saw you," he said, his smile utterly wicked.

"Have you?" she whispered, surprised that she could even speak.

His leg was warm, muscled, insistent, slipping between hers. Her heart beat against the cavern of her chest as her breath came hot and fast.

She let him guide her, touch her, would have begged him to do more if she knew what to ask for or how. When he spread her legs, she opened for him. When his fingers touched her, she arched her hips, and when he murmured praise, she cried aloud and crested.

Feeling her own surrender was both intoxicating and erotic.

There were no shadows here, no fear. Even her surrender was praised rather than mocked. There was only Ian and long, slow, drugging kisses that made her feel as if she were part of him. She felt as if she could easily drift away in a mist of sensation.

He lowered his head, his lips near her ear, mur-

muring in a voice rough with need, "I'm going to come into you now, Emma. I don't think I can wait any longer."

Emma shuddered. A throbbing began at the exact point where his fingers lingered. She spread her legs, making room for his hips to nestle there, gasping when she felt him hard and hot against her. He reached down and guided himself into position, entering her with single-minded determination.

His heat flowed around her, through her, into her, spearing her.

His hands were everywhere, his hips driving her against the mattress. She was no longer Emma but someone else, undefined and unknown. What she felt was too primitive, too powerful to be called pleasure.

"Emma," he said between clenched teeth, his voice harsh.

Each time he surged into her, he lifted her with him. Her body bowed in response, his rhythm demanding surrender and submission.

Sensations she'd never considered, nor imagined, shimmered over her skin, turned her bones to liquid, made her sigh in helpless wonder. She was poised upon a precipice, held there by a thin filament, before being catapulted into the air.

Emma felt her entire body clench, then shudder, again and again. She clung to him, wrapped her feet around his muscled calves and held him, at the mercy of a rhythm of pleasure so intense it shattered her.

He made a sound like a growl, a low rumbling sound of pleasure or approval. She buried her face against his throat and allowed herself to cry out.

She might die of this.

She might die of *him*.

When it was over, when every muscle trembled and every nerve quivered, she simply held him. Words would have been wrong and completely unnecessary.

This wasn't permanent. Nothing about this interlude was anything more than temporary. But, for now, that was enough.

This coupling was as perfect as dawn and as endless as night.

Twice in the next hours, he took her again. Once, she was on top, the depth of his possession almost causing him to lose control before he pleasured her.

He loved the way she looked right at that moment, her eyes heavy lidded, her cheeks flushed with passion. She bit her bottom lip, lifted up, then lowered her hips, pleasuring herself on him.

He took up the rhythm she'd begun, surging into her, planting himself in her so deep she made a sound in the back of her throat. He raised one hand to stroke his fingers across her face, trace the fullness of her bottom lip.

"Did I hurt you? Emma?"

She shook her head from side to side, her nails digging into his skin. He understood then that she was adrift in sensation, lost to anything but pleasure.

Next, she was on all fours in the middle of the mattress, and the sight of her, naked and rosy, curved and delectable, was so arousing that Ian knew that this sight would remain with him until the day he died.

When she lay spent, he used his mouth on her, driving her up and over again. Tears wet her face when she climaxed, and he swallowed her sobs in a kiss.

While she slept, he lay on his side, his head propped on his hand, and watched her. Her lips were swollen from his kisses; her cheeks were flushed.

The rumors had portrayed her incorrectly. Yet no one had said anything about Emma's beauty or mentioned that a look of determination appeared on her face more often than not. The rumors hadn't mentioned the fear that showed in her eyes, either. The only thing they'd gotten right was her withdrawal from society.

She stole his breath away.

An odd feeling, one almost momentous in its rarity, hit him then. He wanted—needed—to remember this moment for the rest of his life. He needed to remember this overwhelming surge of lust mixed with tenderness, forever remember how weak, and paradoxically strong, he felt at this moment.

A warning too strong to ignore.

He'd been a damn fool for attempting to procure the mirror in the first place. He'd climbed across a roof, into a woman's boudoir, and abducted her. To make matters worse, he'd seduced Emma, without compunction, without thought, wanting her so desperately that he would have begged if she'd not acquiesced.

She'd shocked him with the fierceness of her passion, in the freedom of it, meeting him thrust for thrust, gasp for gasp. Yet when that hunger had been sated, the hint of it was there, threatening to return.

Even now he wanted her.

He was due to be married. He should be thinking of Rebecca, not Emma. He should recall Rebecca's face, her voice, her laughter. But Rebecca had never been more than a friend. Not once had he thought of her with longing. He'd never kissed her the way he'd kissed Emma, never lusted for her.

Marriage was something that one was expected to do. He wasn't adverse to getting married. At least his engagement had kept his mother from making not so veiled hints about his marital status. Instead of reminding him that he was still a bachelor, she'd taken to uttering comments such as, "When you are married, Ian . . . " or, "When I have a new daughter, Ian . . . " as if she were counting the days.

So was he, but not in the same manner.

Perhaps he should seek out a church and get down on his knees and pray to the Almighty to grant him some sense. Or if that wasn't possible, some restraint.

Ian slid from the bed, walked into the adjoining chamber and ran the taps for the tub. Twice, he went to the doorway to see if the clanking of the boiler and the rush of water had awakened Emma, but she still slept.

He bathed—regrettably, alone—and dressed, slipping from the room without returning to the bed. A farewell kiss wasn't wise. Kissing Emma would lead to more.

He needed to travel to Chavensworth today. More importantly, he needed to send Emma home before he couldn't.

When Emma woke, Ian was gone.

She lay there for a few moments, taking stock first of the room, then of herself. The room was curiously empty without Ian. Her body simply felt odd. Pleased, almost, if a body could be said to have sensations separate from that of the mind. She didn't ache anywhere. Instead, it was as if she'd just created a lovely and stirring piece of music. A symphony, created by her body, a body that had never even hinted at possessing such an ability. If she were an instrument, then perhaps Ian the Brigand was the virtuoso.

Last night she'd wanted to be the Emma of her youth, and yet this morning she'd transcended that person and become someone entirely different. She wanted to stretch, to fall back on the bed, stare up at the ceiling and marvel about the sheer deliciousness of how she felt for a few hours.

Emma sat up, her feet dangling over the edge of the mattress. Naked, she sat in Ian's room and wondered how she could have gone from wanting to be a pattern biscuit to being an exotic creation—a cake steeped in brandy and saved for special occasions.

She smiled at herself and walked into the bathing chamber. All prisoners were not cared for with such regard, but she was fortunate to have found herself a gentleman jailer. In addition to providing such luxurious accommodations, there was also a new toothbrush, some tooth powder, washcloths, and towels that felt so soft as to be clouds and not towels at all.

Naked, she surveyed herself in the mirror. The curve of her shoulders, the shape of her breasts, all these things were familiar to her, as uniquely her as her memories. She'd had a bruise once, on her left arm, an ugly thing that had spread from elbow to shoulder. A mark left by Anthony. There, on her right breast, she'd had a bruise as well, one that Anthony made during one of his entertainments. She'd screamed that night, and he'd been pleased at the show she provided his guests.

To Anthony, she'd been a vessel, nothing more.

To Ian, she'd been a participant in passion.

What she'd experienced with Ian was nothing like

the games Anthony played, and as far from that debauchery as the sun was from a candle's light.

After taking care of her morning ablutions, she returned to the bedroom. On top of the bureau was the brush the young maid had placed there yesterday. She sat on the edge of the bed, still naked, and began to brush her hair. This brush was heavier than the one she'd used the night before. Silver backed, it looked to be an heirloom, and she couldn't help but wonder to whom it belonged. Ian's mother? Or his sister?

He'd caused it to be brought here, she knew that well enough. Just as she knew that the items in the bathroom had been placed there at his request. She was being surfeited with kindness and regard from the same man who'd ravished her only hours earlier.

No, not ravished.

She finished brushing her hair and sat in the sunlight. Today she'd return to Chavensworth, not an errand she wanted to perform. After that she'd have to return home. Perhaps only hours from now. Regardless of how strange and delightful this interlude, she would have to return to her true life and her real existence.

She was not simply Emma Harding. As much as she might wish it, she was someone else.

When the door opened, she didn't move to cover herself. Somehow, she'd known he would come to her, an answer to boredom's prayer.

She smiled in welcome when Ian entered and closed the door.

"We need to leave for Chavensworth," she said, making no move to cover herself.

"Not now," he said, his gaze turning to the window. Morning lit the sky, light seeping in between the closed curtains. "You're not going anywhere for hours." He looked at her, daring her to question him, to defy his lust, to deny that hers matched his.

In moments his clothes were flung over the bedroom floor, his enthusiasm and haste causing her to laugh in a way she hadn't laughed in years.

In answer, she held out her arms to him.

Chapter 12

They left for Chavensworth immediately after luncheon, the distance to Anthony's ancestral home short enough that they could return to London by end of day. As they pulled away from the square, she glanced at Ian.

"Are you not going to blindfold me?"

He only sent her a look, and she smothered her smile.

The closer they came to the great house, the more Emma regretted returning. She could have sent a maid or footman with detailed instructions as to the mirror's location. But it was all too possible that the new Duke of Herridge's staff would not admit a maid or footman. They could not, however, bar the Duchess of Herridge from the door.

The new Duke of Herridge, Anthony's cousin, was not in residence. He, like Anthony, preferred to live in London. Would he use Chavensworth as a place to hold his revels? Thankfully, that was none of her concern.

For most of the journey, Ian had been reading, a paper he explained he needed to review before writing an introduction. Something to do with the effects of decaying flesh. She'd been grateful when he didn't go into more detail.

The air was heavy but there was no storm on the horizon. Perhaps emotion rendered the atmosphere so still.

She and Anthony had been married in London, at Anthony's request. She'd only seen Chavensworth a week later. The sheer size of the house amazed her, as did the Italianesque architecture and beauty of the structure. Over the years, however, she'd ceased recognizing its beauty, only remembering the events within its walls.

Today was no different. As they topped the rise, Chavensworth visible at last, Emma felt herself tightening, the fluttery feeling deep inside her stomach increasing until she thought she was going to be sick. Intellectually, she knew Anthony was dead. Emotionally, he lingered on, coupled with memories of Chavensworth. This journey was a test. If she could return to Chavensworth, she could do almost anything.

"Emma?"

She glanced across the carriage. On Ian's face was a look of concern. They had barely spoken since London, more her inclination than his. She didn't know quite how to address a man who was little more than a stranger to her. Yet she'd lain in his arms, and he knew her more intimately than any man had, even Anthony.

With Anthony, she'd done her duty, docile and receptive. With Ian, she'd been a participant in the act of love.

Perhaps that's why she felt so shy with him now. The person she'd been last night and this morning was not the same person she was now. Had the change been precipitated by the donning of her mourning dress?

The Duchess of Herridge had returned. The Ice Queen lived again.

For all her resolve to remain decorous now, she didn't regret having been Emma for a little while. At least once in her life she'd been wild and unrestrained, not because of fear or drugs, but because she'd wanted someone. She'd desired him.

"We're almost there," she said, extending one finger toward Chavensworth, gratified to see that her hand did not shake. Her trembling was inside and not visible.

"I've seen it before," he said.

Even though it was impossibly difficult to do so, she forced her gaze to his face. Had he attended one of Anthony's infamous entertainments, and she'd not recognized him? During those gatherings, the men had all been naked, their faces sometimes covered with grotesque masks of animals—horses, bulls, goats.

Dear God, please do not let him have been there.

"This is a well-traveled road," he said. "I use it when I travel by carriage instead of train."

"Then you've never been a guest at Chavensworth?" she asked, feeling as if her heart paused to hear his response.

His answer, when it came, was in a soft, and almost kind, voice.

"No, Emma," he said. "I have never been a guest at Chavensworth. Your husband and I did not travel in the same circles."

"You can consider that commendable, Ian," she

said, relief making her almost dizzy. "I did not care for most of the people in Anthony's circle."

Did he know what had gone on at Chavensworth? She glanced away, concentrating on the view outside the window, a view that did not encompass the great house, only the passing countryside. All the land for miles around Chavensworth belonged to the Duke of Herridge's estate. Anthony had been quite wealthy but only in property. Her inheritance had provided the income for his debaucheries. An irony that she'd always fully appreciated.

"What is she like? Lady Sarah?" she asked, desperate to change the tenor of her thoughts. She could not bear her memories.

"Unlike what you might think Anthony's daughter to be," he said, not questioning her sudden change of subject. Did he know how difficult this was? It seemed he did from his intent look. "Stubborn, amusing, very much the chatelaine of her home. She's extremely loyal. If she thought you posed any harm to those she cared about, Sarah would likely take a claymore to you."

"I should very much like to meet her one day," she said, surprised to find that it was true. She'd never cared to meet Anthony's daughter, thinking that Sarah must be somewhat like her father. Now she wanted to know what kind of woman inspired such friendship that Ian was willing to steal for her.

"I think you would like her," he said.

"But would she like me?"

He didn't answer for a moment, but when he did, his words brought a blush to her cheek. "I think she would, very much, Emma. But then, I think anyone who got to know you would like you. The trouble is, I doubt you allow many people to do so."

She hadn't a response to that, simply because his words were too close to the truth. She'd found, in the last few years, that it was easier to keep her own counsel than to attempt a friendship.

The men and women who came to Chavensworth were not people with whom she wished to be acquainted.

"I shall miss you," she said, not expecting to say the words.

He put his papers down on the seat beside him, giving her all his attention. The directness of his look was a little disconcerting but she didn't glance away.

"You're to be married," he said.

"As are you."

Neither of them made a response. The passion they'd shared was here in this carriage, not in the form of a memory but alive and real, growing each passing moment.

"I envy Lady Sarah," she said. "To have such a friend as you. Is that what she is to you?" Implicit in her question was yet another—is she anything more?

"Her husband, Douglas, is one of my closest friends," he said. "I've not known her long but I think to count her among them."

She nodded.

"I shall miss you as well, Emma," he said.

For a moment she wished he would expound upon his feelings, tell her something that she might be able to recall for weeks and months to come. As it was, she would forever remember the exact tone of his voice when he said those words.

She turned her head and directed her attention to the approach to Chavensworth. The last time she had been here was on the occasion of Anthony's death, funeral, and interment. There had been no necessity to return after that.

Thankfully, the new Duke of Herridge had kept Williams on when he'd assumed control of Chavensworth. The majordomo greeted her now, his bald head ringed by a tuft of white hair, his stocky figure immaculately attired in the Duke of Herridge livery.

Despite what had happened at Chavensworth, the man was utterly proper. Did he cling to all his rules and regulations in order to make some sense of his life? Did the proprieties soothe him in some way?

Perhaps one day she would ask him. Or perhaps she never would, clinging to the proprieties herself.

"Your Grace," he said, unable to control his surprise. "It is good to see you again. Are you well?" He stepped forward, then caught himself and remained the proper distance from her.

She'd not seen the man for eighteen months, but in the intervening time he'd not changed. Had it not been for Ian's presence beside her, it might have been one of those innumerable occasions when she'd been summoned to Chavensworth. A pawn in one of Anthony's games or simply a fly to his spider.

Emma smiled at him. "I am," she said. "But I need your assistance." She glanced behind her to where Ian stood. "My friend and I need your assistance."

Williams looked at Ian and bowed. No doubt he was curious, but one did not question a duchess, even a widowed duchess, so he remained silent.

"How may I assist you, Your Grace?"

"I left behind a mirror, Williams. A hand mirror. Would you have any objection if I look for it in the Duke's Suite?"

"Someone asked about a mirror just yesterday, Your Grace."

Surprised, Emma exchanged a glance with Ian. "What did you tell him?"

"He stated that he was from your uncle, Your Grace. I explained that I would not divulge any information without Your Grace's permission. Nor was I about to give him anything that belonged to you. Or allow him access to any of the ducal apartments."

She blinked several times. "Thank you for your loyalty, Williams."

Williams bowed again. "Would you prefer for me to fetch it for you, Your Grace? Or to summon the housekeeper? Mrs. Turner is still with us."

That would be the best solution, would it not? But she didn't want to meet with Mrs. Turner, not having seen the woman since the day of Anthony's funeral. They shared a terrible secret, and Emma would be content if she never saw the housekeeper again.

"I'd like to look for myself, if it would be all right. If you think His Grace would not object."

Williams bowed once more.

"His Grace is not in residence, Your Grace. He has not been since . . . "

She supplied the words so that he would not be uncomfortable. "Since acquiring the title," she said.

"Quite so, Your Grace," he said, bowing once more. "His Grace has given instructions for substantial changes, however. You might not find the suite in the same condition as you left it."

"Is the gold wall still intact?"

"Yes, Your Grace. The duke would not alter that, since it is one of the treasures of Chavensworth."

She smiled her thanks and made her way to the

grand staircase. At the base of the stairs, Ian held out his arm. She knew it wasn't for balance but support. She glanced at him, wanted to thank him, but her face was immobile, her features frozen into the expressionless mask she'd always worn at Chavensworth.

Dear God, she did not want to be here.

He reached out and placed her hand on his arm. She nodded, all she could manage at the moment. Reluctance held her limbs stiff, her joints immovable. She would not be able to climb that staircase even if the bottom floor was on fire.

Somehow, though, she was. With Ian beside her, with his firm arm beneath her hand, she took one step and then another, her right hand clenched in a death grip on the ornate banister. Snippets of conversation flew by her ears, trailing on ribbons of sound. She heard laughter, too bright and too loud to be without enhancement of some sort—tobacco, alcohol, or the Chinese powders with which Anthony liked to experiment. From some faroff place in her memory, a woman screamed, and she couldn't remember if there had been ecstasy or terror in the sound. As she climbed the stairs to the second floor, the buzz of words rivaled her heart's beating for dominance.

Dear God, please don't let me be here. Let this be a dream, as she'd wished on all those other nights. But she hadn't been dreaming then, and she wasn't now.

"I would have spared you this if I could have," Ian said. Although he had spoken softly, the words echoed around her, companion to the ghosts of all those other memories.

She could not look at him, could not respond in any way. She was no longer frozen—she'd become one of the specters that haunted Chavensworth, one of the wraiths. She was no more substantial than a filament of fog. She was ethereal and almost angelic, save for the tenor of her thoughts and the content of her recollections.

They were at the top of the steps now. Without stopping, without allowing herself to think, she began to walk toward the Duke's Suite. Ian followed her without speaking, and she wanted to let him know how much she appreciated his presence and how vital it was right at this moment.

Impulsively, she held out her hand, and he grabbed it. She entwined her bare fingers with his, gripping so tightly that it must have been painful. But he didn't say anything, only held on, as if he knew her connection to him was the only thing anchoring her to reality. Otherwise, she might go catapulting into the past.

She hesitated at the door to the Duke's Suite, then placed her left hand on the carving, her fingers trailing over the vines and flowers. Still, Ian didn't speak. Another man might have attempted to cajole her, ease her terror, fill the silent seconds with words. Instead, he held her hand tightly and stood beside her, a friend when she most desperately needed one.

You'll do what I say, Emma. A ghostly voice. *I doubt I need to persuade you of the need to obey me, now, do I?* A voice she'd not heard in eighteen months. *You're such a willful creature. Why do you make me keep training you, my dear?*

He was dead. He was dead. He was dead—a refrain she'd uttered for days, weeks at a time. She bowed her head, took a deep breath, and opened the door.

Chapter 13

The door opened on oiled hinges. The staff at Chavensworth had always been commendable and diligent about maintaining the property.

As she stepped into the Duke's Suite, she straightened her shoulders. How many times had she held herself tight, telling herself not to reveal any emotion? Remaining the Ice Queen had been the only way she'd stayed sane. The only way she'd occasionally won in the eternal battle with Anthony.

"If you'll tell me where it is, I'll retrieve the mirror," Ian said from beside her.

She glanced over at him and smiled, the first genuine expression she'd had since entering Chavensworth. But she didn't answer him, needing to face the ghosts herself.

Except they were no longer in residence. The massive four-poster bed was missing from the dais. Good, that was one sight she didn't have to see. The vanity had also been removed, as well as the armoire.

On the opposite wall were three rows of five cupboards with gold leaf doors. Each door bore a separate painting, scenes of the estate. A treasure, Williams had said, and she supposed it was.

But to her, Chavensworth was Hell.

She opened the farthest cupboard on the bottom left-hand side but the mirror wasn't there. Neither was it in the middle row, or the top. Ian began on the right-hand side of the wall, and the two of them met in the middle.

"It isn't here," she said, dismayed. Had she made the journey to Chavensworth for nothing?

He didn't respond but she could almost hear his unspoken question.

"I put it here," she said. "I never took it out again."

She could remember the moment on her wedding night when Anthony had given it to her.

This is for you, my dear, on the occasion of our wedding. I doubt this mirror has ever witnessed beauty as vibrant as yours, however.

Probably the last kind comment he'd ever made to her. There hadn't been an audience that night, only two people consummating their marriage. One of them had been a satyr in bridegroom's clothing, the other a woman too innocent of what was to come.

She looked around the room and realized that even though the furniture was gone, the memories still lingered.

"Of course I'm disappointed," Ian said. "But I can honestly say that I've done my utmost to retrieve the Tulloch Sgàthán. And so have you."

She closed the last cupboard and turned to him.

"Damn it, Emma," he said, startling her by pulling her into his arms.

She knew better than to fight. She wasn't as strong as a man. Yet Ian did nothing more than extend his arms around her waist and rest his cheek against the top of her head.

A strangely comforting embrace, and one she'd not expected from him. Her head turned, her cheek resting against his chest. She took a deep breath, exhaled it, and allowed her fists to unclench.

How very odd that she suddenly felt as if she were going to cry.

She became aware that he was saying something, whispers so quiet that she could barely hear him.

"On the seventeenth, air was allowed into the chamber with no filter apparatus attached. On the nineteenth, observation was made that there was no decay present. On the morning of the twentieth, however . . . "

She pulled back and asked him, "Are you quoting your speech?"

He looked a little embarrassed. "No, I was reciting the notebook I keep of my experiments."

"Why?"

He only shook his head.

"Why did you embrace me?" she asked.

He put his hand on her face, a touch no more substantial than a breath. His thumb brushed her chin, rested on the slight hollow below her bottom lip, held her prisoner while his fingers touched her cheek.

Tenderness softened his dark eyes as a small and intimate smile curved his lips. Words fled her as his other palm pressed against her opposite cheek, fingers spearing into her hair, thumb resting on the corner of her mouth.

She was held in thrall by his touch, so soft and gentle, as if she were the most delicate and rare of treasures.

"Because," he said, his voice a whisper, an ache of sound, "I couldn't bear the look on your face."

Could moments be frozen? Could time be convinced to remain still? Would she be able to recall this moment for a thousand lifetimes? If she could remember Anthony, then Providence should allow her to remember this as well.

She wished he would look away, that he would study something else in the suite other than her. She might point out the painting of the lavender fields on one of the cupboard doors. Or the view from the windows of those same fields.

For long moments they simply looked at each other. Finally, she stepped back and his arms dropped.

She turned to leave the Duke's Suite, closing the door behind her with a feeling of relief. From the windows on the landing she could see the sun bright in the western sky, a presage to dusk and nightfall.

"I'm sorry we made the journey for nothing," she said. "Perhaps Anthony disposed of it."

He didn't respond, merely came to her side. He was still looking at her, his gaze intent.

"I'm less concerned about the mirror than I am you, Emma."

She glanced at him.

"He cannot hurt me anymore, Ian. Anthony is dead, and there is another Duke of Herridge."

He didn't look as if he believed her. She couldn't blame him; memories of Anthony survived even the grave.

Williams was standing at the base of the stairs. When she reached him, he bowed again.

"Did you find your mirror, Your Grace?"

She shook her head. "Would you convey a message to the housekeeper, Williams?"

"Of course, Your Grace."

"Would you tell her," she said, "that if she locates the mirror, to send it to me in London? It's gold, with a ring of diamonds around the face of it."

"It would be my pleasure, Your Grace. Before you leave, may I provide refreshments?"

"Thank you, Williams, but no. We need to return to London before dark."

Once again Williams looked at Ian. Again the questions were not forthcoming. If he had been the type to gossip, she would have discovered that fact before today. There had been enough fodder for all sorts of talk when Anthony was alive.

"Thank you, Williams," she said. She leaned forward and in a thoroughly improper gesture kissed the middle-aged majordomo on the cheek. "For all your kindnesses."

He didn't say a word as she and Ian left Chavensworth.

Silence was a third passenger in the carriage all the way back to London.

Darkness had descended upon London by the time his carriage halted in front of Emma's home. A footman opened the door, but before she could exit, Ian leaned forward and placed his hands on the edge of the seat on either side of her.

This would be the last time he saw her. The knowledge didn't sit well with him, and because it didn't, a warning bell rang in his mind. What kind of man was betrothed to one woman and thought constantly of another? Not an honorable one, for a certainty, and he'd always prided himself on his integrity.

What forces had been put into motion by his entering her home? For that matter, what emotions had been released by seducing the Duchess of Herridge? How would they deal with both?

He would soon be home, working on his experiments, being laird to his community, and preparing for his wedding.

"I don't want to leave you here," he said.

"I'll be fine."

"I'll be in Scotland, Emma," he said. "Too far away if you need me."

She held up her hand as if to forestall any further words, then tempered the gesture with a small smile.

"I shall not need you, Ian. But thank you."

What the hell did he say to her? He felt caught between his honor and his wishes, between his obligations and his needs.

"Forgive me," he said.

Her smile altered character, became a little sadder. "Please don't say that. Do you think I fault you for what happened between us?" She looked down at her clasped hands. "I wanted it as much."

How did he leave her?

She was the one to open the carriage door.

"Then I wish you the very best of good fortune in your future, Duchess," he said as she made to leave the vehicle.

What was she thinking when she looked at him with such a steady regard? Was she remembering the passion they'd shared? Or the laughter that had so effortlessly flowed between them?

"May you find all that you want in life, Duchess."

Another warning bell rang.

"I think I liked it better when you called me Emma,"

she said, as she gripped her skirts with one hand and reached for the strap beside the door with the other.

He watched her climb the steps to her town house, telling himself that this strange interlude was over. The fact that he deeply regretted leaving her was something he would have to reconcile, along with his bruised and dented honor.

Emma pushed down all the emotions threatening to overwhelm her, and entered her home.

"Good evening, Your Grace," the majordomo said.

He said nothing about her three-day absence. Nor did he mention that she arrived home looking a little worse for wear, since she was attired in the same dress she'd worn three days ago. He was simply deferential, as he'd always been, his demeanor the same for her as for a stranger.

Williams had managed never to lose his humanity in the performance of his duties.

Her uncle appeared in the doorway to her left.

"Emma."

She turned to face him, waiting for some sort of explanation. Or even a greeting. He said nothing, merely raised one eyebrow.

In this light, he looked nothing like her father. Perhaps he never had, and she'd only wished to see some familial resemblance. The man who greeted her now was thin, his narrow face pinched into an expression of displeasure.

"You've returned," he finally said.

"Are you surprised?"

"Merely grateful. Plans are in place for your wedding. How would I explain the absence of the bride?"

She was nothing more than a walking bank draft, a funding source for his gambling. This marriage he so desperately wanted for her must be valuable to him in some fashion.

"Who was he?"

"My abductor?" she asked. "I have no idea."

He asked for no more details. Nor did he move to explain himself.

The last three days had proven she was not a coward. She'd been someone else, a woman named Emma, who'd chosen what to feel and how to act, irrespective of society's rules or a man's dictates.

"I know you didn't ransom me, Uncle," she said. "Did you hope I'd be killed?"

"How dare you address me in such a tone," he said, his voice quietly chilling.

"You'll find I dare a great deal," she said, no doubt shocking him.

"Then we have nothing more to say to each other." He turned and, without another word, walked back into his library.

Emma followed him, knowing that the issue must be put to rest now, when she was fueled with courage.

She entered the library, took a deep breath, and clasped her hands in front of her. "I've thought about it a great deal, Uncle," she said. "I do not wish to marry again."

"Your abduction has made you courageous, Emma."

She wasn't that brave or she wouldn't have stepped aside when he approached her. The odor of camphor surrounded him like a noxious cloud. Did he bathe in it?

"You will marry, Emma. When I say. To whom I say. You will do whatever I want. Whenever I want it."

His voice echoed with Anthony's arrogance.

"No."

He shoved her so hard that her back hit the wall. She immediately recovered, straightening her shoulders and facing him.

"Anthony trained you well," her uncle said. He took another step toward her. "You don't show fear. How very admirable of you, Emma. But, then, you've had a great deal of experience at being the Ice Queen, haven't you?"

Her gaze flew to his face.

"Oh, yes, I know," he said, his thin lips curving. "So reticent, so decorous. But the world doesn't know, does it, Emma, that you're the worst whore in London?"

She could taste salt on the back of her tongue, but she forced the nausea away.

"I witnessed your performance more than once. Anthony was rather . . . masterful, in his way."

This wasn't a conversation. Nor did it require her participation. If it followed the pattern of Anthony's diatribes, she would be flogged with each point until she bled from it. All she had to do was endure.

"Perhaps I should let slip that what society speculates about is true. All the fluttering old ladies, gossiping at their afternoon tea. You couldn't go anywhere without whispers. Is she the one? Yes, it's her. The Herridge Whore."

She didn't blink or move her gaze from his face. She'd once read a newspaper account of a famous explorer and his expedition in the wilds of Africa. What she remembered now was his insistence that one should never show fear, especially in the presence of a predator. She'd learned that lesson on her own.

"What do you think society would do then, Emma? You'd spend your life in isolation."

As a threat, it lacked teeth. She'd spent the last four years in a self-imposed isolation and would do so again, if necessary.

He gave her a considering look.

"Perhaps that wouldn't matter to you," he said, as if guessing her thoughts.

She remained silent.

"Marry Bryce, Emma," he said, his smile feral, his tone thoroughly pleasant. "If you don't, I shall have to do something I'd abhor."

"What do you mean?" she asked, feeling as if her throat were closing. Her heart had, strangely, slowed its beat, as if to ready her for death. Her feet were blocks of ice and her fingers cold.

He reached out and touched the cameo at her throat. She jerked away as if he'd touched her, instead.

"How many men do you think you could take, Emma? Before you agreed to wed?" He smiled. "We've a few stable lads who'd be more than happy to bed you for free. Imagine their joy if I pay them for it. Add in another dozen or so men I can easily find on the east side of London and you'd have your fill in a few hours. I'm willing to say ten before you change your mind. Shall we have a wager on it?"

"You can't be serious," she said, pushing the words past numb lips.

He moved away to lean against his desk. He folded his arms, regarding her with that small smile. "It's your choice, my dear Emma. Strictly your choice."

She shook her head.

"How very foolish you are. Of course I'm serious.

You mustn't doubt that. What shall it be? Marriage? Or will you push me to do what I must? Of course, there's every possibility you'll find yourself with the pox at the end of it. Or with child." He shrugged. "Regardless, you'll be married."

"Is that why you didn't ransom me, Uncle? Because you wished me dead?"

His face changed. The appearance of affability faded, to be replaced by another emotion, one that caused her to take a step to the side, away from him. Why had she never seen his hatred before now?

"Let me set up my own establishment," she said. "Give me enough money to do so. You keep the remainder."

"Perhaps you could hold out to twelve. Or your experience as the Herridge Whore might have made you receptive to at least two dozen."

"You can have all of my inheritance," she said. "Surely, the solicitors can arrange it."

"What's it to be, Emma? Marriage? Or will you choose the least acceptable alternative?"

Her composure was as thin as her skin. Inside, she was screaming. Her mouth was dry and her palms wet. Not only did she suspect that he would do what he threatened, but that he would thoroughly enjoy the spectacle.

"Do you owe this man money, Uncle? If so, pay him from my inheritance."

He didn't respond.

No one would help her. Not the staff, all of whom got their pay and instructions from her uncle. She'd broken off her friendships when it had been only too obvious what kind of monster she'd married. She hadn't wanted her friends tainted by Anthony. Ian was gone, back to Scotland to marry.

"Well, Emma?" He smiled. "What shall it be?"

She forced herself to breathe deeply. "You know the answer, Uncle," she said, her voice tight. "I'll marry him, of course."

"There, I knew you were a smart girl."

The past wasn't dead after all—it lived and breathed here in this room. Her tormenter had changed identities, that's all.

She turned on her heel and left the room before she could do or say anything that would only put her in more jeopardy.

Chapter 14

"There is nothing you can do to change his direction, Ian?"

Ian forced his attention away from the motion of the whiskey in his glass and to his mother. They sat in his Edinburgh home, one of the few homes he'd inherited that he didn't particularly like. It was old, cramped, and crowded, but for some reason his mother preferred to live here rather than at Lochlaven. The Edinburgh house was always filled with visitors, and was a center of activity—because of his mother.

He couldn't say that she'd decorated the house as much as simply *filled* it. The entire house was so crowded as to be impossible to navigate. In this room, a flowered carpet covered the floor, and on top of it rested a sofa, two armchairs, and a scattering of square and round tables. Every bit of furniture was draped in a crimson fabric with fringe, from the tables to the mantel to the flower pots.

Lochlaven was a sparsely furnished haven in comparison.

"Bryce is going to go his own way, Mother," he said.

His train journey to Edinburgh had been interminable. Under normal conditions, he would have continued on to Inverness as soon as possible, then taken his carriage to Lochlaven. But he needed to tell her of his meeting—confrontation—with Bryce, and as the Countess of Buchane was to leave for the continent soon, now was as good a time as any.

"He's getting married," he said. "To an heiress, evidently. He was quite proud of that fact."

The Countess of Buchane sat in the adjoining chair, her eyes wide.

She'd always appeared too young to be his mother. With her light brown hair and hazel eyes, she was a pretty woman—an impression that lasted until she smiled. Then, some magic of nature rendered her unmistakably beautiful.

She'd contemplated remarriage more than once, only to change her mind at the last moment. He'd accused her of enjoying the attention of being courted, and she'd only laughed in response. But he'd made note of the fact that she never denied the charge.

"Is that the best thing for him?" she asked.

He glanced at his mother and stifled his smile. Despite his age, or his sister's, or Bryce's for that matter, his mother was determined to orchestrate their lives. The fact that she had quite an exciting life of her own was their only saving grace. She traveled often, leaving the three of them to tend to their own lives without difficulty.

His mother was generous and never refused Bryce funds when he requested them. What Bryce didn't know, however, was that the simple request for money also triggered her well-developed protective instincts. Now the same impulses were in play, and unless he dissuaded his mother, she would travel to London to see Bryce herself.

"It's what he wants," he said. "You can't make his decisions for him, Mother," he added, knowing that she'd ignore the caution.

Ian's father and his cousin had been close; it had been natural for her to swoop down and gather up Bryce when he was orphaned at ten and bring him to Lochlaven to live.

From that moment, his second cousin was one of the family, and nothing would dissuade the countess from treating him like another of her children.

The fact that Bryce had resented her kindness from the moment he arrived at Lochlaven was something his mother had never been able to discern.

Bryce would make his own way, whether or not his mother interceded. People did.

Would Emma?

She was going to be married. Someone would wed the sad young Duchess of Herridge. Would the fool ever understand what darkened her lovely blue eyes? Or why she sometimes looked as fragile as a glass tube?

Because he was a man who studied, investigated, and pulled apart the skeins of the mysteries of his life, he didn't flinch from examining his own thoughts.

Was what he felt for her simple lust? Had it been, he could have controlled his baser impulses with some difficulty but controlled them nonetheless. What he'd felt for her, what he'd experienced with her, had been something different.

What would he call it?

The need to conquer? Part of it, yes, not the whole. He'd dominated but had also been overwhelmed, by tenderness, by protectiveness, by emotions he'd never felt.

Strangely enough, he'd first wanted to talk with her, learn her secrets, know her mind, and perhaps offer up to her the gift of his knowledge. He wanted to introduce her to all those things that amused, charmed, or intrigued him, if only to see if she felt the same.

"Ian?"

He glanced over to see his mother staring at him.

"You haven't heard a word I've said, have you? What's wrong?"

Unless he acted quickly, his mother's concern for Bryce would be transferred to him.

"Sorry," he said. "Wool-gathering."

"Was London successful, then?"

"Yes," he said slowly. "I believe it was."

"Rebecca will be pleased to see you."

He regarded his mother steadily. "You like her a great deal, don't you?"

His mother returned the look. "I would like anyone you chose."

"Did I choose her? Or did circumstances do it?" He couldn't, for the life of him, remember making a conscious decision to marry Rebecca. Perhaps it was something he and Albert had discussed, hunched over their microscopes. Perhaps it was simply a sliding forward into something that felt companionable.

"Are you having second thoughts, Ian?"

More like third and fourth thoughts, but he only smiled.

"Were you happy with my father?"

"Yes," she said simply. "From the beginning. So much so that I can't imagine being married to anyone else."

From the beginning—that's what it was. From the moment he'd seen her from the window of her sitting room. From the first words out of her mouth. From the first time her chin rose imperiously and her finger pointed. He was hers, and she was his from the beginning.

His mother leaned forward. "Love is not an easy emotion, my dearest. It's not soft and pretty and filled with romance. Love is difficult because it demands all of you." She looked away, and he wondered where her thoughts were. With his father? In those early days of her marriage? "Your father was not an easy man to love," she said, turning back to him. "He was stubborn, overbearing, frugal to a fault, and was more than content to remain at Lochlaven for the rest of his days."

"Yet he traveled to Edinburgh often enough with you. And to the continent as well."

She smiled, and the expression had a great deal of mischief in it. "I'm not necessarily an easy woman to love, either. But he did. We did. All I would ask of you is that you feel the same for Rebecca."

He didn't. He wouldn't. He couldn't.

He stood, suddenly needing to move. "I'll go back to London," he said. "And bring Bryce physically back to Lochlaven if I must. Will that reassure you?"

She looked at him curiously. "Do you think that's necessary, Ian?"

He smiled at her, the decision coming easily to him. "I've got to return to London regardless, Mother," he said. "It's no trouble at all."

He placed his whiskey on the table before approaching her.

"If I bring Bryce home, you'll welcome him with open arms, won't you?"

"Of course," she said, obviously surprised at the question.

"Even though his behavior isn't necessarily honorable?"

She nodded.

"You'll forgive him again, won't you?"

"Love again, Ian. It forgives anything."

"I may call upon you to do some forgiving on my behalf," he said, bending to kiss her cheek.

She still looked confused. As well she might, because he was grinning like an idiot.

Emma could feel time trickle away like water through her fingers. She read, toiled on her needlework, or paced in her sitting room until she was certain that she had created a permanent pattern in the polished wooden floor.

She grew so adept at deciphering the sounds around her that she could tell what time of day it was by the tasks being performed: the sweeping of the floors, the muffled conversation of the maids as they moved on their knees brushing the carpet, the splash of water as the floors were damp mopped, the clank of the boiler as baths were drawn.

Her mourning gave her a reason to hide in her chamber, and she took full advantage of it. She also refused to go to meals with her uncle, and for once he didn't object. Why should he? He'd already won his battle.

Her return home had been without fanfare. Not one of her servants had been curious. Nor had she explained to Juliana where she'd been or why. Instead, knowing that the girl sometimes went to her uncle with information she would much rather not share, Emma remained silent.

She was conscious of every passing hour, and with it, the knowledge that there was nothing she could do. Without her agreement, with her whole repugnance, she was going to be married again. The alternative was frighteningly real. She didn't doubt that her uncle would do whatever was necessary, in his mind, to accomplish his goal.

For some reason, that goal was her second marriage.

The view outside her window held a great deal of fascination for her. The scenes of life being lived by people unrestrained by their titles or the expectations of others were more interesting than her own existence.

The young girl across the square, today attired in pale yellow, always accompanied by her governess, reminded her of herself. She couldn't help but smile one day when the girl raced away from the older woman and hid behind a pillar. How many times had she wished to do the same but never quite possessed the courage?

Oh, Ian.

Her life felt as if it should be in two parts—before her abduction, and after.

How foolish she was to recall a man she'd known for only three days. Yet in those three days, she'd learned wonder, delight, and the true meaning of yearning. For the first time in her life she'd felt true passion. She'd lusted and hungered and given in to all the sensations she'd only witnessed before. She'd lain in his arms and felt only a sense of feminine victory, not humiliation or shame.

Three days, that was all. Three days could not change the course of her lifetime. Three days did not have the power or the ability to mold her, or to alter her to a substantial degree.

Somehow, they had.

"Your Grace?"

She turned her head to see Juliana entering her sitting room.

"Someone is at the door to see you."

For an impossible moment her heart raced.

"Show him upstairs," Emma said, carefully schooling her features so as to not betray her excitement.

It had to be Ian.

Juliana looked conflicted but turned, finally, to do her bidding.

A few minutes later a footman attired in Herridge livery stood at her bedroom door. Emma bit down her disappointment as she stared at the man.

"Your Grace," he said, bowing low. "I was tasked with bringing this to you."

"This" turned out to be a carved mahogany box that he handed to her. She recognized it immediately.

She opened the box to find the Tulloch mirror cradled on a small pillow. Resting on top of it was a note from the housekeeper. The mirror had evidently been retrieved from the Duke's Suite when renovations were begun and tucked away for safekeeping.

"Thank you," she said, dismissing both the footman and Juliana. They left her sitting room, closing the door softly behind them.

She should call for one of her own footmen and have him deliver the box to Ian. He'd be in Scotland, but his staff could forward it to him. At least she'd help him succeed in his task of delivering the mirror to Lady Sarah.

Emma set aside the note from the housekeeper, gripped the handle of the mirror and extracted it from the case to admire the back. There had been writing on it; she'd remembered that correctly. The language was Latin: *Animadverto vestri, visum posterus.* To see the truth of the future?

The handle was adorned with a pattern of trailing vines. Inset around the back of the mirror were at least a hundred small diamonds. They winked in the afternoon light, as if summoning the sun itself.

Her fingers trailed over them. How odd a juxtaposition—ugly and beautiful at once. Not unlike how she viewed Chavensworth.

Slowly, she turned the mirror over, and the sun abruptly vanished. Now she remembered why the mirror had been so disconcerting when Anthony gave it to her. What should have been her reflection was, instead, dark brown glass. All those years ago, she'd put it away, disturbed by something she couldn't recall.

Now, however, she stared into the glass. The mirror began to lighten, the brown fading first to beige, then to blue. She felt, suddenly, as if she were not in her chamber in London at all but standing in the midst of a blue sky. Behind her was an ocean glittering in the sunlight.

The woman in the mirror was laughing, her eyes alight with humor. Her cheeks bloomed with color, and Emma could almost feel the surge of true joy that swept through her at that moment.

In her dream—because that's all it could be—her

reflection reached out a hand to someone just beyond the mirror's curved frame.

Abruptly, the brown surface of the mirror reappeared, and in its shadowed darkness Emma saw herself as she was now, her face pale, her brows drawn together in puzzlement or refutation. The stranger in the mirror was gone, vanished. No, she'd never been there at all—only wishful thinking had created a woman suffused with joy.

With trembling fingers she placed the mirror back in its wooden case and closed the top. Standing, she walked to the other side of the room and rang the bellpull. While she waited for a footman to appear, she went to her secretary, and wrote a note to Ian.

Please convey this to Lady Sarah.

Six small words, when she wanted to say so much more.

Had the mirror demonic properties? Or was it possible that it had the power to display one's greatest hope and desire? In her case, a wish for happiness, for love, for the utter joy she felt pulsating through the image in the mirror.

Perhaps it simply lured the viewer to sit and watch what might have been, to become so immersed in a world of fantasy that the real world simply faded away.

She walked to the window and stood looking out at the square.

Could she summon him with a wish? Could she open the window and he would suddenly be there, a rooftop brigand come to carry her away? What had begun in fear ended in delight, days she would never forget. Days that were out of time, and out of place, and never to be replicated.

She'd made him moan.

His eyes had darkened with lust because of her. Her hands had gripped him and caused him to swell, as if she were some sort of sorceress. That dangerous, masculine instrument had been tamed by the warmth of her palms and the softness of her lips.

He'd ripped the dreariness of her widow's veil aside, and allowed her to see a different world, tinged not by black but colored lemon and gold and azure and green.

He was more magic than any mirror.

In his bed, she'd no longer felt alone, had no longer been aloof and isolated. She'd belonged to him because she'd had no choice in the giving of herself. He'd demanded it, and she succumbed and surrendered, and in doing so had felt a greater freedom than she'd ever known.

She would never forget him, even though she needed to try.

When a footman appeared, she gave him instructions.

"Just the name Ian, Your Grace?"

She only nodded. But the moment the footman reached the door, she called him back.

"Never mind," she said, uncaring what the footman thought. Ian wasn't there, and the mirror would only sit and wait for him. She reached out and took the box from him, forcing a smile to her face.

The Ice Queen she had been would never have offered an explanation, but she did now. "I've changed my mind. I'll make alternate arrangements."

He left the room, no doubt to tell his fellow servants that the Duchess of Herridge had gone odd.

She ran her hand over the wooden box. She'd never pitied herself, but she did now. Poor Emma, trapped by a vision that she probably imagined, of a life she'd never have.

A foolish thing, pity, almost as foolish as longing.

Chapter 15

Less than a week after returning home, Emma was married, only meeting her bridegroom twenty minutes before the ceremony in the drawing room.

Bryce McNair didn't smile, only nodded at her, as if he were pleased to be wed to a woman garbed as a blackbird, the only concession to this day a small jet brooch at her throat.

Despite his youth, he already bore the signs of dissipation. His brown eyes were bloodshot and the swelling beneath them would sag with age, creating pouches. One day he would bear a striking resemblance to the hounds at Chavensworth.

For now, however, he was society's version of handsome, with his blond hair cut short, and attired in an immaculate gray suit with silver links on the cuffs of his snowy white shirt. He appeared a prosperous bridegroom on the occasion of his wedding, and if he smelled too much of whiskey, she could only surmise it was because of his Scot's heritage and the fact he was celebrating his marriage to an heiress.

Emma wished she was as thrilled to be marrying him as he was to be marrying her.

She couldn't help but recall her father's words,

spoken on the occasion of her wedding to Anthony. "Your mother and I did not know each other well when we married, my dearest Emma, but we went on to fall in love with each other. There is not one day I do not deeply miss her."

Her wedding to the Duke of Herridge had been a spectacular ceremony, costing thousands of pounds, effectively announcing to the world that Emma Harding had become a duchess. This wedding, held in the drawing room and attended by the servants, her uncle, and the minister, was a penurious contrast.

She was no longer a pattern biscuit. Now she was more like a trickle of water, one that easily changed its path. Yesterday she'd been Emma, Duchess of Herridge. Today she was Emma McNair, wife of Bryce McNair, stranger.

All her earthly possessions now belonged to Bryce. Her uncle would no longer have control over her fortune, her allowance, or her properties.

For that alone, she was grateful.

At the wedding dinner, Bryce did not pass up the glasses of wine offered with each course. At the end of the meal she doubted he had the ability to stand up, and certainly did not do so when she stood.

Instead, he raised a glass to eye level, looking at her through the crimson wine, and proposed a toast. "To you, my lady wife. Emma."

Her uncle followed suit but he, at least, stood at her departure. She couldn't have cared less what he did. From the moment he'd threatened her with rape, she'd become the Ice Queen once more. Even tonight, disgusted by both of them, she was careful not to reveal any emotion.

"If you do not mind," she said, "I will retire."

"I shall join you shortly, wife," Bryce said, the effect of the wine slurring his voice more than a little.

She only nodded, leaving the room, and wishing she could leave the house as well. But there was no respite to be found, no security, no sanctuary, unless it lay within the confines of her own mind. And even there she felt tortured. Too many memories resided there, all too willing to be recalled on this night, of all nights.

Juliana was waiting for her in her chamber.

They barely spoke, but then they rarely had. Their relationship was nothing more than that of servant and mistress. Even though it was Emma's fortune that paid the other's salary, Juliana was London born and bred, cultivating a "civility to all, servility to none" attitude that made Emma feel, sometimes, as if Juliana were doing her a favor by acting as her maid. Her loyalty was held in reserve, for herself. Perhaps that was wiser, especially in the Duke of Herridge's household.

Sometimes Anthony had dismissed someone from their employ simply because the young man had blond hair and he wanted to see brunette or black. One year, he'd taken to employing only footmen with blue eyes. The next year, it had been brown. During one eventful year, he'd fired the majority of the servants, simply because he wanted to see new faces.

Juliana had served her more than adequately. She was always there when needed, always prompt. She kept Emma's wardrobe in perfect order, ironed impeccably, attended to her jewelry, straightened her room, arranged and cared for cut flowers, and was available to offer any assistance that Emma required.

The fact that she could barely tolerate Juliana had,

at its roots, the fact that Anthony had selected the maid for her.

She stood immobile as Juliana closed the drapes before returning to help her off with her skirt and hoops. Night had come suddenly, with no warning of dusk, or setting of the sun on the horizon. One moment it was afternoon, and the next it was dark, as if the earth had simply shut its eyes to sleep.

She knew only too well what would come now. The only difference between Bryce and Anthony would be youth and cruelty. How much did Bryce wish to become a bridegroom? What was he willing to do to accomplish the consummation of this marriage?

The last man to touch her had brought her joy.

She deliberately blocked off those other thoughts, memories only days old. Instead, she thanked Juliana and dismissed her, wishing to finish dressing in private.

Please, God, let him at least be gentle. God would not see that prayer as too onerous, would He? Would that be considered too selfish of her? Was she simply supposed to endure what her husband chose to do to her?

But at least this husband would not take her on a stage in full view of a hundred people.

She was no longer the Duchess of Herridge, and for that she ought to thank Bryce. No longer would she be known as Anthony's widow, but the shocking Emma Harding who, months after the duke's death, married a no one. Not a peer but a Scot.

Society would deem her reckless and foolish, and probably willful as well.

If no one called upon her, that was fine. If no one sought her company, that was acceptable. If no invitations were extended to her and her new husband, she would be able to tolerate the exclusion.

As long as she could tolerate the wedding night.

Tonight she would wear a deep lavender peignoir and wrapper, and forgo the nightgowns that had been dyed black. The color didn't matter. Nor did the bridegroom, and wasn't that a sad thought?

Peter, Earl of Falmouth, watched as his niece's bridegroom became increasingly drunk. The young man might be decidedly clever but he was vastly unsophisticated in other areas—such as holding his liquor. From what he'd seen of the man, it was a chronic problem.

The damn fool was a dangerous liability.

This marriage was a payment, one of the few he could afford. A marriage to an heiress in return for Bryce's silence. Now all he had to worry about was keeping the idiot quiet.

"You and I have friends in common, Your Lordship," McNair had said on that fateful day a month ago.

He'd known the man by appearance only but had agreed to see him because of McNair's insistence.

"Is this a social call, McNair?" he'd asked, taking a seat behind the desk he purchased not long after coming to live with Emma. His niece had needed someone to care for her—and her fortune—after the tragedy of her husband's death.

"One of business," McNair said.

The expression on Bryce McNair's face had been genial, but the Earl of Falmouth didn't give a flying farthing about McNair's mood.

"Then state it."

"I find myself low on funds," McNair said. "Here

I was, rousting around in my mind for the perfect opportunity to raise some capital when it struck me. I had been overlooking the very means by which to do so."

"What is it you want?"

"I know things, Your Lordship. Things I shouldn't know, perhaps. But I'm a cautious man, one who watches my step. I'm also a curious one."

"What the devil are you talking about?"

"I have, you might say, a penchant for overhearing things. Interesting things. You might say that I have an ability for being in the right place at the wrong time."

"What the hell do you mean?"

"I was at Chavensworth that night," McNair said.

"What night would that be?"

"The night the Duke of Herridge died. Unexpectedly. Before his time. Tragically."

They'd exchanged a look, and for a few moments Peter couldn't breathe.

"I was often at Chavensworth, Your Lordship. As were you. The gambling was almost as good as the wenching."

"I never indulged in the wenching, as you so colorfully put it."

"But you did indulge in the gambling, as I recall," McNair said.

He hadn't any choice. He'd no money of his own, and he'd been dependent upon Anthony for assistance. If he wagered and lost at one of Anthony's parties, the duke covered his losses. Anywhere else, and he had to find a way to fund his markers.

"How very convenient of the duke to die when he

did, Your Lordship. You owed quite a bit of money at the time, didn't you?"

The damn fool didn't know anything.

But what if he did?

McNair looked directly at him, and Peter restrained his shudder only barely. He motioned to the chair beside the desk. For a moment he thought that Bryce would refuse, but then he rounded the desk and sat.

"Are you married, McNair?" he asked.

The other man smiled, but it didn't ease the cool look in his eyes.

"I have it within my power to grant you more money than you've ever seen in your entire lifetime," Peter said, smiling. "What would you say if you could control a vast fortune?"

He named the cumulative amount of Emma's inheritance. The other man's eyes widened, and the cool look vanished.

"In return for what, exactly, Your Lordship?"

"Eternal silence?" Peter smiled. "Is that too much to request? What you think you know might prove to be embarrassing should it be repeated. People might give it some credence."

McNair watched him with hooded eyes. "Not to mention that the authorities would be interested."

"Are you married, McNair?" Peter asked again.

This time the young man answered. "I am not."

"Have you any objection to be married?"

"To your niece?"

"My niece." Peter sat back, studying McNair.

"Your proposal sounds interesting, Your Lordship. But why would you be so quick to turn over the administration of that fortune?"

"I would, of course, expect to be remunerated from time to time. An allotment, if you will." He smiled. "Shall we toast to it?" Peter had asked, going to the sideboard and selecting his finest brandy.

He sat back now, sipped at his own wine with moderation and watched as Bryce became increasingly more intoxicated. The fool would be easy enough to manipulate. A great deal easier than Anthony had been.

Men like Bryce McNair didn't come to the well only once. He would continue to come until the well was dry. Better to let him think he was getting all the water at once.

He'd been tempted, though, to take little Emma's offer of her fortune. Tempted, until he realized that he'd have the same problem with McNair. No, this way was better. A little longer, perhaps, but more secure in the end.

Life could not get much better, could it?

The door opened and her bridegroom stood framed in the doorway, both hands braced on either side of the frame. His waistcoat was unbuttoned, his jacket discarded somewhere, and his shirt half out of his trousers.

"My lady wife," he said, beaming at her. "I am here, your bridegroom."

She walked through the sitting room to face him.

"Come in," she said, in a voice much softer than his.

He bent, picked up a bottle of wine, holding it aloft triumphantly as he entered the room.

"I bring gifts!" he said, in a voice that bordered on a shout.

The very last thing she wanted was for all the servants to hear her wedding night.

"Bryce," she said, hoping to calm him, "come and sit down. Let me pour you some wine."

He smiled brightly at her, an expression that made her wonder exactly how old her bridegroom was. Was he her junior? At the moment, he was acting like a boy, and she felt ancient.

Unbidden, Ian came to mind. She could not bear it if she remembered Ian now. Later, when she was alone, she would think of him, and dream of him, and remember him.

Not now, please God.

Bryce sat in a chair by the window, stretching out his legs. She took the bottle of wine from him and placed it on the top of the bureau.

"I'll just request some glasses," she said. She rang for the maid and then stood at the door. When the girl arrived, she conveyed her request, and returned to Bryce's side to tell him that the glasses would be coming shortly.

To her very great surprise, her bridegroom had fallen asleep, his head at an angle, his mouth gaping open.

A good wife, a proper wife, would have eased him to the bed. She would have begun to disrobe him so that he was more comfortable, or at least remove his shoes and loosened his neck cloth.

Emma did none of those things. She just extinguished the lamp beside the chair and tiptoed into her bedroom, grateful that, for this night at least, she'd been given a respite.

Chapter 16

The day after her marriage, Emma awoke to find her husband asleep in the chair in exactly the same position she'd left him.

Instead of attempting to wake him, she summoned her maid. When Juliana arrived, she greeted her at the door.

"Does my husband have a valet?" she asked.

"I do not believe so, Your Grace," Juliana said.

"Is there anyone among the footmen who could be promoted to the position?"

Seeking Juliana's opinion would be considered a mark of respect in the servants' quarters, not to mention the power it would give the girl.

Juliana drew herself up to her full height and smiled, one of the few times Emma had ever seen that particular expression on her maid's face.

"Robert, Your Grace. He's new to Your Grace's employ but he's a fast learner and an honest man."

"Send Robert to me, then," she said. Before Juliana left her, however, she stopped the girl. "I'm no longer to be addressed as Your Grace," she said.

Juliana only nodded, before hurrying to inform Robert of his potential position.

She had certainly begun a new life, hadn't she? First, by attempting to garner Juliana's support, and secondly, by evincing some concern for her husband.

Bryce needed a valet, and this morning would certainly be a testament to Robert's tenacity. If he could get Bryce dressed and about, she would promote him to the position of gentleman's valet immediately.

Ian took the first available train back to London. Thankfully, there were no accidents on the line, and the trip was relatively uneventful. Except, of course, for his thoughts. Even though he'd brought his notes with him, as well as his journal, he hadn't been able to concentrate.

Sitting back against the seat, he closed his eyes and imagined Emma at Lochlaven, strolling through the formal gardens, admiring the roses and the sight of the island in the distance. Or sitting on the edge of the lowest of the brick fortifying walls. She would swing her legs back and forth, hands braced on the wall on either side of her, her gaze fixed on the mist-blanketed hills.

He didn't care what plans the Earl of Falmouth had for Emma. He didn't even care about his own engagement. Both impediments could be dealt with, and although he was certain he was going to make quite a few people angry, he would deal with that as well.

His title was just as old as that of the Earl of Falmouth, if not more illustrious. His wealth was a match, if not greater, than Emma's. His prospects for the future were bright, his reputation sound. Emma's uncle would have no reasonable argument to prevent their marriage. Even if he did, that was an obstacle he was more than willing to face headlong.

Besides, he was not going to be stopped by the man who'd struck Emma.

If nothing else, he would take Emma to Scotland, and the world could go hang.

Granted, the circumstances of their meeting had been odd, but there hadn't been anything strange about the way they'd come together. Ever since he met her, she'd been lodged in his mind. He didn't want to banish her either from his thoughts or his life.

He'd always handled those responsibilities he'd inherited, as well as those he'd taken on, including the welfare of the people who depended upon him for their livelihood. He had never been profligate. Sometimes, he'd been wise. Sometimes, foolish, witness the decision he'd made on that night only a short time ago. Yet, the act of being a burglar had changed his life.

In return for all those years of restraint, he wanted something now. He wanted Emma, Duchess of Herridge. He didn't want a day to pass without seeing her face. Nor did he want to sleep alone in his bed. He wanted to tell her about his experiments, and banish that look that occasionally came over her face—a combination of fear and defiance.

Their future would not be easy, at least not immediately.

First, he needed to tell her who he was. Not a thief, not a brigand, but the Earl of Buchane, the Laird of Trelawny, the last in a line of distinguished and country-loving Scotsmen. When it was time, he would take her to Scotland and show her his home, proud

owner that he was. Perhaps he'd even brag about all
his exploits or show her the letters of commendation
he'd received. He would reveal Lochlaven to her as
he'd learned it from his childhood, with wonder and
excitement and joy.

He felt as if he were about to embark on a great
and lifelong adventure, and couldn't wait to reach
London.

Peter eyed the bank draft in his hand with satisfac-
tion. This amount could easily be replicated. All he
need do was to go to the young bridegroom sitting
in front of him.

How quickly Bryce had acclimated to being wealthy.
He sat in the library attired in pressed clothing, freshly
shaved, his bloodshot eyes the only indication of his
overindulgence of the night before.

"Thank you. You're very generous."

"Consider it a parting gift, if you will," Bryce
said.

"What do you mean?" A sensation like melting ice
traveled down Peter's spine.

"I want you out of here, with all possible haste,"
Bryce said.

Peter placed the bank draft on the surface of the
desk with great precision, lining it up so it was in
the exact center of his blotter, just below the crystal
sander.

"Do you think to dictate to me?" he asked.

Bryce smiled. "Exactly so, Your Lordship. One word
from me and the authorities would be very interested
in speaking with you." Bryce stood and regarded him
with an expression too much like contempt.

"You're a fool to think I'll tolerate your threatening me."

"What are you going to do about it, Your Lordship?"

"Do you think to keep it all for yourself?" Peter stood as well, biting back his smile. The young fool was as stupid as he'd thought.

Bryce chuckled. "You'll need to find other living arrangements, Your Lordship. This is now my house, and you're not welcome here."

"Be careful," Peter said softly. "Be very careful in your threats."

Bryce smiled again, a particularly annoying expression. "Have you forgotten what I know?" His smile faded. "Do you think I'm going to just sit back and wait until you do to me what you did to the Duke of Herridge?"

His smile returned with an edge to it. "We're leaving this morning," he said. "We'll be back in a few weeks. Make sure you're gone by the time we return."

An apologetic Robert had delivered a summons from her new husband to Emma. She was required in her uncle's library. She was raising her hand to knock on the door when the shouting began.

Nearby, a few of the servants stopped what they were doing, each of them looking toward the room with no effort to hide their interest. They didn't even have to try to listen. Both her uncle and Bryce were so loud that no doubt passersby heard them on the street.

They were arguing about money. She'd witnessed the same type of disagreement between Anthony and her uncle. She never understood why Anthony was so incensed over the amount of money her uncle gambled away when it was quite evident that Anthony was attempting, in his own way, to decimate her fortune.

Being an heiress didn't make her a fool.

Yet money had never given her any freedom. She could buy almost anything she wished, as long as a man approved. She could travel almost anywhere, as long as she was chaperoned and accompanied by a male escort. She could engage in good works and make contributions to any charity she wished, as long as it was sanctioned by a male relative.

At times, she didn't want to be wealthy. Or at least wealthy enough to be sold, bartered, and haggled about such as now.

The door abruptly opened and she was face-to-face with Bryce. Robert had evidently helped him wash and dress, because other than bloodshot eyes, there was little evidence of the night before in the man she saw now.

"We'll be leaving shortly," he said. "Pack your trunks."

"Where are we going?" she asked, conscious of her uncle's presence in the doorway. She edged away from him.

Bryce turned and faced her uncle. The words were for her but the challenge in them was for the Earl of Falmouth.

"To Scotland," he said. "It's time my boorish relatives learned of my great good fortune." He sent a thin smile in her uncle's direction, then turned and left her.

She could hear him striding through the main hall and then the sound of the front door opening and closing. Since she did not want to remain in her uncle's company, Emma turned and left, retreating to the safety of her suite.

By noon her trunks were packed. She'd refused the dresses her uncle had had made, defiantly remaining in mourning. Now, she allowed Juliana to pack the three dresses with white cuffs and white collars. But there were only seven dresses in all and two bonnets, a fraction of the wardrobe she'd once had.

"Will you take your jewelry case . . . " Juliana's words stumbled to a halt as the two women looked at each other.

"It's all right," Emma said. "It will take some time to get used to calling me Mrs. McNair. I'll leave my case here. I shall not be wearing any jewelry for a while."

She sent Juliana on an errand, and while her maid was out of the room, went to her desk where she'd hidden the Tulloch Sgàthán. She placed it in the bottom of the trunk holding her dresses, creating a well amidst the paper and carefully draped skirts.

Ian had said it belonged in Scotland, and perhaps there would be a way to send it to Lady Sarah once she was there. Besides, she didn't want to leave it behind, feeling a sense of responsibility for this one object greater than anything she'd ever owned.

An hour later she and her new husband were ready to leave.

At the carriage, her uncle exchanged a look with Bryce that wasn't the least friendly. She'd never known him to hold back his remarks but he was evidently doing so now. She turned away when he would have addressed her.

The Earl of Falmouth could go to hell on a fast horse for all she cared.

"I wish you a safe journey," her uncle said, stepping back and allowing the carriage door to be closed.

The last time Emma had been in a carriage with a man, the man had been Ian. The comparison between him and Bryce was not a fair one. Although they were similar in build, Bryce lacked Ian's commanding presence or Ian's enthusiasm and intelligence.

"Have you really asked my uncle to leave?"

"I have. It's my house now. If you have any objections as to how I manage my business, keep it to yourself."

All her life she'd known that her possessions were truly not hers but belonged to the man closest to her. How quickly Bryce had assumed his role as master of her domain.

"My uncle is of a stubborn bent," she said, pushing back her resentment.

"I think you will find that I'm even more stubborn," he said, reaching into the cupboard on the side of the carriage, a place that had normally kept a selection of books, a traveling clock, and writing implements and paper. From it he extracted a silver flask, removed the cork, and proceeded to drink his fill.

She glanced away, her eyes meeting Juliana's. Her maid was not happy to be taking this journey, but her displeasure showed in her eyes and the set of her mouth, not her words.

At the station, Bryce arranged their tickets, relegating Juliana to the second-class carriage while they occupied the first class with sixteen other people.

"You did not want to bring Robert?" she asked him when they'd settled.

"I can care for myself," he said, closing his eyes and

effectively ending their conversation. "I don't need a valet to do it for me."

He'd needed help this morning, but it was a comment she didn't voice. Emma had the feeling that she would become accustomed—once again—to holding back her thoughts, as well as her feelings.

The hours passed slowly but he was finally back in London. At King's Cross Station, Ian hired a carriage to take him to Emma's home. The sky was turning dark, the sunset announced with joyous orange and pink streaks.

Traffic was snarled and difficult, a commonplace occurrence for London's streets. Ian found himself impatiently drumming his fingers on his knee as they made their way through the congestion.

The hired carriage was commanded by a coachman who understood his need for haste. When they reached the house on Alchester Square, Ian opened the carriage door and called up to the man, complimenting him on his speed.

"I'll pay you double your hire if you wait for me," he added.

The man nodded, touched his hand to his hat, and wrapped the reins around the brake.

Ian took the steps two at a time, knocked on the door, and found himself face-to-face with a majordomo not unlike Patterson.

The man didn't speak, only inclined his head.

"I need to see Her Grace," Ian said, just now realizing that he'd never called Emma by the title. Her Grace. How apropos for her. "The Duchess of Herridge," he added, realizing he was being foolish. He felt like he was a boy again, a rash, improvident youth.

He couldn't help but smile at the dour man.

"I regret, sir, that Her Grace is not at home."

He knew that game quite well—he'd played it himself.

"Tell her it's Ian," he said. "She'll want to see me."

What if she didn't?

The majordomo opened the door a little wider, so that his not inconsiderable bulk was revealed. A bulwark of flesh. Did the man think to intimidate him? Nothing could at this point. Not plans, not geography, not a future all mapped out by strangers. He needed to see Emma, and he needed to see her now.

"I regret to say, sir, that she is truly not at home. The Duchess of Herridge was married yesterday, and left London this afternoon."

Sounds abruptly stopped.

Ian couldn't hear the vague distraction of the traffic a few streets away. The world narrowed to his breath, his heartbeat.

He stared at the majordomo like a dumb animal. When the man began to close the door, Ian did nothing to stop him. He didn't slap his hand across the carved panel or insert his foot in the space of the open door. He merely stared, and when the door closed with a substantial click, he remained where he was for a few moments before turning and very carefully, and very precisely, descending the steps.

The carriage was still where he left it, the coachman smiling as he approached.

He couldn't think.

The silence of his own mind was strangely abrasive, rubbing against his composure. He had to think. He had to move.

"Where to now, sir?"

Ian looked up at the driver. He should give him directions. Where, though, should he go? Where could he go?

Instead of giving the man his London address, or directing him back to the train station, Ian called out a list of the various establishments Bryce liked to frequent.

Darkness fell over London as he entered the carriage.

He'd try to locate his cousin, but if that chore was not immediately fruitful, he'd leave for Lochlaven. He needed to be home. He needed to return to his work. That was the only thought in his mind.

He didn't want to think of Emma.

Pain is a part of love. He remembered reading that once. Which part, however? A sliver, or the whole of it?

Somewhere past the border they encountered a storm. Wind buffeted the car in which they traveled, causing it to sway. Coupled with the sheer speed of the train, Emma found it difficult to do anything but stare out the window and wonder if the next turn would lead to her death.

Bryce snored beside her.

When the train slowed, she uttered a grateful prayer. A man dressed in a uniform passed through the car, speaking to the passengers. She waited until he drew abreast, then raised one hand to capture his attention. More properly, her husband should have flagged the gentleman down, but her husband was still in his sodden sleep, leaving her with no other choice.

"Is something wrong?" she asked.

"No, madam," he said, his face arranged in a pleasant aspect. "But we are going to be stopping on the siding soon. It's safer in the storm."

She, for one, was glad.

"We'll stay the night there," he continued. "And reach our destination in the morning."

She thanked him, and lay her head back against the seat. Would she be able to emulate Bryce and find sleep? She doubted it. Instead, she looked out at the night, careful to think only of the present. It wouldn't do to focus on the past, or even speculate on the future. The *now* was challenging enough.

The wind intensified until the car nearly rocked on the tracks. None of the other passengers in the first class compartment looked disturbed, so she pretended a calm she didn't feel.

Lightning rushed from cloud to cloud like a knight in silver armor, thunder following a moment later in a clash of sound. Evidently, she was going to have to deal with storms, speed, and unfamiliar travel by herself. Her new husband was neither consoling nor considerate.

Yet if he had been, would she have been able to reciprocate? She didn't want Bryce's avowals of undying love. She wouldn't have believed him, regardless. But she had not been prepared for his total disdain for her.

The train slowed further, the sound of the wheels on the tracks oddly comforting. Several moments later they ground to a stop, and only then could she hear the pounding of the rain on the car's roof.

One good thing about the train resting on the siding for the night. Her wedding night would be delayed.

But it would come, soon enough, and she needed to prepare herself for it. The sooner she banished all memory of Ian, the better. Should she be so reluctant to do so?

And why did that seem to be the most terrible chore she'd ever given herself?

Chapter 17

"**W**hat's the delay?" Bryce asked, his voice too loud. Several people in the train station glanced at him, but he didn't moderate his tone.

The man standing at the entrance to the baggage car turned to face Bryce.

"There's a problem, sir, with your trunks. They cannot be found."

"What do you mean, they can't be found?"

"We've had a bit of a muck up, sir. We're sorting it out now. If you don't mind waiting a few minutes."

Bryce's face turned red. "I do mind. I've already engaged a carriage, and I've been on your damn train for days."

Not days but certainly one whole day, and a few hours beyond that on the Highland Railway. Enough time that Emma felt soiled and in need of a good wash. Perhaps a soak in a tub like the one in her house in London. She craved hot water, perfumed salts, and the mechanical clank of the boiler as a backdrop to the slosh of water.

Even the *idea* of a bath was enough to make her sigh in longing.

"I'm sorry, sir, but we're sorting it out now."

"See that you do. I want my trunks, and I want them now! I've got a crate of damn fine wine in there!"

The man touched his fingers to his hat, turned, and disappeared into the baggage car.

Emma did not like being the object of so many stares. She motioned to Juliana to follow her to a bench some distance from the train.

Bryce evidently was not at his best in the morning, despite the fact that he'd slept the whole night. She was not as refreshed but certainly not going to take out her ire on the hapless man trying to make sense of the baggage issue.

"Are we to take a carriage for the remainder of the journey, madam?" Juliana asked.

"I believe so," Emma said.

However, Bryce had not conveyed anything more to her. He'd simply announced that they were going to Scotland, and here they were, in Inverness, after hours and hours of travel, tired, and without their trunks.

"Will it take long, madam? I'm only asking because of our meals." Juliana scanned the interior of the station. "There seem to be numerous places for us to purchase something. Shall I do so?"

Emma nodded. "Please," she said.

She only had a small amount of money with her, the allowance her uncle doled out each quarter. Normally, if she wanted to buy something, she sent a servant after it, and the bill was proffered to her uncle. Since she wasn't in the mood to go to Bryce with a request for funds, she gave what she had to her maid with the instructions that Juliana was to use her own judgment in how it was spent.

"You might want to purchase some wine as well," she told Juliana.

Perhaps some spirits would mollify Bryce. A drunkard and a bully, what a delightful man she'd married. Yet even with those failings, Bryce McNair was a substantially better husband than Anthony had been.

A few minutes later Bryce strode toward her, his expression thunderous, his face still red.

Emma stood, preparing for the expected confrontation.

"Why aren't you at the carriage?" he asked.

Since she had no idea where the carriage was located, that was an unfair accusation.

"Have they found all our trunks?" she asked, as calmly as possible.

"All but one. It's one of yours. You'll have to do without it. At least the fools didn't lose my crate of wine."

She stared at him. "I can't do without one of my trunks," she said. "I only have two."

He stopped and turned, making no effort to hide his irritation. "We're leaving now. Whatever you need, you can replace."

He began to walk, glancing back at her. Evidently, she was to follow him. He continued for some distance, finally stopping beside the carriage he'd hired.

When Juliana joined them a few moments later, Bryce addressed her maid. "Where have you been?"

Juliana gave him a look as if to remind him that she was a lady's maid and not subject to the treatment he might give other servants. "Getting a meal, sir. A selection of meats and cheeses."

Bryce reached out and uncovered the basket on Juliana's arm. "Any wine?"

"A bottle of red."

"Only one?"

He shouted up to the coachman. "Open up the case of wine from London," he ordered. "This day won't be a total loss." He waved his hand in the air as if that were a signal to follow him before rudely entering the carriage before Emma and her maid.

Emma stared after him, wondering how two people could have such a conflicting opinion of the same thing. It had been an absolutely miserable day and didn't look as if it were going to get any better.

Ian couldn't find Bryce anywhere in London, which was just as well because he was in a mood to pay him off and send him packing to America or Australia—as far away from Scotland and England as possible.

Bryce seemed to be lacking in compatriots, let alone friends, but his creditors were only too easy to locate. Evidently, his second cousin had fled London owing a great deal of money. Ian paid off seven men who held markers for Bryce, and requested statements from two gaming establishments.

By the time he decided to return to Scotland for the second time in as many days, he was in a raging mood.

He scrawled off a letter to his mother that managed to be moderately polite. His lies, however, niggled at him all the way to the station. He'd told her that Bryce would be at Lochlaven, that she needn't worry about him, and to enjoy her visit to France.

When he returned home, he would spend a good long time in the church in the neighboring village, praying for forgiveness of his many sins.

* * *

For the next hour, Emma occupied herself by studying the scenery. Unlike the train, a carriage ride was slow enough to appreciate the changing topography.

The road hugged Loch Ness for the majority of their journey, and in places seemed too narrow to accommodate a carriage. When they turned at a crossroads, she lost sight of the lake, and several minutes later was surprised to enter a forest. For a quarter hour they were surrounded by trees, the forest swallowing the sounds of the carriage wheels and making her feel as if they were cocooned in silence. When the trees thinned and they were suddenly bathed in bright sunlight, Emma gasped aloud. Surrounding them were tall blue-gray mountains that she hadn't seen before, as if they'd crept up on them unawares while they traveled through the forest.

Scotland exceeded her expectations.

She'd never traveled, other than to Chavensworth and back to London, and as a young girl between their country home and London. Traveling to Scotland had always been something that she'd wanted to do. She'd once had a forbidden thought that if Anthony were to die, she'd be permitted some degree of freedom. She could travel as she willed, see the world and all the places within it that sparked her curiosity. However, freedom hadn't come. Instead, her uncle had taken over not only her fortune but her future.

A future that looked dire unless she changed it.

Very well, she'd not been prepared to love Bryce McNair. After all, he was a stranger. But she had been inclined to tolerate her new husband, to withhold judgment until such time as his character was revealed to her. She'd thought they might be, if not friends, then amiable acquaintances, people who'd been forced together by circumstance and who could find a common purpose.

This man, however, in just a few short hours, was proving to be unlikable. The idea of loving him was as incredible as her wishing Anthony back from the grave.

Ian would have told her their destination. Ian would have described the whole of the journey to her. Or, if he'd noticed she was bored, would have offered to share his scientific journals with her. Or described an experiment. He would not have treated her as if she were an inconvenience, an annoyance.

How very strange that she'd compared her husband to Ian and not Anthony, as if Ian were someone who had mattered in her life.

She'd known him only three days, hardly long enough to judge a man's true worth. She'd labeled him a thief and a brigand, but he'd turned out to be a scientist and a mystery. Perhaps that was an indication of how wrong she could be. Perhaps Bryce would become a much more enjoyable person in time.

Perhaps she'd gone about this marriage all wrong. Had she truly made an effort to be a good wife? Had she tried to become acquainted with Bryce?

"Tell me about your family," she said, forcing a smile to her face.

He chuckled but she didn't think she'd amused him with her question.

"My family, my dear wife? I have no family."

"Then why are we in Scotland?"

"Did the Duke of Herridge tolerate your curiosity?" he asked, reaching for the last bottle of wine. Bryce had already finished the bottle Juliana purchased, as well as a second bottle. Only one remained of the two the coachman had removed from the crate.

So much for attempting to be pleasant. It was hard to converse with a drunkard.

He drank from the bottle without apology for his bad manners or the fact that he evidently had no intention of sharing the wine with anyone. He sat back against the seat and regarded her steadily. She returned his look, perhaps one of the first times she'd ever attempted to stare a man down.

This marriage was going to be different from the beginning. She was prepared to feel reluctance, perhaps even repugnance, boredom, impatience, and frustration, but she would not tolerate fear.

She was not going to be afraid again.

"Will you answer my question?" she said finally. "Or am I to be left in ignorance as to your family and our destination?"

He addressed the window, his gaze on the passing countryside. "You'll nag until I tell you all my plans, won't you?"

"I do not consider it nagging to be kept informed."

"I'll wager you never talked to your duke in such a tone," he said.

She didn't respond, merely waited.

"My parents died when I was young," he said finally. "I was brought up in a household of relatives. I was, you might say, the poor relation. The one without any funds who was dependent upon those with a benevolent nature."

Of course he would want to parade his new heiress

in front of those people. However, she didn't particularly want to be on display.

She exchanged a glance with Juliana, then forced herself to look away.

"I'm sure I shall like Scotland," she said. "I've never traveled here before."

"I don't give a flying farthing if you like it or not, dear wife." He smiled, the expression almost genuine but not mirrored in his eyes.

"Will we stay at an inn tonight? Or is that another question you choose not to answer?"

Several moments passed in silence.

"We should reach Lochlaven by afternoon," he said.

"Are you quite all right, madam?" Juliana asked a moment later. "You've become very pale." She reached over and patted one of Emma's gloved hands.

"Lochlaven," Emma repeated very calmly.

"My family's home."

The air cooled around her. Her face felt too warm, especially around her hairline. She untied her bonnet and removed it, thrusting it into Juliana's hands.

She turned toward the window, closing her eyes, and praying that her stomach did not disgrace her.

When she could, she glanced over at him. "I thought you said you have no family."

"Let's just say it's where my relatives live."

Lochlaven? She could not go to Lochlaven. The one place in the entire world she should not go, and it seemed it was their destination.

She looked at Juliana with panic in her eyes, needing some reassurance that she hadn't heard the word. But of course, all Juliana did was look back at her

curiously. Of course, she didn't know. No one knew.
No one knew that a Scot named Ian, a brigand of the
worst order, a scientist with talent for passion, lived
in a place called Lochlaven.

Dear God, what was she to do?

Bryce looked over at her disinterestedly. "If you're
taking ill, Emma, I will not order the carriage to
stop."

If he could have married a fortune without it being
affixed to a body, he no doubt would have done so.
If only she could have handed him her fortune in a
bag and bid him be on his way, that would solve her
problems, too. But no, this new husband was making
her life miserable.

Nor did the future look very promising.

"How long shall we be at Lochlaven?" she asked.

"I have not yet decided. It has a great deal to do
with our welcome. My cousin is the Earl of Buchane
and the Laird of Trelawny and sees himself as father
to the family. There's an equal chance that we will
be feted with Scottish hospitality as being asked to
leave. That is, if he remembers our last meeting. The
welcome might be less, shall we say, welcoming."

"What is your cousin's name?" she asked, needing
the confirmation, the words spoken aloud.

He glanced at her. "McNair," he said. "Ian
McNair."

Chapter 18

Emma sat in the corner of the carriage, trying not to think. When she thought, she remembered, and when she remembered, she wanted to smile. Bryce would think that the smile was directed at him and nothing could be further from the truth.

She was faced with two impossible and contradictory futures. She was married to Bryce. She was traveling to Ian.

Both could not happen.

She slitted open her eyes and looked at Bryce. His head lay back against the seat, his mouth hanging open. Either he was supremely relaxed or inebriated. Try as she might, she couldn't see much familial resemblance. Ian's hair was black, while Bryce was fair. The color of their eyes was similar, their physique possibly alike.

In the whole of her life, Emma had never once questioned her destiny or her duty. It had simply been there, like her hands or feet, part of what made her who she was. She was the Earl of Falmouth's daughter, and as such, expected to marry well. She'd done that. She'd been the Duke of Herridge's wife and had endured her marriage as well as she could have. As Anthony's widow, she'd behaved impeccably, unless you counted three days stolen from her hermitage.

She'd sought comfort in prayers, and tried to understand why God had allowed those nights at Chavensworth. But she'd never been angry at God until this moment.

This was too much.

This trial might break her.

She thought back to their conversations. Had Ian ever said anything about his family? Had he mentioned Bryce at all? He'd been hesitant to speak of himself, only mentioning Lochlaven when she'd pressed him.

A thought occurred to her, one that had her sitting upright. Juliana glanced at her curiously, but she didn't speak to her maid. Instead, she stared at her drunken husband.

Dear God, was she going to have her wedding night at Lochlaven?

Surely God would not be so cruel.

Unless Bryce was unable to perform at all.

Two bottles rolled on the floor of the carriage, another was wedged between Bryce's body and the side of the carriage. She pulled it free with two fingers, noted that it was empty, then gingerly placed it on the floor.

"Are you given to such bouts of drunkenness often? I ask merely because I would like to be prepared for the rest of our marriage."

He blinked at her, his eyes bleary, his smile mocking.

"You're dead," he said calmly. "You are sitting there on that chair, Mother, but I know you're dead."

She exchanged a quick look with Juliana, who was wearing an expression of shock no doubt the twin of hers. She'd never witnessed such an effect of spirits on a man.

Bryce moaned, as if he knew she was thinking uncharitable thoughts of him. She glanced at him again. His skin appeared pale and there were droplets of moisture upon his brow.

She glanced at Juliana. "Do you think he's ill?" she asked.

Juliana only looked helplessly at her, and Emma realized how unfair it was to solicit her assistance. Juliana was a lady's maid, not a sickroom attendant.

Should she try to wake him?

Unwilling wife or not, she really should be of some assistance to Bryce, if for no other reason than to protect his pride. It would not do to reach Lochlaven with him in such a condition.

"Bryce." She raised her voice and repeated his name.

He didn't move or respond.

She leaned forward and placed her hand on his knee, but he didn't react to her touch, even when she coupled the gesture with speaking his name again.

He didn't rouse.

Now she was truly becoming worried. She'd never seen anyone so thoroughly inebriated that he couldn't be awakened.

She looked for her reticule, found it, and withdrew the small crystal bottle of *sol volatile*. As Juliana watched, she uncapped the vial, reached across the seat and held it beneath Bryce's nose.

He didn't move.

She glanced at Juliana. Her maid reached out and took the bottle from her. From time to time the mixture needed to be refreshed, but from Juliana's look as she sniffed the pierced top, the *sol volatile* was still pungent.

"Something's wrong," Emma said. "If he didn't

react to smelling salts, then perhaps he's truly ill and not inebriated it all."

"What shall we do, Your Grace?"

"I don't know," Emma said, feeling more helpless than she ever had in her entire life.

His lips were so pale they could barely be discerned from the rest of his sallow face. As the moments passed, his breathing grew increasingly labored. Why hadn't she seen that he was ill?

Because his being drunk was so much more convenient. She could feel superior, and justified in disliking him.

Shame warmed her as she moved to sit beside Bryce. She placed her hand on his forehead. His skin was clammy and cold.

He began to retch, and as Juliana drew back her skirts, Emma reached up and opened the grill above Bryce's head.

"Driver," she said, raising her voice so the coachman could hear. "Stop the carriage as soon as you safely can."

A moment later the carriage slowed, and finally came to a stop.

The man Bryce had hired in Inverness opened the door a few minutes later. "Is there a problem, madam?" he asked, removing his hat.

"Please assist my husband," she said, grateful that after one look at Bryce, the man understood what was needed.

Bryce might have been correct about the distance to Lochlaven, had they not been required to stop so often on the way. As the hours passed, he was increasingly ill, and the coachman had been pressed into service more than once to lead him away so he might have some privacy. On the last occasion, the man came back and spoke to Emma, his voice earnest.

"Madam," he said. "There's blood."

"Then we should attempt to reach Lochlaven as quickly as possible," she said, pretending a calmness she didn't feel.

The coachman led Bryce back to the carriage, and Emma lent her assistance in getting her husband onto the seat. Bryce was trembling, and when she placed her palm against his forehead, it was to find that his skin was even colder than before. He curled into a ball in the corner of the carriage.

Concerned, she turned to the coachman.

"Go as quickly as you can," she said. At least it wasn't raining and the roads were fair.

"Aye, that I'll do," he said, putting his fingers to the brim of his hat and nodding at her.

In minutes they were on their way again.

"Do you think it's the cholera, madam?" Juliana asked, in as subdued a voice as she'd ever heard from her maid.

"I don't know," Emma said, wishing she was more experienced.

Juliana made a point of drawing as far away from Bryce as she could.

As the carriage began to crest a hill, Emma glanced out the window to see the glint of sunlight on water. At the end of a thickly forested spear of land sat a sprawling, four-storied rectangular house in the Palladian style. Or perhaps it was five floors tall, if those small windows just beneath the roof led to servants' quarters and were not simply to ventilate the attics. She counted twelve chimneys, which meant there were least forty-eight fireplaces in the structure.

A large house, a prosperous dwelling, even situated as it was in the middle of a Scottish glen. She knew it was Lochlaven immediately from Ian's description.

Lochlaven was ringed by a stone wall constructed of a material darker in hue than the yellowish brick of the house itself. Easily twice the height of a man, the wall was marked by arched doorways and pediments topped with stone orbs.

A gravel drive curved in front of the pediment-topped door. Two pillars flanked the three steps to the entrance.

As soon as the carriage stopped, and without being instructed, the driver descended from his perch and ran to the door. His urgent knocking was answered immediately by a young maid attired in a white starched cap and matching apron. She glanced at the coachman and then at the carriage before saying something to him and disappearing from sight.

The coachman returned to the carriage and opened the door, leaning inside to speak to Emma.

"Assistance is coming, madam," he said. "It's a matter of minutes now."

She reached out and touched the coachman's sleeve. "Thank you for your kindness," she said softly. "Thank you, also, for getting us here safely."

The man look abashed at her thanks. "I was only doing my job, madam."

"With great skill," she said, forcing a smile to her face.

True to his word, assistance was on its way. Several brawny young men, followed by two maids and an older woman, were coming toward the carriage.

The older woman held up her hand, halting the group a safe distance away.

"You have someone ill?" she asked, her caution evident in the fact that she didn't approach the carriage or allow her staff to do so.

Emma couldn't blame her. They could be anyone, and the passenger they carried could be ill from any number of horrid diseases.

"I am Mrs. McNair," she said calmly, feeling strange announcing herself for the very first time. "My husband, Bryce McNair, is ill."

The older woman's face changed instantly. "Mr. Bryce? Oh, why didn't you say so?" She immediately began to direct the actions of her staff.

In no time at all Bryce was whisked from the carriage and up the steps, disappearing into the sprawling house, leaving Emma to follow.

Ian was tired and annoyed.

Even though he'd opened his case, withdrawn his papers, and attempted to concentrate on his letter from a French confederate, he couldn't concentrate. His reasoning was that if he submerged himself in his work, he'd be able to banish any thoughts of the Duchess of Herridge—or whatever her name was at the moment.

He finally got to the second page of the man's missive by the time they made it to Glen Affric, west of Loch Ness, a place that never failed to elicit his awe.

Strong breezes carried the scent of the pine woods to him as bright sunlight glittered off the waters of Loch Ness. As he traveled through the forested part of the glen, shadows draped the carriage, and a hundred—or a thousand—birds chattered overhead as if they spoke of his travels. When they were through the forest, the steep peaks of mountains greeted him and the river sang its welcome.

Caledonia.

He put aside the letter, opened all the shades, and watched as his homeland unfolded, scenery that never failed to move him on an elemental level.

The ruins of two castles dotted the landscape. Strong people had settled here, men and women like his own forebearers. They'd created a civilization in a land that offered little pity but compensated with an endless beauty.

Whenever he traveled through this part of the glen, he remembered the "Highlanders' Farewell," a song his nurse had sung him.

Thy brave, thy just, fall in the dust,
On ruin's brink they quiver,
Heaven's pitying ee is closed on thee,
Adieu, adieu forever.

His memory furnished the sight of Annie, with her bright smile and curly blond hair. He'd missed her greatly when she left him when he was seven, going to live in Inverness with her new husband. He'd visited her there twice in the last few years, a yearning to recapture his past causing him to seek her out. She had five children of her own, some of them near grown, a reminder to him that his own family was waiting to be born.

His future stretched before him, and where once it was bright and filled with promise, now it appeared more than a little drab and dour.

Damn Emma, and while he was at it, damn himself, too.

Chapter 19

E mma turned to Juliana, who had accompanied her from the carriage.

"I'll wait here, madam," Juliana said, sinking down on a bench in the foyer.

Emma didn't argue with her but followed Mrs. Jenkins and the two men carrying Bryce.

Lochlaven smelled clean and fresh, as if the breeze from the lake blew away any scents. She disliked large houses, knowing there were unopened rooms, not often visited, where secrets sat waiting to be revealed. Or perhaps that had only been Chavensworth.

"The architect Sir William Bruce began the house in 1686, for the second Earl of Buchane. The second earl was instrumental in restoring Charles II to the throne," Mrs. Jenkins said as they continued down the corridor.

"I see," Emma said, feeling that some acknowledgment, if not fawning, was in order as Mrs. Jenkins spoke of the house.

"Lochlaven has only been moderately restored, for the convenience of the family, of course. We've added a small gatehouse to the rear of the property for a boiler. There is hot water available in all the bathing chambers," she said proudly. "However, we are too remote for some conveniences." She glanced at Emma. "We do not have gas lighting but I doubt you'll notice the difference. Our maids are very industrious in cleaning the oil lamps and trimming the wicks."

"I'm sure," Emma said, wondering what she was expected to say. She'd never been involved in the day-to-day operation of Chavensworth, and her uncle had taken over her home in London. Prior to that, she'd been a young girl living in her father's household.

"His Lordship does not like the ringing of bells," the housekeeper continued. "Therefore, you shall have to judge your own lateness by the clock in your chamber. We do not, of course, have a clock in the sickroom."

"You have a chamber set aside as a sickroom?" Emma asked, surprised. Normally, when a family member became ill, his bedroom was stripped and prepared for the duration of the illness.

"A modification of His Lordship's," the housekeeper said, halting before a long table in a wide hallway. "If anyone at Lochlaven becomes ill, he is sent here immediately and treated by Dr. Carrick, if he's available. If not, the earl has had several girls trained in London to care for the ill." She turned to Emma. "I do not want you to think that we have a great deal of illness at Lochlaven, for such is not the case. We are probably one of the healthiest places in all of Scotland because of the earl's measures."

"Then I am most fortunate to have come," Emma said. "I'm afraid Bryce is very ill."

Mrs. Jenkins looked as if she would say something, then restrained herself. She merely pursed her lips and moved to the table. On it was a pitcher of water, a basin, and a clear glass jar containing a bluish liquid.

"One of the measures the earl has instituted," she said. "You must not enter the sickroom until you've washed your hands in this solution."

"What is it?"

Mrs. Jenkins glanced at her impatiently but then must have realized that Emma was a guest, and not one of the servant girls she commanded. Her expression smoothed somewhat, and she answered. "It is His Lordship's recipe," she said. "He believes that washing the hands will limit the spread of illness."

"Has it?"

"We have not had any outbreaks of cholera at Lochlaven," she said. "And most of our people are remarkably healthy."

Juliana's question in the carriage came back to her. What if Bryce's illness was contagious? What if she'd brought disease to Lochlaven?

"We are also privileged to have a physician staying here," Mrs. Jenkins said. "Dr. Carrick, whom I mentioned before, is a friend of His Lordship's, and assists him in his discoveries. If you'll excuse me, I'll go and fetch him now."

Emma turned to the housekeeper. "What should I do, Mrs. Jenkins?"

Mrs. Jenkins had already turned and was walking down the corridor. At her question, she glanced over her shoulder at Emma.

"I would go to your husband's side."

Implicit in that comment was a criticism. A well-deserved one, at that. A truly devoted wife would not have asked what she should do but would simply have accompanied Bryce.

She was not proving to be devoted at all.

Emma washed her hands in the blue solution, dried them, and entered the sickroom.

The carriage was traveling downhill, a landmark of sorts, for the approach to Lochlaven. There was the loch, a sheet of pewter stretching to the edge of the horizon, and beyond, the house itself, perched above the loch at the end of a promontory of densely wooded pines.

Lochlaven. His home, inheritance, responsibility, and haven, it seemed to wait impatiently for his return. He found himself leaning forward, as if to urge the carriage onward.

A strange vehicle sat in the drive, forcing his driver to park behind it. Had Albert purchased a new carriage?

He entered his home to find a young woman sitting on the bench in the foyer. At his entrance, she stood, but before he could address her, he heard Albert barking orders.

Curious, he followed the voices down the corridor. Two footmen left the sickroom and halted at the sight of him, before one of them called to the housekeeper.

Two women emerged from the room, one of them his housekeeper, Mrs. Jenkins.

Ian knew, before he turned his head. He knew, in some deep part of him that allowed for hideous coincidences and absurd shocks, who the other woman would be. There she was, standing in an errant ray of sunshine streaming in through the sickroom window. Black as a crow, swathed in ebony from the wilted brim of her bonnet to the toes of her shoes peeking out from beneath her full skirts. Even the shawl around her shoulders and held at her waist with her wrists was black.

She looked as if she might cry.

The hidden part of him jumped up and ran to her like he was a small boy. Inside, the child he was twirled her around joyously, yelling at the top of his lungs, *You're here! You're here!*

Emma. Dear God, it was Emma.

She looked up at him in that next moment, her eyes solemn, her mouth unsmiling. A perfect face, one that was rendered beautiful not by its expression but simply by nature. Yet he'd seen her smile, and it had given life to the sculpture. He wanted her to smile right at this moment, at the most inopportune time. He wanted to jostle her into laughter, ease the misery on her face.

He wanted to apologize to her, and he wasn't certain for what. The fact that she was here, and he was acting the fool? The fact that he couldn't stop staring at her? Or the fact that he was no doubt causing consternation not only to her but to everyone who witnessed his behavior?

Instead of a greeting, he came to stand directly in front of her, as if blocking her passage.

Several people spoke to him but he ignored all of them.

Slowly, he reached out his hand and touched her cheek with his fingertips, as if to ensure himself that she was real.

"You're here," he said, in a voice that sounded as if he'd just awakened.

"Your Lordship, it's Mr. Bryce. He's very ill," Mrs. Jenkins said at his side.

He glanced at his housekeeper.

"Bryce?" he said.

Mrs. Jenkins nodded.

He looked back at Emma. "You've married Bryce," he said. "You're his heiress."

What did he expect her to say? That Fate was a capricious bitch who'd played them both false? But this was no time for recriminations or explanations.

"He's very sick," Emma said. "He has been for the last two hours. The doctor is with him now."

With her words, she gifted him with sanity and released him from the power of her presence.

As he began to wash his hands, another tune his nurse had hummed on their outings came to him.

O I loved a lass and I loved her so well
I hated all others who spoke of her ill
But now she's rewarded me well for my love
For she's gone and she's married another.

How damnably appropriate.

Nestled in the corner of the house, the sickroom boasted two sets of windows, both now open to the early afternoon breeze. In most sickrooms there was a scarcity of furniture, the thought being that the fewer furnishings, the better. In this room, however, there was a small round table on either side of the bed, an overstuffed chair in the corner accompanied by another table and lamp, and the sickroom cabinet taking up most of the far wall.

Bryce was unconscious, the pallor of his skin tending toward yellow. He smelled of sickness, garlic, and wine, a curious and noxious combination.

Dr. Carrick was bent over the bed, examining him.

Albert Carrick, rotund, short, and looking perpetu-
ally confused, was singled out from the rest of men
his age by his remarkable thatch of curly black hair. If
his wife, Brenda, did not trim it on a regular basis, Albert's hair would have reached his shoulders, invaded
his ears, and obscured his eyes. Albert's hair was a
living entity, a creature that demanded its own life,
leading Ian to think that he should have nicknamed
his friend Samson.

At Ian's entrance, Albert straightened. "Welcome
back, Ian," he said, but his expression was not his
usual cheerful one. He was frowning, a fact that Ian
immediately noted. "Did the symposium go well?"

Ian nodded. They could discuss London later.

"What's wrong with him?" he asked.

"I'm not quite sure," Albert said, continuing his
examination. He bent over Bryce again, to smell his
breath, before unbuttoning his coat and shirt to pal-
pate his chest. Bryce's shoes had been removed, but
otherwise he was still fully dressed, the stains on his
clothing attesting to the misery of his journey.

Mrs. Jenkins bustled around the end of the bed.
Emma sat on the chair in the corner, remaining silent.
Only when Albert turned and bowed slightly to her
in that European way of his, and began to ask her
questions, did she speak.

"Has he been ill for very long?"

"Since around noon," she said. "I thought him
inebriated," she added, staring down at the floor. She
looked up a moment later, and continued. "It wasn't
until later that I realized he was ill."

"When you determined he was ill, how did you
make that judgment?" Albert asked.

She listed the symptoms Bryce had experienced

during the day. Albert nodded at each one of them.

"Is it cholera?" Emma asked finally.

"I can see why you would think that," Albert said. "The symptoms are indeed similar. But no, Mrs. McNair, I can promise you that it is not cholera."

"Then what is it?" Ian asked.

Albert turned to him, removed his spectacles and regarded him with a somber look.

"I do not know," he said. "But unless we discover why he's become so ill, it is only too possible that your cousin may die."

Emma stood. "Die? Is he that ill?"

Dr. Carrick and Ian looked at each other but neither was forthcoming with an answer.

"I should like to know what he's had to eat or drink in the last day, Mrs. McNair," Albert said.

Emma thought back. "My cook in London prepared a hamper for us for the train," she said.

"Which you all ate?"

She shook her head. "Juliana had her own food," she said. "This was just for Bryce and me."

"But you both shared the contents?"

She nodded.

"Anything else?"

"Juliana purchased some meats and cheeses in the Inverness station."

"Did all of you eat from that?"

"Only Juliana and I. Bryce limited himself to wine."

"Has anyone else in your party become ill?" Albert asked.

She shook her head. "No one."

"You said you thought Bryce was drunk," Ian said. "Why?"

"Because he'd finished three bottles of wine," she said. "One from Inverness, and two from the crate he'd brought with him from London."

"Where are the empty bottles?" Ian asked.

"Still in the carriage," Emma said.

A moment later Ian left the room.

Emma turned to the doctor.

"Is there not something you can give him? Some medicine to make him well?"

Dr. Carrick regarded her with kind brown eyes. "We may do more damage until we know, exactly, why he is so ill."

She abruptly sat down again.

He came to stand at her side. "Several diseases can mimic his symptoms, Mrs. McNair. A severe tumor of the bowel, for example."

No one had ever mentioned the word "bowel" in her presence. Yet this Scottish physician didn't look the least disturbed to have been indelicate. His lack of embarrassment spared her the hypocrisy of having to appear offended. After what she'd seen at Chavensworth, she doubted anything would ever shock her again.

"You should consider yourself very fortunate that you are not sick as well," he said.

She looked up at him. "Do you think it is contagious, then?"

"No, Mrs. McNair," he said, "I do not."

She stared after him as he left the room.

At the door, Ian hesitated, turning to the woman seated on the bench in the foyer.

"Are you with Emma's party?"

She nodded, and stood. "I am her lady's maid, sir."

"Have you experienced any illness?"

"I am feeling a little queasy, sir, but other than that I seem to be fine."

He nodded, then felt compelled to reassure her. "I don't believe that Mr. McNair is suffering from anything that might be contagious. You needn't worry about your health."

She so obviously forced a smile to her face that he wanted to congratulate her on the effort.

"Thank you for saying so, sir," she said.

He waved her back down onto the bench and left the house, heading toward Emma's carriage.

Ian found the wine bottles on the floor. Withdrawing his handkerchief, he wrapped it around the necks of the bottle before lifting them. Until he knew exactly what they were facing, it wouldn't be wise to touch the bottles with his bare hands.

He returned to the house, entering the foyer and crossing to the door of his laboratory.

Once, the ground floor of Lochlaven had been comprised of a morning room, a drawing room, and a dining room. After his father's death, Ian had transformed the house to his standards, converting the ground floor primarily to his laboratory and library. He'd left the drawing room intact but removed several dozen items of bric-a-brac, and a great deal of fringe, so that it was more masculine. The better to accommodate those visitors who traveled to Lochlaven to discuss some of his newest discoveries.

He was well aware that when he married, his wife would probably rearrange the rooms once again to suit her preference. Thankfully, Rebecca had not been overly concerned with the decor, even though he'd caught her looking at several pieces of furniture speculatively. In moments like those he was tempted to ask her thoughts. He knew from past experience, however, that she would only smile and deny that she was giving any consideration at all to rearranging his furniture. Therefore, he'd given up the habit of asking her.

His laboratory, of which he was so proud, encompassed the entire eastern wing of Lochlaven. Here was where he worked in cooperation with Albert, Rebecca's father. Although Albert had begun his scientific inquiries as a physician, he'd become fascinated with the disease process itself. From Albert, Ian had learned countless things, and the relationship, begun as a scientific one, matured to become one of friendship and affection.

Ian passed through the outer room and into the heart of his laboratory. He placed the bottles on one of the long tables arranged against the wall, pouring their contents, each no more than a spoonful of wine, into a series of beakers. One by one he placed a strip of bright copper foil into the beaker as well, and then heated each glass vessel until the contents were almost to the boiling point. With a pair of tongs, he removed the strips of foil, took them to the sink, and washed them first in water, then alcohol, and lastly ether. He needed to allow the strips to dry without heat before he began the next step.

Returning to his worktable, he pulled up a stool, readied his microscope and a series of slides. Once the foil pieces were dry, he rolled each piece into a scroll, inserting each into a glass tube about four inches long. He positioned a holder in the middle of the tubes and moved to another worktable. Instead of using an oil-based lamp, which rapidly blackened any glass vessel, he changed the wick of one of the spirit lamps and lit it, positioning each tube with the holder over the hottest part of the flame.

Albert came into the room then, settling himself on the adjoining stool and watching Ian.

"You're performing the Reinsch's test, then?"

He nodded.

"Your cousin is very ill, " Albert said softly. "I do not know if he can survive this."

"We're not even certain what 'this' is," Ian said, not moving his gaze from the heating tube and, inside, the piece of copper foil. Once one tube was heated sufficiently, he moved on to the next.

Albert only smiled, as if he knew that Ian was willing to lie to himself for the moment.

A few minutes later the last tube had been heated and the solution oxidized.

Ian moved to the microscope, opening each of the tubes. Albert took one, and he the other two, smoothing the foil onto a slide.

The contents of the first bottle proved negative. He glanced over at Albert, who was examining the foil in his own microscope.

He shook his head.

The third piece of foil was not so innocuous. In the single eyepiece, Ian could see what he'd suspected but hadn't wanted to find.

"What is it?" Albert asked.

"Octahedral crystals," Ian said, his voice carefully expressionless.

"Meaning arsenic."

Ian nodded. "Meaning arsenic. Bryce was poisoned."

Chapter 20

A s she sat vigil over Bryce, Emma was grateful for the training of her marriage. Being the Ice Queen meant that she could hide her emotions behind a thick wall of reserve. Nothing could touch her. Not even the fact that she was in the one place on earth she shouldn't be, too close to the one man on earth who fascinated her.

Dr. Carrick finally returned to the sickroom. He and Mrs. Jenkins spoke together for a few moments, their conversation too low for her to hear. Finally, Dr. Carrick departed, leaving Mrs. Jenkins alone with her and Bryce.

"We need to undress your husband, Mrs. McNair," the housekeeper announced, turning to her.

Emma looked at her, aghast.

"Mrs. Jenkins, if I may depend upon your discretion," she said, standing.

The other woman looked formidable in her dark blue skirt and pristine white starched blouse. A small apron covered the front of her skirt, no doubt for decoration only. At her waist she wore a fabric sash of a lighter blue, and looped through the end of it was an enormous round key chain filled with keys, symbols of her position.

"What is it, Mrs. McNair?" she said, folding her hands together in front of her, almost as if she were praying.

"I have only been married for two days, Mrs. Jenkins. My husband and I are strangers to each other."

Emma could feel the flush mount from the pit of her stomach, up her chest to flood into her cheeks. She looked away from the other woman, unwilling to see the look of censure on her face.

"Had circumstances been different," Emma continued, "I would, of course, assist you. But as it is . . . " Her words trailed away.

"Mrs. McNair," the housekeeper began, "your husband is either going to die shortly, or he is going to live, thanks to the efforts of Dr. Carrick and His Lordship. If he lives, then you are going to have to become accustomed to caring for a man. It's not necessarily a pleasant occupation, I grant you. But it is a necessary one for each woman to learn. If he dies, wouldn't you feel better knowing that you had given him as much Christian charity as possible prior to his death?"

Emma glanced at the housekeeper. "Would it be Christian charity for me to view his naked body?"

"There is no need to be indelicate," the housekeeper said.

Evidently, there was no other choice but to act as Bryce's wife.

Emma removed her shawl, folded it tidily, and placed it on the chair she had occupied. Next, she removed her bonnet and put it atop her shawl before unfastening her cuffs. She rolled each sleeve up a

couple of turns, before moving to the side of Bryce's
bed and facing Mrs. Jenkins.

"What shall we do first?" she asked.

A small smile was playing around Mrs. Jenkins's lips, almost as if she were amused by Emma's
ignorance.

If Mrs. Jenkins only knew. She had seen a score of
naked men in her life, thanks to Anthony's debauchery,
but she'd never undressed one.

When Anthony insisted that she participate in his
entertainments, it had been as a judge. She'd sat on a
thronelike chair elevated upon a stage in Chavensworth's elegant ballroom. Cushions and fabric were
spread across the floor, a perfect backdrop for the
nakedness of those who participated in Anthony's
bacchanalias. She was forced to adjudicate whose
lovemaking was more energetic, whose body was
more beautiful, or which man had the most impressive equipage.

She was not, thankfully, permitted to participate in
the games themselves. She was, after all, the Duchess
of Herridge, and expected to be pure and pristine. As
innocent as any wife of Anthony's could be. Her womb
was to be inviolate until such time as she gave birth
to an heir. God, in His infinite mercy, had protected
her by keeping her barren.

Once a month, however, as if to remind her of her
place, Anthony chose to give his audience the sight
of him mounting his wife. He called such tableaux
the "Rape of the Maenad," and it was a popular
occurrence.

The rumors had, of course, proliferated. How could
they not, given the identity of the players, the Earl
of This and the Duke of That and their respective

wives or mistresses? The Countess of Maden, once
set upon by two men and two women in the middle
of the ballroom to her utter delight, had looked right
through Emma a week later when the two women
encountered each other in London.

Let Mrs. Jenkins think she was some London miss,
unequipped for marriage, instead of who she was, all
too aware of the frailties of males, especially those
hedonistic creatures like the man spread out on the
bed before her.

It might even be amusing to be considered
innocent.

"The trousers first, I think," Mrs. Jenkins said. "And
then his coat and shirt."

Emma realized she shouldn't have bothered being
concerned, since Mrs. Jenkins was unfurling a sheet
on top of Bryce and undressing him from beneath it
by benefit of touch.

The entire situation could have been accelerated
by simply divesting Bryce of his clothing and then
covering him with the sheet. Instead of suggesting
it, Emma remained properly silent.

Together they removed Bryce's trousers by each
grabbing a section of the waist and easing the garment
over his hips, then down each leg. Since Bryce was a
tall, muscular man, currently unconscious, the effort
was considerable and the task they'd given themselves
one not easily accomplished.

Once the trousers were off, they faced each other
across the bed, then began to remove Bryce's under-
clothing. The symptoms he'd experienced for the
entire day had left his clothing and skin soiled, but
Mrs. Jenkins didn't flinch, merely pulling the garment

out from beneath the sheet and dropping it onto the floor.

Emma sincerely hoped that the housekeeper planned to burn his clothing.

"You said there were girls trained in nursing?" Emma asked. "Could one of them assist me in washing him? He cannot be expected to remain in this condition."

Mrs. Jenkins surveyed the man on the bed.

"I'll go and fetch Glenna now," she said, and left the room.

As soon as the housekeeper was gone, Emma removed the sheet. Bryce's coat and shirt were in the same deplorable condition as his trousers and underclothes.

Emma gripped one cuff with two fingers and focused determinedly on removing Bryce's coat. Before she was done, Mrs. Jenkins returned, followed by a young girl dressed in an almost identical fashion— dark blue skirt and white blouse. Her dark blue apron was larger, however, and she wore a small blue cap atop her blond hair.

Surprise kept Emma silent as the housekeeper introduced them.

"This is Glenna," she said. "She'll assist you in bathing your husband, Mrs. McNair."

Glenna's cheeks were flushed as she bobbed her head in greeting.

"Please ring if there's anything else I can provide for you," Mrs. Jenkins said.

Emma nodded, waiting until the housekeeper left the room before turning to Glenna.

"You never said you were from Lochlaven."

Glenna smiled. "I was just finishing up my stay at the Hospital for Invalid Gentlewomen," she said. "His Lordship had sent me to Miss Nightingale's Training School for Nurses."

The young maid who had served her so well at Ian's home wasn't a maid at all but the nurse now standing in front of her.

"I have the greatest admiration for His Lordship," Glenna said, as if she could read Emma's thoughts. "I'd never say or do anything to embarrass him."

"I would imagine that a nurse must need a great deal of discretion," Emma said.

Glenna smiled. "His Lordship neither wanted your identity known or his."

Emma tucked that knowledge away to think about later. Right now, Bryce needed attention.

Glenna assisted her with removing Bryce's jacket and shirt, then went to the far side of the room, opening the large cabinet. Inside was a sink, in addition to several drawers and cupboards. Glenna filled a basin with water and returned to the side of the bed. Emma was startled to see steam rising from the top of the basin.

"You have hot water in the sickroom as well?" she asked.

The girl nodded. "His Lordship does not like disease," she said, placing the basin on the table closest to her. "He believes that hot water aids in curing sickness."

She returned to the cabinet, opened one of the drawers, and removed a selection of toweling and clothes.

"Why did you return to Lochlaven, to such a remote place?"

Glenna looked surprised at the question. "It's my

home." She dipped the cloth into the basin, wrung it out, and gently washed Bryce's face. "I'm married now but my training's not gone to waste at Lochlaven. I'm a midwife as well, and there are scores of babies born all around Lochlaven."

She washed Bryce's chest, emptied the basin, refilled it, and returned to his bedside. Emma contributed by drying what Glenna washed.

"It's hard to be gone from Lochlaven." She glanced at Emma. "If you're born to it, I mean."

Emma had never had such longing for a location. Even their country home was just that, a house in the country where her father rode horses and she played in the gardens. Nothing there inspired her loyalty or rendered her miserable when she left.

Glenna had worked her way down to Bryce's masculine bits, and bathed those with the nonchalance of a woman who'd seen better.

"I'll need to find his trunk," Emma said. "In order to change him into clean clothes."

"No need for that," Glenna said. "We've garments here."

She returned to the large cupboard, where she bent and opened one of the bottom drawers. From it, she picked up one folded garment, looked back at the bed as if measuring Bryce, then selected another.

The garment turned out to be a snowy white nightshirt.

"This will suit him fine for now," Glenna said. "I'll give the rest of the clothes to the laundress and see what she can do with them. But he isn't going anywhere for a little while."

Emma helped Glenna dress her husband, a task at least as difficult as removing Bryce's clothes. When he was dressed in the voluminous nightshirt, and tucked beneath the sheets with a blanket warming his feet, she turned to the nurse.

"Do you really think he'll get better?"

A look of caution crossed Glenna's face. "I don't know," she said softly. "That's not for me to decide. That's for the good Lord, Dr. Carrick, and His Lordship."

Without further comment, Glenna began to clean up around the bed, emptying the basin in the sink in the cupboard, gathering up the towels and placing them in a hamper also located in the large cupboard. When she was done, she closed the doors and all evidence of a sickroom was concealed. Finally, she gathered up Bryce's soiled clothing and went to the door. Before she left, she turned and glanced back at Emma.

"I have a birth a mile or so away," she said. "Otherwise, I'd be more than willing to sit with him tonight. It doesn't look to be a long affair. Mary's had two children already. When I return, shall I spell you for a while?"

"That's not necessary," Emma said. "Perhaps tomorrow," she added.

A look stretched between them. If Bryce survived until tomorrow.

Glenna nodded her head once and left the room.

Emma stood beside the bed, her fingers drumming on the sheet next to Bryce's arm. If he'd been someone she knew, she might have talked to him, told him about her impressions of Lochlaven or spoke to him of her earnest wish that he get well.

Despite the fact that the law had joined them, he was as much a stranger as anyone plucked from a London street and delivered here.

Still, perhaps she should make the effort to be a good wife.

"We're at Lochlaven," she said, finding a topic of conversation that might, possibly, interest him, since he'd been so intent on reaching their destination. "From what I've seen, it's quite a lovely place. Do you know it well?"

"He lived here as a boy."

She turned to see Ian, standing in the doorway. He wore a garment not unlike a frock coat but constructed of a blue linen fabric, unbuttoned and revealing a white shirt and black trousers.

Had he appeared so tall and large in London? Or had her memory of him attempted to diminish him in size so he'd have less effect on her thoughts? Either way, the Earl of Buchane, her brigand, towered in the doorway.

She'd feared this moment for hours. Being alone with him now was not made easier for the anticipation.

Skeins of feeling wrapped around her, threatening to cut off her breath. She knew how quickly he fell asleep, how he woke as if sodden with sleep. She knew he had a pattern of three moles on his hip, and how his eyes darkened to black when he was aroused, and that he liked his toast crispy on both sides. She knew that he laughed with abandon, and had a wicked sense of humor, hands that delivered magic, and that when he kissed her, she lost both her thoughts and her inhibitions.

But she hadn't known that she was to come here, to this place, to him.

She turned her head, deliberately refusing to look at him. Instead, she contemplated the man in the bed.

"Do you know what's wrong with him?" she asked.

"Yes," he said, coming inside the room. "He was poisoned."

Shocked, she turned to stare at Ian.

"Poisoned?"

He nodded. "Arsenic," he said. "Relatively common. Easy enough to procure."

She could barely breathe. "Are you sure?" She stared down at Bryce, wondering if she could have gotten him help any sooner than she had.

A thought occurred to her.

"I didn't poison him, Ian," she said.

She forced herself to look in his direction, startled to see that he was staring at her, his expression one of surprise.

"I never thought you had," he said. "Why would you think that?"

"I've never made any secret of my antipathy for this marriage," she said. "It was arranged without my cooperation. Without my participation."

"Then why did you agree to it?" he asked.

The words were calm but the look in his eyes was turbulent.

Why was he angry?

"Are Scottish women so free, then? Are they allowed to disobey their relatives?" she asked. She was not going to tell him of her uncle's threat. To do so would be to solicit his pity, and she didn't want pity from Ian McNair.

Bryce moaned, and anything Ian might have said vanished in his concern for his cousin.

He bent over the bed, gently pressing Bryce's closed lids upward, one at a time, examining his eyes.

"Dr. Carrick is preparing a solution that Bryce will need to drink. The next twenty-four hours will not be easy for him."

"Nor has the past day been a pleasant one," she said.

He glanced over at her. "Will you stay with him?"

She nodded.

Silence stretched between them, a silence so filled with words that she could almost see them written in the air. Forbidden words. Words society would condone even less than her setting up an establishment of her own. But she was not society's darling anyway, was she? Having married before her mourning was officially over. Already dressed appropriately for this husband's death.

And when he died—if he died—would she mourn a stranger? He deserved her show of grief more than Anthony had.

Ian came to stand on the other side of the bed. When Glenna had stood in that exact spot, the bed had been a wide barrier, almost a wall. Ian could stretch his hand across the sheets and touch her.

He was too close and she was too aware of him.

She looked at Bryce's drawn face. "I don't know anything about him," she said. "I don't know what he likes to eat, or his favorite book, or the name of his best friend." She glanced over at Ian. "We haven't conversed very much," she said, remembering her wedding night, when Bryce had consumed two bottles of wine, topping it off with half a bottle of brandy. "I don't even know his occupation."

"He gambles," Ian said flatly. "Until now, he's been able to support himself with the habit."

She nodded, not unduly surprised.

Dr. Carrick entered the room then, two bottles and a metal spoon in his hand. He approached the bed, nodding to both Ian and Emma.

"Ian, if you will support his shoulders, we shall be about getting this medicine into the boy."

"What is it?" Emma asked as Ian came to her side of the bed. She moved down so he did not stand so close.

"Ferric oxide with magnesia," Dr. Carrick said, holding up the first bottle. "Followed by a tartar emetic." He studied her for a moment. "Will you be up to it, madam? He's going to be very sick."

She shouldn't have judged him so harshly. He hadn't been drunk; he'd been ill.

"Yes, I'm up to it," she said firmly.

Ian placed his arm behind Bryce and raised him almost to a sitting position. Dr. Carrick administered the two medications with some difficulty but finally managed to get Bryce to swallow some of it.

"He will begin to experience the cure within hours, madam," Dr. Carrick said, without turning to address Emma. "It might well be worse than what you've endured already today, I'm afraid."

She nodded, understanding everything he wasn't saying.

Dr. Carrick walked to the cupboard, opened it, and removed a bowl, placing it on the side of the bed.

"Please have a maid summon me if his condition changes."

He ticked off a number of symptoms for which Emma should be alert, and she nodded after each one.

"Will he live?" she asked when the doctor finished.

The question hung in the air, neither man answering

it. Finally, Dr. Carrick spoke. "I have no idea. Now, it's in the hands of the Almighty. There was a great deal of arsenic in the wine, madam. Enough to dispose of most of the rats in Edinburgh. Whoever did this to him of a certainty wished him dead. If we could have reached him sooner, perhaps I would be more hopeful."

She watched as he left the room, carrying the medications with him.

"Will he not need another dosage?" she asked, turning to Ian.

He shook his head. "If it doesn't work, there's nothing more to be done. Another dosage would be toxic to his system."

She'd been married twice, and might soon be widowed again. What did that make of her that she couldn't truly mourn either husband?

Evening pressed against the window, demanding notice. Ian strode to the corner and lit a small lamp, then shielded the light with a darkened shade. The result was a column of light beside the chair but not enough illumination to disturb a patient in the bed.

He returned to the side of the bed and stood too close.

She wanted him to leave the sickroom, wanted it with a desire so fierce that she nearly spoke the words. His presence was disturbing, because it brought back so many feelings, the strongest of which was regret.

Her future was immutable, as if chains bound her. What she wanted or what she wished was as foolish as wanting Anthony to have been a different man.

She focused her attention on the man in the bed, watching the slow rise and fall of Bryce's chest.

"Who would want to poison him?" she asked, giving

voice to the question that had been in her mind ever since Ian pronounced the diagnosis.

He glanced at her, his face stoic and impossible to read.

"Bryce has a great many enemies," he said. "He's not an easy man to love."

"But enough to kill him?"

They exchanged a long look before he turned and left the room, leaving Emma feeling more alone than she'd felt in her life.

Chapter 21

Emma settled as comfortably as she could in the chair, thinking that if she were truly a good wife, she would ask for a Bible and spend the time in contemplation of mortality. Instead, her life lay before her as if it were a daguerreotype. Instead of churches and basilicas, important moments in her life were preserved and displayed for her to see now.

She didn't want to remember; she especially didn't want to remember Chavensworth.

She lay her head back against the chair, exhausted and knowing that she couldn't sleep. Someone must watch over Bryce. She stood, walked to the cupboard and opened it quietly. Following Glenna's movements, she obtained a towel, a cloth, and filled the basin with a little hot water. Returning to the side of the bed, she bathed Bryce's face and spoke to him in low and measured tones.

"I'm so very sorry this happened to you," she said. "But you're in good hands. Dr. Carrick seems quite competent, as does Ian."

It wouldn't do to think of Ian.

Her task done, she returned the bowl to the sink, squeezing out the cloth. She hung up the cloth and used a towel to dry the bowl before placing it back in the cupboard.

She returned to Bryce's side, smoothing his hair back from his brow. He hadn't truly stirred since Dr. Carrick and Ian forced the medication into him. There were none of the side effects she dreaded. Instead, Bryce looked to be hovering between sleep and death.

At least he was here, with people who loved him, with people who knew him.

She smoothed the sheets, folding them below his chin, ensuring they were tucked in. She stood there for a moment, wondering what else she could do to ease his misery.

Finally, she returned to the chair, sitting once more, and wishing that she could at least loosen her corset. She sat as her governess taught her, knees together, feet together, and hands loosely clasped on her lap, a pleasant if distant smile curving her lips. Her bonnet was on top of her shawl on the floor beside her. That was not proper. Nor was the wish to remove her snood and loosen her hair. Or unfasten her shoes so she might wiggle her toes and cool her feet.

The curtains had been drawn against the night, but she stood and parted them with one hand, staring out at the gleaming silver reflection that was the lake in moonlight.

How could one bear to live here and see such beauty day after day?

Chavensworth was considered a structure of immense beauty, and perhaps it was to someone who didn't know what went on within its walls. But it was beauty created by man, and nothing as spectacular as that wrought by God.

There was such utter peace in this place, which was a ridiculous reason to suddenly wish to weep. Being at Lochlaven loomed as a challenge greater than any she'd faced in her lifetime. On one hand, there was duty—caring for Bryce, the worry, the sincere and heartfelt prayers. On the other hand, there was temptation—Ian, with his slow smile and piercing gaze, who brought back memories of forbidden passion.

One was expected of her, and one was illicit.

How like her to resent one and long for the other.

Perhaps this was Eden, and she was Eve. Adam was Bryce, ill and failing. And Ian the snake who lured her to forbidden fantasies. And above it all, God watched and waited for her to make the wrong choice.

Was Eden the last time women had been given an opportunity to choose? And because they'd chosen wrong, were they forever to be dominated by man?

She was tired, that's why she was thinking of God and Eden.

"You haven't eaten."

She turned to find Ian standing in the doorway, a tray in his hands.

A smile curved her lips. "Have you turned maid now? Brigand, scientist, laird, and maid."

"If you think so," he said. He entered the room and placed the tray on a small table beside the chair. "I prefer to think of it as caring for my guests."

A young man followed him, carrying an overstuffed chair the match of the one already in the room. He lowered it slowly next to the first chair and stepped back, waiting.

"That's all, Broderick," Ian said. "Thank you."

How very proper he was, made even more so against the tenor of her thoughts.

"Thank you," she said, realizing she was hungry. "You are an exceptional host."

"I wish I could've welcomed you here under different circumstances," he said.

She looked up at him, wondering at the comment. Did he mean under circumstances where Bryce was not ill? Or under entirely different circumstances, where she was not married at all?

Oh, how foolish she was to even think such a thing.

He went to the cupboard and opened it, removing a small collapsible table. The clever contraption was folded flat, but as she watched, he unfolded it and moved it in front of the chair.

"If you'll sit," he said, motioning to the chair, "I'll serve you."

Amused, she sat, and watched as he unfurled a napkin and handed it to her.

"I brought you tea," he said, pouring her a cup from the small teapot in the corner of the tray.

"You're very kind."

He smiled. "You've had a bad two days."

"How did you know I've been married two days?" she asked.

He didn't answer. Instead, he sat next to her and poured a cup of tea for himself.

"Has Bryce treated you well?" he asked.

"Is that a question you should ask?"

His smile faded. "Perhaps not," he said.

He didn't say anything for a few moments but she

had the impression that he was weighing something in his mind.

"What is it, Ian?"

He looked surprised at her question. "We know each other too well, I think, Emma."

She shook her head. He could not say things like that to her. Not now.

Just when she was about to tell him that it would, perhaps, be better if he left her, he spoke again. "Bryce was one of your husband's hangers-on. He liked being in the duke's circle of acquaintances. Did he tell you?"

She had the strangest feeling in the pit of her stomach, as if she were in a carriage going too fast, or in a train taking a curve.

"No," she said. "He didn't. Did he ever go to Chavensworth?"

Her voice was barely a whisper, not much more than a thought, but he heard her. Did he hear the fear in the question as well?

He must have, because the look he gave her was one filled with a soft and gentle emotion. Pity? Compassion?

Shame seemed to cradle his answer in a soft down, so that she felt the words rather than simply hearing them.

"On numerous occasions," he said.

She looked away. She had an answer, then, to Bryce's treatment of her. Her new husband had seen her as the Ice Queen of their revelries.

"Were you a visitor to Chavensworth?" She'd asked him the question before and his answer had been no. Would he be more honest now?"

"I loathed the Duke of Herridge," he said. "Even if I had been invited, I would not have attended. I'd heard enough about his parties to be disgusted from afar."

She heard the edge in his voice, the sharply defined anger, and felt the blood drain from her face.

Had Bryce told him? Had he a gift for description? Had he conveyed all of the horror and depravity of those nights?

She didn't particularly like being an object of pity. Nor did she want to be a target for scorn. But those were the only two choices left her, having been the Duchess of Herridge as well as the Ice Queen.

Emma didn't know what to say. Words were like tiny moths in the face of a gale. However frantic their flutters, they were incapable of changing anything.

She closed her eyes, wishing herself away from this room, from him. Wanting to be a child again, capable of changing the course of her life. The implausibility of that wish, the sheer impossibility of it, forced her to look at him.

She would not be a coward here and now.

"You know what happened, then," she said, her voice carrying the faintest whisper of fear. "You know what I did."

She didn't think he was going to answer her. He refilled his cup, moved the table, and stretched out his legs. Finally, he sat back and looked at her, his eyes flat, his face somber.

"How could I not? I traveled to London often enough to hear the rumors. A beautiful duchess with skin like alabaster, naked and aloof. Available to see, to dream of, but never to touch."

"No wonder you were so filled with contempt for me that first night." How very calm she sounded. There was no shame in her voice, or humiliation, while her skin felt shriveled with it. Her lungs were too constricted, and tears were too close.

"I had nothing but rumors by which to judge you, Emma. It was only later when I realized they could not be true."

"They were," she said flatly. "I was the Ice Queen, as Anthony labeled me."

He smiled at her, the expression too tender for this room and their respective roles. He didn't touch her. Nor did he say a word. But in the silence she could almost feel his compassion.

"Pity the girl I was," she said, her voice steady. "There's no need to pity me now."

"Because he's dead."

She smiled. How quick he was.

"Because he's dead," she said.

She stood and moved to the window, waiting until she was certain she could speak without her voice trembling.

"You should have told me, then, that you knew," she said, her voice vibrating with emotion.

She was only too familiar with the looks of derision from men and women alike. As if they'd said to her: We choose to participate in Anthony's entertainments. You have no such choice. And because she didn't, she was less of a human, less of a woman, less of a person.

"When, exactly, do you propose that I should've told you, Emma? Around the same time you told me you were going to marry my cousin?"

She glanced at him, startled at his vehemence, and

when she saw his expression, she almost took a step back.

He was as angry as she.

"In the garden, when we had breakfast together? Or the night in my bed? When, exactly, should we have been honest with one another?"

"You dared me to be honest," she said, her anger dissipating as she recalled his words. "And I made the choice not to be."

Moonlight glittered on the water. She had no fondness for boats or vessels of any kind, but right at the moment, the lake offered some type of freedom. What would it be like to simply take one of those boats and sail away?

"I didn't know Bryce's name then," she said. "But if I had, I'm not certain I would have mentioned it. So perhaps your accusation is correct. I didn't tell you everything."

"And I didn't demand it."

"One of us should have," she said, daring herself to turn and face him. His expression had softened, his eyes revealing too much emotion. She glanced away again.

"The truth would have done no good," he said. "It wouldn't have stopped me from wanting you or taking you to my bed. As for Chavensworth, and the Duke of Herridge, a starved dog is not responsible for his emaciation, Emma."

Her smile broke free. "I know you didn't mean to liken me to a dog, but I get your point well enough." She didn't look away. "Don't paint me as an angel, Ian. I fervently wished for his death. I prayed for it each night, may God forgive me."

"Then you should thank God for His blessing," he

said bluntly. "Otherwise, I would take great pleasure in killing the bastard for you."

She stared at him, wide-eyed. "I don't know what to say. No one's ever offered to kill someone for me."

"He deserved it, didn't he?"

She looked down at the floor. The boards were bare, well waxed. Were carpets not allowed in here because of disease? She would have to ask Ian later, some other time when other—more important—words weren't trembling on her tongue.

"Someone evidently thought so," she said, glancing at him. "Enough to murder him."

Chapter 22

⟨⟨◦⟩⟩

His face was immobile, his eyes flat and unreadable.

"Are you going to tell me exactly what you mean, Emma?"

Her gaze moved to Bryce's bed, then resolutely back to him.

"I've never told anyone before," she admitted. "Only one other person knows for sure. The housekeeper at Chavensworth."

She came and sat on the edge of the chair, clasping her hands tightly together.

"We thought he'd died because of his heart," she said. "Anthony was not a young man, despite his actions. He was found in his library, seated behind his desk. Only later, when the body was being prepared for burial, did the marks become visible."

She wrapped her arms around her waist.

"There were bruises all over his neck. Bruises that looked like finger marks. Someone had strangled him."

"Why didn't you go to the authorities?"

She smiled. "And admit that a great many people

had reason for killing Anthony? The fathers of the servant girls he raped at Chavensworth? The husbands of the wives he used as trophies? The men he humiliated? Even me? It wasn't a case of finding someone with a motive to kill Anthony but eliminating all of those who did."

"Not to mention that what happened at Chavensworth wouldn't simply be rumor anymore," he said. "The press would have publicized all the lurid details."

She nodded. "Perhaps."

"You allowed a murderer to go unpunished, Emma."

She stared down at her hands. "I allowed a murderer to go unpunished," she agreed. "I gave instructions that the coffin was to remain closed for the wake. I attended the funeral and Anthony's interment, and never once thought to contact the authorities."

"And the housekeeper?"

She smiled again. "Servants wear a mask around us, have you ever noticed? At least the ones who worked for Anthony did. I saw more emotion in Mrs. Turner's eyes that day than I ever had before. She felt only relief that he was dead. I know that she'll never speak of it."

Her smile vanished as she looked over at him. "Do you want to know the horrid truth, Ian? Anthony's sins were greater than those of his murderer. The only emotion I've ever seen expressed at news of his death was relief."

He sat back in the chair, his gaze focused on Bryce's face.

"Someone killed him," he said. "Someone who might have poisoned Bryce."

"I didn't kill him," she said. "Any more than I poisoned Bryce."

The look of surprise on his face was gratifying. "Don't be absurd," he said.

"Is it absurd?" Again she clasped her hands together. "I certainly wanted Anthony dead." She glanced at the bed. "I didn't want Bryce as a husband."

"The Duke of Herridge was a man of some stature. You wouldn't have been able to strangle him."

She nodded. "I could have hired someone to do it for me."

"No, you wouldn't have."

She regarded him steadily.

"Why do you have such faith in me?"

"Because of the look of sadness in your eyes, Emma. If you'd murdered Anthony, I doubt you would be as sad."

She was so overwhelmed by his words that she had to look away.

"But you may have an admirer," he said, startling her.

"An admirer?"

Slowly, he turned toward her. "Did you never think of that? Anthony could have died because of what he did to you. And Bryce could have been a target because he was your husband. Someone who can't bear you to be married might have killed them both."

She'd never thought of such a thing.

"Is there anyone who's expressed an interest in you?"

"Other than you?"

"Shall we both suspect each other?" His smile robbed the words of their sting. "We're a pair, aren't we?"

But they weren't, a fact she had to keep reminding herself.

"After Anthony died, I made a list of people who might want him dead. I am not exaggerating when I say it was a very long list."

"What about men who were interested in you?"

She smiled. "I was the Ice Queen. No one was allowed to speak to me."

"There must have been someone."

She was not going to tell him what it was like to be naked and shamed in front of a hundred or more people, held captive to her thronelike chair by threats.

If one of the revelers won a round of a game, or pleased Anthony in some way—by loaning a daughter or sister or wife for the night—he allowed the man to mount the three steps to the stage in order to taunt her.

Sometimes the winner was masked, but more often than not, he was naked in face and body. All activity on the ballroom floor ceased so that Anthony's guests could witness the reward. The winner would circle the throne, stretch out a hand to Emma, fingers never quite touching. Sometimes he'd simply whisper to her all those delightful things he'd do to her if she were available to him. Sometimes he'd hint that Anthony was tired of her, and close to accepting that he'd never have an heir from her, so that she'd be fodder for their games soon enough.

Could one of those men, or one in the audience, have developed protective feelings for her? The idea that a visitor to Chavensworth might be behind Anthony's death and Bryce's poisoning was horrifying. The idea that he might think she felt something for him was even more frightening.

"I'll try to remember," she said, wishing he hadn't asked it of her.

As if he knew she couldn't bear any more talk of Chavensworth, he handed her another cup of tea.

"Eat your dinner," he said softly.

She smiled her thanks and finished the dinner he'd brought for her, saying nothing when he reached for one of the rolls held in a small silver container. When she was done, Emma sat back against the chair, closed her eyes and took a deep breath. She was exhausted but determined to sit up with Bryce.

The hours passed slowly, ticking by without a clock to measure them.

They spoke of commonsense things, the time of night, the weather, Bryce's condition. Emma bathed her husband's face and hands again, and placed her palm on his forehead, thinking it odd that it was the first kind gesture she'd made toward him. When she turned, it was to find Ian staring at her, a look in his eyes she couldn't decipher.

A few times they were silent, as if each wanted to absorb the nearness of the other. Words were unnecessary and would have been an intrusion.

In the lamplight Ian was even more handsome. His Celtic ancestors had bequeathed him high cheekbones, a sharply defined jaw, and lips that, although full, could be thinned in anger or irritation all too quickly.

He was not as controlled as other men she'd known. He left no doubt of his opinions on certain matters. There was a passion about him that carried into his daily life—a fascination with the work he'd chosen, an interest in the world around him, irritation at politics. He would love as deeply as he would hate, and the woman in his life would have no doubt of his feelings for her.

She wanted to ask him to move away. Or to speak of his fiancée, perhaps. Another person needed to be in this room. A chaperone, someone other than an ill husband. A minister, a confessor, a fiancée, even the housekeeper would do. Someone to keep her silent, to keep her from saying those things that would not be wise to say.

Words such as: *Hold me. Do not kiss me, because I have no right to ask you that. But simply hold me, so that I can be reminded of those hours when you did more. Hold me, so that I can feel your arms around me, and your chest against my cheek, so that I might hear the booming beat of your heart and be reminded of a sunny morning in London, of hedonism so perfect that every single moment of it was more real than this scene.*

Ian's night beard darkened his cheeks. Shadows lay beneath his eyes. His shirt was creased from sitting for so long, and sometime in the passing hours he'd removed his shoes and stockings, leaving his feet naked and bare. Although horribly improper, his bare feet touched her in a silly way, made her want to move a footstool close and lift his feet upon its pillowed softness, push him gently back into the chair and cover him with a blanket. *Sleep,* she might say, if she were allowed such intimacies. *Sleep, Ian, and I'll watch over you and him.*

She found herself envying the woman he would marry, and that thought, forbidden as it was, had the power to make her realize that what she was doing was wrong. Wrong in the worst of all ways.

"You should leave," she said softly, so as not to disturb Bryce.

He turned to look at her. She almost asked him not to look at her in such a way but stopped herself. He mustn't know how she was affected by him, how her body recognized him as if it were a separate entity and not subject to her will.

Try as she might, she couldn't quite forget what it had been like to be in Ian's arms, to have passion sweep through her at his touch. She'd required no aphrodisiacs, no spirits or drugs to induce her euphoria.

She stood, walked to the window and parted the curtains again.

"No one would understand if they found us together."

"You're my cousin's wife. Why shouldn't we watch over him together?"

"Because Bryce and I have never had a wedding night," she said, staring out at the darkness.

She gave him the truth when it would probably have been better to hide it. Yet he knew the deepest and ugliest secrets she'd hidden for years. What was a bit more candor?

She turned to face him.

"Because I've been in your bed," she said softly, "and it's something I can't quite forget. Because I vowed that I would never be like those women at Anthony's entertainments who bragged of their infidelity."

He stood and walked toward her, but she held up her hand as if to block his approach.

The night was late and she was tired. Too tired, perhaps, to hold back her emotions. Even now they were very near the surface. She was suddenly surfeited by an overwhelming grief, although not for Anthony or Bryce.

She mourned for him, for Ian.

What would her life have been like if she shared it with him? What would each day bring if she allowed herself to be loved by him?

That was the reason he should leave. Not because of what anyone else might think but because of what she might do. She was too close to going to him, to framing his face with her hands, to pulling his head down so she might kiss him. Not in gratitude or friendship or a dozen other reasons, but in passion, in desire, to answer her body's needs and perhaps to ease the ache in her heart.

Slowly, she dropped her hand. "If you hold any affection for me, Ian," she said gently, "you'll leave."

"Hardly fair, is it, when you utter your request in such a fashion?"

He really shouldn't smile like that. He really shouldn't look at her with that expression in his eyes, as if he knew quite well what a temptation he was.

"Your Lordship," she said, startled when the words sounded like an endearment rather than some measure of propriety. "Please."

"I don't like leaving you alone. Bryce might sicken still further."

"Ian. Please."

He studied her, as if he meant to imprint her face on his memory for all time.

"I'll send a maid to you," he finally said. "To help or just to keep you company."

She should thank him for understanding. Instead, she remained silent, all too afraid that she'd revealed too much to him already.

At the door, he turned and faced her once again.

"Why did your uncle agree to this marriage?" he

asked. "Why Bryce? He hasn't a title or any wealth to speak of."

They exchanged a long look.

"I don't know," she said. "I knew they were acquaintances, and thought they had some degree of friendship for one another. But they were arguing the morning we left for Scotland."

"What about?"

"Money," she said.

"If it was a Scot he wanted, I was available," he said, words that were as explosive as pouring lamp oil into a fireplace.

She held her hands tightly clasped, feeling her heart swell and ache.

"You weren't available," she said. "You're to be married."

Had he forgotten?

"I would have changed my plans," he said softly.

She didn't think she could bear any more. She felt the tickle of one small tear trailing down her cheek, and turned her head so that he couldn't see.

"Please leave, Ian," she said. This time her voice didn't sound so calm or untouched. This time it sounded as if she were grieving.

Ian left her because she asked, not because he wanted to do so. He stood at the window in his bedroom, unable to sleep. The night was deeply shadowed, cast into relief by a midsummer moon, full and pendulous like a woman's breast. The shape of it, the size of it, the sheer magnificence of it jeered at him, reminded him of how long it had been since he'd lain with a woman.

Hell, since he'd been desperate for a woman.

Only since London. A matter of days, not weeks or months. Mere days, and yet it felt like a lifetime, a very long and very celibate lifetime.

She was in his home. Emma, the Duchess of Herridge, rumored to be among the most dissolute women in London, now married to his cousin. A complicated, fascinating, mysterious woman who intrigued him, nested in his thoughts, kept him awake.

Emma, his cousin's new bride.

His ill, possibly dying, cousin.

Guilt knifed through him.

In his youth he'd been a sensualist, well on his way to dissolution himself. His curiosity had saved him, and he'd channeled all that force and energy into scientific discovery. Tonight it was as if he were twenty again, hot blooded and yearning, as needy as a bull in rut.

He slammed his hand flat against the pane of glass, daring it to break, almost welcoming the resulting injury. Instead, it held, shimmering with the force of his blow, defying him.

He wanted his wife to be a partner, needed someone to be with him, to listen to his frustrations, to accept those gifts he wanted to give, to share his dreams, and the successes of the future. He needed someone to stand hand in hand with him and create a perfect circle, or perhaps a wall. A bulwark against the world, in the shelter of which he could receive support and provide it as well.

Ian knew, deep inside where he'd always known, that Rebecca was not that person. Rebecca wanted a charmed life, one in which there were no challenges, one in which her husband did not go out and actively seek problems to solve.

In his heart he wanted a woman who knew life itself, who'd been through enough and experienced enough that each day was recognized as the gift it was.

He wanted Emma, and she was the one woman he couldn't have.

Yet despite her name, despite the fact that there were documents proclaiming her to be his cousin's wife, despite anything she might have signed, despite the damned entry in a London register, despite anything or anyone, she was his.

The knowledge was like a shard of glass embedded in his skin.

Despite the presence of the young girl seated beside her, and Bryce in his bed, Emma felt as if she were totally and completely alone.

Perhaps she would become as inured to loneliness as she had to fear.

Fear had been a constant and unremitting companion during her marriage. Fear was Anthony's sword, and he had no qualms about wielding it.

At first Emma thought she would always be afraid, but then she learned that human nature grows only too comfortable with strong emotion. Fear dulled her, smoothed all her emotions to one level. She was never so afraid again, but then she was never so happy, either.

As for now, she was very certain that she wouldn't continue to be so miserable or so lonely. In time, perhaps, it would ease, and she wouldn't feel very much at all.

Bryce's condition began to worsen an hour later. If Ian hadn't been true to his word and sent a sleepy maid to sit with her, Emma didn't know how she would have cared for him alone.

Thankfully, the young maid took the bowls away to empty them, but there was nothing they could do about the miasma that hung over the sickroom. When Bryce wasn't moaning and becoming wretchedly sick, he was attempting to pull the covers from his body. Either the poison or the antidote had made him acutely sensitive to any touch, so much so that when she brushed his hair from his forehead, he arched his head back and nearly screamed.

She didn't know what else to do other than continually wipe his face and hold his head when he became sick. In a little while she had to remove his nightshirt and change the bedding since it had become so soiled.

An hour passed, then another, and just when she thought he couldn't become any sicker without dying, Bryce began to rally. His face, up until now chalk white, showed some traces of color. His lips were no longer blue. His stomach did not revolt as much, giving her some hope that he might be able to drink some water. One sip at a time was all he could tolerate but at least he'd begun to drink something.

The maid left the room with the soiled linen, returning in the next quarter hour with a supply of fresh linens and some lavender to help sweeten the air. Mrs. Jenkins followed her, taking in Emma's appearance with one swift look.

"I've brought you some tea, Mrs. McNair," she said, placing the tea on the table.

Emma smiled her thanks and sipped at it, finding the tea so strong it nearly etched her teeth. Still, it would keep her awake.

"He survived the night," Mrs. Jenkins said. "That's a very good sign."

Emma glanced at the gap in the curtains. Dawn had come an hour earlier.

"Can you sit with him a few minutes?" she asked. "Long enough that I can change and wash?"

Mrs. Jenkins looked shocked at the request. A moment later Emma understood why.

"I haven't even shown you to your room," the housekeeper said, obviously discomfited. "Forgive me for being so inhospitable."

"I'm right where I should be," Emma said, hoping to ease the other woman's embarrassment. "Has my maid been seen to?" How very odd that she'd forgotten Juliana's presence until just this moment.

"Yes," Mrs. Jenkins said. "We have servants' quarters in abundance at Lochlaven. She was given a choice of rooms."

"And my trunk?" Her lone remaining trunk. She'd not had time to open it to see what belongings she had left.

"Taken to your room, of course."

Mrs. Jenkins gestured to the young maid who'd been so helpful in the last three hours. "Take Mrs. McNair to her room, Isobel, then get some rest for yourself."

The young girl nodded and left the room, glancing back to ensure that Emma was following her.

"Glenna's returned," Mrs. Jenkins said. "She can look after your husband while you sleep."

Emma shook her head. "I'll be back as soon as I wash and change."

Caring for Bryce would be penance, of sorts, for her thoughts and longing for a man not her husband.

Chapter 23

⟨ ◦◦ ⟩

The room Emma had been given was a lovely one, the equal of her suite in London. The furniture might even be finer than what she owned. The secretary was small and feminine, ornately carved, with legs that tapered to small lion's feet. The carpet had been loomed with such detail that the woolen roses looked as if they carried a scent.

Her remaining trunk sat on the carpet in front of the armoire. Juliana had not yet unpacked it. Since all her trunks looked the same, Emma had no idea what clothing she had left until she withdrew her key and opened it.

The answer stared her in the face, prompting a sense of sorrow so deep it startled her. She'd lost the mirror. The Tulloch Sgàthán had been in the bottom of the second trunk, the one now lost, the one holding her dresses.

In the back of her mind she'd not quite believed what she'd seen in its reflection. Instead, she wanted to look again, knowing full well that it was foolish. Knowing, too, that what she was doing was not far removed from scrying, and wasn't that practice more suited to witches than to former duchesses?

Now she would never know if what she'd seen had been real. She would never again see that look of utter joy on her face, or wonder at its cause.

Sighing, she stood, staring down at all her intimate garments, her nightgowns and chemises, her sewing kit, all items that she could have done without. How did she replace her dresses?

Perhaps there was a town nearby, and a seamstress with time to spare.

She looked down at herself. Not only was she end-lessly tired of black, but the dress was stained to the point of being ruined.

How hypocritical of her to still wear black. As if being proper now could ever mitigate the past. An-thony still lived as long as she talked of him. He still lived every time she recalled one of his entertainments. He still drew breath whenever she felt shame.

Since she couldn't change, she washed as well as she was able, brushed her hair and rearranged it in the snood.

Before she returned to the sickroom, she went in search of Juliana. She found her maid, escorted to the fourth floor by Mrs. Jenkins herself. The housekeeper smiled when Emma expressed her thanks, turned and walked back the way she'd come.

"Have you been treated well?" Emma asked of Juliana.

Her maid looked quite rested. Emma bit back her annoyance.

"I have, madam."

Juliana said nothing further but her gaze encom-passed Emma's soiled dress. She looked down at herself.

"The trunk that is missing is the one containing my dresses. I have nothing into which to change."

"Perhaps I could take the garment to the laundress," Juliana said. "Honestly, madam, I do not believe that it could be assisted by sponging it."

"I don't have the time for you to sponge it now. I'm due back in the sickroom."

Juliana's expression of disgust was so fleeting that Emma might well have imagined it, but she didn't think so.

"Mr. McNair cannot help being sick, Juliana," she said. "He was poisoned."

She related the events of the night before and the results of the tests Ian had done.

"I'm very sorry, madam," Juliana said. The words were proper but her tone was jarring. As if she didn't feel anything for Bryce except dislike.

Even Emma could feel pity for the man's suffering.

"If you'd like to return to London," she said bluntly, "I'm sure there would be no difficulty arranging transportation for you."

Emma wasn't entirely certain she could do without a maid, but perhaps there was a girl at Lochlaven who might wish to be in her employ. Someone whose loyalties wouldn't be devoted, unambiguously, to whichever man held the purse strings. Except for Bryce, for whom Juliana had seemed to have some antipathy.

"Have I given any displeasure, madam?" Juliana asked stiffly.

She was tired, and not inclined to enumerate all of those occasions in which her maid had undermined her. "Unpack my trunk if you would," she said, turning to leave. "My room is the second on the left on the third floor," she added.

"After I've performed that task, madam? What can I do to further assist you?"

In London, she would probably have a list of chores for Juliana. However, this was Scotland, and she neither wanted to impose upon her host or take the time to find some tasks for her maid.

"I think you should offer your services to Mrs. Jenkins. While you're doing that, I think it might be wise of you to consider whether or not you wish to remain with me."

Whenever Emma was this tired, she had a tendency to say exactly what she thought. Perhaps this conversation with Juliana was overdue. She turned to face her maid.

"I don't like sly people, Juliana. I don't wish to be in the company of those who go behind my back. I've embarked upon a new marriage, a new life, and I don't wish to continue with behavior that has disturbed me in the past. If you cannot be loyal to me, then I wish you'd leave. I shall give you a good letter of recommendation, and a list of women who would value your many services."

"I should not like to go back to London, madam," Juliana said, staring at the floor.

Emma noticed that the other woman conveniently avoided mentioning her loyalty or lack of it.

"Very well," she said, and turned away, not quite able to banish the feeling that something wasn't right, that there was something she needed to know. She pushed the feeling away and descended the staircase.

The layout of Lochlaven was very strange, and

evidently designed for the pleasure of its inhabitants and not its visitors. The second floor was where the drawing room and dining room were located. She'd learned that much from her conversation with Mrs. Jenkins yesterday. The bedrooms were located on the third floor, while the servants' quarters were above, on the fourth. While the public rooms took up all of the second floor, the first was almost entirely converted to Ian's laboratory.

A wide corridor led from the front door to what she thought was the main door of the laboratory. It was open, and she stood just beyond the threshold for a moment, clasping her hands together. The view to her right captured her attention, and she began to walk toward the wall of windows.

The land where Lochlaven sat curved inward, a bay sheltering the house. A small island lay in the center of the bay, its contours forming an exact opposite curve, almost as if a giant had sliced the island from the mainland, casting it adrift.

On the island sat a structure of some sort, and the longer Emma stared, the more she could discern its shape. A castle, perhaps. Or a fortress once used by the McNairs, in days gone by.

The lake was golden, a repository for the rays of the morning sun. She could smell the clean, fishy odor, see the enormous kelp bed shimmering in the water, almost as if nature had placed it there as a natural barrier to the island—a moat of seaweed.

The room in which she stood was nearly empty, except for two long tables sitting against adjoining walls. Stacks of papers covered most of the surface, along with a series of crates, their markings clearly indicating they'd come from Germany.

The next room was as cluttered as the previous room had been empty.

Men were always surrounded with possessions that proved they belonged somewhere. Here, in this laboratory, Ian had marked his place in the world. The microscopes and tables, the beakers, tubes, and odd, squat little bottles with soot-darkened wicks stated as clear as a placard that he was the master of this domain.

What did she have? What did any woman have? A corner of a room outfitted with a small and comfortable chair. A basket filled with needlework and a lamp that could be adjusted for the task at hand. A home, lent to her by a husband, a father, an uncle. A place in society that she hadn't wanted.

She heard voices in the other room, and she approached slowly, uncertain whether she should call out and announce her presence, or simply retreat.

The decision was taken from her the moment a woman turned and saw her in the doorway.

"Oh, how long have you been standing there? Come in, come in."

The woman, barely older than a girl, approached her, hands outstretched, her auburn curls pinned in an array of ringlets at the back of her head that bounced when she walked. Her warm gray eyes sparkled with welcome, as did her smile.

"You must be Mrs. McNair. May I call you Emma? We are soon to be relatives, you see."

Emma didn't know whether to stretch out her hands in return. She gripped her hands together tightly and pasted a smile on her face, hoping she appeared more convivial than she felt.

The girl glanced behind her. "Oh, Ian, please introduce us properly, I beg you."

"Emma," he said, "I'd like you to meet my fiancée, Rebecca Carrick. Rebecca, Emma McNair, Bryce's wife."

"How horrible that such a thing should have happened on your wedding journey, Emma."

Emma exchanged a glance with Ian. Was his fiancée so innocent that she didn't realize that Bryce's poisoning had to be deliberate? This was no accidental ingestion. Someone wished him dead.

Or perhaps he hadn't told her everything.

She instantly and acutely disliked Rebecca's innocence, whether feigned or not. She, herself, had never been quite that naive. Or perhaps what she was feeling was simply jealousy, because no one had wished to protect her to the degree they evidently sheltered Rebecca. Not even her father, who'd been so eager for her to marry the Duke of Herridge.

"Forgive my intrusion," Emma said.

"It is no intrusion," Rebecca said. "I would have called upon you in the sickroom if Ian had not specifically forbidden me." She tossed a chiding look toward Ian.

Emma's smile was firmly fixed and might not ever fade. "Do you know of any local seamstresses?" She glanced over at Ian. "One of my trunks was lost at the Inverness Station. The one containing all of my dresses."

A gasp escaped Rebecca. "Oh no, you poor dear. How absolutely hideous a journey you've had! You must take one of my dresses, although I have nothing in black. But must it be black?"

What on earth should she say to that? That she must remain in black to mourn a man she detested, loathed, and reviled? That she must remain in black or else face ostracism from society? She had done that by marrying before her two-year mourning period was over.

Helplessly, Emma allowed her hands to fall to her sides. "No," she said. "It doesn't have to be black."

In any other place she would have scandalized society by going from black to a lighter color immediately with no half measures—such as purple or lavender—in between. But here, in Scotland, no one knew her. Nor did she doubt that anyone cared overmuch what she wore.

She glanced at Ian again.

His eyes darkened as he watched her.

She looked away, feeling a rush of heat as she remembered a conversation about a nightgown.

"I couldn't impose," she said.

"Of course it's no imposition," Rebecca said. "We're going to be practically sisters."

Rebecca might have been naive but she possessed the single-minded will of a spoiled child. Before Emma could protest, she was being swept back up to the third floor, to the suite of rooms Rebecca occupied, all the while being regaled with tales of the lavish wedding to come in a matter of weeks.

"We'll have it on the island, of course," she said. "At the very top of the hill. Is that not romantic?"

Emma nodded.

"I shall be wearing the loveliest gown," Rebecca said. "Of course you must attend me, dearest Emma."

Dear God, please don't let me be here for that spectacle.

"I'm certain Bryce will have recovered by then," Emma said. "I'm almost certain we'll have returned to London."

She didn't know any such thing. Her future was amorphous, and uncertain, at least as far as she knew. Did Bryce have his own home, other than Lochlaven? Did he have any family, other than Ian? What were his plans for their future? Surely it was to return to London? What was to happen to her?

How odd not to know.

She'd begun the day draped in black, and by mid-morning found herself attired in a lovely blue dress that surprisingly matched the shade of her eyes. How that had come about, she didn't know, but according to Rebecca, it was Fate.

"It was simply meant to be, my dearest Emma. It's a dress I've worn but once, and it doesn't suit me half as well as it does you. You must take it with my blessings. And this one as well."

"This one" turned out to be something in a jaunty yellow, with delicate embroidery on the cuffs and yoke. Even the full skirt had a trace of embroidery at the hem. It was one of the prettiest dresses Emma had ever seen, and highly inappropriate.

"I can't take your clothes," she said helplessly. It was one thing to not wear black, but yellow?

"Oh, you must," Rebecca said, pressing the dress on her.

And that, it seemed, was that.

Chapter 24

Ian's father had realized that being the Earl of Buchane and the Laird of Trelawny might be ancient and noble titles but they didn't carry the same sense of obligation as a hundred years earlier. His clan had spread out, most members no longer dependent upon the Earls of Buchane for their livelihood. A great many McNairs, those not employed at Lochlaven or in the nearby village, were now living in cities like Edinburgh or even closer, Inverness.

Lochlaven didn't require Ian's constant attention. Therefore his avocation, science, was an apt way for him to spend his time. Or perhaps his father had simply approved because he'd had similar leanings, being interested in the stars and the heavens beyond this planet.

Two years ago Ian had commissioned a small building behind Lochlaven. His mother had not been happy about the construction, or the fact that he'd taken up some of the garden to do so. However, after the building was finished and the exact purpose of it made clear, she and other periodic visitors to Lochlaven had expressed their wholehearted approval.

Along the exterior wall, in heavy glass boxes with

brass fittings, he'd placed several selections of raw meat. In two of the boxes, the meat had been left exposed to the air. Two of the boxes contained a filter of sorts, to purify the air before it reached the beef. A fifth and sixth box held a different type of filter, a mixture of chemicals that created a vitreous solution through which the air had to pass to reach the meat.

According to his hypothesis, the meat in the boxes without the vitreous filters would deteriorate faster than those with them. So far he'd been able to repeatedly prove his experiment as well as his hypothesis.

The odor in the room was substantial enough for him to wish that he had built a larger building for his experiments. Thankfully, he'd considered the decay of his experiments and taken measures to establish cross ventilation. Today he opened both doors and windows on the exterior walls toward the lake and the ones facing Lochlaven. The fresh breeze from the lake added to his instant comfort.

Although his primary study featured bacteria in water, he was even more fascinated with what bacteria could do. For the last two years, he'd been working with other scientists in France to prove that bacteria could be airborne, and could have an injurious effect on human tissue.

He prepared several slides for study from each of the boxes, and carefully placed them in the wooden case created for carrying them.

"Ian, may I speak with you?"

He looked up to see Emma standing in the doorway. The strangest expression flitted over her face before she began backing out of the building. She clamped one hand over her mouth, and the other waved him away as if she didn't want him to see her discomfiture.

"If I'd known you were going to come here," he said, following her outside, "I would've warned you. The smell does take some getting used to."

He hadn't seen her transformation, even though Rebecca insisted upon telling him.

"She's a very pretty woman, Ian," she said. "And now, dressed in something other than that smothering black, she looks so much younger as well."

The woman standing in front of him did not resemble the widowed Duchess of Herridge. This woman, unknown to him until now, might have been closer to the girl she'd once been.

She took another step backward, removed her hand from her mouth and smiled, as if amused by her own reaction.

Oh, Emma, don't smile at me. Don't lean toward me. Don't stretch out your hand as if you want to touch me. Don't, above all, look at me as if your happiness depended upon the words I might say or whether or not I smile at you in the next moment.

Or perhaps that was simply fanciful thinking on his part. After all, she'd banished him the night before. Of the two of them, she was wiser.

"How long has it been since you slept?" he asked, noting the shadows below her eyes.

"I can sleep later," she said.

"How is Bryce?"

"That's what I came to ask you about," she said. "Is there anyone we should notify? Anyone who would want to be with him in his illness?"

"Is he worse?" he asked, alarmed.

"No. Dr. Carrick thinks the fact that he survived the night a very good sign. At the same time, I can't help but think that if I were his mother, or a relative, I would want to know if he was ill."

"The only family Bryce has is here at Lochlaven. My sister is due to arrive any day, a visit she'd scheduled some time ago. My mother has left for the continent, so I didn't think to send word to her."

Emma nodded, looking away again. Words were fragile things between them.

In front of Rebecca, he'd wanted to go to her and take her in his arms, comfort her about the loss of her trunk. Her presence was a temptation, not only to his libido but to his very honor.

She played with the placket at the front of her bodice. He'd unbuttoned a similar set of buttons himself, had stroked his fingers from her throat to the lace at the top of her chemise, before divesting her of the rest of her garments. He had undressed her, feverishly, impatiently, revealing the woman beneath the black-crowed appearance. Revealing her as she truly was—beautiful, alluring, and passionate beyond his wildest imagining.

Emma said something else, words he didn't hear, all his senses focused on the actions of her fingers. He wanted to stop her, calm her restless hand, or replace those fingers with his own. The swell of her bodice amply covered her beautiful breasts, but he knew too well how they appeared, how they felt, how the texture of her skin lured his tongue, his lips.

He wanted to suckle her, hear her open-mouthed gasps. He wanted her on his lap, in his arms, beneath him. Ian forced himself to look away and take several calming breaths. It would not do to pounce upon Emma in the garden.

"I see that Rebecca was able to assist you in the matter of your clothing," he said. If he invoked Rebecca's name, perhaps it would remind him that they were to be married soon. Or that Emma was already married.

She looked beautiful and too much a temptation.

Emma looked down at herself, smoothed her hands over the material of her skirt, and nodded. "I didn't know she would be here," she said. "In residence."

"She's Dr. Carrick's daughter. She visits with her father, sometimes."

Emma nodded. "She's been very generous," she said in a low tone.

"Do you begrudge her generosity?" he asked.

Her gaze flew to his face. "Why would you say that?"

"There's a note in your voice I can't quite place," he said.

"Are you that familiar with my moods and how to determine them?"

"Yes."

That admission silenced both of them. He'd only known her for three days. But it seemed like so much longer, perhaps because she'd been in his mind for so long—first before he ever met her, then constantly after the interlude in London.

"I came back for you," he said abruptly.

Her look of confusion was almost enough to keep him silent.

All his life he'd been rational, dedicated to careful constructs, cause and effect thinking. Right at the moment, however, he felt different, *was* different, not quite himself.

"I came back for you," he said. "I came back to

London to find that you had married. If I'd made it a few hours earlier, I would've reached you before you said your vows."

She took a step back, away from him. Her hand went to her throat, flattened against her chest. If anything, her complexion paled even further.

Now would come the recriminations or the questions. Why are you saying such a thing to me? How can you say such a thing to me now? But she surprised him and remained silent, her face stricken, her eyes wide.

In that moment, Ian realized how much he'd hurt her. She didn't have to say a word. Her expression was enough. Or perhaps he simply felt her dawning disbelief and her pain.

"Emma," he said, taking a step toward her.

She turned and left him, nearly flying down the gravel path, leaving him feeling idiotic and cruel.

He had come for her. What was she to make of that? That he wished to rescue her? Or make her his mistress? She should have asked him for clarification but was so startled by his admission that she had to leave him as quickly as possible.

The Ice Queen was melting.

He couldn't say such things to her. He shouldn't say such things to her. They were both bound, both wrapped in ropes of honor and morality.

How ironic that after all this time, she, who prided herself on being the most decent of the venal people she knew, was now wishing she had their ability to slip the bonds of propriety.

If she was anyone other than herself, she might have taken advantage of his offer to become his mistress, if that's what he'd thought to offer her. If she was anyone but Emma Harding, formerly the Duchess of Herridge, she might have flirted with him even now, with Bryce still in his sickbed, and his fiancée in residence.

Or had he wanted more? Had he wanted her to be his wife? Dear God, please no. She could not bear that.

She could not bear seeing him each day.

She shouldn't have gone to see him now.

When he first answered the door, his hair had been a little mussed, as if he'd threaded his fingers through it in exasperation. Impatience had molded his features, revealing that he wasn't pleased at the interruption.

But when he'd seen her and come to her, striding across the floor in that way of his, his lips had curved in a welcoming smile.

How easily they could alter each other's moods.

She felt her heart stop, then begin beating again, so loudly and furiously that it made her breathless.

He couldn't say those things to her. He couldn't expect her to simply brush them aside. Had three days in London made the same difference in his life that they'd made in hers? Try as she might, she hadn't been able to forget him.

Now she was at his home, his guest, his prisoner, again. She felt as if she were a fly in the web of a particularly attractive spider, so charming and so handsome that by the time he crawled across his web to eat her alive, she practically begged him to nibble on her.

Bryce needed to get well quickly. They needed to leave Lochlaven. They needed to find some other place to live, if not in London, then Scotland. Anywhere.

Her fortune would allow them to do so. And if it

didn't, if it was gone, she would take up washing, darning socks, becoming a servant in someone else's home.

Anything but remain at Lochlaven and lose her immortal soul.

And her heart.

Four of the rooms in Ian's laboratory opened up into each other. He'd had the doors removed and the door frames enlarged so they could accommodate the massive laboratory tables, should he wish to move them from one room to another.

This part of his laboratory faced north and a view of the island. The sight of the castle was always a reminder to him that he was doing exactly what he'd planned so many years ago as a boy. Even then, instead of simply exploring and pretending he was an adventurer on those outings to the island, he'd been equally interested in what people couldn't see. He'd overturned rocks and boulders, taken samples of water from the springs, and examined the very soil of the island.

His most expensive acquisition, and his most beloved one, sat on the table facing the loch, the brass plate bearing the mark of its maker: ANDREW PRITCHARD, PICKETT STREET AND 312 & 263 STRAND, LONDON. The microscope was made of solid brass, except for the lenses, which were ground of optical quality glass. A rosewood case with fourteen ivory-knobbed drawers sat beside it. Two of the drawers held the new slides he'd purchased in London, waiting for his examination and discovery.

The microscope was not unlike the one given to him by his father when he was sixteen, and which now sat in his London laboratory. The construction was the same—the long, slender column of brass resting on a tube connected by several screws to a tripod. At the base was a refracting mirror, bringing light to the slide and thereby aiding in the magnification. The difference between the two microscopes lay only in the strength of the lenses.

Over the years, he'd become impatient with the available lighting. Consequently, he chose the brightest spot in the room to assemble his microscope, and assisted the process by always having a lamp directly behind the instrument.

What he truly coveted, however, was an apparatus similar to the one displayed at the International Exhibit in London four years ago. That device was the most brilliant artificial light ever produced, and this spectacular accomplishment had been achieved using a magnetoelectrical device invented by Professor Holmes.

He'd occasionally given some thought to erecting a mirror on a tripod and setting it on the expanse of lawn running down to the shore of the lake. On sunny days it could be tilted to reflect light into his laboratory.

Mirrors inevitably made him think of the Tulloch Sgàthán, which led to thoughts of Emma.

Pushing thoughts of her aside—a great deal more difficult than he'd expected—he pulled a stool toward the table, uncaring that the legs scraped across the wooden floor, and removed his microscope from its case.

He worked for a little while, recording the results of slides he'd made earlier.

When Albert entered the room, he looked up.

"I hear Bryce is better," Ian said.

Albert didn't look as pleased as he'd expected.

"I'm a little concerned about his color," he said. "There are signs of jaundice, which is never good."

"What can we do for him?"

Albert sighed. "Nothing at the moment. Arsenic is not an easy poison to survive."

"Will he? Survive?"

Albert looked directly at him, not attempting to hide anything. "I don't know, Ian. I've done all I can. Nature will have to reason the rest of it out."

Their camaraderie was of long standing. Ian had asked Albert to come and work with him nearly ten years ago. The physician had eagerly limited his practice with patients for that of research, and spent more than two weeks a month at Lochlaven. Occasionally, his wife, Brenda, joined him. Sometimes Rebecca did as well, as she had on this visit.

Albert donned his laboratory coat, settling beside him on a neighboring stool. His microscope was older than Ian's but as much an extension of the man as his hands.

In addition to the laboratory at Lochlaven, Albert had a small lab set up at his home in Inverness. Ian had thought nothing of giving him the funds to do so. Albert was an invaluable collaborator. Without his assistance, Ian knew he couldn't have achieved as much as he already had or as much as he wanted to in the future.

In his experiments, Ian was very quick to discard a hypothesis when it was clear it could not be proved. He was a nimble thinker, focused forward, and not spending any appreciable time mourning what had not been or could not be.

His personal life was proving not to be that simple.

Ian looked through the eyepiece of the microscope, but instead of viewing the bacterium he expected, only saw only a blur. He hadn't yet inserted the slide.

Placing both hands flat on the table, he stared out at the view of the lake. The day was a bright and sunny one, calling to him as it rarely did.

Emma was here. Emma, to whom he'd been cruel. Emma, who was wearing a blue dress and had smiled at him.

Dear God, he was losing his mind.

"Have you told Emma what you think?" he asked.

Albert looked up from his microscope. "I didn't. Do you think it's necessary?"

"I think she should be warned," Ian said, standing and removing his lab coat and placing it carefully on the stool he'd occupied.

Albert, intent on his own work, merely waved him away without taking his gaze from the eyepiece.

The curtains had only been opened an inch or two in the sickroom, the morning light muted. The maid was nowhere in sight, and he was annoyed by her absence.

Emma sat in the corner, her gaze on him as he entered. He concentrated on Bryce for the moment. Today his cousin's face was not as pale. There was color in his cheeks, and he was breathing easier than yesterday.

Ian fervently hoped that Albert was wrong and that Bryce was recovering, and quickly.

"Where's Glenna?" he asked.

With someone else here, if she insisted upon staying in the sickroom, she could at least doze in the corner.

"She went to get some lunch," she said.

"She should not have left you alone."

He felt like an utter fool. But then, that shouldn't be any surprise to Emma. From the moment he'd met her, he'd behaved unlike himself. Or—and this was a thought he put away to examine later—perhaps more like the person he'd always secretly been.

"I want you to rest."

Evidently, those were the wrong words to say. Belatedly, he realized that it might have sounded like a command rather than concern.

She stood, the movement so slow that he suspected she was as tired as she appeared. She hadn't slept last night, and he doubted if the night before that had been restful.

"If you do not sleep soon," he said, "we shall have to bring in another bed for you. Bryce will not be the only one who's ill."

She walked to the opposite side of the bed, fiddling with the edge of the sheet that covered Bryce. As if putting Bryce between them might moderate his thoughts, or keep him from wanting her.

What had she said the night before? Something about not being like the women she'd seen at Chavensworth? No hedonism, then. No loose morality for Emma. Despite the look in her eyes, despite the memory of that night and that day together, there could be nothing between them.

But dear God, he wanted to stretch his hand out and touch her shoulder, measure the smooth curve of her arm. He wanted to hold her hand and stare down at the back of it, studying the knuckles and the small, almost invisible tracery of veins. Then turn it over and kiss each line on her palm.

Perhaps he was no better than the Duke of Herridge with his appetite and his lack of honor.

"Will you promise me to get some rest? I worry about you."

Her glance focused on the actions of her hands as she smoothed the sheets.

"Is it wrong to tell you that I worry about you?" he asked. "Is that, too, forbidden?"

She raised her gaze to him finally. "It should be. If it isn't, it should be."

Emma had been at Lochlaven two days, and already his life was upside down. He'd been catapulted into emotions he wasn't prepared to feel, hungers he'd never known.

A lie, and he wasn't used to lying to himself. He'd felt the hunger ever since meeting her.

"I'm going to see Mrs. Jenkins," he said, angry at her, at himself, and mostly at the circumstances. "I'll find someone to watch Bryce. Right now, however, you're going to get some rest."

She looked surprised at his vehemence. He waited for her to protest, to argue with him. He anticipated an argument, perhaps even welcomed it.

To his surprise, she only sighed, looked down at Bryce, then back up at him.

"You'll stay with him until then?"

"I'll stay here," he said.

She was so pale he was afraid she'd faint. If he could have trusted himself alone with her, he would have escorted her up the stairs and to her room. But he only stood where he was, watching as she left the sickroom. At the door, she hesitated and glanced back at him. For the longest moment, they exchanged a look, one filled with memory. He wanted that glance to mean something, an admission, a conciliation, a surrender.

He needed to ensure that Bryce grew as healthy as quickly as possible and that his cousin and Emma went somewhere else for their honeymoon. Otherwise, he was quite certain he was going to do something to shame his family name.

Chapter 25

❧

Ian's sister and her husband arrived shortly after Glenna returned to the sickroom. He arranged for another girl to replace her an hour later, then left the room to greet his sister.

Their carriage rolled up in front of Lochlaven but no one exited. He watched them from the front door knowing, from prior experience, exactly what was happening inside the carriage. Fergus was kissing his sister and his sister was reciprocating with great enthusiasm.

If he didn't like his sister so much, she would have embarrassed him with her adoration of her husband, Fergus.

Although they'd been married for two years, their passion for each other showed no signs of lessening, a fact that gave him—until London—some hopes for his own union.

Now, however, he knew that the only chance for his marriage was to change the bride. Unfortunately, the woman he had in mind was already wed.

He gave Fergus and Patricia a few more minutes before striding down the gravel drive and opening the carriage door himself.

The two of them pulled apart, not looking the least embarrassed for being found in such circumstances. The entire world could have faded away, and as long as Fergus and Patricia were in the same room, they would be equally content.

Their marriage was one he envied. In strength and emotionality, it easily equaled that of their parents.

"Shall I go away for a few moments?" he asked, smiling at them.

"An hour or so might suffice," Patricia said, smiling back at him.

He laughed, helped Patricia from the carriage before embracing her.

Marriage suited her. She'd always been a pretty girl but she was radiant now, her black hair a perfect complement to her fair skin and brown eyes.

Fergus, on the other hand, would never be anything but what he was, a big redheaded bear of a man with a full beard. Rumor had it that he was a master negotiator in addition to being a very prosperous merchant. Fergus owned a fleet of ships as well as numerous business concerns in Edinburgh and London.

"Bryce is here," Ian said as he walked with both of them to the door.

Patricia stopped and looked up at him. "Bryce? Why ever for?"

He exchanged a long look with Patricia. "He's married."

"But why has he come back to Lochlaven?"

"We're his only family," he said.

Patricia made a most unladylike sound. "You know better than that. We've always tried to be family to Bryce. He's the one who refused us. At every occasion, he pushed us away. Why now?"

"I think it's because he married well," he said.

"And he wanted to show her off?" In the middle of the foyer, Patricia stopped, folded her arms and stared at him. He realized that she wasn't going to advance upward until he answered her questions.

"I think that's exactly why he came, to show her off."

"The poor thing," Patricia said.

Not exactly the description he would give the former Duchess of Herridge but he didn't illuminate his sister either to Emma's nature or his feelings for her.

"Where are they?"

"He's very ill," Ian said.

That comment drew her up short.

"What do you mean?" she asked.

He decided to give her the brief version. "Bryce became ill on the journey here," he said. "I've put him in the sickroom. Dr. Carrick is treating him."

She glanced at Fergus. "Is it something that we should be concerned about, Ian?" she asked.

Evidently, the brief version wasn't going to be satisfactory.

"He was poisoned," he said. "Arsenic."

She returned to Fergus's side. Her husband wrapped one arm around her shoulders but Patricia didn't seem to notice.

"Poisoned? By whom?"

"We haven't been able to determine that. Bryce hasn't awakened yet."

"Do you think he will?"

He gave her the truth. Patricia would ferret it out anyway. "I don't know. Dr. Carrick doesn't know. He's survived this long, which is a good sign."

"Where is his wife? Is she with him?"

Before he could answer Patricia's questions, she began to walk toward the sickroom.

He exchanged a glance with Fergus. Once Patricia was in the mood to do something, little stopped her.

"She's not there," he called out.

She halted so suddenly that her skirts swung around her as she turned.

"Where is she?"

"She was up tending to Bryce all night, Patricia. She's gone for a well-deserved rest."

She advanced on him, and once again he exchanged a glance with Fergus. What had he revealed? Something important, or Patricia wouldn't be looking at him with that calculating gleam in her eye.

"You can meet her later," he said.

"Tell me about her."

Now *that* he was not going to do. He saw Mrs. Jenkins lingering in the hall, and summoned her to his side.

As the two women greeted each other, he took the opportunity to slip away, retreating to his laboratory. He was only postponing the inevitable. Patricia would find a way to assuage her curiosity, one way or another.

Perhaps he should warn Emma.

Emma sat on the edge of the bed. Although she was tired, so tired that she felt empty inside and incapable of speech, sleep felt as far away as a distant country.

Juliana hadn't been in her room when she'd entered it. Nor had her trunk been unpacked. Rather than summoning the girl, Emma simply opened her trunk, withdrew a nightgown, and undressed herself.

She wasn't up to dealing with Juliana at the moment. She wasn't up to dealing with anyone else, either, especially Ian McNair.

Emma pressed her hands against the edge of the mattress, staring at her bare feet.

For the four years of her marriage, she'd held onto a sense of decency. Even if propriety had only been a façade, she'd clung to it in desperation. Yet here she was, of her own accord, admitting to wanting to be immoral.

The fact that her union was legal and binding dictated that she act in certain ways, despite what she wished or felt or wanted.

She needed her sleep. But for the first time in a very long time, she lay back on the bed, her hands folded atop her stomach, and wished for dreams. Let her recall that day in London. Let her remember those hours in Ian's arms. Let her body feel that passion, that fevered longing, once again. Let her feel all of that desire, if only in her sleep.

Dinner that night was a boisterous affair, with Patricia and Fergus relaying tales of their recent travels. Despite the company, and the conviviality, Ian found himself irritated. The cause wasn't hard to determine—Emma was not at the table.

He directed his attention toward his fiancée. Rebecca's cheerfulness had never been grating before, and he knew quite well why it annoyed him right at the moment. Because a woman with calm, assessing blue eyes was not seated across from him. A woman whose expression was more often solemn than happy, whose smiles were so rare that he ached to coax them from her.

Rebecca was of such an amiable disposition that she

rarely frowned. There was nothing mysterious about her past, nothing that she wished to keep hidden. She was just as she appeared, a doctor's daughter excited about her future, planning on becoming a countess, and overjoyed at the prospect.

At the moment, she was looking at his sister fondly. Did Rebecca think that their marriage would be as warm and loving as Patricia's?

He should warn her now, pull her aside and tell her, in words that would no doubt be hurtful, that he couldn't demonstrate that same type of feeling toward her. He didn't have it in him. He didn't possess the capacity for such emotions any longer.

They'd been stripped from him by a certain woman with soft blue eyes.

He forced his mind away from those thoughts and concentrated on his dinner. Because Patricia was a particular favorite of the staff, most of the people employed at Lochlaven had appeared in various guises during this dinner.

Duties that would normally be performed by a footman in London were easily done by young women at Lochlaven. As one of Cook's helpers began to serve the courses, another decanted a bottle of wine, pouring each glass half full.

He stopped her when she came to his side, took the bottle and inspected it. Something niggled at him. Something he'd forgotten or not noticed.

Ian stood and pushed back his chair, glancing at the four of them. Albert was concentrating on his dinner. Patricia and Fergus were speaking in low tones to each other. Rebecca looked up at him in surprise.

"If you'll excuse me," he said, "There's something I must do."

"Now, Ian?" Rebecca asked.

"Most assuredly now," he said.

He entered his laboratory, went to the rubbish bin and carefully picked up the three wine bottles he'd discarded. He hadn't been paying attention at the time, but one of the bottles was different, the slope of its shoulder not as pronounced, and the punt deeper. Two of the wine bottles were the same.

He knocked on Mrs. Jenkins's door, apologizing for the intrusion when she answered a moment later.

"You're never an intrusion, Your Lordship," she said with a smile. "What can I do for you?"

"My cousin brought a case of wine with him. Do you know where it is now?"

She thought for a moment. "I believe all his belongings were taken to his room. The one that he's always used," she added. "Would you like me to see?"

"It's not necessary," he said. "I'll check myself."

"If you're certain, Your Lordship," Mrs. Jenkins said.

He smiled his thanks and left her, taking the stairs to the third floor. Bryce's room was across the hall from his own suite.

What had Bryce done to get himself poisoned? Ian suspected it had its roots in London.

He opened the door to Bryce's room, to find two trunks and a crate stacked in the corner. He rang for a maid and when she arrived instructed her to have one of the stable lads carry the crate to his laboratory.

He should have examined the crate before. Maybe it wasn't a suitor, an admirer of Emma's, after all. Maybe the answer to who had poisoned Bryce was closer to home.

Chapter 26

❦

Thank God Emma didn't care for wine.

Ian couldn't help but wonder if her avoidance of spirits had something to do with having been the Duchess of Herridge. No doubt she'd witnessed the effect of alcohol on others, and didn't wish to experience the same lowering of inhibitions in herself.

Except with him.

He pushed that thought away and motioned to the young man to place the crate on the table next to his microscope. The lid of the crate had been opened, then carelessly fastened again.

Ian opened each full wine bottle in order of its placement in the crate. When each bottle had been tested, he discovered exactly what he'd suspected. None of the other bottles in the crate contained arsenic, which meant that the contaminated bottle was one of the three. Which one?

He glanced at the mantel clock. Hours had passed since he left the dining room, and thankfully, everyone had left him alone. At the moment, however, he needed to see Emma.

After leaving the laboratory, he strode toward the sickroom. When he saw Glenna there, sitting in the glow of the lamp and evidently comfortable with her knitting, he only smiled in greeting, then glanced at Bryce.

"How is he?"

"He stirred a little while ago, Your Lordship," she said. "I think, in a few days, he'll come out of it completely."

"Good," he said, nodding. "Good."

Without another word, he left the sickroom, heading for the foyer of Lochlaven and the grand stairs that led him to the upper floors.

He walked to the door of the room she'd been given, hesitating only slightly before rapping on the door with his knuckles. She was probably still asleep, and he had no right to disturb her.

If she didn't answer his first knock, he'd simply wait until morning. But just as he was beginning to turn away, she opened the door.

Her coloring was somewhat better but she still looked tired.

She held onto the edge of the door, and in the space, he could see that she was dressed for night in a filmy gown of black. Her widow's nightgown.

He resolutely kept his gaze on her face, congratulating himself on his resolve.

He braced his hands on either side of the door, leaning toward her. "Would your maid have any reason to want to kill Bryce?"

Confusion shadowed her face.

"Juliana? Why do you ask?"

"Because Bryce drank three bottles of wine. One of them was poisoned. The other bottles in the crate weren't poisoned."

Her eyes widened. "None of the other bottles?"

When he shook his head, she folded her arms in front of her, her gaze on the floor.

"The chances are that Juliana poisoned the wine she bought in Inverness. Were you with her the whole time?'

She shook her head. "I was with Bryce," she said. "I'd sent her off to get food for the journey."

"So she would have had the opportunity," he said.

A moment later she looked up at him. "If you're going to see her, I'm coming with you."

He waited in the hallway while she dressed. When she joined him, Emma was attired in Rebecca's blue dress.

"We must see about a seamstress for you," he said.

She glanced quickly at him and then ahead. "I hope not to be here that long," she said. Abruptly, she halted and looked at him. "I do apologize for the bluntness of my comment. It's just that, for a variety of reasons, it would be better if we continue our journey as soon as Bryce has recovered."

"To where?"

Instead of answering him, she only shook her head.

"You're welcome to stay here as long as you wish," he heard himself saying, the exact opposite of what he should have said. He should have bid her on her way, done anything in his power to ensure that she and his cousin were soon gone. Instead, he'd issued an invitation.

"This is Bryce's home," he said. "The only one he's known."

She halted again, and in deference to the hour,

whispered the question. "If this is his only home, and you are his only family, then why does he seem to have such antipathy for you?"

"Does he?"

He continued walking, simply because it was easier to be about his errand than to answer her question.

She caught up with him soon enough.

"I would not have expected you, of all people, to avoid answering a difficult question."

"Why am I any different than anyone else?"

"Because you are."

They were at the stairs now, and instead of taking them, he turned to face her.

She looked up at him, her face cast into shadow. The scent she used wafted up from her body, warm and seductive, urging him to recall those hours when she was in his bed. He wanted, almost desperately, to kiss her, to grab her hand and pull her down the stairs and into his suite. He'd bar the door to everyone, say to hell with every virtue he'd learned. If it didn't concern Emma, he didn't care.

Instead, he remained where he was and gave her a version of the truth, not about his need but about his past. "From the moment Bryce came to Lochlaven," he said, "he resented us. We were prepared, Patricia and I, to consider him our brother. He didn't want to be part of our family. Why?" He shrugged. "I don't know. Perhaps it was because he disliked feeling like a poor relation, even though none of us ever said anything to him about his parents. I can't give you an answer. Dealing with scientific principles is one thing, Emma. Dealing with people quite another."

"Thank you," she said to his surprise. "For your honesty. For answering me."

He began to mount the steps.

"I didn't give you an answer," he said. "I gave you an explanation for not having one."

"Yes. But you might have just simply told me it was none of my concern. Men do that with women, sometimes."

He glanced at her over his shoulder. "Not at Lochlaven," he said, faintly amused. "My mother and Patricia are extremely strong women. They're Scots. They're McNairs. They will not take a subservient role to anyone."

"I imagine Rebecca is the same," she said softly.

Since he didn't know what to say to that comment, he remained silent.

Juliana wasn't answering her door.

Ian knocked once more, as quietly as he could, so as not to disturb the other occupants of the wing. But after a few moments it was all too evident that Juliana wasn't going to respond.

Emma stepped forward. "Perhaps it would be better if I rouse her," she said.

"Is she a heavy sleeper?"

"I don't know. Whenever I rang for her, she appeared promptly." He stepped back as she grabbed the handle of the door and swung it inward.

Servants' quarters were rarely equipped with locks, and this chamber was no exception. Although it was small, however, it was furnished with everything necessary: a narrow bed, a set of dressers, a ladder-back chair that served as a bedside table, and a series of pegs for clothing.

Everything was neat and tidy, and quite empty.

"She might be in another room," Emma suggested.

"Perhaps she developed an affection for one of the male servants."

He glanced at her. "In two days?" he asked. "Was she given to doing such things?"

"I'm woefully unfamiliar with Juliana's personal life, her habits, or her predilections," she said.

"She might be in another room," Ian conceded.

"But you don't think so."

"No, I don't think so," Ian said.

Emma turned to face him, her hands clasped together in front of her. She felt as if she were riding in the train again, her stomach none too steady.

"If she left, that doesn't mean she's guilty. I came very close to dismissing her," she said, conveying her last conversation with Juliana.

"Nor does it prove her innocence," Ian said.

They left Juliana's room, and as they descended to the third floor, Emma was consumed with worry.

"How did she leave Lochlaven?" she said. "Where did she go? How?"

"Why are you so concerned about her?" Ian asked, halting in front of her door.

"She was in my employ," Emma said. "Her welfare is my concern."

"Even if she's proven to be a poisoner?"

Emma considered his question for a moment. "Perhaps not." A moment later she spoke again. "I don't understand. How can some people do such egregious things? How can anyone place themselves in the role of God and decide who should live and who should die?"

"How can anyone force another to do his bidding?" Ian asked.

She looked up at him. "For power," she said. "All despots crave power."

"Perhaps murder is no different."

He was standing too close.

Her mouth trembled but she held it tight. Each of her hands gripped the opposite forearm, holding herself tightly. Her legs felt like liquid.

She should excuse herself, close the door. Yet she didn't leave, even now. She looked up at him, noticing that his deep brown eyes were ringed with a thick black border, and his lashes were full and thick. As she stared, his mouth thinned, his expression growing fierce, the Scottish warrior of his heritage becoming all too evident.

She wanted to look lower, to take in the column of his neck, the shape of his shoulders beneath his white shirt, the width of his chest. But she kept her eyes on his. Something flared there, something that warned her to step away. Although her heart tripped in its haste, beating furiously and too fast, she didn't move. How could she? Her breath was gone, and her will melted beneath the heat she felt. Her cheeks were flushed; her skin felt too tight.

This was not right.

"Ian, I've lost the mirror," she said abruptly. "The Tulloch Sgàthán." The fact that she'd forgotten, until now, to mention that fact to him was a blessing in disguise. Her remark altered the tension between them and caused him to frown.

"The housekeeper at Chavensworth found the mirror and sent it to me. I placed it in my trunk, the one that was stolen."

If anything, his frown grew more thunderous.

She didn't know what else to say to him. There were no further explanations she could make, nothing that would ease the news she'd just conveyed.

"If you would communicate with Lady Sarah," she said, "and tell her that I would be more than happy to compensate her for the cost of the mirror."

What value could she put on such an obviously old object?

"Did you steal your own trunk?" he asked.

"Of course I didn't," she said. "Nor am I assuming too much blame. It's simply that it was in my possession, and I feel responsible."

Ian took a step toward her and she was forced to move back until she could feel the door frame behind her.

He bent his head until his lips were close to her ear.

"You feel responsible for your murderous maid. You feel responsible for an act of thievery that you could not control. What else do you feel responsible for, Emma? The sun shining? The fog across the lake?"

She raised her hand, as if to press it against his chest and push him back. At the last moment, however, reason returned to her. She couldn't touch him. If she did, it would be like stoking a banked fire. Fiery embers would float in the air followed by flames.

"You take too much on yourself," he said.

She welcomed the irritation she felt. Who was he to question her character?

An honorable man, who, from what she'd observed, cared for those in his keeping. He was as responsible. Too much so, perhaps.

"Perhaps I assume responsibility for those things

I cannot control, in order to avoid shame for those actions I could have altered and didn't."

For the longest moment he said nothing. The seconds ticked by like heartbeats, and she was conscious of each one.

"What would he have done to you if you'd refused to play the part of Ice Queen?" he asked softly.

She closed her eyes, unwilling to answer that question. But he was implacable.

"Emma," he said. "What would he have done? What would Anthony have done if you'd not agreed to appear in his revels?"

She would not tell him. In the end, Anthony and her uncle had not been that far apart in their threats.

"My father once beat me for telling a lie," he said. "It was a lesson I learned quite well. I learned not to lie to my father and I learned something else."

He leaned closer, his forearm braced against the door. As if he were creating a shelter of his body in which she could feel secure.

"I don't like pain."

He was looking at her. She could feel the intensity of his stare.

"So, to avoid being raped, you became the Ice Queen."

She nodded. She truly did not want to have this conversation. And if Providence insisted upon this conversation, she most especially did not want to have it with *him*.

"See the facts as they are, Emma. Like it or not, you were no match for the Duke of Herridge. Not in depravity, or cruelty, or a dozen other character defects I'm certain he possessed. The situation was one of inequality. But even more than that, can you truly fault yourself for not seeking out pain?"

"I should have done something," she said.

"Such as?"

She shook her head. "I don't know but something."

"How many times have you asked yourself that question? How many times since he died have you chastised yourself for your behavior?"

A faint smile curved her lips. "A great many," she admitted.

"Then I propose to you, my dearest Emma, that in all this time, and with all that thought, if you cannot think of a single thing that you might have done, there was *nothing* to be done. You simply had to endure, and you did that. Don't fault yourself for surviving him."

She lifted her eyes to his face. His words eased her heart a little, but even more so was the fact that he'd called her "dearest Emma."

She turned and slipped behind her chamber door.

"Good night, Ian."

"Sleep well, Emma," he said.

As she closed the door, she wondered why his words felt almost intimate, dangerously so.

Chapter 27

Rebecca sailed into the sickroom a few days later.

"There you are, dearest Emma," she said, unconsciously repeating Ian's words to her.

Following her was a stranger, a tall and striking woman with dark brown eyes and black hair. From the shape of her features, and her high cheekbones, Emma guessed that she was face-to-face with Ian's sister.

A moment later that guess was confirmed as Rebecca made a great show of introducing her future sister-in-law.

"This is Patricia. We're going to be sisters, soon," she said. She looked confused for a moment, then smiled brightly at Emma. "But then, you and she are sisters already. Are you not?" She turned to Patricia. "Do you not think of Bryce as your brother?"

Patricia glanced at her and smiled, leaving Emma to wonder if the expression was as forced as it appeared.

"Of course we do," Patricia said.

She directed her attention to Emma.

"I am so sorry to meet you under such circumstances, Emma. Ian refused to let me come and visit with you until today. Welcome to Lochlaven, although I can't think that your visit here has been very pleasant."

"Which is the reason why we're here, of course," Rebecca said brightly. "You must come with us to the island."

Bryce stirred, and Emma stood and left the room, gesturing to the other women to follow. "I don't wish to disturb him," she said in the hallway.

"How is he?" Patricia asked.

Before she could answer, Rebecca spoke. "My father says that each day he grows stronger." She turned to Emma again. "So there is no way at all you can refuse to accompany us. Patricia has promised to assist me in the planning of the ceremony, and I thought it would be an opportunity for you to see the island, first of all, and secondly, for all of us to become better acquainted."

"I really shouldn't leave Bryce," Emma said.

"You've spent enough time in the sickroom of late. You never take your meals with us. It's almost as if you're hiding in here. Being in the fresh air would be good for you. Once Bryce has recovered, we will take him to the island as well and make a monumental family event of it."

"Glenna is truly a very good nurse," Patricia said. "I'm sure Bryce would be fine, but we can verify that with Dr. Carrick."

Emma sent a grateful look to Patricia.

"I do so want you to come with us," Rebecca said. "There is so much to plan. Mother Barbara is coming for the wedding," she added. "I want everything to be just perfect."

Patricia carefully studied the pattern of the runner below her feet, giving Emma the impression that her mother did not care for the appellation "Mother Barbara."

"Do I need anything?" Emma asked, capitulating.

Today, she'd worn the yellow dress she borrowed from Rebecca, and it had lightened her mood, somehow.

"Just your bonnet," Patricia said. "The sun is hotter than you expect."

She didn't have a bonnet, other than the bedraggled black thing she'd worn on the trip to Scotland, but rather than mentioning the lack—and be given one of Rebecca's—she remained silent. A few hours in the sun wouldn't be a bad thing, especially since, as Rebecca accused, she'd been hiding in the sickroom.

Hiding, and praying that Ian wouldn't visit, that he wouldn't come and inquire about Bryce or her. That he wouldn't, above all, smile at her, or talk to her in that soft, low tone of his.

Rebecca left, after providing the details about the outing, Patricia following in her wake, an amused smile on her face. She exchanged glances with Emma and her look seemed to say: *I feel the same as you. Together, however, we might be able to tolerate her.*

The island was best viewed from Lochlaven's herbaceous gardens, a discovery Emma made as she followed the procession to the dock. The gardens were beautiful in their splendor, and so filled with heady scents that she wanted to stay and savor the air itself.

She had always wanted to have a garden just like this, to watch the plants grow and know that she'd had some small part in their existence. Circumstances had always prevented it, however. As the Duchess of Herridge, she was not allowed to toil in the earth. "That's what gardeners are for, Emma." In London, the only green space was in the rear of the house where the horses were exercised.

Twice, Rebecca glanced back at her impatiently, as if questioning why she lingered. Twice, Emma smiled and followed, sedately but punctually, to where the garden sloped down to the dock.

Patricia greeted her with a smile, then turned to a large man standing beside her.

"Fergus, darling," she said, "this is Emma. Our cousin Bryce's wife."

Fergus turned and smiled at her. His neatly trimmed beard and mustache was the same shade of red as his hair. His hands reached out and encompassed hers, and Emma felt as if she'd been gripped by a giant.

"A pretty little thing you are," he said in a rough burr of a voice. "Bryce found himself a jewel, he did."

"Thank you," Emma said, a little startled.

"Fergus, you mustn't embarrass Emma. Not so soon, at least," Patricia added, reaching up and patting the side of his face with one hand.

He turned his attention to his wife.

"No one can be as beautiful as you, my love," he said, dropping Emma's hands and directing all his attention toward Patricia. No one existed but the two of them.

She turned her head to find that Ian had arrived. She hadn't expected him to accompany them. Would she have accepted the invitation if she'd known he'd be present?

Probably, and chided herself for doing so.

Ian helped Rebecca into one of the boats, while

Fergus assisted Patricia. A young man introduced himself as Broderick and held out a hand to her. Emma accepted it with gratitude, getting into the second boat with him and two large baskets. She'd never been in a boat, and the experience of not having any balance whatsoever was disconcerting.

Broderick didn't speak as they crossed the lake, the waves surging so strongly beneath the hull that Emma wondered if the lake had its own tide. Or was it somehow linked to the North Sea? The wind was howling, as if it had gathered speed for a thousand miles and now its sole aim was to push them back to shore. Neither Broderick nor any of the occupants of the first boat looked uneasy. Emma could only guess that the wind was always this brisk and the water always this turbulent.

She could understand why the first McNairs had chosen the island for their fortress. It was easily defensible since there was no beach, no welcoming shore, only a series of large boulders sitting like jagged teeth along the edge of the island. Over the years, someone had cleared a way through the boulders, and it was there they docked.

The others left their boat with practiced ease, while Emma relied heavily on Broderick's kindness. He reached behind him, grabbed the two baskets, and together they followed the others.

Around her were thickly forested trees, tall pines, maples, and elms. The birds sang prettily in the vicinity, a rustle in the undergrowth signaling the alarm of creatures not often disturbed.

The path, soft with loamy soil, dried leaves, and pine needles, wound upward from the beach to the highest point of the island.

To her left, sitting in forlorn isolation, were the ruins of the McNair castle. Emma stopped to study it for a moment, moving to the side of the path so Broderick could move past. Lochlaven was barely visible through the trees, and it struck her that the two structures were separated by both a narrow inlet of water and centuries.

The damp breeze was a caress against her cheek, the sunlight filtering through the trees a soft welcome. Emma would have liked to linger in that one spot, but their party was in pursuit of the summit. She cast one longing look toward the ruins of Lochlaven Castle before lifting her skirts and following them in silence.

She'd never been given to adventure. Her life had been mostly sedate, until her marriage to Anthony. This journey to Scotland had proven to her that travel was not easy, nor as exciting as she'd once imagined. Train travel was a bit frightening, and riding in a boat could be difficult on the stomach.

"Are you all right, Emma?"

She looked up to find that Ian had separated from the rest and come back to see why she was falling behind.

"I must confess that my mind was wandering," she said. "I was not as intent upon my destination as I was my thoughts."

He stepped to the side of the path and waited until she came level to him, then matched his strides to hers so they were climbing to the peak together.

"Were your thoughts that onerous?"

"I think they were, yes," she said. "I was thinking that travel wasn't as pleasant as I envisioned it to be.

Perhaps that's the same with all things we imagine. They're never quite as attractive in reality."

He didn't say anything in response. Nor did she glance over at him to see his reaction to her words.

"I discovered how your maid left Lochlaven," he said a few minutes later. "The supply wagon. We send it once a week to Inverness, and it's just now returned."

She glanced over at him.

"According to the driver, she decided to return to London. She said that she'd never agreed to come to Scotland."

Emma stared down at the path. "That's true," she said.

"That doesn't mean she's innocent," he said.

"I know." Juliana had been on her mind for the last three days. Try as she might, however, Emma couldn't come up with a reason why the maid would have wanted to murder Bryce. Nor was he yet conscious and able to give them any information.

Ian shrugged. "I'm going to send some men to Inverness to see if they can find her. Perhaps she knows something. I'm not as forgiving as you."

"You think I was wrong in not reporting Anthony's murder," she said.

"Yes," he said simply. "At the same time, I can understand why you didn't."

"I just wanted it over," she said. "I just wanted to forget those years."

"Is that what you do?" he asked. "When circumstances are too difficult, you simply pretend they didn't happen?"

She glanced at him to find him studying her, his eyes turbulent.

"Anthony, yes."

"And me?"

It wouldn't be wise to tell him that she hadn't yet found a way to pretend that the interlude in London hadn't happened.

She only shook her head, a wordless admission that she couldn't answer his question.

"I haven't forgotten."

"Do you think you should mention that now? When Rebecca might hear? Or Patricia?"

"My sister and her husband have eyes and ears for no one but themselves," he said.

She glanced ahead to where Patricia and her husband were holding hands as they walked.

"And Rebecca?"

"Do you think," he said softly, "if you and I were engaged to be married, that we'd hold hands? Or after we've been married for two years, still look at each other in such a way?"

She was entirely too warm, and it wasn't the summer afternoon that was affecting her.

"Ian," she said softly, "please do not do this."

"A man can think. There aren't any penalties for thoughts."

"As long as they remain unvoiced," she said.

He stopped, turned and looked at her.

Had anyone else ever looked at her the way Ian did? Did he study her to imprint her in his thoughts and his memory? As if he knew how she should look and was measuring the reality of her against an image he'd already formed in his mind. As if he wanted to know every one of her thoughts and value them, unspoken.

"Being around you, Emma, is sometimes hell."

She stared at him. What did she say to that? How did she defend herself?

"We should avoid each other, then," she said.

For a few moments the only sound was the leaves and the twigs crunching beneath their feet.

"You've already been avoiding me," he said.

She sent an irritated glance toward him, one that he correctly interpreted, if his smile was any indication.

"Avoiding me only lessens the time we spend together, Emma. It has no effect on my thoughts."

She stopped in the middle of the path and turned. "Ian, you mustn't think of me. I mustn't think of you."

Dappled sun danced through the leaves and played upon his shoulders. He might have been a Celt of old, one of the original McNairs. A man destined to know his own future and still stride confidently toward it.

He was a devastating person to know, and by knowing him—remembering him—she also had to fight against him. He was a much greater temptation than any she'd ever known. Those years at Chavensworth felt simple now and almost easy compared to the chore and the necessity of pushing Ian away.

Because one part of her, perhaps the whole of her, didn't want to be proper and moral. She wanted, even now, to walk into his embrace and allow him to hold her. She could tell herself it was a farewell gesture, but that lie died before it could be born. She dared not touch him, or think about those days in London, or dream of his kiss.

He reached out and plucked a bit of leaf from her shoulder. But his hand lingered, the warmth of his fingers felt even through her dress. The pretty yellow dress Rebecca had given her.

She bowed her head and concentrated on the shine of his shoes, the drape of his trousers at the ankle. Anything but his eyes and the tender expression that shouldn't be there.

"I always thought I was strong," she said softly.

"And you don't think so now?"

She merely shook her head from side to side.

Emma regretted this moment more than any other moment in her entire life. She regretted the need to step away from him, turn and continue on her way. She resented having to do something so virtuous, and so terrible. He was a man with whom she might have found happiness. He was a man she respected and admired, and had perhaps come to love. Her experience with love was lamentable, but if it meant that a person felt unfinished, unaware, and only half alive without another, then it was truly love she felt for this man.

A forbidden love that no one would understand.

"Forgive me, Emma. I would not add to your burdens."

"Then do not seek me out anymore, Ian. Please. We only knew each other for three days," she said softly. "We don't know the important things about each other."

"On the contrary," he said. "I know the depth of your courage. I know what kind of books you like, that you love flowers, that you've never experienced simple pleasures. I know you're afraid to feel, and yet you give of yourself with such freedom that it awes me. What else is more important than that?"

Silence surrounded them, as if even the forest creatures and the birds quieted to listen to his words.

She forced herself to look at him directly. "Are you asking me to be an adulteress, Ian? Are you asking me to be what everyone thinks I am? Immoral and profane?"

"No," he said softly.

"Then what do you want from me?"

He placed his hand on the back of his neck and looked up as if seeking guidance from the clouds. Finally, he blew out a breath and looked at her.

"This is not the conversation I meant to have with you," he said. "I wanted to talk to you about Juliana."

She halted on the path and waited.

"I went back and tested all three bottles again. At first I thought it would be impossible because there was little of the wine left, but there was enough."

"What did you find?"

"The bottle containing the arsenic was from the crate. Not the bottle Juliana purchased in Inverness."

She understood immediately. "The crate from London," she said.

He nodded.

"The crate from your uncle's cellar."

Chapter 28

~ C ~

Suddenly, Rebecca was advancing on them, her skirts held up with both hands, her smile fixed and determined.

"What are you two talking about back here? You both look so earnest and serious."

"Bryce," Emma said, finding the ability to lie came quickly and easily to her.

Let Ian judge her for that.

Rebecca's face instantly transformed into a sympathetic look.

"My dear Emma, I am certain he is on the road to recovery. I am quite certain he is going to be well any day. Don't you agree, Ian?"

Instead of answering her, he looked ahead. "I think we're nearly there, are we not?"

"Ian, you know the island far better than I," Rebecca said, sending him a fond smile.

Ian turned to Emma. "We're nearly at the summit. There are some ruins here. Roman, I suspect."

Rebecca grabbed Ian's right arm with both her hands and smiled up at him.

"Dear Ian, have you told Emma of our plans for our wedding? I was saying, just this morning, that

she really should plan to attend. Don't you agree?"
she said.

"Of course," he said.

Emma smiled politely, an effort that was nearly
beyond her.

Please, God, do not let me be here when Ian marries.

"Ian says that he met you in London," Rebecca said.
"Before you and Bryce were married."

Emma glanced at Ian, uncertain how to respond.
Why on earth had he said that? How did she tell
Rebecca that he'd pretended to be a burglar? Or that
she'd realized, all too soon, that he wasn't exactly the
brigand he pretended to be?

What would Rebecca say if she told her the truth?
*I was a slave to passion, dear Rebecca, and Ian was my
master.*

He might still be.

"Instead of discussing the past," Patricia said,
coming down the path, "I'm more concerned with
the future. Whose idea was it to have your wedding
ceremony on the island? Yours or Ian's? He's always
loved this place ever since he was a boy."

Rebecca smiled at her future sister-in-law. "It was
Ian's but I confess I really don't care where the cer-
emony is held. It's simply enough that I get to marry
Ian."

"Which is exactly how my wife felt about marrying
me," Fergus said, generating a smile from his wife.

The glance they shared was filled with passion, but
there was nothing of licentiousness or lust in their
gaze. Instead, this was love, so direct and so forceful
that Emma could not help but feel it.

Rebecca no doubt felt the same, because she sighed
a little.

"When Ian and I are married," she said, smiling up at him with artless candor, "we shall be just as much in love."

Emma excused herself and began to walk ahead.

Rebecca must have said something amusing because both Fergus and Ian laughed.

A charming young woman. No doubt innocent and virtuous, as well. Why did that thought annoy her?

The forest abruptly fell away as they reached the summit. The area was larger than she imagined, the top of the hill flattened as if by a giant's hand. Pine needles were layered over what looked to be limestone, or perhaps granite, some grayish stone that sparkled in the afternoon sun.

From here she had a view all around the island, as well as the lake stretching to the horizon.

Broderick began to open the baskets, spreading a cloth on the ground. The top of the hill was a lovely place for an outing, and an even more magnificent spot for a wedding ceremony.

Sadness surrounded her, seeped inside her, as if it were a damp and pervasive fog. Emma held herself tight, walking closer to a low wall that looked out of place for this hilltop. The wall stretched only about nine feet in length, of pale red brick that had crumbled in places. She peered over it to find herself looking down to a sheer drop. At the bottom were jagged boulders. Perhaps the Romans had built this as a retaining wall. Or a caution to anyone not to venture too close to the edge.

Were these the ruins Ian meant?

She turned to ask, only to find him with his head bent toward Rebecca, their conversation evidently a personal one.

Envy curled in her stomach. Rebecca would have him with her during all the small, unimportant moments that made up life. She'd be able to smile at him across a table, have him hold her hand, have him touch her face with tenderness in his fingertips and mirrored in his eyes.

Rebecca would be his companion for all those years, for decades of conversations, of mundane questions interspersed with laughter. Rebecca would be the one to bear his children, hear his tales of triumph, and cajole him from despair.

Suddenly, she wanted to be away from all of them. She wanted to be alone, a condition in which she'd found herself in the last eighteen months, one that suited her best. Without people there was no one to criticize her, no one to speculate on her past, no one to whisper tales that may or may not be true. No one to hurt her.

When she was a child, her mother had vanished for long stretches of time, creating niches of silence for herself. Sometimes she'd be found in the upstairs parlor. Sometimes Emma viewed her in the garden, sitting on a bench, staring at the flowers so intently it was as if she were listening to them. For years she wanted to know why her mother was so content in her own company, and now she knew why.

Silence was a friend. The absence of people meant safety. People could hurt you. Or if they didn't hurt you, they lured you to think that you could be someone you weren't. Someone who could laugh and be at ease, who could trust and believe in an impossible future.

What she was feeling was not a physical pain. This was a sorrow so vast and so deep that it felt as large as the lake surrounding the island.

Turning, she began to walk back the way she'd come, glancing over her shoulder at the others. No one noticed her departure. Broderick was intent upon laying out luncheon. Fergus and Patricia were immersed in each other. Rebecca had both hands clamped around Ian's arm as if she were afraid she'd fall without his support.

Emma began to follow the path, descending into the forest again. Without the others, she could hear the sounds of the birds. In that moment she wished she could become a creature of the forest itself. She would let her hair flow free, dress in a simple shift, and converse only with the squirrels, the foxes, and the birds.

When she saw the abandoned castle through the trees, she stepped off the path, holding her skirts up a little higher than was proper, and began to walk toward the original home of the McNairs.

The castle was little more than a moss-covered ruin, three walls leaning toward each other. No roof remained, and only fallen stones marked where the rest of the castle had stood.

The air was thick and heavy, the pattern of light filtering through the trees almost magical. Emma wondered if she'd stumbled onto an enchanted spot. If she remained motionless, would the castle rise up, the ruins reforming into walls and rooms and roofs until the structure was whole again? Then the structure would speak to her in a thickly burred voice, in an accent from an earlier time. A voice with sorrow in it, or even anger that it had come to being this: a blight upon the landscape, when it had once housed warriors.

She walked through the nearly knee-high grass, scrunching up her skirt with both hands.

The McNairs of an earlier day must have had to bring in all their food by boat, along with those items they could not make themselves and for which they'd traded.

From here she could see the promontory of land on which Lochlaven had been built. How long ago had the McNairs left their island fortress? When their fortunes improved? When they longed for more civility, and less barbarity?

She would ask Bryce. Surely he would know of his family's history.

As to her own history, she could not imagine her uncle a murderer. Perhaps, if the poison was in only one bottle, it had been an accident of some sort.

Emma bowed her head, the silence surrounding her. In this place, peopled only by ghosts, she felt curiously at peace. Not happy or content but resigned.

Perhaps she was not destined to know love, not the way she'd always longed for it. Yet there were other compensations to life, and she would have to find them, list them, review them daily so as to gain hope and wisdom and the courage to live completely and without resentment.

"I cannot blame you," Patricia said.

Emma whirled to find that Ian's sister had followed her and was standing only a few feet away. For once she was not accompanied by Fergus.

"You've escaped us," Patricia said. "Quite well, too. If I didn't know for certain you've never been here, I might think you know your way around the island."

She advanced on Emma, smiling. When she reached her side, Patricia's voice softened. "Is it Rebecca? She can be cloying, can't she?"

"I just wished a few moments to myself."

"I'm always a little concerned about women who are excessively sweet," Patricia said, as if Emma hadn't spoken. "I haven't the temperament. All you need do is ask Fergus—he will verify that only too quickly." She raised an eyebrow at Emma. "Are you sweet, Emma?"

Emma smiled, amused. "Unfortunately, I'm not. There are times when I would truly like to be. But I haven't the temperament, either."

"I think we shall be fast friends, you and I. Now, if we could only convince Rebecca to do something utterly wicked."

"Wickedness is overrated," Emma said.

Patricia laughed.

"Have you known Rebecca long?" Emma asked.

Patricia considered the question before answering. "I have. Nearly ten years. Ever since she was a little girl, coming with her father to Ian's laboratory."

She leaned closer to Emma. "I think this marriage is a bit of convenience, myself. There she was, of marriageable age, the daughter of someone my brother respects a great deal. And there he was, quite a catch, an earl, wealthy, intelligent, and beyond handsome." She smiled. "He's my brother but I'm as good a judge of masculine beauty as anyone. Do you not think him handsome?"

Emma didn't quite know how to answer that question. If she gave Patricia the truth—that every time she saw him, her heart beat faster—that comment would give her feelings away, would it not? So she settled for a smile that assuaged Patricia well enough.

"I wish he'd find someone to love," Patricia said, her voice growing pensive. "Someone not convenient at all but to match his temperament. Instead, I think he halfway offered for Rebecca because of money."

It was quite ill-bred to speak of money, having it or not having it. Still, Emma couldn't quite tamp down her curiosity.

"What do you mean?"

"Oh, Ian has plenty of it. But she has nothing. Dr. Carrick doesn't practice as a physician any longer. If it wasn't for Ian's money, I don't doubt they'd be in dire straits."

She looked a little shamefaced. "There I go. At least I told you I wasn't sweet. I have a termagant's temper, my Fergus says. Of course, I fuss at him sometimes, only to apologize in the most appropriate way." She smiled again and the same look came into her eyes that Emma had seen earlier that day—the look of a completely satisfied woman.

Emma followed Patricia back to the path. A few minutes later she and Patricia reached the summit. Their luncheon had been arranged, and everyone but the two of them was sitting on a large cloth Broderick had spread on the ground.

There were no formal seating arrangements, as there might have been at dinner. Rebecca sat beside Ian, and on Ian's other side, Broderick. Beside him was Fergus, who Patricia joined. Emma sat on Patricia's right side, with no one next to her, feeling as out of place now as she had earlier.

Rebecca began to speak of the wedding ceremony, how Ian would be wearing a kilt, and she a sash across her dress.

"There isn't a McNair tartan, per se," Rebecca said. "But I found one that I think will do." She tilted her chin down and looked up at Ian. A coy look that Emma had seen performed more than once by women of Anthony's acquaintance.

She looked away rather than watch the spectacle. Perhaps she simply needed to be in Rebecca's company a little longer. After all, the girl had done nothing to her. Rebecca had gone out of her way to be charming and welcoming.

Her own character, mottled and filled with holes, was to blame for her irritation and no doubt the reason she was getting a spearing pain over her left eye.

Sitting here under a cloud-filled blue Scottish sky, the breeze from the lake blowing gently across her face, it was almost possible to believe that nothing was amiss in her life. The day was bucolic, the company charming, but just below the surface pulsed too many questions for which she had no answers.

Who had poisoned Bryce? Had it been an accident or a deliberate and evil act?

What was she supposed to do about these unwanted and unwelcome feelings for Ian McNair?

Would Bryce be so easily convinced by a few fluttering lashes? She'd have to attempt it. Anything to get him quickly out of his sickbed and into a carriage.

In this lovely setting, with the breeze brushing against her cheek with the tenderness of a lover, Emma made a vow. She would do everything within her power, with no reservations, with patience and determination, to be a good wife to Bryce. If he was unhappy in their marriage, it would not be because of any lack of effort on her part.

Ian glanced at her from time to time. She wanted to tell him that she was fine, thank you, and that he should not express any concern as to her health. He mustn't be tender, or considerate, and above all he should not talk to her in a low tone, the one that made her feel as if his voice were caressing her.

Patricia suddenly looked up, then spoke to Ian. "Do you see that?" she asked, pointing toward the house.

All of them looked toward Lochlaven. For a moment Emma didn't know what Patricia meant but then another flash of light came from an upstairs window, as if a mirror had been angled to reflect the light. The flash came again, then a third time.

Ian stood. "Something's wrong," he said. He glanced down at Patricia, then the rest of them. "It's our signal to come home," he said. "Our parents used it when we stayed too long on the island."

"Ian," Patricia said, joining him. "Look."

Emma stood and walked to where the others were congregating.

A woman with bright blond hair—Glenna?—stood in the garden, waving her arms over her head.

"Something has happened to Bryce," Emma said.

Everyone was looking at her with various degrees of compassion. Finally, she glanced at Ian.

"I'll take you back, Emma," he said.

A look of displeasure slipped over Rebecca's face. "Nonsense, Ian. Broderick will be more than happy to do so." She nodded at the young man and he smiled in response.

Emma started toward the path she'd taken earlier, beginning to descend the hill, paying no attention to the tracery of shadows from the overhanging trees. The silence of the forest was not a fitting backdrop to her tumultuous thoughts.

"Emma," Ian said from behind her.

Evidently, he'd won the battle on who would row her back to the house. She wanted to ask him if Rebecca was angry that he'd accompanied her. Doing so, however, would be petty.

Instead, she said, "You're going to tell me it could be anything," she said. "That it doesn't have anything to do with Bryce at all."

"I was," he said, smiling lightly. "I take it you wouldn't have listened."

"What else would be important enough for people to signal you on the island?"

He didn't hesitate. "Nothing."

Soon she was at the rocks. Ian untied one of the boats and helped her in, then sat opposite her. Although he was the equal of Broderick in strength, it couldn't have been easy to row against the lake's current. Yet there was no sign of exertion on his face, as if he had done this many times before and was accustomed to it.

The look in his eyes, however, was almost as turbulent as the waters beneath them.

"I should have kept you in my room," he said.

He looked at her, as if he knew quite well that her heart was suddenly racing, the blood heating her skin throughout her body. "You wouldn't have wed, and we could have been together."

"For a little while," she said.

The water lapped against the side of the boat, as if vying for attention.

"Nothing would have changed," she said. "I would have still been forced to marry Bryce."

"Not if I had spirited you away to Scotland," he said. "I've a fortune of my own. There is nothing your uncle could have done if I'd married you in Scotland."

Why was he doing this? Why was he heaping misery onto misery?

She looked directly at him, almost daring herself to tell him the truth.

"If you'd taken me away to Scotland, I would have been horrified."

Then, perhaps, but not now. She'd learned too much in a matter of weeks, not the least of which was what she felt for him.

They were almost back at Lochlaven and she glanced at the dock in relief.

"It's too late now, Ian. It's too late to be a brigand, and too late to wonder what would have happened, and too late to feel regret. It isn't our time."

"It's never too late to feel regret, Emma," he said, pulling to the dock. "It's never too late for that. I'll feel that for the rest of my life."

"Your Lordship! Your Lordship!" Glenna shouted, running to the end of the dock. "It's Mr. Bryce."

"What is it, Glenna?" Ian was calmer than she, if his tone of voice was any indication.

"He's awake, Your Lordship, and calling for his wife."

Chapter 29

"**W**ill you come with me?" Emma asked, turning to him.

"I think it best if you greet Bryce alone."

They exchanged a look, one that revealed her reluctance only too easily.

"Send word to me if he's feeling well enough for visitors," he said. "I'll visit him later. There's something I need to do right now."

A task he should have performed the moment he returned from London.

If Glenna had not been standing there, he would have bent and placed a kiss on Emma's forehead and whispered that she was stronger than she knew. Instead, he only smiled at her, watched her walk away with Glenna, then turned and headed for his laboratory.

He'd been groomed to be the Earl of Buchane, as well as the Laird of Trelawny. His heritage had been taught him by a succession of good men, each of them handpicked first by his father, then his mother. He'd been grateful to each and every one of them for the knowledge they'd shared. Albert Carrick, however, was the teacher he'd selected in his adulthood, the man who fed his mind and inspired his enthusiasm.

For years he'd been Albert's apprentice, fascinated by Albert's quick and dexterous mind. When he'd first begun to investigate the theory of spontaneous generation, Albert had played devil's advocate, questioning every one of his hypotheses. If he was considered a man of science, it was because of Albert.

Yet the words he would speak today would probably destroy that strong bond between them.

Albert was hunched over his microscope, his attention on what most people couldn't see and didn't know—would never know—existed.

When Ian entered, Albert looked up and grinned. "I think you need to see this last batch of water from the spring," he said. A moment later his grin slipped. "What is it, Ian? Bryce?"

"He's awake," Ian said. "Thanks to you."

"Then what's put that frown on your face?"

"I've come to ask you to release me from our arrangement," Ian said abruptly. "I realize you have no obligation to do so, Albert, but I ask because I believe it would be the best for both Rebecca and me."

"You don't want to marry my girl, then?" Albert asked.

There were so many ways he could phrase the next words, so many excuses he could give Albert. But the man was the closest he'd ever had to a father since his own had died. Besides, Albert deserved the truth.

"There's someone else," he said. "If I cannot stop thinking of her now, when I'm engaged, how will I stop when I marry?"

"And if she's married?" Albert asked, his voice deceptively calm.

Ian had seen Albert in a temper, and he was capable of destroying a room. Nevertheless, he answered him, again with honesty.

"Then that makes me a fool, doesn't it?"

"I must tell you, Ian, that I'm disappointed."

Ian moved to the stool next to Albert and sat. He leaned forward, clasped his hands between his spread knees and nodded. "I know, and I'm sorry."

"Are you sure about this, Ian?" Albert asked. "Thoughts can change, feelings can be altered."

"I'm sure," Ian said. "I cannot marry one woman when I'm thinking of another."

Albert nodded.

"Then you'll tell her? As soon as you can?"

Ian nodded.

"Will this hurt us, Albert?" Ian asked.

Albert slowly straightened his shoulders.

"I would miss you, if you decided not to work with me anymore," Ian said. "At the same time, I would understand if you chose not to."

Albert studied him for several moments. "Is that what you want, Ian?"

"I want what's best for you, old friend. We can always communicate by post. And we've had enough experience working separately during those times I travel to London."

Albert bent his head, his intense gaze fixed not on Ian but the brass microscope in front of him. For the longest time, he didn't speak.

"She's my girl, Ian. My only child. I'll need to take her home."

"I know you think that I haven't acted with honorable intent, Albert. If so, then I'm sorry. But I couldn't be false to Rebecca. I have too much admiration for you, and fondness for her."

Albert nodded, as if he'd expected Ian's speech, and paid it as little heed as he did the sight of the lake from the window.

"I'll finish up this series," he said, his voice curiously devoid of emotion. "And then I'll take her home."

"What about the work, Albert? Our partnership?"

"That I'll decide as I go," Albert said. "As I go."

Albert said nothing further, only retreated to his microscope. A moment later Ian did the same. Sometimes, science was easier than dealing with people.

By the time she and Glenna made it to the sickroom, Bryce was half propped up on two pillows, looking not completely well but certainly less ill than he had yesterday.

Emma halted in the doorway and regarded the tableau with surprise.

In the intervening days, Bryce's beard had grown. Now, a young man was shaving him, having arranged a towel around his neck, and equipped with a wicked-looking straight razor, a cup filled with lather, and a bowl of hot water.

"Good afternoon," Emma said, entering the sickroom fully. Although it might have been expected to feel shy around the man, they were, after all, married. And had been for nearly two weeks now. Yet in all that time, she'd exchanged less than a few dozen words with Bryce.

He glanced in her direction.

"I understand we're at Lochlaven," he said.

His voice came slowly, as if he were unaccustomed to words. Or perhaps it was simply painful for him to speak.

She walked to the end of the bed, clasping her hands in front of her.

Glenna took over for the young man, rinsing the soap from Bryce's face and then drying it, each of her motions quick and efficient. The woman did everything with an economy of movement, as if she reasoned out each task beforehand, to determine the best way to bathe a patient's face, or fold a sheet, or even to care for a patient's more intimate needs.

"You were poisoned, Bryce. Who would wish to do such a thing?"

He looked unsurprised. Had Glenna already told him?

"Dare I think that that is genuine emotion I see on your face, Emma? Were you worried about me?"

Her years of experience in not revealing her emotions served her well. If she'd not crumbled when facing Anthony, she certainly wasn't going to do so in front of Bryce McNair.

"Yes," she said. "I should not like to think of anything happening to you. Especially arsenic poisoning. You were very ill."

He closed his eyes, and the gesture wasn't that of a man recovering from illness as much as one who was deliberately shutting her out. Still, she didn't move away from the bed.

"Do you know of anyone who might have done this to you?" she asked softly, uncaring that Glenna was standing so close and could hear every word. "Or why anyone might wish you ill?"

"No," he said, another rebuff.

She made her way to the chair in the corner and sedately sat.

He opened his eyes and looked over at her. "You've given up your widow's clothing," he said. "Was that in anticipation of my survival?"

"No," she said calmly. "It was because you were sick all over my dress, and if you remember, you didn't care enough to find my trunk in Inverness."

He only smiled, an expression that prickled the skin at the back of her neck.

Although it wasn't necessary for her to love her husband, Emma wished she could respect him. So far, however, his actions hinted at a man whose character was lamentably weak.

Yet who was she to criticize others, coveting a man not her husband?

Long after Glenna finished her chore and Bryce had fallen back asleep, Emma sat where she was. It wasn't her role as wife that kept her in place but the vow she'd made on the island.

Ian stood at the window, staring up at the white nothingness of the moon, as if someone had torn a hole in the fabric of the sky and not yet patched it.

A reiver's moon, it was called in the old days, when Scottish lairds and their clans rode across the glens to steal cattle from their neighbors. McNairs hadn't gone reiving for a hundred years or more but he had a sudden yearning to get on a fast horse and ride the hills around Lochlaven.

"Father said you wished to talk with me," Rebecca said from behind him.

He turned from the window to face her. He'd prepared carefully for this meeting, wearing one of his

London suits, his hair carefully combed, his shoes polished to a shine.

Perhaps he simply wished her last memory of him to be a good one.

She took a seat on the sofa, reaching for the tray he'd ordered for this meeting. Rebecca began to pour. Although he didn't want any tea at the moment, he took the cup and saucer she handed him.

"You're breaking our engagement, aren't you?" she said, surprising him. "There's no other reason for you to look so somber. Either that, or father is ill, and I know that isn't true, so it must be our marriage."

"Yes," he said, grateful to her for making it so easy. "I'm breaking our engagement. Although I'd much rather it be said it was your decision."

She nodded. "You haven't been the same since returning from London," she said.

"I'm sorry for that," he said.

She still wore a smile, as if she were perfectly amiable about the change of plans. He knew better. She was no longer going to be a countess. The elevation in rank had interested her almost as much as becoming his wife.

But perhaps he was being unkind, and for this meeting he should summon up his compassion and regret. At the moment, however, what he truly felt was an overwhelming sense of relief, an indication that he'd made the right decision.

"She's married, Ian," Rebecca said softly, startling him.

She looked directly at him. Had he been so obvious? Or was Rebecca simply more astute than he'd realized?

"I know, Rebecca."

"She's married, and it pains you, doesn't it? It hurts you. It truly hurts you."

"Rebecca—" he began.

She shook her head. "We've always been honest with each other, you and I, Ian. There's never been a time when we found it necessary to lie."

Except now, with her guileless gaze spearing him.

"You hold yourself differently when you're around her," she said.

"I don't know what you mean."

She smiled. "You either hold your hands behind your back or they're balled into fists. Your shoulders are tight and even your jaw is clenched. As if you need to hold onto yourself in case you do something shocking."

She looked down at the tea tray before returning her gaze to his face. "Is that what you feel, Ian? As if you're going to do something shocking?"

He didn't answer her because there wasn't a damn thing he could say. He could lie but he disliked telling falsehoods, especially now. Besides, what could he say to explain what he felt for Emma?

Rebecca had it only half right. He might have been able to restrain his body. His mind was another matter entirely.

"I told myself you loved me, but I think you only wished to marry me because it was convenient," she said, her tone conveying no emotion whatsoever, as if she were reciting a paragraph from some scientific treatise. "Because you and my father work together."

He remained silent. If she wanted the truth, let silence speak for him.

She nodded, as if unsurprised that he didn't defend himself, or their engagement.

After a moment she stood, graceful and womanly, possessed of all the virtues and talents he could wish in a wife. Rebecca's heart was warm and open; her demeanor was generous and sweet. She would have supported him in any of his endeavors; she would have been a good mother to their children.

But a complicated and confusing woman fascinated him. A woman who was not free to be his wife. One whose past darkened the whole of her future, and for whom it would be necessary to continually hold up a lamp to dissipate the shadows around her. Yet despite the very real barriers between them, his mind was occupied with Emma. His body only followed suit, and to his dishonor, Rebecca knew it.

Virtue and vice—perhaps that's what they were in his mind. Or something even more elemental. He felt a warm affection for Rebecca. But what he felt for Emma was something deeper, darker, and less decipherable.

"You cannot have her, Ian. Don't you know that?"

He smiled. "I know that only too well, Rebecca."

She held herself straight and tall, a small and pleasant smile curving her lips. Her gaze, however, was uncomfortably sharp as she studied him.

"I wish you would have looked at me the way you look at her. Just once, Ian. But you never did."

He didn't have an answer, silence being the best recourse. What he felt for Emma could not be explained; it was enough that it existed, even if it was never reciprocated in the future.

Together, the two of them would be honorable. She would be loyal to Bryce, and he would be loyal to her.

A damnable thing, really, since he'd never set out to be a martyr and the role didn't fit him well.

Chapter 30

Emma spent most of her days attending to Bryce. Her meals were taken on a tray in either her room or the sickroom. She left his side late and arrived early, and by such means was able to avoid the other inhabitants of Lochlaven with the exception of Mrs. Jenkins. The housekeeper visited once a day, to ensure that Emma and Bryce had everything they needed.

She couldn't help but wonder if Ian had requested Mrs. Jenkins to do so.

Surprisingly enough, she'd dealt quite well without her maid. But then, she always had, accepting Juliana's presence as a necessary evil. Still, Juliana's disappearance niggled at her. Had Ian sent men to look for her? Rather than seek him out and ask, she decided it was better to live in ignorance.

Bryce and she never talked. When he was awake, which wasn't often, it was to complain of the light or the silence or the feel of the nightshirt or a dozen other things that bothered him.

The third day following Bryce's awakening, Emma was sitting in the chair, her gaze on the lake beyond, an unopened book on her lap. From her viewpoint she couldn't see anything of the island, which was just as well.

"I knew you'd be here," Patricia said.

Emma looked up and smiled at Ian's sister.

"Fergus and I are leaving tomorrow, and I did want to spend some more time with you. Will you join us for dinner tonight?"

"Is it that time already?"

"Nearly," Patricia said, her smile oddly kind.

Emma felt a little uncomfortable being the recipient of Patricia's kindness. She wasn't the type of woman to whom other people were considerate. She was the former Duchess of Herridge, a woman envied for her title, if not her inherited wealth.

But Patricia didn't know any of that, and if she was kind, it was due to the circumstances of Bryce's illness.

"I know that Glenna stays with him at night," she said, glancing at the sleeping Bryce. "Perhaps she could simply come earlier. I really think it's important that you come to dinner, Emma."

There was something in her expression, something Emma couldn't read.

"After all, it will only be Fergus, Ian, and myself."

In the silence, Emma wondered if Patricia was waiting for her to ask about the whereabouts of Ian's fiancée. Finally, she could bear it no longer. "Will Rebecca and Dr. Carrick not be in attendance?"

Patricia came and sat beside Emma, in the very same chair Ian had used so many nights ago. He was very careful never to visit Bryce when she was there, and she found that both a blessing and a curse. He was making it so much easier for her, and at the same time she missed the sight of him.

"Didn't you know?" Patricia said. "They've broken their engagement."

Emma gazed down at her clasped hands.

"No," she said slowly, "I didn't know."

"Ian swears it was Rebecca's decision, but I know that she would never do such a thing. But I, for one, applaud it. I never thought that he and Rebecca would suit."

Bryce stirred and both women looked over at the sickbed.

"Should he not be up and about by now?" Patricia asked.

"Glenna and I both think so," Emma said. "But he seems very weak. He can't hold a cup, and it's nearly impossible for him to rise to a sitting position by himself."

Patricia turned to her. "Is that common in arsenic poisoning?"

"I don't know," Emma said. "I had it in my mind to ask Dr. Carrick, but I haven't seen him in the last few days. I didn't know it was because he'd left Lochlaven."

"He may be returning. Not Rebecca, of course. You see, you should come to dinner and tell Ian that Bryce needs a doctor's care."

"Could you simply not send him word?"

"No," Patricia said firmly. "You shall have to do it." She stood. "I'll tell Cook that you'll not require a tray tonight. You will join us?"

She only nodded, and Patricia smiled, then turned and left the room.

When it was time, Emma left the sickroom, climbing the stairs in the rear of the house to avoid the laboratory entrance and anyone who might be wandering about. When she entered her room, she went to the bathing chamber, ran cold water into the basin, and washed her face.

Finally, she surveyed herself in the mirror, content with her appearance. If her eyes had a few shadows beneath them, if she was paler than was attractive, if her expression held a little misery, that was to be expected due to Bryce's illness.

The dining room was located in the middle of the large house, a room directly opposite a comfortable-looking parlor. She hesitated at the door, startled to see that the three of them were standing at the window, laughing as they stared at the island. This room, too, faced the lake, now shrouded by night.

Ian saw her first, turned, and extended his hand to her. Amidst the laughter, it felt as if there was a sudden and unexpected silence as he stood there, watching her, his eyes darkening as his lips firmed.

"Come and join us, Emma," he said. "We're watching for ghosts."

She blinked at him, surprised. "Ghosts?"

Ian caught her hand and pulled her close to the window, then reluctantly released her.

Patricia turned to face her. Her smile was bright and welcoming, the beauty of her face enlivened by amusement.

"Ian and I have always vied to be the first to see one of the ghost ships of the McNairs. Evidently, our clan was filled with pirates, those who roamed the seas in search of treasure."

"And women," Ian added.

"Then they'd bring them home to the island and make them wash and clean," Patricia said.

"I think it's the other way 'round," Fergus said. "The women charmed them into capturing them and giving up all their chests of treasure."

Emma couldn't help but smile at their amusement.

"Is tonight a good night for ghost ships?" she asked.

"Every night is," Patricia said, "but especially when the wind is high and the moon is full."

One of the maids at the doorway interrupted their sport by carrying in a tray. Soon the four of them were seated at a long mahogany table adorned with a white lace runner, several silver pieces, and an array of lovely Spode dinnerware in shades of crimson, black, and gold.

A heavily carved mahogany sideboard sat on the far wall, adorned with a selection of silver and china. The long table easily sat twelve, each of the chairs upholstered in a peacock blue fabric. A carpet of a similar hue covered the floorboards. On the wall closest to her sat a massive fireplace, but instead of the customary mirror hanging over the mahogany mantel, a family portrait held pride of place.

A gray-haired man sat on a chair, and behind him stood a woman with her hand on his shoulder. The boy and the girl seated on either side of the older man were so alike in coloring and appearance that Emma knew this was the younger Ian and his sister Patricia.

What had life been like for him growing up here, at Lochlaven? Or had he gone away to school at an early age? She'd never been so curious about a man. Nor had she wanted to share memories of a time far in the past.

She would be better served by seeking to know more about Bryce. What had his early life been like? Had he resented the fact that his cousin was earl and not himself?

Who had poisoned him? A question that was never far from her mind, but she was no closer to understanding now than she'd been when first learning of the diagnosis.

Their dinner consisted of roast loin of mutton, currant jelly, Jerusalem artichoke soup, and a selection of vegetables, including brussels sprouts, potatoes, and fried broccoli. Not only was the meal delicious but it was a surprisingly delightful experience. Fergus kept them amused with tales related to him by the captains of his ships.

At the end of dinner, Patricia reached for Fergus's hand, then looked at Ian.

"I do wish our visit could have been longer," she said. "But there is a reason why we need to return to Edinburgh."

Fergus was looking at her with a mixture of pride and tenderness.

"You're going to be an uncle, Ian."

"Would it be indelicate of me to say that it was about time?" he asked, standing and going to his sister. He pulled her up and enveloped her in a hug. "I think you'll be a wonderful mother."

He pulled back and they stared at each other, both smiles identical.

"Mother," Ian said. "Does she know?"

"Not yet."

"Then bless you, dear sister, for giving her something to do other than focus her not inconsiderable energies on me."

He released her and went to Fergus, clasping his brother-in-law on the shoulder. "If it's a girl, Fergus, be prepared for her to run you a merry race, much as my sister did."

"And if it's a boy?" Fergus asked, a twinkle in his eye.

"Then he shall be handsome and intelligent, of course. And give you no trouble whatsoever."

Patricia's laughter was contagious. Emma found herself smiling, genuinely happy for the couple. She added her well wishes to those of Ian's. After a flurry of partings, the two of them left the dining room, leaving her alone with Ian.

They stood, almost at opposite ends of the table, almost in the same pose: each bracing one hand flat against the mahogany surface.

She looked over at him to find him watching her.

"Patricia's son might well be the next Earl of Buchane," he said.

She looked down at the surface of the table, newly cleared by the industrious maids. All that was left was the table runner, and her finger stroked the intricate pattern of the lace as she spoke.

"Then it was foolish of you to break your engagement."

"I had no other choice," he said, turning to stare out the window. "You came to Lochlaven. No matter what happens in the future, I will always remember you here. How can I marry one woman when I can't forget another?"

He turned and faced her.

"When I find release by my own hand," he said, "I think of you. When I wake hard, I think of you. Do you want to know how many nights I lay on my bed, unable to sleep with even a sheet against me, because I want you?"

She couldn't breathe.

He strode to her side, pulled her into his arms, bent his head and pressed his lips against her temple.

"I remember how we were together, Emma. I can't forget it. I can't forget you, God help me."

She bowed her head. "I can't do this, Ian."

He dropped his hands but didn't move. Her palms flattened against his chest, and for a moment, just a moment, she allowed herself the luxury of pretending that she belonged right there, so close she could feel the beat of his heart.

"The seventh day showed an unexpected decrease in bacterium involvement, consistent with the aqueous filter manipulation. However, most of the pattern involved—"

"Ian?"

He stepped back.

"What are you saying?"

"I'm just reciting my notes."

"Why?"

"So I can focus on something other than you," he said.

He'd done that once before, at Chavensworth. He was still breathing with some difficulty, his cheeks bronzed, the glitter of his eyes attesting to how swift and powerful passion rose between them.

The amusement she felt was laced with sadness. How wonderful he was, this earl with the scientific mind. How fascinating. How intriguing.

"When will Bryce be well enough to travel?" he asked.

"He needs to see a physician," she said. "He's still very weak."

"I'll arrange it. When he is well enough to travel, where will you go?"

"Back to London, no doubt."

"To your uncle's? Is that safe? Especially in light of what we suspect?"

"We don't have proof, however. Nor has Bryce been forthcoming with any answers."

"Have you asked him?" Ian said, evidently surprised.

She nodded. "He simply closes his eyes and refuses to speak with me."

"I don't want you going back to London, Emma."

She smiled. "That's not your decision, Ian. The house is mine," she said. "Or Bryce's, now. It will be safe enough."

"As your money is Bryce's. With any luck, he won't gamble it away."

"My uncle is a gambler," she said. "At least I have some familiarity with the vice. Anthony was always complaining about how much my uncle lost. He periodically threatened to refuse to give him any more funds."

She wrapped her arms around her waist.

"That's what they were arguing about," she said, the words coming back to her. *Do you think I'm going to just sit back and wait until you do to me what you did to the Duke of Herridge?*

Emma turned, staring at Ian, and repeated the words to him. "At the time, I thought they were talking about money. But if they weren't . . . " Her words faded away.

"Then it's something worse," he said.

Chapter 31

"**W**e need to talk with Bryce," Ian said.

She glanced at the mantel clock. "Tonight?" she asked, surprised.

"Tonight," he said.

They descended the stairs together in silence.

Bryce was sleeping when they entered the sickroom. Ian went to the corner, spoke to Glenna, and a moment later she gathered up her knitting, stuffed it in a cloth bag, and left the room without a word spoken.

Emma moved a ladder-back chair closer to the bed and sat, trying to pretend a composure she didn't feel.

How very odd that she sat at her husband's bedside with the man she loved in the same room, and felt no hypocrisy. She, who had lived with an understanding of society's duplicity, had no shame about her own.

Why was that?

Because she knew that, despite her wishes and her wants, she would not act on her feelings. Instead, she would be the very best wife to Bryce that she could be. Not because she loved him or even thought that she might come to love him, but because loving someone else had changed her.

She pitied Bryce because, while he acted as if he wanted none of the softer emotions, he was human, and people deserved to be loved. She pitied him, also, because someone wanted him to die.

Ian stood on the other side of the bed. He reached out one hand and placed it on Bryce's shoulder. A moment later he shook his cousin gently.

"Bryce," he said. "You need to wake up."

Bryce's lashes fluttered and he blinked a few times before groggily waking. A smile curved his lips when he saw Ian.

"Cousin," he said, his words a little slurred. "It's about time you came to see me. Where's the vaunted McNair hospitality?"

"I've been to see you many times, Bryce," Ian said.

Bryce's expression slid from forced amiability to something darker, a dislike he didn't bother to conceal.

"I'm so sorry to have put you to any trouble." He glanced over at Emma. "I see you've met my bride. Did she tell you she was an heiress?"

Ian folded his arms and looked down at his cousin.

Emma suspected that if Ian said something protective, they might not learn anything from Bryce. Let her husband say what he wanted about her. It simply didn't matter. She shook her head, a signal to Ian. He frowned at her but remained silent.

She placed her hand on her husband's arm.

"Bryce, you need to tell us who you think could have poisoned you," she said.

Ian leaned down and braced himself with one hand above Bryce's pillow.

"You mentioned a carriage trying to run you down in London," he said. "Was that before or after you told the Earl of Falmouth that you knew he'd murdered the Duke of Herridge?"

She stared at Ian, shocked. But she was not the only person startled by Ian's question. Bryce was looking at Ian in surprise.

"You're very clever, cousin," he said.

"Before or after?"

"After."

Emma stared at Bryce, hearing that one word and understanding the import of it.

Ian straightened, glanced over at Emma, his expression barely restrained. "Perhaps it would be better if you left the room, Emma."

"So that you can shout at each other? I'm not leaving."

Bryce glanced over at her, his mouth twisting in a grimace. "Your uncle is wrong, you know. He told me that you were a compliant sort. You haven't been, since the day we married."

"Nor do I intend to be, for the extent of our marriage," she said, quite amiably. "However long my uncle allows you to live, that is."

Bryce frowned.

Ian folded his arms again, stared down at his cousin. "I agree with Emma. Sooner or later, her uncle is going to succeed in killing you."

"You're very cordial with my wife, Ian. Have you fucked her yet? I've been told she's quite a spirited little mare after she's been put to the crop."

Violence suddenly shimmered in Ian's eyes.

Emma stood, stepped around the bed and placed her hand on Ian's arm. "Please," she said softly.

"So you have fucked her," Bryce said, closing his eyes. "At least one of the McNairs has dipped his wick in the heiress."

Emma could feel the tenseness of the muscles beneath her hand. She squeezed Ian's arm, a wordless plea for his restraint.

"The Earl of Falmouth will keep trying to kill you," Ian said, biting out the words. "Although, at this point, I say let him have you."

Bryce remained with his eyes closed, long enough for Emma to wonder if he was going to speak at all.

Was this what her married life was going to be like? Bryce being crude or no more receptive than a block of stone? At least he hadn't pretended an affection he didn't feel. Nor would she.

Bryce opened his eyes, turned his head and smiled. "What do you suggest I do, Ian? Go to the authorities? If I come forward, I also admit to extortion."

"Is that why my uncle forced this marriage?" Emma asked, needing verification from him. "Because of what you knew?"

"You were a payment," Bryce said. He didn't look at her, but concentrated on Ian instead. "I would have preferred cash."

Before either man could say another word, Emma escaped the sickroom.

Ian found her in the garden, after going to her room, the drawing room, and a dozen other chambers within Lochlaven. Emma was sitting on one of the stone benches his grandfather had erected in a particularly lovely part of the garden. The herbs and flowers overflowed their borders, so that when someone walked along the path, a scent of spice floated through the air.

The lights of the laboratory illuminated this part of the garden, cast the plants into shadow, gave midnight the color of silver.

He walked to where she sat, standing in front of her, remaining there until she looked up at him. Her eyes were surprisingly dry but the stricken look on her face was still in place, as if Bryce's words had etched that look on her features.

"I can't go back in there," she said, her voice trembling with emotion. "I can't go back to that life. It's diseased and depraved. I can't be married to *him*."

She stared out toward the lake, now a black mirror for the sliver of moon.

"I wondered why my uncle was so insistent on my marriage," she said. "Now I wonder if it wasn't simply because Bryce knew too much." She glanced at Ian. "Could it be because he wanted to be able to kill Bryce, and being married to me would keep him within reach?"

She stood, walked some distance away, her arms wrapped around her waist, then slowly returned.

"What kind of people do I have in my life?" she asked, a question he took as rhetorical. "What kind of monsters surround me?"

"Your fair share," he said.

He lifted his hand to place it on her shoulder, then withdrew it. She didn't want comfort. She wanted him to hear her, to see her, to understand her.

What she didn't understand was that he already did.

"Everyone needs someone to love them," she said.

"I had my father, but after my marriage to Anthony, I wondered if he truly loved me as much as he did the idea of having a daughter who was a duchess. My uncle loved my money more than me. I always knew that." She stared off toward the island. "I was twice the fool, wasn't I?"

"To want to be loved? By your uncle? Perhaps."

"Now is the time to humor me, McNair," she said, giving him an annoyed look. "Not the time for blunt honesty."

"On the contrary," he said, "you'd resent me if I treated you like an idiot. As everyone else has."

She smiled, a halfhearted expression but a smile nonetheless.

His Celtic forbearers had granted him a spirit of possessiveness, for the land, for Lochlaven, and for this woman. She was his. She'd always been his. From the first moment he'd seen her, he'd claimed her.

He'd enjoyed the company of other women, the passion and laughter shared. None of those moments, none of those women, had ever made him tremble. None of them had ever entwined themselves around his heart.

She was hurting now, and he wanted to ease her, but wouldn't do so with lies or half-truths.

"We're all fools when it comes to love, Emma," he said gently. "We lose our way, our common sense, our ability to think. We find ourselves studying the moon, and wondering why the thought of sleep is impossible. We all need love, Emma. You're not a fool to wish for it."

"What are we going to do now?" she asked.

"There is, unfortunately, nothing that can be done," he said. "Neither you nor your housekeeper reported

Anthony's murder. I doubt, very much, that Bryce is going to willingly admit to the authorities that he's guilty of extortion. Without his testimony, there's no proof your uncle is guilty of murder. Nor is there anything we can do to prove who is responsible for Bryce's poisoning."

"Why did he only poison one bottle?" she asked, a question he'd considered as well.

"Perhaps he didn't have enough time," he said. "They were arguing the day you left for Scotland, you said."

She nodded.

"But even that we can't prove," he added. "He could easily claim that it was contaminated before he received the shipment."

She continued to stare straight ahead. "So there's nothing we can do?" she asked, her voice hollow.

"I think Bryce has probably done it. He's cut your uncle off from any funds, and banished him from your house."

"I wish it had been someone from Chavensworth," she said. "I wish it had been someone who knew me as the Ice Queen and wanted me for himself. That would have been a great deal more tolerable than my own uncle."

"Yours is not the first family to be marked by greed," he said.

"But why did he do it?"

"You touched upon the reason yourself, I suspect. Evidently, your uncle and Anthony had some disagreements about money in the past. Perhaps Anthony gave him an ultimatum."

He hesitated before he asked the question, knowing that it would only cause her more pain.

"Why do you dislike wine, Emma?"

"It makes me sick," she said, turning to look at him.

"Has it always made you sick?"

The realization of what he was asking came swiftly. Abruptly, she sat on the bench.

"Oh, dear God," she said softly. "Ian, you don't think . . . But of course you do. What else could you think?"

She pressed her hands over her face, then dropped them and studied the gravel path.

"No," she said slowly. "It hasn't always made me sick. Not until the last year." She glanced up at him. "Was the wine meant for me?"

"I doubt it. He would need to rid himself of Bryce, first. But I suspect you were next on his list if you returned home a widow."

She wrapped her arms around her waist.

"What do we do now?"

He took a deep breath. Somehow, the words would have to be said. Somehow, he would have to find a way to believe them.

"You and Bryce will go on with your lives, somewhere away from your uncle. You and I will have to find a way to deal with the feelings between us."

"Why does that sound so difficult?" she asked, standing.

"Because it will be."

"Ian," she began, reaching up with one hand as if to place her palm against his cheek.

He stepped back before she touched him. For a moment they just stared at each other. Darkness added a regality to her features. The silence of the garden rendered the moment almost poignant.

She nodded, understanding. She dropped her hand and straightened, growing taller in those moments. Growing older, in a way, or perhaps it was simply that she became distant. The proper former Duchess of Herridge, the Ice Queen, his cousin's wife.

His love.

Chapter 32

The drawing room was strangely masculine, almost Georgian in its purity. The furniture was French but sparse. Only a settee, sideboard, two chairs, and a small table between them occupied the whole of it. No pianoforte sat against the wall, no curio cabinet filled with collections of objects stood in the corner. The walls, a pale French blue, were offset with panels of white, and cornices of carved thistles, like the ones she'd seen in a London garden.

Emma sat on the settee, turning to face the windows. The sky was gray-white; raindrops trickled down the glass. Fog erased the landscape, muted the sounds of the lake lapping at the apron of beach, and seemed to slow life itself. Wind, carrying a hint of autumn in its gusts, whined around the corners of Lochlaven, seeped in through the window pane, whispering her name. *Emma, come and walk with me. Let me billow your skirts, allow me to banish the cobwebs of your memories, and render you fresh and new.*

She almost succumbed.

Had it not been for the advancing wall of cold gray fog, she might have ventured outside while Bryce slept. As it was, she'd escaped to this room, needing some change of scenery.

She brushed the hair from her cheek with the back of her hand, wishing she might find a way to escape. Above all, she wanted to lose herself, become someone else for as long as she was able. Let her be a wraith, a ghost of the fog. Let her feel something other than this horrible emptiness that laced every hour and every minute of her day.

Tomorrow, she would leave Lochlaven.

Bryce was still weak, physically. His will, however, outpaced his body. He was determined to leave Lochlaven and Ian's hospitality with all possible speed.

Dr. Carrick had returned from Inverness three days ago. His demeanor, however, was not the same as it had been. Gone was the ready smile, and his eyes bore a troubled look. Emma couldn't help but wonder if he blamed her for his daughter's broken engagement. She didn't know what to say to him, so they avoided each other for the most part. When he came to examine Bryce, she would slip out of the room, although she had conferred with him about the mystery of Bryce's weakness.

"It is, no doubt, an effect of the arsenic," he said.

"Will he always have it?"

He looked as if he didn't want to answer her, but he finally did. "I don't know, Mrs. McNair. He ingested a great amount of the poison. He's fortunate to still be breathing. A little weakness is small enough price to pay."

Except that it wasn't a "little weakness." Bryce needed help to sit, and although he'd gradually gotten back enough strength in his hand to hold a cup, someone still had to feed him.

Serving as Bryce's nurse would keep her mind occupied, especially after tomorrow when they left Lochlaven.

She turned back from the window, knowing that her respite was drawing to a close. She would need to return to the sickroom, to Bryce's side.

Tears were too close to the surface of late but they wouldn't serve her now. Instead, she needed to show the same determination and stoic resistance she'd demonstrated during her marriage to Anthony.

Once, she'd thought about love in a theoretical way, almost as if it were an emotion she could harness, or an aged cask she could tap at will. She knew now that loving someone changed you from the inside out, made you more receptive to joy, made you think of others before yourself, opened your heart to kindness and laughter.

Love was simply there, like the moon and the stars.

When the heart was opened to love, life changed. Even if it wasn't right or proper or accepted by the world, once love came into a life, nothing was the same. Even if she could never touch him again, could not ever welcome him to her bed and to her body once more, she would love Ian McNair with her whole heart for her whole life.

When it had happened, she had no idea. Yesterday, or the day before, or in London when she'd stood at the window and willed him to return, brigand that he was. Or perhaps it had even happened earlier, that first night when he grabbed her hand and together they'd flown from her house. Or later in a shadowed garden or when she discovered passion in a stranger's arms.

Tomorrow, she would leave Lochlaven, this strange and fey place on the edge of a magical loch. She'd

never see Ian again, or if she did, it would be years
and years from now.

She could not bear this. But somehow, she must.

Glenna rushed into the room, her usual rosy face
leached white, her voice quavering.

"Mrs. McNair," she said, "you must come quickly.
Something terrible . . . please. Come."

Without waiting for Emma, she turned and ran
out of the room.

Emma entered the sickroom only steps behind
Glenna.

"I was gone just for a little while," Glenna said,
her voice trembling. "Just to get some biscuits from
Cook. I thought Mr. Bryce would like some, that it
might tempt his appetite." She turned and looked at
Emma. "He was asleep and I thought it would be all
right. It wasn't long. I swear."

Slowly, Emma approached the bed. Bryce wasn't
asleep. His legs were nearly off the bed, his body
angled strangely. Biscuits were scattered over the floor
along with a silver tray.

"Shall I fetch His Lordship?"

"Yes," Emma said, wrapping her arms around her
waist. "Please do."

Bryce's face was tinged blue, his eyes bulging. Both
hands were clenched, and there was a froth of blood
around his nostrils.

Emma walked around the fallen biscuits and to
the bed. She placed her fingers against Bryce's neck
in a vain attempt to find a pulse.

Arsenic hadn't killed Bryce. But someone had.

She turned and carefully walked to the corner and
sat in one of the chairs arranged there, sitting primly, as
she'd been taught by her governess, her face carefully

expressionless, as she'd been taught by her years of marriage to Anthony. No one looking at her would know what she was thinking or feeling.

The Ice Queen had frozen solid.

She couldn't think of what to do next.

How long did it take for Ian to arrive? She wasn't certain she knew, only that every passing second grew stranger, her mind incapable of resolving what her eyes saw.

She heard a noise and glanced toward the doorway to see Ian standing there, staring at Bryce. A look of disbelief washed over his face, no doubt the match to her own expression. He took a few steps into the room, followed by Glenna. The closer he came to Bryce's bedside, the stiffer he became. His shoulders straightened, his jaw rigid, his expression fixed.

"Emma," he said softly.

She looked up to find him reaching down to grip her hands in his. How very warm he was. Suddenly, she was standing up and his arms were around her.

That wasn't proper, was it? The widow being embraced at the scene of the murder.

She lay her cheek against Ian's chest, feeling as if her bones were turning to liquid. If he hadn't wrapped his arms around her at that moment, Emma was certain she would have lost the ability to stand on her own.

She let him lead her from the room, heard him give instructions to Glenna to summon Dr. Carrick. She wanted to say the words but somehow they wouldn't come—a physician couldn't help Bryce now.

Bryce was buried in the churchyard of St. Andrews Presbyterian Church in the village of Trelawny, his companions in death his mother, father, and baby sister.

Despite the fact that Ian had sent out letters of invitation to the funeral, the occasion was sparsely attended. Albert was present, along with his wife, Brenda; and Rebecca, who refused to look in Ian's direction, although she frowned at Emma from time to time. Patricia and Fergus were not present, Fergus deciding that too much travel would not be judicious for Patricia in her condition. Ian and Patricia's mother, the woman who had insisted that the parentless Bryce be brought home to Lochlaven all those years ago, was traveling in France and could not be reached.

Glenna sat to her right, with Ian beside the nurse, close enough that Emma could look over and see him but not so close as to be improper. Half his face was in shadow, revealing his strong, chiseled features. He stared straight ahead for most of the service. The one time he glanced at her, their gazes locked and each had been forced to look away.

For some reason, the Reverend William Marshall chose to dwell on the thought that Bryce had not been lost but simply gone before God, and that the congregation should give thanks for his three birthdays: his physical birth, his spiritual awakening, and his birthday into glory.

The minister sent several looks in her direction, no doubt in approval for Emma's tears. What would he say if he knew that her grief was for the promise of Bryce, for what he might have been, more than for who he was? She cried for the young boy who'd had no family, for the man who'd refused to be loved, for the invalid who'd been smothered.

Once the service was over, the carriage delivered them back at Lochlaven. Emma exited the carriage with Ian's help but didn't look at him again. Without a word to anyone, she simply mounted the stairs and went to her room, trying not to wonder who, among them, was a murderer.

Chapter 33

Someone at Lochlaven had killed his cousin.
   Someone at Lochlaven was a murderer.

Emma had retreated to her room, and Ian couldn't blame her. He had no explanation to give her, no rationale for what had been done to Bryce. He couldn't even explain it to himself.

Three days passed, and Ian felt as if he existed in a clear glass case not unlike those that held his experiments. He was changing, altering in some profound way, but he didn't know how to measure the change.

The home, of which he was so fond, had ceased to be a haven. Someone who walked among them had killed Bryce. Worse was the fact that, as the days passed, he became more and more certain of the identity of the murderer, and the thought sickened him.

A month ago everything was peaceful at Lochlaven. The winds blew across the lake, the pines gave off their pungent scent, the summer was advancing into autumn.

Emma had come to Lochlaven with Bryce. Glenna had come back from her schooling in London. Patricia and Fergus had visited. In addition, one thing had substantially altered his life in the last month: the fact that he'd broken his engagement to Rebecca Carrick.

Ian walked into his laboratory and closed the door slowly behind him. Only rarely did he lock the door but he did so now, the snick of the mechanism sounding too loud in the silence.

He placed his hand flat against the door and leaned into it, wishing that he could push away his thoughts as easily. Slowly, he turned and walked through the first room, then into the second, reaching the third too quickly. He stood in the doorway and waited until Albert sensed his presence.

The older man was intent upon his microscope, his back curved, his head tucked into his neck like a turtle.

How many times had he seen Albert in such a pose? Ten years of work, a few days of every week—he couldn't even calculate it.

"Good morning, Albert," he said softly.

Albert slowly straightened. "Good morning, Ian," he said, turning slowly on his stool to face Ian. "Did you not sleep well? You don't look rested."

"I didn't, no," Ian said, advancing on his old friend. He pulled a stool close to Albert and sat. "I spent a goodly number of hours thinking."

Albert only smiled. The expression, coupled with that thick mass of black, springy locks, made Albert look like an aging, mischievous cherub.

"We employ thirty-seven people at Lochlaven," Ian said. "Did you know that?"

"I believe you might have mentioned it over the years," Albert said.

"That's not counting the farms, of course, and caring for the sheep."

"I will accept a number of fifty, if it makes you feel better," Albert offered, his smile deepening.

Ian forced an answering smile to his face. "Fifty, then. I know them all well. I've grown up with most of them. The newest employees are daughters and sons or nephews and nieces of those who have served Lochlaven for years."

"Is there a reason for this litany, Ian?"

Ian ignored the question and continued. "Ever since Bryce died, I've considered each man, each woman, and asked myself who could have brought murder to Lochlaven. I thought of Glenna. Then Mrs. Jenkins. A score of maids and footmen."

"Did you consider Emma, Ian?" The older man smiled again, but it was not a genial smile. Instead, it held a touch of bitterness.

"Not once," Ian said easily. "You see, Emma has a core of integrity. She was more than prepared to be a good wife to my cousin. She's also capable of enduring a great deal, a fact most people don't know about her. She's been tested by circumstance, and has behaved with decorum despite it."

"It seems to me that you have a reason, Ian. With Bryce dead, the avenue is clear to Emma."

Ian nodded. "You're right. Of all of us, I probably had the most reason to want Bryce dead. But I have the advantage, because I know I didn't kill him."

The older man didn't flinch as Ian stared at him.

"Imagine my shock when, after thinking of one person after another, I came to you."

No emotion shone from Albert's eyes; his face was

as expressionless as a death mask. Another sign, then, that he was right.

"How much did he pay you?"

"I don't know what you're talking about," Albert said, turning back to his microscope.

"You left for Inverness angry with me. I half expected you not to return. I wouldn't have been surprised to receive a letter from you telling me that you'd decided to sever our acquaintance. Instead, you returned, amiable and seemingly unaffected by what I did."

Albert glanced over at him.

"I told myself it was because you understood my dilemma. I told myself it was because we shared not only a working relationship but a friendship."

Albert smiled. "You neglected one item on your list, Ian. The work is important to me."

"A convenient point," Ian said. "Because it allowed you an excuse to come back to Lochlaven."

"I was obliged to do so regardless," Albert responded. "Some of the equipment here is mine."

Ian looked steadily at the other man. "Did you not trust me to crate it up on your behalf? Another anomaly in your behavior, Albert. Your return to Lochlaven is filled with inconsistencies, and we've both learned to pay attention to those, have we not?"

"What, exactly, are you accusing me of, Ian?"

"Murder."

The word was lobbed into the silence and sat there.

"I realized," Ian continued, "that you had returned to Lochlaven for one thing, to fulfill part of a bargain. One for which you were probably paid a great deal of money. Did the Earl of Falmouth contact you directly, Albert? Or did he have someone else meet with you? Was the money sufficient to silence your conscience?"

Albert turned to face him. "What do you know of a conscience, Ian? I gave up my practice to work with you. I was willing to do with less, and so was Brenda. When you offered for Rebecca, it was an answer to a prayer. We weren't going to be poor any longer. My girl was going to be a countess. And then, you changed. All our dreams were gone, as quick as you please, because you fell in love with a woman you couldn't have. What about your conscience, Ian? What about my life, my Brenda's life, my daughter's?"

Ian stood, walked to the windows and stared out at the lake. "I'm sorry for that, Albert. If you would have told me, I could have helped. I would have given you a salary, if nothing else."

"I didn't need your damn charity."

He glanced over his shoulder at Albert. "What kind of man refuses the act of a friend but accepts blood money from a murderer?"

"His liver was compromised," Albert said. "Bryce would have died soon in any case. No doubt in a great deal of agony."

"So you delivered the coup de grace, did you? How much did you get paid for your act of godliness?"

Instead of answering him, Albert asked a question of his own. "What are you going to do, Ian?"

Ian stared out at the lake. The sunlight was diffuse this morning, as if seen through a filter.

"You have a choice, Albert," he said. "I can take you to the authorities. Or you can surrender yourself."

"You can't prove your hypothesis, Ian."

"I'm convinced I can, Albert, and I'm willing to

expend whatever sum is necessary to prove it. How much were you paid? I'll equal that, at least."

"Five thousand pounds," Albert said. "Enough to ensure a future, a bright one, for all of us."

Sometimes, Ian didn't want a mind that refused to stop until an answer was found. Sometimes, the answer wasn't what he wanted to hear.

"Why did you smother him, Albert? Why not a solution of something injected into a vein? Being a physician, there must be all sorts of ways to kill."

"Do you really want to know, Ian?" Albert asked, his voice soft and almost sympathetic.

"Consider it my unshakable curiosity," he said.

"It's not as if I was prepared for murder," Albert said. "I had to take the opportunity that presented itself. Glenna was out of the room, and Bryce was leaving the next day. I had no other choice. "

Albert stood, looked toward the door.

"You had a choice, Albert. You could have chosen not to kill him."

Albert didn't respond.

"Did he struggle?" Ian asked, feeling numb inside. "Or was he too weak?"

Albert didn't answer him.

"Have you done this before, Albert? I kept wondering that. In your practice, were there other patients you've helped along to death?"

Albert glanced toward the door again.

"You won't make it," Ian said, looking at him over his shoulder. "I've locked the door. Broderick and Samuel are on the other side, waiting."

"What about the choice you mentioned?"

"Let's just say that Broderick and Samuel are there to

ensure you make the right choice. They'll accompany you to the authorities."

"And remain with me at all times, I gather," Albert said.

Ian didn't answer.

Albert smiled. "Regardless of what happens to me, I've cared for my family."

"And killed a man."

"Who was going to die."

"So you say. Who contacted you?"

"The Earl of Falmouth," Albert said. "I would have been paid twice the amount if she'd died as well, Ian. What kind of woman inspires her own uncle to want her dead?"

One who deserves better. An answer he didn't give Albert. Instead, he asked, "How did he know Bryce survived the poison?"

"How should I know?" Albert said, annoyed.

Murder was abhorrent to Ian. Murder was, simply put, the worst act a man could commit. But Albert had compounded that sin, because he'd killed a man who could not fight back.

What responsibility did he himself bear for that act? By not understanding how much Albert had sacrificed, was he somehow guilty as well? A question for which there was no ready—or easy—answer.

Evil had a new face, and it was kind, genial, and topped with curly black hair.

"How did he find you?" Ian asked.

Albert looked annoyed. "I'm well known enough. I'm not the Earl of Buchane but people know me."

"People will certainly know you now," Ian said, walking to Albert's side. "Did you never think what this would do to Brenda and Rebecca? You may have secured their future financially, Albert, but you will always be known as a murderer, and they a murderer's family."

"Then do not do this, my friend," Albert said, reaching up and clapping his hand on Ian's upper arm. "You have to believe me. Bryce was dying."

Ian stepped back, unable to bear the touch of the man he'd considered a surrogate father, the man who'd been his mentor, a man whose mind he'd respected.

Anger shadowed Albert's face. "I've done you a favor, Your Lordship," he said, one of the few times he'd ever addressed Ian in such a fashion.

"How's that?"

"I've cleared the way to the woman you love."

Ian could only wordlessly stare at the older man. A moment later he turned and walked away, leaving Albert for the last time.

Chapter 34

A week passed, seven interminable days since Bryce died, and during that time Emma kept to her room. Isobel brought her meal trays, but Glenna also visited, sharing information about Lochlaven when she did. As the days passed, Glenna was as close to a friend as Emma had known in years. Mrs. Jenkins called upon her once a day, each time inquiring if there was anything she required. Everyone at Lochlaven was extraordinarily kind.

From Glenna, she'd learned that Dr. Carrick had been taken to the authorities in Edinburgh, accompanied by Ian and a number of people from Lochlaven. That Albert had killed Bryce, when he'd labored so long to save him, was one of those facts she could not quite grasp.

Another was that while most people went their entire lives without being touched by violence, she had two murdered husbands to her credit.

Today, she'd retreated to the garden, because the breeze from the lake seemed capable of blowing away her thoughts. It had certainly been turbulent enough to loosen the snood from her hair.

She stared toward the island. The morning light was diffused; the island appeared more distant than it was. She'd been at Lochlaven for a month, and life had changed drastically here in that time.

She'd not loved Bryce but she regretted his death. No one should be murdered. No one should be killed for the sake of greed. No one should have to die before his time.

Ian had returned last night, which meant that she needed to meet with him this morning. A meeting she dreaded, and one that would be difficult. She knew what he would say, could predict his arguments. She would have to be strong, perhaps stronger than she'd ever been.

A seamstress had been employed in the last few days and had somehow—and miraculously—managed to complete a dress and appropriate bonnet for her. The short, sparrowlike little woman spoke almost continually in a low, heavily accented voice, as if she were talking to herself. Not once, however, had she directly addressed Emma, merely moving Emma's arms when necessary, or climbing atop a box to obtain measurements of her waist and bodice. The result was a perfectly acceptable mourning dress.

Standing, she smoothed the skirt of her new dress, then took the graveled path back to the house.

The laboratory door was open. Emma stood there for a moment, gathering her courage. The laboratory, with its view of the lake and light glistening off glass, was too bright. She wanted shadows and darkness for this meeting.

She entered the laboratory and its warren of rooms. Ian was in the second room at the window, a view that looked out over the garden where she'd just been sitting. Had he been watching her? Sadness filled her and threatened to make speech impossible.

"Your uncle is missing," he said without turning.

Startled, she said, "How do you know that?"

"I've been in contact with a firm of investigators in London. I received a telegram from them when I was in Inverness."

"Could he still be in Scotland?"

"I frankly don't care where he is, as long as it's nowhere near you."

She didn't want him to be kind to her or protective.

He turned to face her. "I've news of your maid as well. Juliana has found employment."

"Who would have employed her without a reference?" she asked.

"The Duchess of Meltonshire, I believe. Do you know her?"

She looked away.

"Emma?"

"She was a particular favorite of Anthony's."

"Perhaps Juliana is emulating Bryce."

"Extortion?" She smiled. "The duchess is a very proper personage. She prides herself on her parties, her charities."

"And her reputation?"

She nodded.

He turned. "There's something else," he said. He moved to one of the tables, picked up a sheet of paper and handed it to her. "Juliana telegraphed your uncle once she arrived in Inverness."

I know what you did. Mr. McNair still lives. I'll not have anything to do with your plans.

"It sounds as if she was afraid," Emma said.

"I came to the same conclusion."

"Perhaps I misjudged her," Emma admitted, staring down at the paper. "I wonder if she knew what she did?"

"Told him his plan failed, in so many words? He had no other choice but to find another way to kill Bryce."

"Why couldn't he have waited until Bryce returned to London?"

"He didn't know when that would be. Perhaps he was afraid it would be months, enough time for Bryce to have told someone else what he knew."

"He wouldn't have," she said, certain of that.

She glanced at him. How alone he looked, how separate and apart from anyone. The loss of both Bryce and Albert had shadowed his face, banished his smile, and stripped his eyes of any emotion.

"I'm leaving for London," she said in the silence. "Tomorrow morning."

For the longest moment, he didn't speak. She didn't look at him, directing her attention, instead, to the garden.

"Why?"

"Why? Ian, please do not pretend ignorance as to why I'm leaving. It wouldn't be right for me to stay. Not now."

"No," he said finally.

"No?" She smiled. "For the first time in my life, I'm not obligated to listen to any man, Ian. Not even you. You have no power to keep me here."

He was silent so long that she finally stole a glance at him. He was regarding her somberly, almost as if committing her to memory.

"Is that why you wish to leave? To create your own life?"

No, but if it was an excuse that he'd accept, she'd use it. She nodded, wishing she didn't feel so close to tears.

"Very well," he said. "If you're set to go back to London, then I'll accompany you. Or have you forgotten that your uncle is still a murderer? There are certain conditions I insist upon," he said, in a voice she'd never heard from him.

"What are those?" she asked coolly.

"You allow me to obtain a security staff for you. You have all the locks replaced, in case your uncle has keys. A watchman will be stationed outside your house."

"For how long?"

"Until such time as your uncle has proven not to be a threat."

"And when would that be?"

"When he's dead," he said flatly.

"Very well," she said. It wasn't very difficult to agree to his terms. She might have instituted the very same measures if he'd given her the opportunity.

"Then your life will be your own," he said.

"Why does that seem to annoy you?"

He didn't say anything in response, only turned back to the window, effectively dismissing her. As he did so, she realized that he thought she'd chosen a life of autonomy over a life with him. No, not even that, because he hadn't asked her to stay.

She felt as if she were spinning off wildly in a hundred different directions like a dandelion puff set in motion by a windstorm. She stretched out her hand as if to touch him, then pulled it back.

The world would not understand her remaining at Lochlaven, not so soon after Bryce's death. It would appear as if the two of them feasted on his grave, as if they celebrated his demise.

It wasn't their time.

For a moment she simply stood there, dressed in mourning, and filled with a terrible grief.

Then she turned and walked away, intent on the preparations for her departure.

Chapter 35

At the Inverness Station, Ian left her for a few moments, returning only when the train was nearly ready to leave.

"I've given the station master your address," he said, "and asked him to redouble his efforts to find your trunk."

"That was very kind," she said. "I should like to give the mirror to Lady Sarah."

The loss of the Tulloch Sgàthán weighed heavily on her. She decided to write Lady Sarah once she arrived in London, taking the chance that the other woman wouldn't rebuff her attempts at conciliation. She would explain what had happened and apologize for her part in losing the mirror.

During the journey, Ian was very solicitous, ensuring that she was warm enough, comfortable, purchasing some tea for her. At least once an hour he would ask if she needed something, and she would turn her attention from the passing scenery to him.

"Thank you, no."

They sat opposite each other, a small square table between them. If the other passengers in the compartment wondered at the man with the black armband

and the obvious widow accompanying him, they kept their curiosity muted and undetectable.

Emma not only looked the part of proper widow but felt the part as well. She was truly miserable. However, the harpies of society would be wildly gossiping if they knew the truth. The newly widowed Mrs. McNair was grieving, but not, shockingly, for her husband.

She could recall everything Ian had said to her, every comment, every single word. She could see his face in her dreams, could envision each of his separate expressions and emotions. She could feel the touch of his hands on her, the slide of his body against hers, the laughter that bubbled up from the depths of her when he was being amusing.

At Lochlaven she'd come too close to inviting Ian into her room, closing the door and forgetting the world. She'd wanted to smooth her hands up the broad plains of his chest to his shoulders, link her hands at the back of his neck and hold on. She wanted to marvel at the power of his body over hers, be fascinated at his strength and masculinity compared to her femininity.

She ached for him now, not simply in passion but also in longing. A feeling that was tied to the inside of her, to the open, empty cavern in her chest.

Once in London, a solicitous Ian led her through Kings Cross Station.

"I don't think you should return to your home," he said after he'd hired a carriage. "If you have no friends with whom you could stay, then stay with me."

She smiled.

"To hell with propriety, Emma."

He had not been whispered about, sent looks when she entered a shop, been shunned at a gathering.

She reached over and placed her hand on his arm, the first time she'd allowed herself to touch him since Bryce's funeral. "Ian, I'm going home."

His face closed up but he finally nodded.

The carriage ride through London was as silent as most of the train journey back to England. Dusk had fallen by the time they reached her house, and when the carriage stopped, Emma let out a sigh, almost of relief.

Being with Ian was the most perfect torture she'd ever endured.

She wanted, desperately, to turn to him, to have his arms enfold her, to gain comfort from his embrace. Doing so, however, was so wrong that even the thought of it rang like a bell through her mind.

Now was not the time for friendship, love, or passion.

Before she could mount the steps, Ian touched her arm. She halted and turned to him.

"Allow me to introduce your security detail to you," he said.

Three men exited an adjacent carriage, two of them tall, one of them short, but each possessing a muscular build that strained their jackets.

"My security detail?" she asked.

"One of my conditions," he reminded her.

She nodded.

"They'll be with you at all times," he said. "They'll also approve new hirings, and the entrance of anyone into your home."

"Something else you arranged in Inverness?" she asked faintly.

"Yes."

She met Matthew Harrison, the man in charge of

her security. He was nearly a foot shorter than Ian, and a foot broader, and possessed a large mustache that jiggled when he spoke. He was also Scottish, a fact that was immediately evident when he began to speak.

"We'll not be a hindrance, madam," he said. "You'll not see a whisker of us unless you wish to."

"Thank you, Mr. Harrison."

"We'll just go and search the house now," he said, bowing to her.

She turned to Ian.

"Just how long will I have the services of Mr. Harrison and his cohorts?" she asked.

"I told you at Lochlaven," he said, standing at the bottom of the steps. "When your uncle is dead."

He and Mr. Harrison were deep in conversation. Evidently, that was the only farewell she was going to get from Ian.

She opened the door, nodding to her majordomo.

"Ask Cook to have a tray sent to my room in an hour," she said to him. "Something light."

The man merely bowed, respectful and distant. Or was he disdainful? Perhaps she should be like Anthony and dismiss the whole of her staff. She would replace them only with people who chose to be in her employ.

She turned to look back at Ian just once before the door closed.

It's not our time, dearest Ian.

She wanted, almost desperately, to tell him that. Or to tell him how much she appreciated his care of her. Instead, she forced herself to turn away from him and mount the stairs to her room.

When Emma entered her suite, she closed the door softly, leaning back against the carved panel, her hands behind her. The gas lamps were lit, illuminating the sitting room in a warm yellowish glow. Bryce had slept through his wedding night in that chair. Ian had entered through that window. Everything was exactly the same as it had been.

She was the only one who'd changed.

Emma closed her eyes, unprepared for the onslaught of memory.

No one told me how beautiful you were.

My home is near a lake, and on the lake is an island.

I came back for you.

Words Ian had said to her. Words he'd uttered in a teasing voice, a somber tone, with tenderness.

How was she to bear this?

Emma walked to the window and stood looking down at the street. Ian was still there, his carriage at the curb. The fact that he hadn't left was both oddly reassuring and troubling.

How was she ever to say good-bye to him?

Why must she?

For years she'd pretended that she could be part of society again. That, if she tried hard enough, people would accept her. That, one day, she'd be able to attend a tea or a ball and have people welcome her instead of staring at her with open dislike.

For years she'd told herself that propriety was important, that rules were made to be obeyed, not broken.

Society didn't care about her, other than as fodder for gossip. Even if she were to be restrained, demure, and docile for the next twenty years, she doubted if any of the harpies in society would ever forget all the tales. Instead, she would forever be the stuff of rumors and innuendo. Someone new to London would be immediately regaled with stories of the Duchess of Herridge.

She could never escape. Then why did she try? Why did she care?

Why was she going to allow anyone to dictate her happiness?

The rebellion had been fomenting since Scotland. She'd changed there, become someone else. She suspected she would never again be the Ice Queen.

She wanted to laugh with abandon, or throw something at the wall or the window. She wanted to take off her shoes and walk barefoot in the grass. She wanted to bathe in the lake. She didn't want to be decorous or proper. She wanted to be a hoyden. She wanted to picnic on the island. She wanted to let loose with all of those impulses she'd tamped down during her marriage. All of those un-duchess, impolite, thoroughly human emotions she'd never expressed.

Emma pressed her hand against the glass, remembering that night when Ian entered her room. He'd come for the Tulloch mirror and left with her heart.

What a fool she'd be if she turned down the opportunity to be happy.

As she looked, he approached the carriage and glanced upward, their eyes meeting.

She didn't want to stay here. If she must, she'd defy propriety to be with him. She almost raised the window and called out to him. *Stay. Wait for me. I'm coming!*

The smell of camphor was the only warning she had.

Ian was damned if he was going to leave her.

Her uncle might have departed for parts unknown

but he could always return. He didn't want to leave Emma at the mercy of a killer. Besides, he had the distinct impression that if he left her, she'd never again allow him into her life. She'd become an utterly proper widow, a woman who attempted, in her later life, to make up for all the sins of her youth.

She would martyr herself for propriety.

Couldn't she see the love right in front of her eyes? Couldn't she see that there wasn't anywhere else for her to be but right at his side? In his house, in his life, and in his arms?

Ian knew he should get in his carriage, give the driver the address of his London house, and give her time. But he was reluctant to leave. Instead, he conferred with Harrison and spoke to Emma's majordomo.

He wasn't going to marry anyone else. He wasn't going to form an alliance with anyone else. He didn't even want to *talk* to another woman. Emma was his and had been from the first moment he'd seen her. If she didn't understand that fact, then he would simply have to do something or say something to ensure she did.

His Celtic ancestors had been strong men determined to survive. He felt the same now, as if his very survival depended upon Emma being in his life. Each moment, he couldn't help but feel more and more Scottish.

No more so than now, when the woman he loved had repudiated him.

Perhaps an abduction was in order again.

"You're looking well, Emma," her uncle said, stepping out of the shadows.

She turned.

"You didn't leave," she said. How very composed she sounded.

"I have no funds with which to do so," he replied. "Let's just say that I've expended all the available cash I had."

Her palms felt damp against the fabric of her skirt.

"On a trip to Inverness, perhaps?" she asked. "Or was it the payment for murder that cost you?"

He smiled agreeably. "Does it matter?"

"They searched the house."

"They didn't search the servants' quarters," her uncle said, smiling. "A sad thing, my dear, when I'm forced to hide in a maid's room. She had more in her purse than I have in my pocket. An irony, is it not? I'm almost happy to see you. The wait was endless."

"People are looking for you, Uncle. Or do you think you should be allowed to get away with murder?"

"Bryce? You should thank me for that, my dear. He would have proven to be a disagreeable husband."

"I'm speaking of Anthony," she said.

"Anthony?" His smile broadened. "I always thought you knew what I'd done and approved. You never told anyone that Anthony was murdered. I'd not expected an accomplice, Emma. It made my life so much easier, and I thank you."

He smiled, and it was then she noticed the gleam of madness in his eyes. Or perhaps it had always been there, and she only just now saw it. He strode toward the chair, a bottle of wine in his hand.

"Now, regrettably, it's your turn."

She took a step backward.

"You don't even seem to know that you have money,

Emma," he said. "You would probably be content not to have any money at all. No funds for little Emma."

He grabbed her arm. She jerked away, but he only seized her again, pushing her down into the chair, her skirt and hoop billowing.

"We'll have a toast, you and I. To Anthony. To Bryce."

He pulled the cork from the bottle and held it out to her.

"Drink it, Emma. I promise you, all your problems will vanish if you do so. No more onerous wealth to manage. No more worries about husbands. No more concern for your reputation."

"I don't want any," she said, pushing the bottle away.

"Ah, but I insist." He held out the bottle again. "Oh, you think it's ill mannered to drink from the bottle? Shall I get you a glass?"

"Only if you join me, Uncle," she said. "And drink first."

He laughed. "You've become brave, little Emma."

"I'm not drinking any of your wine."

"But I've learned from my mistake, Emma. It's not the same dosage as Bryce's wine. It's much stronger. You'll not be able to survive like poor Bryce. You'll simply go to sleep."

"You can't think to get away with this," she said. "People know about Anthony. They know about Bryce."

"Do they?" He smiled. "Then they'll just have to know about you as well, little Emma." He held out the bottle. "Drink it."

"No."

"No? Come now, Emma, you've always been such an obedient girl." His smile vanished. "Drink it," he said, his easy manner disappearing. "Or I shall have to force you to do so."

With one hand on the bottle, the other on her chin, he forced her mouth open. She clawed at his wrists with both hands as he tipped the bottle, then angled her head and bit his thumb.

He swore, then backhanded her.

Emma lunged forward, half falling toward the fireplace, wishing her corset wasn't laced so tightly or her skirts weren't so fulsome. She grabbed the poker from its stand, but he was right behind her. He hit her again, and she collapsed to the floor, the side of her face burning. A second later she scrambled to her knees and swung the poker at him, catching him on the shin.

He swore at her, grabbed for the poker, but she managed to stand and swing it again. Her first blow struck his shoulder. The second hit him on the side of the head. He staggered, dazed, and she ran to the sitting room door. Before she could reach it, he grabbed her arm, pulled her around and struck her again, this time with a closed fist.

The poker fell to the floor.

Later, Emma wondered if that horrid sound had really come from her. Mr. Harrison said that it sounded like a wounded animal. One of the men in her security detail said it was the cry of a Scottish banshee.

All Emma knew was that she wasn't going to be poisoned. She wasn't going to die. She was *not* going to be powerless again.

She raced toward the chair, grabbed the bottle and swung it at him. It struck his cheek but didn't break.

He lunged for her, both arms outstretched, fingers like claws.

She bent, scrambled for the poker, then stood facing him, breathless.

"Emma," he said in a singsong voice. "Little Emma. Drink the wine, little Emma. You're proving to be as great a problem as Bryce."

He was Death, and she wasn't going to die. Not before she'd truly lived. Not as the Duchess of Herridge. Not as Bryce's wife. But as Emma, simply Emma.

She could feel the strain of each muscle, the blazing heat of her blood, and the fierce pounding of her heart as she raised the poker with both hands and, with every bit of strength she possessed, struck her uncle again.

This time the blow landed on his neck. He fell to his knees, one hand on the wound. She raised the poker again, ready to strike him again as the door opened.

"Emma," Ian said from behind her. "Emma, it's all right. You're safe."

She still held the poker aloft, aiming for her uncle's head. He wasn't just her uncle at that moment, he was Anthony as well. He was every man who'd ever frightened her or abused her or threatened her.

"I want to kill him," she said, her voice trembling.

"I know," he said softly. "But you won't."

Slowly, she lowered the poker, releasing it from her numb hands and hearing it clatter to the floor.

Ian turned her, saying words she couldn't understand in that beautiful voice of his with its hint of Scotland. She grabbed him with both hands, closed her eyes and held on, feeling his arms wrap around her and knowing he was right. She was finally safe.

* * *

In another time, she would have been a warrior beside him, this shocking former duchess. She would have defended the island at his side, worked to build a castle to shelter their children, wielded a sword with expert skill.

A Celtic woman, for all that she'd been born in England.

A moment later he left her and went to help her uncle up from the floor. Once the man was on his feet, Ian shook him gently, just to ensure that he was fully conscious.

"Are you with us, Your Lordship?" he asked pleasantly.

The man nodded faintly, just before Ian struck him again. He watched with pleasure as the Earl of Falmouth fell face first onto the floor, sliding over the floorboards until he was stopped by the wall.

Ian clenched his fist and released it, shaking his hand. The pain in his knuckles was worth it.

"What will happen to him?" Emma asked from beside him.

He glanced at her. "He'll be given over to the Metropolitan Police."

"Will he go to jail?"

"If I have anything to say about it," Ian said. "For the rest of his life."

She was still trembling, but when he reached for her she moved farther away.

"I'm taking you home, Emma. To my home. You can scream and shout and do anything you wish, but I'm taking you home."

"No, not until we talk," she said.

"Then we'll talk, but you're still coming home with me."

He wasn't leaving here without her. He was never leaving her again. She filled every cell of his body, every crevice, every empty place. Couldn't she see that? Didn't she know? If she didn't, he would spend the rest of his life proving it to her.

She took a deep breath, squared her shoulders and resolutely faced him.

"I'm a shocking woman, Ian," she said. "I've come to understand that, for the rest of my life, rumor will follow me. You have to know that as well."

"Must I?"

"I could damage your reputation. It could harm you irreparably to have your name linked with mine."

He leaned against the wall and folded his arms.

"Would it?" he asked.

"I will never be received in proper society again, not after being the Duchess of Herridge, the Ice Queen," she said, her eyes swimming with emotion.

"Does that matter to you? Being received in proper society?"

She walked to the fireplace, looked with loathing at the bottle of wine now laying on the carpet nearby.

In the stilted silence, he refused to speak. Nor would he beg, although he came damn close.

She turned to face him. "That's what I'm trying to say, Ian. I realized that it doesn't. All that's important to me is what *you* think. To blazes with my reputation or those who would judge me."

"Shall I tell you what I think?"

She looked startled at his vehemence.

"I don't give a flying farthing about your reputation,

Emma. I never have since I learned who you were. If it disturbs you not to be received in London, we'll spend all our time in Scotland, with occasional visits to France."

"We will?" Her eyes widened.

They didn't need to talk anymore. He reached her side in three strides and lifted her up in his arms. He was through the door, down the stairs, and into his carriage before she could utter a word of protest.

She smiled up at him.

"You're abducting me again," she said as he settled her on his lap and reached over to close the door.

"I am. Know one thing, Emma, if you know nothing else. I'm proprietary. You'll need to get used to it."

"I am, too," she confessed. "I was horribly jealous of Rebecca. Not simply because she was going to be able to share your bed, although there was that. But she was going to share your life.

"I may be a pariah, Ian, but I would also be a partner. I would be there to listen to you complain, to hear your theories, to tell you that you're marvelous." She smiled, and cupped the side of his face with her palm. "You are, you know."

"You're going to marry me, Emma," he said, feeling as if his heart was filled with emotion.

"Am I?"

"We're also going to shock the world further, you and I. We'll marry within the week. That will give the harpies something to talk about. The scandalous Earl of Buchane and his countess."

"It might be entertaining to be married to someone I *like* for once."

Ian pulled his handkerchief free and dotted at the cut on her lip. The side of her face was bruised. If she hadn't pummeled the Earl of Falmouth herself, he would have gone back to finish the job.

Emma wrapped one hand around the back of his neck and raised up to kiss him.

He pulled back. "Emma, I don't want to hurt you."

"Then kiss me," she said, and smiled.

What other choice did he have?

Once at his house, he greeted Patterson with a nod, all the while carrying Emma up the stairs. Inside his room, he closed the door and slowly lowered her to her feet before lighting a lamp.

He stood there looking at her. Not touching her, because he didn't quite trust himself at the moment, but simply studying her, knowing that he wasn't ever going to let her go again.

Nothing else mattered but Emma.

She took a step toward him. Something broke inside of her, some last bond holding her prisoner to the past. His arms enfolded her, caught her up close. Her arms wrapped around him tightly, held on as if he were the greatest treasure, one she'd sought all her life. Let the world fade away but for Ian, precious Ian.

Ian would demand all of her, from her thoughts to her passion. She would be his, as he would be hers. He allowed no duplicity in himself and, therefore, none in her. Yet with that realization came another: she could never hide again. She could never again shield herself behind pretense, behind an iron control.

Ian would know all of her.

Could she be that courageous? The answer came swiftly—with Ian, yes.

"It wasn't our time," he said, repeating her words to him. "Before. It wasn't our time. But it is now."

His finesse was gone, his fingers were clumsy, his breath was coming too fast. When they were both undressed, they tumbled on the bed, Ian on top. Naked and smiling, she was the loveliest creature he'd ever seen. His hands caressed her skin, slid over the whole of her in a sense of wonder.

"Ian, please."

She held out her arms to him.

Her eyes were huge, the pupils dark. A flush suffused her face. Even with the bruise on her cheek, she was still beautiful. A last thought before he tenderly kissed her and lost the ability to reason or think.

Her hips moved back and forth, as if she couldn't bear the heat between them. His hand dove between her thighs, explored the soft, swollen folds. His fingers stroked across her dampness, and her thighs clamped against his hand, trapping him, needing him. His fingers moved, gently at first, then bore down with more pressure, circling the opening of her body with such delicate care that her sudden, indrawn breath interrupted their kiss.

He smiled, then bent and drew a nipple into his heated mouth, arousing her with sharp little bites, then soothing her with the tip of his tongue.

Emma could hear the breathless sound of her own voice, feel the grip of her hands on his shoulders, her fingernails scraping gently down his chest. She writhed in his arms as he kissed his way between her breasts and down her stomach to hover at her navel.

He slipped into her heat, clenching his teeth when she closed around him like a fist. A soft cry escaped her as her hands beat against his shoulders, then gripped him with possessive fingers, a push and pull of desire that drove him nearly mad.

"Ian," she whispered, nearly sobbing in her need of him.

Overcome with love, desperate with arousal, he began to withdraw, push himself inside, then withdraw again. He fought his way to sanity through levels of pleasure.

Emma wrapped her arms around his neck, arched up to bite gently at his throat.

"Now, now, now," she said, her voice vibrating with emotion.

He closed his mouth over hers, absorbed her shuddering breaths.

One arm supported his weight as his other hand reached under her, slipped under her beautiful bottom and lifted her up to him. A gasp escaped her, and she clung to him, her lips pressed against his throat.

This was not simply lovemaking. This was mating. This was elemental and fierce and as right and proper as the sun rising or the moon hanging above the earth.

Her surrender summoned his own. He emptied himself into her, barely conscious as he collapsed half on top of her. Her hands slid weakly to the mattress as he murmured an incoherent apology, rousing enough to roll to the side. She turned her head and softly kissed his chest.

"I love you," he said.

"I know." She patted his chest possessively. "You always have."

"I always have," he admitted. "And you?"

"My dearest Ian," she said, emotion thickening her voice. "Must you ask?"

"Yes," he said. "I find I must."

"I love you," she said, placing her palm against his

cheek. "I love you," she repeated, rising up to kiss the curve of his ear. "I love you," she said against his lips when he turned his head to kiss her.

He looked at her, grateful that he'd left the lamp burning. His memory would forever furnish the beauty of her shadowed face.

Ian bent his head and touched his lips to the space between her breasts, a benediction with a kiss. He kissed her throat, then the edge of her jaw.

"I used to believe in science to the exclusion of all else," he said. "Science has rules. Science is measurable. Science can be proven, repeatedly. Fate is something else entirely, but Emma if . . . " His voice trailed off.

Her hand cupped the side of his face. He turned his head to kiss her palm.

She had the strangest thought, a faint recollection of a woman in a mirror, the laughing, loved woman in the Tulloch Sgàthán. She'd been reaching for someone beyond her sight, and as Emma looked at Ian, she knew it had been him. Later, she'd tell him about the mirror, but for now, she only smiled.

"I believe in *you*. Must we believe in anything else but each other?"

He smiled. "No," he said, and kissed her again.

Author's Note

Victorian society has always fascinated me because of its duplicity. On the one hand, Victoria was a virtuous—and staid—Queen. On the other, the Victorian age produced a great deal of pornography, both written and photographic. What went on behind the scenes was often as informative as what happened in public. The orgies at Chavensworth are based on rumors and innuendo of the time.

In Greek mythology, a Maenad (translation: raving one) was a female follower of Dionysus. The Maenads were often depicted as being in a drunken, ecstatic rapture in which they lose all self-control.

Until the Married Women's Property Act of 1870, any money a woman earned, or inherited, automatically became the property of her husband.

The music hall Bryce frequented was modeled on an actual club functioning in 1866.

"I Once Loved a Lass," also known as "The False Bride" is a folk ballad dating from the seventeenth century.

A Collection of Strathspey Reels With a Bass for the Violoncello or Harpsichord, by Alexander McGlashan, 1778, 1781, features "The Highlanders Farewell."

We truly do stand on the shoulders of giants, men who worked in relative obscurity with only an idea. John Tyndall is one of those giants, and Ian's work is patterned after his experiments. In Tyndall's lab, he came up with a way to create pure air by coating the inside of a box with glycerin. What he discovered was that there were no signs of floating microorganisms in the air of the boxes so treated. His work verified Louis Pasteur's demonstration that the presence of germs—or microorganisms—were necessary to the decomposition of flesh. Tyndall developed a method of killing germs that was known as "Tyndallization." He and Pasteur communicated often during the latter half of the nineteenth century.

Aristotle (384 B.C.–322 B.C.) proposed the theory of Spontaneous Generation. According to his theory, all living things are generated from nonliving things. The creature generated was dependent upon properties of the nonliving pneuma—or vital heat—and the five elements he believed comprised all matter: fire, air, earth, water, and aether (the divine substance that makes up the planets and stars). This theory lasted until Louis Pasteur proved it false in 1859.

Since poisoning cases were often reported by the press, and contained those elements that made for reader interest (love, betrayal, and rage), public perception was that the Victorian era was associated with a poisoning epidemic, and that poisoning was a fashionable crime. The truth was that the actual numbers of criminal cases involving poison remained constant throughout the century.

In Victorian England murder by poison was proven mainly by circumstantial evidence, since most forensic tools had not yet been developed. The Reinsch test is one exception. This test was a method to detect arsenic poisoning and was developed in 1841. In the book, Ian performed the test on the remaining contents of the wine bottles. In actuality, the test was performed on bodily fluids.

People were expected to sign the Poison Book when purchasing arsenic in 1866, but it was a common enough occurrence, since arsenic was used for a variety of purposes: to kill rats, as a complexion enhancer, and even as a food dye. (A coloring agent—Scheele's Green—was made from adding copper sulfate to a solution of arsenic and used as a food dye in sweets.)

The treatment for arsenic poisoning was as I described it in the book. However, there are no definitive statistics on survivors, so it's uncertain if the treatment was efficacious.